AMERICAN SHORT STORIES

Selected with an Introduction
by
DOUGLAS GRANT

OXFORD UNIVERSITY PRESS

LONDON   OXFORD   MELBOURNE

1972

Oxford University Press

LONDON .OXFORD NEW YORK

GLASGOW TORONTO MELBOURNE WELLINGTON

CAPE TOWN IBADAN NAIROBI DAR ES SALAAM LUSAKA ADDIS ABABA

DELHI BOMBAY CALCUTTA MADRAS KARACHI LAHORE DACCA

KUALA LUMPUR SINGAPORE HONG KONG TOKYO

ISBN 0 19 281122 3

First published in The World's Classics, 1965

First issued as an Oxford University Press paperback
by Oxford University Press, London, 1972

PRINTED IN GREAT BRITAIN

AMERICAN SHORT STORIES

CONTENTS

INTRODUCTION

THE short story is older by countless centuries than the beginnings of American literature, but the American short story is one of the most distinct and important modern branches of the form. The number and variety of short stories to have appeared in the United States since the publication of Washington Irving's *Sketch Book* in 1820 make it extremely difficult to choose a representative selection within a reasonable space. Any choice should be chronological, of course, but otherwise it would be possible to select with a view to illustrating either the development of the form or its finest achievements. The same writers and the same stories would often appear in either case, but in some instances the choice would differ; authors of historical significance being dropped in favour of the less innovatory but more interesting or formally accomplished. Irving would have to be given room under the first scheme, for example, but could be dispensed with under the second; and the reverse would hold true for Herman Melville.

The absence of Irving from and the presence of Melville in the present selection will indicate that the second alternative has been generally preferred. Irving is the first gap, and there are others to be noticed. Bret Harte not only scored a great popular success with the publication of 'The Luck of Roaring Camp' in 1868, but by setting the tale among gold-miners in California, he showed how local colour could be effectively used. He was also a technically accomplished writer. The shallowness and sentimentality of even his better stories is, however, a sufficient excuse for dropping him. Nor is the group of writers most influenced by Harte—the local colourists—directly represented. Sarah Orne Jewett and Mary Wilkins Freeman, foremost of the group and both from New England, are skilful and charming delineators of local characters and atmosphere, and their exclusion would be a serious loss were this selection primarily illustrative.

The movements most deeply affecting the short story towards the end of the nineteenth century and at the beginning of the twentieth, realism and naturalism, are represented, in the first instance, by Hamlin Garland and, in the other, by Stephen Crane, Jack London, and Sherwood Anderson. The plotting of Garland's 'The Return of a Private' may be weak and obvious, but the honesty and feeling with which its bitter truth is presented are enough to compensate for its shortcomings. Crane's 'The Open Boat', however, is as brilliantly executed as it is intensely visualized, and is justly accepted as one of the best of American stories. Anderson was even more accomplished, though lacking Crane's genius, and 'I Want to Know Why' shows both his skill and his handling of a theme common to many American writers, the initiation of a boy into experience. London seems in comparison a rough and ready popular writer, but his extraordinary energy and narrative power should be enough to save him eventually from the neglect which has followed his astonishing vogue. 'The Heathen' is interesting, too, as it shows him treating, like Anderson, a peculiarly American theme—a blood friendship between men of different colour.

Other writers could have been selected to illustrate these particular phases in the development of the short story. Frank Norris and Theodore Dreiser and Willa Cather all wrote short stories, but their achievement in this respect fell short of their excellence and importance as novelists. The absence of two other writers roughly contemporary with these is also sure to be noticed, and perhaps censured. Ring Lardner and O. Henry—especially O. Henry—were both deservedly popular. Lardner's skilful use of the vernacular is as generally admired as O. Henry's adroit handling of coincidence and surprise, but in spite of their polish Lardner's stories seem meretricious and O. Henry's a matter of trick.

Several of the writers already mentioned were active after the First World War, but the period since then has been dominated by those who first began to publish in the nineteen-twenties or early 'thirties: Scott Fitzgerald, Ernest Hemingway, John Steinbeck, William Faulkner, and Katherine Anne Porter are some of the more obvious names. And the tradition they so powerfully reinforced has been maintained by their successors: Eudora Welty, Truman Capote, J. F. Powers, and Flannery O'Connor, to mention only a few. The choice is bewildering, but it is at least simplified by copyright restrictions and the lack of space. In the present instance, it has been decided to end with Ernest Hemingway, the youngest of the earlier group. Hawthorne's 'My Kinsman: Major Molineux' comes first in this selection, and Hemingway's 'The Short Happy Life of Francis Macomber' last, and handing on undiminished the tradition so remarkably begun.

Hawthorne's story is one of several that might have been chosen to illustrate him. It is almost as difficult to choose stories as writers. Anyone making a selection would wish to avoid the obvious, but there are some stories that must be included either because they represent the author at his best or because of their influence. Crane's 'The Open Boat' would be a case in point: often reprinted and yet a serious loss to any selection, and only to be replaced by his 'The Blue Hotel', which is scarcely less popular. And the selector, too, must be allowed a measure of personal choice. 'My Kinsman: Major Molineux' may be a good story but many would consider less well of it than 'Young Goodman Brown', or some other. I think that it wears the best and that its symbolism is subtler and its psychology more profound; it has the further advantage of being less frequently reprinted.

In spite of the loss of Irving and the others already mentioned, the selection should provide a reasonable survey of the American short story. Irving introduced romance and showed in his tales of 'Rip Van Winkle' and 'The Legend of Sleepy Hollow' how it could be related to the American scene. Hawthorne was the first to raise the short story to an art. He is at times too obviously allegorical and heavily didactic, but in his better stories, and they are many, the symbols, characters, and descriptions are successfully combined to illuminate the sombre truths of the moral conscience.

The unity of Hawthorne's stories depends upon the situation and mood—of Edgar Allan Poe's upon an intelligent grasp of form. The short story, Poe argued, must be 'curt, condensed, well digested'. If the writer's 'very initial sentence tend not to the outbringing of this effect', he observed, 'he has failed in his first step. In the whole composition there should be no word written of which the tendency, direct or indirect, is not to the one pre-established design'. He himself practised this lesson, and however Gothic his imagination, his method was scientific. Each romantic and extravagant effect was calculated to fit into a design. His influence was far reaching, not only in the work of such a skilful follower as Ambrose Bierce, but indirectly in that of every short story writer who understood the advantages of being 'curt, condensed, well digested'.

Only three of the writers in the present selection have so far escaped mention. Mark Twain is the first. Mark Twain's 'Baker's Bluejay Yarn' has been chosen both for its own sake and as an example of the tall tale in the vernacular, typical of the frontier and the western humorist. The tradition persists, and is to be found most recently in Faulkner's work.

The other omissions are Henry James, the greatest of all the American short story writers, and his talented disciple, Edith Wharton. Reading through James's stories in order is to follow one of the keenest of literary intellects endlessly experimenting in the search for the perfect form. He learnt from Hawthorne and Poe among the Americans but he added to what they could teach an inventiveness, a sense of style, and a grasp of character that far exceeded their scope. Though a single story can only illustrate one of James's phases, 'The Beast in the Jungle' shows him at his most creative, self-assured, and mature.

James's reading in contemporary French and Russian literature will remind us that from Irving down, American literature has necessarily been indebted to Europe, often for inspiration and always for enrichment. The short story is evidence of how quickly it has established a tradition and begun to dispense an influence of its own.

DOUGLAS GRANT

My Kinsman, Major Molineux

NATHANIEL HAWTHORNE

(1804–64)

AFTER the kings of Great Britain had assumed the right
of appointing the colonial governors, the measures of the
latter seldom met with the ready and general approbation
which had been paid to those of their predecessors, under
the original charters. The people looked with the most
jealous scrutiny to the exercise of power which did not
emanate from themselves, and they usually rewarded
their rulers with slender gratitude for the compliances by
which, in softening their instructions from beyond the
sea, they had incurred the reprehension of those who gave
them. The annals of Massachusetts Bay will inform us,
that of six governors in the space of about forty years from
the surrender of the old charter under James II, two were
imprisoned by a popular insurrection; a third, as Hutchin-
son inclines to believe, was driven from the province by
the whizzing of a musket-ball; a fourth, in the opinion of
the same historian, was hastened to his grave by continual
bickerings with the House of Representatives; and the
remaining two, as well as their successors, till the Revolution, were favoured with few and brief intervals of peaceful sway. The inferior members of the court party, in
times of high political excitement, led scarcely a more
desirable life. These remarks may serve as a preface to
the following adventures, which chanced upon a summer
night, not far from a hundred years ago. The reader, in
order to avoid a long and dry detail of colonial affairs, is

requested to dispense with an account of the train of circumstances that had caused much temporary inflammation of the popular mind.

It was near nine o'clock of a moonlight evening, when a boat crossed the ferry with a single passenger, who had obtained his conveyance at that unusual hour by the promise of an extra fare. While he stood on the landing-place, searching in either pocket for the means of fulfilling his agreement, the ferryman lifted a lantern, by the aid of which, and the newly-risen moon, he took a very accurate survey of the stranger's figure. He was a youth of barely eighteen years, evidently country-bred, and now, as it should seem, upon his first visit to town. He was clad in a coarse grey-coat, well worn, but in excellent repair; his under garments were durably constructed of leather, and fitted tight to a pair of serviceable and well shaped limbs; his stockings of blue yarn were the incontrovertible work of a mother or a sister; and on his head was a three-cornered hat, which in its better days had perhaps sheltered the graver brow of the lad's father. Under his left arm was a heavy cudgel, formed of an oak sapling, and retaining a part of the hardened root; and his equipment was completed by a wallet, not so abundantly stocked as to incommode the vigorous shoulders on which it hung. Brown, curly hair, well-shaped features, and bright, cheerful eyes, were nature's gifts, and worth all that art could have done for his adornment.

The youth, one of whose names was Robin, finally drew from his pocket the half of a little province bill of five shillings, which, in the depreciation of that sort of currency, did but satisfy the ferryman's demand, with the surplus of a sexangular piece of parchment, valued at threepence. He then walked forward into the town, with as light a step as if his day's journey had not already exceeded thirty miles, and with as eager an eye as if he were entering London city, instead of the little metropolis of a New England colony. Before Robin had proceeded far, however, it occurred to him that he knew not whither to direct his steps; so he paused, and looked up and down the narrow street, scrutinizing the small and mean wooden buildings that were scattered on either side.

'This low hovel cannot be my kinsman's dwelling,' thought he, 'nor yonder old house, where the moonlight enters at the broken casement; and truly I see none hereabouts that might be worthy of him. It would have been wise to inquire my way of the ferryman, and doubtless he would have gone with me, and earned a shilling from the major for his pains. But the next man I meet will do as well.'

He resumed his walk, and was glad to perceive that the street now became wider, and the houses more respectable in their appearance. He soon discerned a figure moving on moderately in advance, and hastened his steps to overtake it. As Robin drew nigh, he saw that the passenger was a man in years, with a full periwig of grey hair, a wide-skirted coat of dark cloth, and silk stockings rolled above his knees. He carried a long and polished cane, which he struck down perpendicularly before him, at every step; and at regular intervals he uttered two successive hems, of a peculiarly solemn and sepulchral intonation. Having made these observations, Robin laid hold of the skirt of the old man's coat, just when the light from the open door and windows of a barber's shop fell upon both their figures.

'Good-evening to you, honoured sir,' said he, making a low bow, and still retaining his hold of the skirt. 'I pray you tell me whereabouts is the dwelling of my kinsman, Major Molineux.'

The youth's question was uttered very loudly; and one of the barbers, whose razor was descending on a well-soaped chin, and another who was dressing a Ramillies wig, left their occupations, and came to the door. The citizen, in the meantime, turned a long-favoured countenance upon Robin, and answered him in a tone of excessive anger and annoyance. His two sepulchral hems, however, broke into the very centre of his rebuke, with most singular effect, like a thought of the cold grave obtruding among wrathful passions.

'Let go my garment, fellow! I tell you, I know not the man you speak of. What! I have authority, I have—hem, hem—authority; and if this be the respect you show for your betters, your feet shall be brought acquainted with the stocks by daylight tomorrow morning!'

Robin released the old man's skirt, and hastened away, pursued by an ill-mannered roar of laughter from the barber's shop. He was at first considerably surprised by the result of his question, but, being a shrewd youth, soon thought himself able to account for the mystery.

'This is some country representative,' was his conclusion, 'who has never seen the inside of my kinsman's door, and lacks the breeding to answer a stranger civilly. The man is old, or verily—I might be tempted to turn back and smite him on the nose. Ah, Robin, Robin! even the barber's boys laugh at you for choosing such a guide! You will be wiser in time, friend Robin.'

He now became entangled in a succession of crooked and narrow streets, which crossed each other, and meandered at no great distance from the water-side. The smell of tar was obvious to his nostrils, the masts of vessels pierced the moonlight above the tops of the buildings, and the numerous signs, which Robin paused to read, informed him that he was near the centre of business.

But the streets were empty, the shops were closed, and lights were visible only in the second stories of a few dwelling-houses. At length, on the corner of a narrow lane, through which he was passing, he beheld the broad countenance of a British hero swinging before the door of an inn, whence proceeded the voices of many guests. The casement of one of the lower windows was thrown back, and a very thin curtain permitted Robin to distinguish a party at supper, round a well-furnished table. The fragrance of the good cheer steamed forth into the outer air, and the youth could not fail to recollect that the last remnant of his travelling stock of provision had yielded to his morning appetite, and that noon had found, and left him, dinnerless.

'O, that a parchment three-penny might give me a right to sit down at yonder table!' said Robin, with a sigh. 'But the major will make me welcome to the best of his victuals; so I will even step boldly in, and inquire my way to his dwelling.'

He entered the tavern, and was guided by the murmur of voices, and the fumes of tobacco, to the public room. It was a long and low apartment, with oaken walls, grown dark in the continual smoke, and a floor, which was thickly sanded, but of no immaculate purity. A number of persons—the larger part of whom appeared to be mariners, or in some way connected with the sea—occupied the wooden benches, or leather-bottomed chairs, conversing on various matters, and occasionally lending their attention to some topic of general interest. Three or four little groups were draining as many bowls of punch, which the West India trade had long since made a familiar drink in the colony. Others, who had the appearance of men who lived by regular and laborious handicraft, preferred the insulated bliss of an unshared potation, and became more taciturn under its influence. Nearly all, in short, evinced a predilection for the Good Creature in some of its various shapes, for this is a vice to which, as Fast-day sermons of a hundred years ago will testify, we have a long hereditary claim. The only guests to whom Robin's sympathics inclined him were two or three sheepish countrymen who were using the inn somewhat after the fashion of a Turkish caravansary; they had gotten themselves into the darkest corner of the room, and heedless of the Nicotian atmosphere, were supping on the bread of their own ovens, and the bacon cured in their own chimney-smoke. But though Robin felt a sort of brotherhood with these strangers, his eyes were attracted from them to a person who stood near the door, holding whispered conversation with a group of ill-dressed associates. His features were separately striking almost to grotesqueness, and the whole face left a deep impression on the memory. The forehead bulged out into a double prominence, with a vale between; the nose came boldly forth in an irregular curve, and its bridge was of more than a finger's breadth; the eyebrows were deep and shaggy, and the eyes glowed beneath them like a fire in a cave.

While Robin deliberated of whom to inquire respecting his kinsman's dwelling, he was accosted by the inn-keeper, a little man in a stained white apron, who had come to pay his professional welcome to the stranger. Being in the second generation from a French Protestant, he seemed to have inherited the courtesy of his parent nation; but no variety of circumstances was ever known to change his voice from the one shrill note in which he now addressed Robin.

'From the country, I presume, sir?' said he, with a profound bow. 'Beg leave to congratulate you on your arrival, and trust you intend a long stay with us. Fine town here, sir, beautiful buildings, and much that may interest a stranger. May I hope for the honour of your commands in respect to supper?'

'The man sees a family likeness! the rogue has guessed that I am related to the major!' thought Robin, who had hitherto experienced little superfluous civility.

All eyes were now turned on the country-lad standing at the door, in his worn three-cornered hat, grey-coat, leather breeches, and blue yarn stockings, leaning on an oaken cudgel, and bearing a wallet on his back.

Robin replied to the courteous innkeeper with such an assumption of confidence as befitted the major's relative. 'My honest friend,' he said, 'I shall make it a point to patronize your house on some occasion, when'—here he could not help lowering his voice—'when I may have more than a parchment threepence in my pocket. My present business,' continued he, speaking with lofty confidence, 'is merely to inquire my way to the dwelling of my kinsman, Major Molineux.'

There was a sudden and general movement in the room, which Robin interpreted as expressing the eagerness of each individual to become his guide. But the innkeeper turned his eyes to a written paper on the wall, which he read, or seemed to read, with occasional recurrences to the young man's figure.

'What have we here?' said he, breaking his speech into little dry fragments. ' "Left the house of the subscriber, bounden servant, Hezekiah Mudge,—had on, when he went away, grey coat, leather breeches, master's third best hat. One pound currency reward to whosoever shall lodge him in any jail of the province." Better trudge, boy, better trudge!'

Robin had begun to draw his hand towards the lighter

end of the oak cudgel, but a strange hostility in every countenance induced him to relinquish his purpose of breaking the courteous innkeeper's head. As he turned to leave the room, he encountered a sneering glance from the bold-featured personage whom he had before noticed; and no sooner was he beyond the door, than he heard a general laugh, in which the innkeeper's voice might be distinguished, like the dropping of small stones into a kettle.

'Now, is it not strange,' thought Robin, with his usual shrewdness, 'is it not strange that the confession of an empty pocket should outway the name of my kinsman, Major Molineux? Oh, if I had one of those grinning rascals in the woods, where I and my oak sapling grew up together, I would teach him that my arm is heavy, though my purse be light!'

On turning the corner of the narrow lane, Robin found himself in a spacious street, with an unbroken line of lofty houses on each side, and a steepled building at the upper end, whence the ringing of a bell announced the hour of nine. The light of the moon, and the lamps from the numerous shop windows, discovered people promenading on the pavement, and amongst them, Robin hoped to recognize his hitherto inscrutable relative. The result of his former inquiries made him unwilling to hazard another in a scene of such publicity, and he determined to walk slowly and silently up the street, thrusting his face close to that of every elderly gentleman, in search of the major's lineaments. In his progress, Robin encountered many gay and gallant figures. Embroidered garments of showy colours, enormous periwigs, gold-laced hats, and silver-hilted swords, glided past him and dazzled his optics. Travelled youths, imitators of the European fine gentlemen of the period, trod jauntily along, half-dancing to the fashionable tunes which they hummed, and making poor Robin ashamed of his quiet and natural gait. At length, after many pauses to examine the gorgeous display of goods in the shop windows, and after suffering some rebukes for the impertinence of his scrutiny into people's faces, the major's kinsman found himself near the steepled building, still unsuccessful in his search. As yet, however, he had seen only one side of the thronged street; so Robin crossed, and continued the same sort of inquisition down the opposite pavement, with stronger hopes than the philosopher seeking an honest man, but with no better fortune. He had arrived about midway towards the lower end, from which his course began, when he overheard the approach of someone, who struck down a cane on the flag-stones at every step, uttering at regular intervals two sepulchral hems.

'Mercy on us!' quoth Robin, recognizing the sound.

Turning a corner which chanced to be close at his right hand, he hastened to pursue his researches in some other part of the town. His patience now was wearing low, and he seemed to feel more fatigue from his rambles since he crossed the ferry, than from his journey of several days on the other side. Hunger also pleaded loudly within him, and Robin began to balance the propriety of demanding, violently, and with lifted cudgel, the necessary guidance from the first solitary passenger whom he should meet. While a resolution to this effect was gaining strength, he entered a street of mean appearance, on either side of which a row of ill-built houses was straggling towards the harbour. The moonlight fell upon no passenger along the whole extent, but in the third domicile which Robin passed there was a half-opened door, and his keen glance detected a woman's garment within.

'My luck may be better here,' said he to himself.

Accordingly he approached the door, and beheld it shut closer as he did so; yet an open space remained, sufficing for the fair occupant to observe the stranger, without a corresponding display on her part. All that Robin could discern was a strip of scarlet petticoat, and the occasional sparkle of an eye, as if the moonbeams were trembling on some bright thing.

'Pretty mistress,' for I may call her so with a good conscience, thought the shrewd youth, since I know nothing to the contrary,—'my sweet pretty mistress, will you be kind enough to tell me whereabouts I must seek the dwelling of my kinsman, Major Molineux?'

Robin's voice was plaintive and winning, and the female, seeing nothing to be shunned in the handsome country youth, thrust open the door, and came forth into the moonlight. She was a dainty little figure, with a white neck, round arms, and a slender waist, at the extremity of which her scarlet petticoat jutted out over a hoop, as if she were standing in a balloon. Moreover, her face was oval and pretty, her hair dark beneath the little cap, and her bright eyes possessed a sly freedom which triumphed over those of Robin.

'Major Molineux dwells here,' said this fair woman.

Now, her voice was the sweetest Robin had heard that night, the airy counterpart of a stream of melted silver; yet he could not help doubting whether that sweet voice spoke gospel truth. He looked up and down the mean street, and then surveyed the house before which they stood. It was a small, dark edifice of two stories, the second of which projected over the lower floor; and the front apartment had the aspect of a shop for petty commodities.

'Now truly I am in luck,' replied Robin, cunningly, 'and so indeed is my kinsman, the major, in having so pretty a housekeeper. But I prithee trouble him to step to the door; I will deliver him a message from his friends in the country, and then go back to my lodgings at the inn.'

'Nay, the major has been a-bed this hour or more,' said the lady of the scarlet petticoat; 'and it would be to little purpose to disturb him tonight, seeing his evening draught was of the strongest. But he is a kind-hearted man, and it would be as much as my life's worth to let a kinsman of his turn away from the door. You are the good old gentleman's very picture, and I could swear that was his rainy-weather hat. Also he has garments very much resembling those leather small-clothes; but come in, I pray, for I bid you hearty welcome in his name.'

So saying, the fair and hospitable dame took our hero by the hand; and the touch was light, and the force was gentleness, and though Robin read in her eyes what he did not hear in her words, yet the slender-waisted woman in the scarlet petticoat proved stronger than the athletic country youth. She had drawn his half-willing footsteps nearly to the threshold, when the opening of a door in the neighbourhood startled the major's housekeeper, and, leaving the major's kinsman, she vanished speedily into her own domicile. A heavy yawn preceded the appearance of a man, who like the Moonshine of Pyramus and Thisbe, carried a lantern, needlessly aiding his sister luminary in the heavens. As he walked sleepily up the street, he turned his broad, dull face on Robin, and displayed a long staff, spiked at the end.

'Home, vagabond, home!' said the watchman, in accents that seemed to fall asleep as soon as they were uttered. 'Home, or we'll set you in the stocks, by peep of day!'

'This is the second hint of the kind,' thought Robin. 'I wish they would end my difficulties, by setting me there tonight.'

Nevertheless, the youth felt an instinctive antipathy towards the guardian of midnight order, which at first prevented him from asking his usual question. But just when the man was about to vanish behind the corner, Robin resolved not to lose the opportunity, and shouted lustily after him.

'I say, friend! will you guide me to the house of my kinsman, Major Molineux?'

The watchman made no reply, but turned the corner, and was gone; yet Robin seemed to hear the sound of drowsy laughter stealing along the solitary street. At that moment, also, a pleasant titter saluted him from the open window above his head; he looked up, and caught the sparkle of a saucy eye; a round arm beckoned to him, and next he heard light footsteps descending the staircase within. But Robin, being of the household of a New England clergyman, was a good youth, as well as a shrewd one; so he resisted temptation, and fled away.

He now roamed desperately, and at random, through the town, almost ready to believe that a spell was on him, like that by which a wizard of his country had once kept three pursuers wandering, a whole winter night, within twenty paces of the cottage which they sought. The streets lay before him, strange and desolate, and the lights were extinguished in almost every house. Twice, however, little parties of men, among whom Robin distinguished individuals in outlandish attire, came hurrying along; but though, on both occasions, they paused to address him, such intercourse did not at all enlighten his perplexity. They did but utter a few words in some language of which Robin knew nothing, and perceiving his inability to answer, bestowed a curse upon him in plain English, and hastened away. Finally, the lad determined to knock at the door of every mansion that might appear worthy to

be occupied by his kinsman, trusting that perseverance
would overcome the fatality that had hitherto thwarted
him. Firm in this resolve, he was passing beneath the walls
of a church, which formed the corner of two streets, when,
as he turned into the shade of its steeple, he encountered
a bulky stranger, muffled in a cloak. The man was proceeding with the speed of earnest business, but Robin
planted himself full before him, holding the oak cudgel
with both hands across his body, as a bar to further
passage.

'Halt, honest man, and answer me a question,' said he,
very resolutely. 'Tell me, this instant, whereabouts is the
dwelling of my kinsman, Major Molineux!'

'Keep your tongue between your teeth, fool, and let
me pass,' said a deep, gruff voice, which Robin partly
remembered. 'Let me pass, I say, or I'll strike you to the
earth!'

'No, no, neighbour!' cried Robin, flourishing his
cudgel, and then thrusting its larger end close to the
man's muffled face. 'No, no, I'm not the fool you take me
for, nor do you pass till I have an answer to my question.
Whereabouts is the dwelling of my kinsman, Major
Molineux?'

The stranger, instead of attempting to force his passage,
stepped back into the moonlight, unmuffled his face, and
stared full into that of Robin.

'Watch here an hour, and Major Molineux will pass
by,' said he.

Robin gazed with dismay and astonishment on the unprecedented physiognomy of the speaker. The forehead,
with its double prominence, the broad hooked nose, the
shaggy eyebrows, and fiery eyes, were those which he had
noticed at the inn; but the man's complexion had undergone a singular, or, more properly, a two-fold change.

One side of the face blazed an intense red, while the other was black as midnight, the division line being in the broad bridge of the nose; and a mouth which seemed to extend from ear to ear, was black or red, in contrast to the colour of the cheek. The effect was as if two individual devils, a fiend of fire and a fiend of darkness, had united themselves to form this infernal visage. The stranger grinned in Robin's face, muffled his particoloured features, and was out of sight in a moment.

'Strange things we travellers see!' ejaculated Robin.

He seated himself, however, upon the steps of the church-door, resolving to wait the appointed time for his kinsman. A few moments were consumed in philosophical speculations upon the species of man who had just left him; but having settled this point, shrewdly, rationally, and satisfactorily, he was compelled to look elsewhere for his amusement. And first he threw his eyes along the street. It was of more respectable appearance than most of those into which he had wandered, and the moon, creating, like the imaginative power, a beautiful strangeness in familiar objects, gave something of a romance to a scene that might not have possessed it in the light of day. The irregular and often quaint architecture of the houses, some of whose roofs were broken into numerous little peaks, while others ascended, steep and narrow, into a single point, and others again were square; the pure snow-white of some of their complexions, the aged darkness of others, and the thousand sparklings reflected from bright substances in the walls of many; these matters engaged Robin's attention for a while, and then began to grow wearisome. Next he endeavoured to define the forms of distant objects, starting away, with almost ghostly indistinctness, just as his eye appeared to grasp them; and, finally, he took a minute survey of an edifice which stood on the opposite side of the street, directly in front of the church-door, where he was stationed. It was a large, square mansion, distinguished from its neighbours by a balcony, which rested on tall pillars, and by an elaborate Gothic window, communicating therewith.

'Perhaps this is the very house I have been seeking,' thought Robin.

Then he strove to speed away the time by listening to a murmur which swept continually along the street, yet was scarcely audible, except to an unaccustomed ear like his; it was a low, dull, dreamy sound, compounded of many noises, each of which was at too great a distance to be separately heard. Robin marvelled at this snore of a sleeping town, and marvelled more whenever its continuity was broken by, now and then, a distant shout, apparently loud, where it originated; but, altogether, it was a sleep-inspiring sound, and, to shake off its drowsy influence, Robin arose, and climbed a window-frame, that he might view the interior of the church. There the moonbeams came trembling in, and fell down upon the deserted pews, and extended along the quiet aisles. A fainter yet more awful radiance was hovering around the pulpit, and one solitary ray had dared to rest upon the opened page of the great bible. Had nature, in that deep hour, become a worshipper in the house which man had builded? Or was that heavenly light the visible sanctity of the place—visible because no earthly and impure feet were within the walls? The scene made Robin's heart shiver with a sensation of loneliness stronger than he had ever felt in the remotest depths of his native woods; so he turned away and sat down again before the door. There were graves around the church, and now an uneasy thought obtruded into Robin's breast. What if the object of his search, which had been so often and so strangely

thwarted, were all the time mouldering in his shroud?
What if his kinsman should glide through yonder gate,
and nod and smile to him in dimly passing by?

'Oh, that any breathing thing were here with me!' said
Robin.

Recalling his thoughts from this uncomfortable track,
he sent them over forest, hill, and stream, and attempted
to imagine how that evening of ambiguity and weariness
had been spent by his father's household. He pictured
them assembled at the door, beneath the tree—the great
old tree, which had been spared for its huge twisted trunk
and venerable shade, when a thousand leafy brethren fell.
There, at the going down of the summer sun, it was his
father's custom to perform domestic worship, that the
neighbours might come and join with him, like brothers
of the family, and that the wayfaring man might pause to
drink at that fountain, and keep his heart pure by refresh-
ing the memory of home. Robin distinguished the seat of
every individual of the little audience; he saw the good
man in the midst, holding the scriptures in the golden
light that fell from the western clouds; he beheld him
close the book, and all rise up to pray; he heard the old
thanksgivings for daily mercies, the old supplications for
their continuance, to which he had so often listened in
weariness, but which were now among his dear remem-
brances; he perceived the slight inequality of his father's
voice, when he came to speak of the absent one; he noted
how his mother turned her face to the broad and knotted
trunk; how his elder brother scorned, because the beard
was rough upon his upper lip, to permit his features to be
moved; how the younger sister drew down a low hanging
branch before her eyes; and how the little one of all,
whose sports had hitherto broken the decorum of the
scene, understood the prayer for her playmate, and burst

into clamorous grief; then he saw them go in at the door, and when Robin would have entered also, the latch tinkled into its place, and he was excluded from his home.

'Am I here, or there?' cried Robin, starting; for all at once, when his thoughts had become visible and audible in a dream, the long, wide, solitary street shone out before him.

He aroused himself, and endeavoured to fix his attention steadily upon the large edifice which he had surveyed before. But still his mind kept vibrating between fancy and reality; by turns, the pillars of the balcony lengthened into the tall, bare stems of pines, dwindled down to human figures, settled again into their true shape and size, and then commenced a new succession of changes. For a single moment, when he deemed himself awake, he could have sworn that a visage—one which he seemed to remember, yet could not absolutely name as his kinsman's—was looking towards him from the Gothic window. A deeper sleep wrestled with and nearly overcame him, but fled at the sound of footsteps along the opposite pavement. Robin rubbed his eyes, discerned a man passing at the foot of the balcony, and addressed him in a loud, peevish, and lamentable cry.

'Hallo, friend! must I wait here all night for my kinsman, Major Molineux?'

The sleeping echoes awoke, and answered the voice; and the passenger, barely able to discern a figure sitting in the oblique shade of the steeple, traversed the street to obtain a nearer view. He was himself a gentleman in his prime, of open, intelligent, cheerful, and altogether prepossessing countenance. Perceiving a country youth, apparently homeless and without friends, he accosted him in a tone of real kindness, which had become strange to Robin's ears.

'Well, my good lad, why are you sitting here?' inquired he. 'Can I be of service to you in any way?'

'I am afraid not, sir,' replied Robin, despondingly; 'yet I shall take it kindly, if you'll answer me a single question. I've been searching, half the night, for one Major Molineux, now, sir, is there really such a person in these parts, or am I dreaming?'

'Major Molineux! The name is not altogether strange to me,' said the gentleman, smiling. 'Have you any objection to telling me the nature of your business with him?'

Then Robin briefly related that his father was a clergyman, settled on a small salary, at a long distance back in the country, and that he and Major Molineux were brothers' children. The major, having inherited riches, and acquired civil and military rank, had visited his cousin, in great pomp, a year or two before; had manifested much interest in Robin and an elder brother, and, being childless himself, had thrown out hints respecting the future establishment of one of them in life. The elder brother was destined to succeed to the farm which his father cultivated in the interval of sacred duties; it was therefore determined that Robin should profit by his kinsman's generous intentions, especially as he seemed to be rather the favourite, and was thought to possess other necessary endowments.

'For I have the name of being a shrewd youth,' observed Robin in this part of his story.

'I doubt not you deserve it,' replied his new friend, good-naturedly; 'but pray proceed.'

'Well, sir, being nearly eighteen years old, and well-grown as you see,' continued Robin, drawing himself up to his full height, 'I thought it high time to begin the world. So my mother and sister put me in handsome trim, and my father gave me half the remnant of his last year's salary, and five days ago I started for this place, to pay the major a visit. But, would you believe it, sir! I crossed the ferry a little after dark, and have yet found nobody that would show me the way to his dwelling;— only an hour or two since, I was told to wait here, and Major Molineux would pass by.'

'Can you describe the man who told you this?' inquired the gentleman.

'Oh, he was a very ill-favoured fellow, sir,' replied Robin, 'with two great bumps on his forehead, a hook nose, fiery eyes,—and, what struck me as the strangest, his face was of two different colours. Do you happen to know such a man, sir?'

'Not intimately,' answered the stranger, 'but I chanced to meet him a little time previous to your stopping me. I believe you may trust his word, and that the major will very shortly pass through this street. In the meantime, as I have a singular curiosity to witness your meeting, I will sit down here upon the steps, and bear you company.'

He seated himself accordingly, and soon engaged his companion in animated discourse. It was but of brief continuance, however, for a noise of shouting, which had long been remotely audible, drew so much nearer, that Robin inquired its cause.

'What may be the meaning of this uproar?' asked he. 'Truly, if your town be always as noisy, I shall find little sleep while I am an inhabitant.'

'Why, indeed, friend Robin, there do appear to be three or four riotous fellows abroad tonight,' replied the gentleman. 'You must not expect all the stillness of your native woods here in our streets. But the watch will shortly be at the heels of these lads, and——'

'Ay, and set them in the stocks by peep of day,' interrupted Robin, recollecting his own encounter with the drowsy lantern-bearer. 'But, dear sir, if I may trust my ears an army of watchmen would never make head against such a multitude of rioters. There were at least a thousand voices went up to make that one shout.'

'May not a man have several voices, Robin, as well as two complexions?' said his friend.

'Perhaps a man may; but Heaven forbid that a woman should!' responded the shrewd youth, thinking of the seductive tones of the major's housekeeper.

The sounds of a trumpet in some neighbouring street now became so evident and continual, that Robin's curiosity was strongly excited. In addition to the shouts, he heard frequent bursts from many instruments of discord, and a wild and confused laughter filled up the intervals. Robin rose from the steps, and looked wistfully towards a point whither several people seemed to be hastening.

'Surely some prodigious merry-making is going on,' exclaimed he. 'I have laughed very little since I left home, sir, and should be sorry to lose an opportunity. Shall we step round the corner, by that darkish house, and take our share of the fun?'

'Sit down again, sit down, good Robin,' replied the gentleman, laying his hand on the skirt of the grey coat. 'You forget that we must wait here for your kinsman; and there is reason to believe that he will pass by in the course of a very few moments.'

The near approach of the uproar had now disturbed the neighbourhood; windows flew open on all sides; and many heads, in the attire of the pillow, and confused by sleep suddenly broken, were protruded to the gaze of whoever had leisure to observe them. Eager voices hailed each other from house to house, all demanding the explanation, which not a soul could give. Half-dressed men hurried towards the unknown commotion, stumbling as they went over the stone-steps that thrust themselves into the narrow foot-walk. The shouts, the laughter, and the tuneless bray, the antipodes of music, came onwards with increasing din, till scattered individuals, and then denser bodies began to appear round a corner at the distance of a hundred yards.

'Will you recognize your kinsman if he passes in this crowd?' inquired the gentleman.

'Indeed, I can't warrant it, sir; but I'll take my stand here, and keep a bright look-out,' answered Robin, descending to the outer edge of the pavement.

A mighty stream of people now emptied into the street, and came rolling slowly towards the church. A single horseman wheeled the corner in the midst of them, and close behind him, came a band of fearful wind instruments, sending forth a fresher discord, now that no intervening buildings kept it from the ear. Then a redder light disturbed the moonbeams, and a dense multitude of torches shone along the street, concealing by their glare whatever object they illuminated. The single horseman, clad in a military dress, and bearing a drawn sword, rode onward as the leader, and, by his fierce and variegated countenance, appeared like war personified; the red of one cheek was an emblem of fire and sword; the blackness of the other betokened the mourning that attends them. In his train were wild figures in the Indian dress, and many fantastic shapes without a model, giving the whole march a visionary air, is if a dream had broken forth from some feverish brain, and were sweeping visible through the midnight streets. A mass of people, inactive, except as applauding spectators, hemmed the procession in; and

several women ran along the side-walk, piercing the confusion of heavier sounds with their shrill voices of mirth
or terror.

'The double-faced fellow has his eye upon me,' muttered Robin, with an indefinite but an uncomfortable idea
that he was himself to bear a part in the pageantry.

The leader turned himself in the saddle, and fixed his
glance full upon the country youth, as the steed went
slowly by. When Robin had freed his eyes from those
fiery ones, the musicians were passing before him, and the
torches were close at hand; but the unsteady brightness of
the latter formed a veil which he could not penetrate. The
rattling of wheels over the stones sometimes found its
way to his ear, and confused traces of a human form
appeared at intervals, and then melted into the vivid light.
A moment more, and the leader thundered a command to
halt: the trumpets vomited a horrid breath, and then held
their peace; the shouts and laughter of the people died
away, and there remained only a universal hum, allied to
silence. Right before Robin's eyes was an uncovered cart.
There the torches blazed the brightest, there the moon
shone out like day, and there, in tar-and-feathery dignity,
sat his kinsman, Major Molineux!

He was an elderly man, of large and majestic person,
and strong, square features, betokening a steady soul; but
steady as it was, his enemies had found means to shake it.
His face was pale as death, and far more ghastly; the
broad forehead was contracted in his agony, so that his
eyebrows formed one grizzled line; his eyes were red and
wild, and the foam hung white upon his quivering lip.
His whole frame was agitated by a quick and continual
tremor, which his pride strove to quell, even in those circumstances of overwhelming humiliation. But perhaps
the bitterest pang of all was when his eyes met those of

Robin; for he evidently knew him on the instant, as the youth stood witnessing the foul disgrace of a head grown grey in honour. They stared at each other in silence, and Robin's knees shook, and his hair bristled, with a mixture of pity and terror. Soon, however, a bewildering excitement began to seize upon his mind; the preceding adventures of the night, the unexpected appearance of the crowd, the torches, the confused din and the hush that followed, the spectre of his kinsman reviled by that great multitude—all this, and, more than all, a perception of tremendous ridicule in the whole scene affected him with a sort of mental inebriety. At that moment a voice of sluggish merriment saluted Robin's ears; he turned instinctively, and just behind the corner of the church stood the lantern-bearer, rubbing his eyes, and drowsily enjoying the lad's amazement. Then he heard a peal of laughter like the ringing of silvery bells; a woman twitched his arm, a saucy eye met his, and he saw the lady of the scarlet petticoat. A sharp, dry cachinnation appealed to his memory, and, standing on tiptoe in the crowd, with his white apron over his head, he beheld the courteous little innkeeper. And lastly, there sailed over the heads of the multitude a great, broad laugh, broken in the midst by two sepulchral hems; thus, 'Haw, haw, haw,—hem, hem,—haw, haw, haw, haw!'

The sound proceeded from the balcony of the opposite edifice, and thither Robin turned his eyes. In front of the Gothic window stood the old citizen, wrapped in a wide gown, his grey periwig exchanged for a night-cap, which was thrust back from his forehead, and his silk stockings hanging about his legs. He supported himself on his polished cane in a fit of convulsive merriment, which manifested itself on his solemn old features like a funny inscription on a tombstone. Then Robin seemed to hear the voices of the barbers, of the guests of the inn, and of all who had made sport of him that night. The contagion was spreading among the multitude, when, all at once, it seized upon Robin, and he sent forth a shout of laughter that echoed through the street;—every man shook his sides, every man emptied his lungs, but Robin's shout was the loudest there. The cloud-spirits peeped from their silvery islands, as the congregated mirth went roaring up the sky! The Man in the Moon heard the far bellow; 'Oho,' quoth he, 'the old earth is frolicsome to-night!'

When there was a momentary calm in that tempestuous sea of sound, the leader gave the sign, the procession resumed its march. On they went, like fiends that throng in mockery around some dead potentate, mighty no more, but majestic still in his agony. On they went, in counterfeited pomp, in senseless uproar, in frenzied merriment, trampling all on an old man's heart. On swept the tumult, and left a silent street behind.

.   .   .   .

'Well, Robin, are you dreaming?' inquired the gentleman, laying his hand on the youth's shoulder.

Robin started, and withdrew his arm from the stone post to which he had instinctively clung, as the living stream rolled by him. His cheek was somewhat pale, and his eye not quite as lively as in the earlier part of the evening.

'Will you be kind enough to show me the way to the ferry?' said he, after a moment's pause.

'You have, then, adopted a new subject of inquiry?' observed his companion, with a smile.

'Why, yes, sir,' replied Robin, rather drily. 'Thanks to

you, and my other friends, I have at last met my kinsman, and he will scarce desire to see my face again. I begin to grow weary of a town life, sir. Will you show me the way to the ferry?'

'No, my good friend Robin,—not tonight, at least,' said the gentleman. 'Some few days hence, if you wish it, I will speed you on your journey. Or, if you prefer to remain with us, perhaps, as you are a shrewd youth, you may rise in the world without the help of your kinsman, Major Molineux.'

The Black Cat

EDGAR ALLAN POE

(1809–49)

FOR the most wild, yet most homely narrative which I am about to pen, I neither expect nor solicit belief. Mad indeed would I be to expect it, in a case where my very senses reject their own evidence. Yet, mad am I not—and very surely do I not dream. But tomorrow I die, and today I would unburden my soul. My immediate purpose is to place before the world, plainly, succinctly, and without comment, a series of mere household events. In their consequences, these events have terrified—have tortured —have destroyed me. Yet I will not attempt to expound them. To me, they have presented little but horror—to many they will seem less terrible than *baroques*. Hereafter, perhaps, some intellect may be found which will reduce my phantasm to the commonplace—some intellect more calm, more logical, and far less excitable than my own, which will perceive, in the circumstances I detail with awe, nothing more than an ordinary succession of very natural causes and effects.

From my infancy I was noted for the docility and humanity of my disposition. My tenderness of heart was even so conspicuous as to make me the jest of my companions. I was especially fond of animals, and was indulged by my parents with a great variety of pets. With these I spent most of my time, and never was so happy as when feeding and caressing them. This peculiarity of character grew with my growth, and, in my manhood, I derived from it one of my principal sources of pleasure. To those who have cherished an affection for a faithful and sagacious dog, I need hardly be at the trouble of explaining the nature or the intensity of the gratification thus derivable. There is something in the unselfish and self-sacrificing love of a brute, which goes directly to the heart of him who has had frequent occasion to test the paltry friendship and gossamer fidelity of mere *Man*.

I married early, and was happy to find in my wife a disposition not uncongenial with my own. Observing my partiality for domestic pets, she lost no opportunity of procuring those of the most agreeable kind. We had birds, goldfish, a fine dog, rabbits, a small monkey, and *a cat*.

This latter was a remarkably large and beautiful animal, entirely black, and sagacious to an astonishing degree. In speaking of his intelligence, my wife, who at heart was not a little tinctured with superstition, made frequent allusion to the ancient popular notion, which regarded all black cats as witches in disguise. Not that she was ever *serious* upon this point—and I mention the matter at all for no better reason than that it happens, just now, to be remembered.

Pluto—this was the cat's name—was my favourite pet and playmate. I alone fed him, and he attended me

wherever I went about the house. It was even with difficulty that I could prevent him from following me through
the streets.

Our friendship lasted, in this manner, for several years,
during which my general temperament and character—
through the instrumentality of the fiend Intemperance—
had (I blush to confess it) experienced a radical alteration
for the worse. I grew, day by day, more moody, more
irritable, more regardless of the feelings of others. I suffered myself to use intemperate language to my wife. At
length, I even offered her personal violence. My pets, of
course, were made to feel the change in my disposition.
I not only neglected, but ill-used them. For Pluto, however, I still retained sufficient regard to restrain me from
maltreating him, as I made no scruple of maltreating the
rabbits, the monkey, or even the dog, when by accident,
or through affection, they came in my way. But my disease
grew upon me—for what disease is like alcohol?—and
at length even Pluto, who was now becoming old, and
consequently somewhat peevish—even Pluto began to
experience the effects of my ill-temper.

One night, returning home, much intoxicated, from
one of my haunts about town, I fancied that the cat
avoided my presence. I seized him; when, in his fright
at my violence, he inflicted a slight wound upon my hand
with his teeth. The fury of a demon instantly possessed
me. I knew myself no longer. My original soul seemed, at
once, to take its flight from my body; and a more than
fiendish malevolence, gin-nurtured, thrilled every fibre
of my frame. I took from my waistcoat pocket a pen-knife,
opened it, grasped the poor beast by the throat, and
deliberately cut one of its eyes from the socket! I blush,
I burn, I shudder, while I pen the damnable atrocity.

When reason returned with the morning—when I had

slept off the fumes of the night's debauch—I experienced a sentiment half of horror, half of remorse, for the crime of which I had been guilty; but it was, at best, a feeble and equivocal feeling, and the soul remained untouched. I again plunged into excess, and soon drowned in wine all memory of the deed.

In the meantime the cat slowly recovered. The socket of the lost eye presented, it is true, a frightful appearance, but he no longer appeared to suffer any pain. He went about the house as usual, but, as might be expected, fled in extreme terror at my approach. I had so much of my old heart left, as to be at first grieved by this evident dislike on the part of a creature which had once so loved me. But this feeling soon gave place to irritation. And then came, as if to my final and irrevocable overthrow, the spirit of PERVERSENESS. Of this spirit philosophy takes no account. Yet I am not more sure that my soul lives, than I am that perverseness is one of the primitive impulses of the human heart—one of the indivisible primary faculties, or sentiments, which give direction to the character of man. Who has not, a hundred times, found himself committing a vile or a silly action, for no other reason than because he knows he should *not*? Have we not a perpetual inclination, in the teeth of our best judgement, to violate that which is *Law*, merely because we understand it to be such? This spirit of perverseness, I say, came to my final overthrow. It was this unfathomable longing of the soul *to vex itself*—to offer violence to its own nature—to do wrong for the wrong's sake only—that urged me to continue and finally to consummate the injury I had inflicted upon the unoffending brute. One morning, in cool blood, I slipped a noose about its neck and hung it to the limb of a tree—hung it with the tears streaming from my eyes, and with the bitterest remorse at my heart—hung it *because* I knew that it had loved me, and *because* I felt it had given me no reason of offence— hung it *because* I knew that in so doing I was committing a sin—a deadly sin that would so jeopardize my immortal soul as to place it—if such a thing were possible—even beyond the reach of the infinite mercy of the Most Merciful and Most Terrible God.

On the night of the day on which this cruel deed was done, I was aroused from sleep by the cry of 'Fire!' The curtains of my bed were in flames. The whole house was blazing. It was with great difficulty that my wife, a servant, and myself, made our escape from the conflagration. The destruction was complete. My entire worldly wealth was swallowed up, and I resigned myself thenceforward to despair.

I am above the weakness of seeking to establish a sequence of cause and effect between the disaster and the atrocity. But I am detailing a chain of facts, and wish not to leave even a possible link imperfect. On the day succeeding the fire, I visited the ruins. The walls, with one exception, had fallen in. This exception was found in a compartment wall, not very thick, which stood about the middle of the house, and against which had rested the head of my bed. The plastering had here, in great measure, resisted the action of the fire—a fact which I attributed to its having been recently spread. About this wall a dense crowd were collected, and many persons seemed to be examining a particular portion of it with very minute and eager attention. The words 'strange!' 'singular!' and other similar expressions, excited my curiosity. I approached and saw, as if graven in bas-relief upon the white surface, the figure of a gigantic *cat*. The impression was given with an accuracy truly marvellous. There was a rope about the animal's neck.

When I first beheld this apparition—for I could scarcely regard it as less—my wonder and my terror were extreme. But at length reflection came to my aid. The cat, I remembered, had been hung in a garden adjacent to the house. Upon the alarm of fire, this garden had been immediately filled by the crowd—by some one of whom the animal must have been cut from the tree and thrown, through an open window, into my chamber. This had probably been done with the view of arousing me from sleep. The falling of other walls had compressed the victim of my cruelty into the substance of the freshly-spread plaster; the lime of which, with the flames and the *ammonia* from the carcass, had then accomplished the portraiture as I saw it.

Although I thus readily accounted to my reason, if not altogether to my conscience, for the startling fact just detailed, it did not the less fail to make a deep impression upon my fancy. For months I could not rid myself of the phantasm of the cat; and, during this period, there came back into my spirit a half-sentiment that seemed, but was not, remorse. I went so far as to regret the loss of the animal, and to look about me, among the vile haunts which I now habitually frequented, for another pet of the same species, and of somewhat similar appearance, with which to supply its place.

One night as I sat, half stupefied, in a den of more than infamy, my attention was suddenly drawn to some black object, reposing upon the head of one of the immense hogsheads of gin, or of rum, which constituted the chief furniture of the apartment. I had been looking steadily at the top of this hogshead for some minutes, and what now caused me surprise was the fact that I had not sooner perceived the object thereupon. I approached it, and touched it with my hand. It was a black cat—a very large one—

fully as large as Pluto, and closely resembling him in every respect but one. Pluto had not a white hair upon any portion of his body; but this cat had a large, although indefinite, splotch of white, covering nearly the whole region of the breast.

Upon my touching him, he immediately arose, purred loudly, rubbed against my hand, and appeared delighted with my notice. This, then, was the very creature of which I was in search. I at once offered to purchase it of the landlord; but this person made no claim to it—knew nothing of it—had never seen it before.

I continued my caresses, and when I prepared to go home, the animal evinced a disposition to accompany me. I permitted it to do so; occasionally stooping and patting it as I proceeded. When it reached the house it domesticated itself at once, and became immediately a great favourite with my wife.

For my own part, I soon found a dislike to it arising within me. This was just the reverse of what I had anticipated; but—I know not how or why it was—its evident fondness for myself rather disgusted and annoyed me. By slow degrees, these feelings of disgust and annoyance rose into the bitterness of hatred. I avoided the creature; a certain sense of shame, and the remembrance of my former deed of cruelty, preventing me from physically abusing it. I did not, for some weeks, strike, or otherwise violently ill-use it; but gradually—very gradually—I came to look upon it with unutterable loathing, and to flee silently from its odious presence, as from the breath of a pestilence.

What added, no doubt, to my hatred of the beast, was the discovery, on the morning after I brought it home, that, like Pluto, it also had been deprived of one of its eyes. This circumstance, however, only endeared it to my wife, who, as I have already said, possessed, in a high degree, that humanity of feeling which had once been my distinguishing trait, and the source of many of my simplest and purest pleasures.

With my aversion to this cat, however, its partiality for myself seemed to increase. It followed my footsteps with a pertinacity which it would be difficult to make the reader comprehend. Whenever I sat, it would crouch beneath my chair, or spring upon my knees, covering me with its loathsome caresses. If I arose to walk, it would get between my feet, and thus nearly throw me down, or, fastening its long and sharp claws in my dress, clamber, in this manner, to my breast. At such times, although I longed to destroy it with a blow, I was yet withheld from so doing, partly by a memory of my former crime, but chiefly—let me confess it at once—by absolute *dread* of the beast.

This dread was not exactly a dread of physical evil— and yet I should be at a loss how otherwise to define it. I am almost ashamed to own—yes, even in this felon's cell, I am almost ashamed to own—that the terror and horror with which the animal inspired me, had been heightened by one of the merest chimeras it would be possible to conceive. My wife had called my attention, more than once, to the character of the mark of white hair, of which I have spoken, and which constituted the sole visible difference between the strange beast and the one I had destroyed. The reader will remember that this mark, although large had been originally very indefinite; but, by slow degrees—degrees nearly imperceptible, and which for a long time my reason struggled to reject as fanciful—it had, at length, assumed a rigorous distinctness of outline. It was now the representation of an object that I shudder to name—and for this, above all, I loathed,

and dreaded, and would have rid myself of the monster
had I dared—it was now, I say, the image of a hideous—
of a ghastly thing—of the GALLOWS!—oh, mournful and
terrible engine of horror and of crime—of agony and of
death!

And now was I indeed wretched beyond the wretchedness of mere humanity. And *a brute beast*—whose fellow
I had contemptuously destroyed—*a brute beast* to work
out for *me*—for me, a man, fashioned in the image of the
High God—so much of insufferable woe! Alas! neither
by day nor by night knew I the blessing of rest any more!
During the former the creature left me no moment alone;
and, in the latter, I started, hourly, from dreams of unutterable fear, to find the hot breath of *the thing* upon my
face, and its vast weight—an incarnate nightmare that I
had no power to shake off—incumbent eternally upon my
heart!

Beneath the pressure of torments such as these, the
feeble remnant of the good within me succumbed. Evil
thoughts became my sole intimates—the darkest and most
evil of thoughts. The moodiness of my usual temper
increased to hatred of all things and of all mankind; while,
from the sudden, frequent, and ungovernable outbursts
of a fury to which I now blindly abandoned myself, my
uncomplaining wife, alas! was the most usual and the
most patient of sufferers.

One day she accompanied me, upon some household
errand, into the cellar of the old building which our
poverty compelled us to inhabit. The cat followed me
down the steep stairs, and, nearly throwing me headlong,
exasperated me to madness. Uplifting an axe, and for-
getting, in my wrath, the childish dread which had hitherto stayed my hand, I aimed a blow at the animal which,
of course, would have proved instantly fatal had it

descended as I wished. But this blow was arrested by the hand of my wife. Goaded, by the interference, into a rage more than demoniacal, I withdrew my arm from her grasp, and buried the axe in her brain. She fell dead upon the spot, without a groan.

This hideous murder accomplished, I set myself forthwith, and with entire deliberation, to the task of concealing the body. I knew that I could not remove it from the house, either by day or by night, without the risk of being observed by the neighbours. Many projects entered my mind. At one period I thought of cutting the corpse into minute fragments, and destroying them by fire. At another, I resolved to dig a grave for it in the floor of the cellar. Again, I deliberated about casting it into the well in the yard—about packing it in a box, as if merchandise, with the usual arrangements, and so getting a porter to take it from the house. Finally I hit upon what I considered a far better expedient than either of these. I determined to wall it up in the cellar—as the monks of the Middle Ages are recorded to have walled up their victims.

For a purpose such as this the cellar was well adapted. Its walls were loosely constructed, and had lately been plastered throughout with a rough plaster, which the dampness of the atmosphere had prevented from hardening. Moreover, in one of the walls was a projection, caused by a false chimney, or fireplace, that had been filled up, and made to resemble the rest of the cellar. I made no doubt that I could readily displace the bricks at this point, insert the corpse, and wall the whole up as before, so that no eye could detect anything suspicious.

And in this calculation I was not deceived. By means of a crowbar I easily dislodged the bricks, and, having carefully deposited the body against the inner wall, I propped it in that position, while, with little trouble, I re-laid the whole structure as it originally stood. Having procured mortar, sand, and hair, with every possible precaution, I prepared a plaster which could not be distinguished from the old, and with this I very carefully went over the new brickwork. When I had finished, I felt satisfied that all was right. The wall did not present the slightest appearance of having been disturbed. The rubbish on the floor was picked up with the minutest care. I looked around triumphantly, and said to myself, 'Here at least, then, my labour has not been in vain.'

My next step was to look for the beast which had been the cause of so much wretchedness; for I had, at length, firmly resolved to put it to death. Had I been able to meet with it, at the moment, there could have been no doubt of its fate; but it appeared that the crafty animal had been alarmed at the violence of my previous anger, and forebore to present itself in my present mood. It is impossible to describe, or to imagine, the deep, the blissful sense of relief which the absence of the detested creature occasioned in my bosom. It did not make its appearance during the night—and thus for one night at least, since its introduction into the house, I soundly and tranquilly slept; aye, *slept* even with the burden of murder upon my soul!

The second and the third day passed, and still my tormentor came not. Once again I breathed as a free man. The monster, in terror, had fled the premises for ever! I should behold it no more! My happiness was supreme! The guilt of my dark deed disturbed me but little. Some few inquiries had been made, but these had been readily answered. Even a search had been instituted—but of course nothing was to be discovered. I looked upon my future felicity as secured.

Upon the fourth day of the assassination, a party of the police came, very unexpectedly, into the house, and proceeded again to make rigorous investigation of the premises. Secure, however, in the inscrutability of my place of concealment, I felt no embarrassment whatever. The officers bade me accompany them in their search. They left no nook or corner unexplored. At length, for the third or fourth time, they descended into the cellar. I quivered not in a muscle. My heart beat calmly as that of one who slumbers in innocence. I walked the cellar from end to end. I folded my arms upon my bosom, and roamed easily to and fro. The police were thoroughly satisfied, and prepared to depart. The glee at my heart was too strong to be restrained. I burned to say if but one word, by way of triumph, and to render doubly sure their assurance of my guiltlessness.

'Gentlemen,' I said at last, as the party ascended the steps, 'I delight to have allayed your suspicions. I wish you all health, and a little more courtesy. By-the-bye, gentlemen, this—this is a very well-constructed house.' (In the rabid desire to say something easily, I scarcely knew what I uttered at all.) 'I may say an *excellently* well-constructed house. These walls—are you going, gentlemen?—these walls are solidly put together;' and here, through the mere frenzy of bravado, I rapped heavily, with a cane which I held in my hand, upon that very portion of the brickwork behind which stood the corpse of the wife of my bosom.

But may God shield and deliver me from the fangs of the Arch-Fiend! No sooner had the reverberation of my blows sunk into silence, than I was answered by a voice from within the tomb!—by a cry, at first muffled and broken, like the sobbing of a child, and then quickly swelling into one long, loud, and continuous scream, utterly anomalous and inhuman—a howl—a wailing shriek, half of horror and half of triumph, such as might have arisen only out of hell, conjointly from the throats of the damned in their agony and of the demons that exult in the damnation.

Of my own thoughts it is folly to speak. Swooning, I staggered to the opposite wall. For one instant the party upon the stairs remained motionless, through extremity of terror and of awe. In the next, a dozen stout arms were toiling at the wall. It fell bodily. The corpse, already greatly decayed and clotted with gore, stood erect before the eyes of the spectators. Upon its head, with red extended mouth and solitary eye of fire, sat the hideous beast whose craft had seduced me into murder, and whose informing voice had consigned me to the hangman. I had walled the monster up within the tomb!

Benito Cereno

HERMAN MELVILLE
(1819–91)

In the year 1799, Captain Amasa Delano, of Duxbury, in Massachusetts, commanding a large sealer and general trader, lay at anchor, with a valuable cargo, in the harbour of St. Maria—a small, desert, uninhabited island towards the southern extremity of the long coast of Chili. There he had touched for water.

On the second day, not long after dawn, while lying in his berth, his mate came below, informing him that a strange sail was coming into the bay. Ships were then not so plenty in those waters as now. He rose, dressed, and went on deck.

The morning was one peculiar to that coast. Everything

was mute and calm; everything grey. The sea, though undulated into long roods of swells, seemed fixed, and was sleeked at the surface like waved lead that has cooled and set in the smelter's mould. The sky seemed a grey mantle. Flights of troubled grey fowl, kith and kin with flights of troubled grey vapours among which they were mixed, skimmed low and fitfully over the waters, as swallows over meadows before storms. Shadows present, foreshadowing deeper shadows to come.

To Captain Delano's surprise, the stranger, viewed through the glass, showed no colours; though to do so upon entering a haven, however uninhabited in its shores, where but a single other ship might be lying, was the custom among peaceful seamen of all nations. Considering the lawlessness and loneliness of the spot, and the sort of stories, at that day, associated with those seas, Captain Delano's surprise might have deepened into some uneasiness had he not been a person of a singularly undistrustful good nature, not liable, except on extraordinary and repeated excitement, and hardly then, to indulge in personal alarms, any way involving the imputation of malign evil in man. Whether, in view of what humanity is capable, such a trait implies, along with a benevolent heart, more than ordinary quickness and accuracy of intellectual perception, may be left to the wise to determine.

But whatever misgivings might have obtruded on first seeing the stranger, would almost, in any seaman's mind, have been dissipated by observing that the ship, in navigating into the harbour, was drawing too near the land, for her own safety's sake, owing to a sunken reef making out off her bow. This seemed to prove her a stranger, indeed, not only to the sealer, but the island; consequently, she could be no wonted freebooter on that ocean.

With no small interest, Captain Delano continued to
watch her—a proceeding not much facilitated by the
vapours partly mantling the hull, through which the far
matin light from her cabin streamed equivocally enough;
much like the sun—by this time crescented on the rim of
the horizon, and apparently, in company with the strange
ship, entering the harbour—which, wimpled by the same
low, creeping clouds, showed not unlike a Lima intri-
guante's one sinister eye peering across the Plaza from
the Indian loop-hole of her dusk *saya-y-manta*.

It might have been but a deception of the vapours, but,
the longer the stranger was watched, the more singular
appeared her manœuvres. Ere long it seemed hard to
decide whether she meant to come in or no—what she
wanted, or what she was about. The wind, which had
breezed up a little during the night, was now extremely
light and baffling, which the more increased the apparent
uncertainty of her movements.

Surmising, at last, that it might be a ship in distress,
Captain Delano ordered his whale-boat to be dropped,
and, much to the wary opposition of his mate, prepared
to board her, and, at the least, pilot her in. On the night
previous, a fishing-party of the seamen had gone a long
distance to some detached rocks out of sight from the
sealer, and, an hour or two before day-break, had returned
having met with no small success. Presuming that the
stranger might have been long off soundings, the good
captain put several baskets of the fish, for presents,
into his boat, and so pulled away. From her continuing too
near the sunken reef, deeming her in danger, calling to his
men, he made all haste to apprise those on board of their
situation. But, some time ere the boat came up, the wind,
light though it was, having shifted, had headed the vessel
off, as well as partly broken the vapours from about her.

Upon gaining a less remote view, the ship, whcn made signally visible on the verge of the leaden-hued swells, with the shreds of fog here and there raggedly furring her, appeared like a white-washed monastery after a thunder-storm, sccn perched upon some dun cliff among the Pyrenees. But it was no purely fanciful resemblance which now, for a moment, almost led Captain Delano to think that nothing less than a ship-load of monks was before him. Peering over the bulwarks were what really seemed, in the hazy distance, throngs of dark cowls; while, fitfully revealed through the open port-holes, other dark moving figures were dimly descried, as of Black Friars pacing the cloisters.

Upon a still nigher approach, this appearance was modified, and the true character of the vessel was plain — a Spanish merchantman of the first class; carrying negro slaves, amongst other valuable freight, from one colonial port to another. A very large, and, in its time, a very fine vessel, such as in those days were at intervals encountered along that main; sometimes superseded Acapulco treasure-ships, or retired frigates of the Spanish king's navy, which, like superannuated Italian palaces, still, under a decline of masters, preserved signs of former state.

As the whale-boat drew more and more nigh, the cause of the peculiar pipe-clayed aspect of the stranger was seen in the slovenly neglect pervading her. The spars, ropes, and great part of the bulwarks, looked woolly, from long unacquaintance with the scraper, tar, and the brush. Her keel seemed laid, her ribs put together, and she launched, from Ezekiel's Valley of Dry Bones.

In the present business in which she was engaged, the ship's general model and rig appeared to have undergone no material change from their original warlike and Froissart pattern. However, no guns were seen.

The tops were large, and were railed about with what had once been octagonal net-work, all now in sad disrepair. These tops hung overhead like three ruinous aviaries, in one of which was seen perched, on a ratlin, a white noddy, a strange fowl, so called from its lethargic somnambulistic character, being frequently caught by hand at sea. Battered and mouldy, the castellated forecastle seemed some ancient turret, long ago taken by assault, and then left to decay. Towards the stern, two high-raised quarter galleries—the balustrades here and there covered with dry, tindery sea-moss—opening out from the unoccupied state-cabin, whose dead lights, for all the mild weather, were hermetically closed and caulked—these tenantless balconies hung over the sea as if it were the grand Venetian canal. But the principal relic of faded grandeur was the ample oval of the shield-like stern-pieces intricately carved with the arms of Castile and Leon, medallioned about by groups of mythological or symbolical devices; uppermost and central of which was a dark satyr in a mask, holding his foot on the prostrate neck of a writhing figure, likewise masked.

Whether the ship had a figure-head, or only a plain beak, was not quite certain, owing to canvas wrapped about that part, either to protect it while undergoing a refurbishing, or else decently to hide its decay. Rudely painted or chalked, as in a sailor freak, along the forward side of a sort of pedestal below the canvas, was the sentence, '*Seguid vuestro jefe*,' (follow your leader); while upon the tarnished head-boards, near by, appeared, in stately capitals, once gilt, the ship's name, 'SAN DOMINICK,' each letter streakingly corroded with tricklings of copper-spike rust; while, like mourning weeds, dark festoons of sea-grass slimily swept to and fro over the name, with every hearse-like roll of the hull.

As at last the boat was hooked from the bow along toward the gangway amidship, its keel, while yet some inches separated from the hull, harshly grated as on a sunken coral reef. It proved a huge bunch of conglobated barnacles adhering below the water to the side like a wen; a token of baffling airs and long calms passed somewhere in those seas.

Climbing the side, the visitor was at once surrounded by a clamorous throng of whites and blacks, but the latter outnumbering the former more than could have been expected, negro transportation-ship as the stranger in port was. But, in one language, and as with one voice, all poured out a common tale of suffering; in which the negresses, of whom there were not a few, exceeded the others in their dolorous vehemence. The scurvy, together with a fever, had swept off a great part of their number, more especially the Spaniards. Off Cape Horn, they had narrowly escaped shipwreck; then, for days together, they had lain tranced without wind; their provisions were low; their water next to none; their lips that moment were baked.

While Captain Delano was thus made the mark of all eager tongues, his one eager glance took in all the faces, with every other object about him.

Always upon first boarding a large and populous ship at sea, especially a foreign one, with a nondescript crew such as Lascars or Manilla men, the impression varies in a peculiar way from that produced by first entering a strange house with strange inmates in a strange land. Both house and ship, the one by its walls and blinds, the other by its high bulwarks like ramparts, hoard from view their interiors till the last moment; but in the case of the ship there is this addition: that the living spectacle it contains, upon its sudden and complete disclosure, has, in contrast with the blank ocean which zones it, something of the effect of enchantment. The ship seems unreal; these strange costumes, gestures, and faces, but a shadowy tableau just emerged from the deep, which directly must receive back what it gave.

Perhaps it was some such influence as above is attempted to be described which, in Captain Delano's mind, heightened whatever, upon a staid scrutiny, might have seemed unusual; especially the conspicuous figures of four elderly grizzled negroes, their heads like black, doddered willow tops, who, in venerable contrast to the tumult below them, were couched sphynx-like, one on the starboard cat-head, another on the larboard, and the remaining pair face to face on the opposite bulwarks above the main-chains. They each had bits of unstranded old junk in their hands, and, with a sort of stoical self-content, were picking the junk into oakum, a small heap of which lay by their sides. They accompanied the task with a continuous, low, monotonous chant; droning and drooling away like so many grey-headed bag-pipers playing a funeral march.

The quarter-deck rose into an ample elevated poop, upon the forward verge of which, lifted, like the oakum-pickers, some eight feet above the general throng, sat along in a row, separated by regular spaces, the cross-legged figures of six other blacks; each with a rusty hatchet in his hand, which, with a bit of brick and a rag, he was engaged like a scullion in scouring; while between each two was a small stack of hatchets, their rusted edges turned forward awaiting a like operation. Though occasionally the four oakum-pickers would briefly address some person or persons in the crowd below, yet the six hatchet-polishers neither spoke to others, nor breathed a whisper among themselves, but sat intent upon their task, except at intervals, when, with the peculiar love in negroes of uniting industry with pastime, two-and-two they sideways clashed their hatchets together, like cymbals, with a barbarous din. All six, unlike the generality, had the raw aspect of unsophisticated Africans.

But that first comprehensive glance which took in those ten figures, with scores less conspicuous, rested but an instant upon them, as, impatient of the hubbub of voices, the visitor turned in quest of whomsoever it might be that commanded the ship.

But as if not unwilling to let nature make known her own case among his suffering charge, or else in despair of restraining it for the time, the Spanish captain, a gentlemanly, reserved-looking, and rather young man to a stranger's eye, dressed with singular richness, but bearing plain traces of recent sleepless cares and disquietudes, stood passively by, leaning against the main-mast, at one moment casting a dreary, spiritless look upon his excited people, at the next an unhappy glance toward his visitor. By his side stood a black of small stature, in whose rude face, as occasionally, like a shepherd's dog, he mutely turned it up into the Spaniard's, sorrow and affection were equally blended.

Struggling through the throng, the American advanced to the Spaniard, assuring him of his sympathies, and offering to render whatever assistance might be in his power. To which the Spaniard returned, for the present, but grave and ceremonious acknowledgements, his national formality dusked by the saturnine mood of ill health.

But losing no time in mere compliments, Captain Delano returning to the gangway, had his baskets of fish brought up; and as the wind still continued light, so that some hours at least must elapse ere the ship could be brought to the anchorage, he bade his men return to the sealer, and fetch back as much water as the whale-boat could carry, with whatever soft bread the steward might have, all the remaining pumpkins on board, with a box of sugar, and a dozen of his private bottles of cider.

Not many minutes after the boat's pushing off, to the vexation of all, the wind entirely died away, and the tide turning, began drifting back the ship helplessly seaward. But trusting this would not long last, Captain Delano sought with good hopes to cheer up the strangers, feeling no small satisfaction that, with persons in their condition he could—thanks to his frequent voyages along the Spanish main—converse with some freedom in their native tongue.

While left alone with them, he was not long in observing some things tending to heighten his first impressions; but surprise was lost in pity, both for the Spaniards and blacks, alike evidently reduced from scarcity of water and provisions; while long-continued suffering seemed to have brought out the less good-natured qualities of the negroes, besides, at the same time, impairing the Spaniard's authority over them. But, under the circumstances, precisely this condition of things was to have been anticipated. In armies, navies, cities, or families—in nature herself—nothing more relaxes good order than misery. Still, Captain Delano was not without the idea, that had Benito Cereno been a man of greater energy, misrule would hardly have come to the present pass. But the debility, constitutional or induced by the hardships, bodily and mental, of the Spanish captain, was too obvious to be overlooked. A prey to settled dejection, as if long mocked with hope he would not now indulge it, even when it had ceased to be a mock, the prospect of that day or evening at furthest, lying at anchor, with plenty of water for his people, and a brother captain to counsel and befriend, seemed in no perceptible degree to encourage him. His mind appeared unstrung, if not still more seriously affected. Shut up in these oaken walls, chained to one dull round of command, whose unconditionality cloyed him, like some hypochondriac abbot he moved slowly about, at times suddenly pausing, starting, or staring, biting his lip, biting his finger-nail, flushing, paling, twitching his beard, with other symptoms of an absent or moody mind. This distempered spirit was lodged, as before hinted, in as distempered a frame. He was rather tall, but seemed never to have been robust, and now with nervous suffering was almost worn to a skeleton. A tendency to some pulmonary complaint appeared to have been lately confirmed. His voice was like that of one with lungs half gone, hoarsely suppressed, a husky whisper. No wonder that, as in this state he tottered about, his private servant apprehensively followed him. Sometimes the negro gave his master his arm, or took his handkerchief out of his pocket for him; performing these and similar offices with that affectionate zeal which transmutes into something filial or fraternal acts in themselves but menial; and which has gained for the negro the repute of making the most pleasing body-servant in the world; one, too, whom a master need be on no stiffly superior terms with, but may treat with familiar trust; less a servant than a devoted companion.

Marking the noisy indocility of the blacks in general, as well as what seemed the sullen inefficiency of the whites, it was not without humane satisfaction that Captain Delano witnessed the steady good conduct of Babo.

But the good conduct of Babo, hardly more than the ill-behaviour of others, seemed to withdraw the half-lunatic Don Benito from his cloudy languor. Not that such precisely was the impression made by the Spaniard on the mind of his visitor. The Spaniard's individual unrest was, for the present, but noted as a conspicuous feature in the ship's general affliction. Still, Captain Delano was not a little concerned at what he could not help taking for the time to be Don Benito's unfriendly indifference toward himself. The Spaniard's manner, too, conveyed a sort of sour and gloomy disdain, which he seemed at no pains to disguise. But this the American in charity ascribed to the harassing effects of sickness, since, in former instances, he had noted that there are peculiar natures on whom prolonged physical suffering seems to cancel every social instinct of kindness; as if forced to black bread themselves, they deemed it but equity that each person coming nigh them should, indirectly, by some slight or affront, be made to partake of their fare.

But ere long Captain Delano bethought him that, indulgent as he was at the first, in judging the Spaniard, he might not, after all, have exercised charity enough. At bottom it was Don Benito's reserve which displeased him; but the same reserve was shown toward all but his personal attendant. Even the formal reports which, according to sea-usage, were at stated times made to him by some petty underling (either a white, mulatto, or black), he hardly had patience enough to listen to, without betraying contemptuous aversion. His manner upon such occasions was, in its degree, not unlike that which might be supposed to have been his imperial countryman's, Charles V., just previous to the anchoritish retirement of that monarch from the throne.

This splenetic disrelish of his place was evinced in almost every function pertaining to it. Proud as he was moody, he condescended to no personal mandate. Whatever special orders were necessary, their delivery was delegated to his body-servant, who in turn transferred them to their ultimate destination, through runners, alert Spanish boys or slave boys, like pages or pilot-fish within easy call continually hovering round Don Benito. So that to have beheld this undemonstrative invalid gliding about, apathetic and mute, no landsman could have dreamed that in him was lodged a dictatorship beyond which, while at sea, there was no earthly appeal.

Thus, the Spaniard, regarded in his reserve, seemed as the involuntary victim of mental disorder. But, in fact, his reserve might, in some degree, have proceeded from design. If so, then in Don Benito was evinced the unhealthy climax of that icy though conscientious policy, more or less adopted by all commanders of large ships, which, except in signal emergencies, obliterates alike the manifestation of sway with every trace of sociality; transforming the man into a block, or rather into a loaded cannon, which, until there is call for thunder, has nothing to say.

Viewing him in this light, it seemed but a natural token of the perverse habit induced by a long course of such hard self-restraint, that, notwithstanding the present condition of his ship, the Spaniard should still persist in a demeanour, which, however harmless—or it may be, appropriate—in a well-appointed vessel, such as the *San Dominick* might have been at the outset of the voyage, was anything but judicious now. But the Spaniard perhaps thought that it was with captains as with gods: reserve, under all events, must still be their cue. But more probably this appearance of slumbering dominion might have been but an attempted disguise to conscious imbecility—not deep policy, but shallow device. But be all this as it might, whether Don Benito's manner was designed or not, the more Captain Delano noted its pervading reserve,

BENITO CERENO   49

the less he felt uneasiness at any particular manifestation
of that reserve toward himself.

Neither were his thoughts taken up by the captain
alone. Wonted to the quiet orderliness of the sealer's comfortable family of a crew, the noisy confusion of the *San
Dominick's* suffering host repeatedly challenged his eye.
Some prominent breaches not only of discipline but of
decency were observed. These Captain Delano could not
but ascribe, in the main, to the absence of those subordinate deck-officers to whom, along with higher duties,
is entrusted what may be styled the police department of
a populous ship. True, the old oakum-pickers appeared
at times to act the part of monitorial constables to their
countrymen, the blacks; but though occasionally succeeding in allaying trifling outbreaks now and then between
man and man, they could do little or nothing toward
establishing general quiet. The *San Dominick* was in the
condition of a transatlantic emigrant ship, among whose
multitude of living freight are some individuals, doubtless,
as little troublesome as crates and bales; but the friendly
remonstrances of such with their ruder companions are
of not so much avail as the unfriendly arm of the mate.
What the *San Dominick* wanted was, what the emigrant
ship has, stern superior officers. But on these decks not so
much as a fourth mate was to be seen.

The visitor's curiosity was roused to learn the particulars of those mishaps which had brought about such
absenteeism, with its consequences; because, though
deriving some inkling of the voyage from the wails which
at the first moment had greeted him, yet of the details no
clear understanding had been had. The best account
would, doubtless, be given by the captain. Yet at first the
visitor was loth to ask it, unwilling to provoke some distant rebuff. But plucking up courage, he at last accosted

Don Benito, renewing the expression of his benevolent interest, adding, that did he (Captain Delano) but know the particulars of the ship's misfortunes, he would, perhaps, be better able in the end to relieve them. Would Don Benito favour him with the whole story?

Don Benito faltered; then, like some somnambulist suddenly interfered with, vacantly stared at his visitor, and ended by looking down on the deck. He maintained this posture so long, that Captain Delano, almost equally disconcerted, and involuntarily almost as rude, turned suddenly from him, walking forward to accost one of the Spanish seamen for the desired information. But he had hardly gone five paces, when with a sort of eagerness Don Benito invited him back, regretting his momentary absence of mind, and professing readiness to gratify him.

While most part of the story was being given, the two captains stood on the after part of the main-deck, a privileged spot, no one being near but the servant.

'It is now a hundred and ninety days,' began the Spaniard, in his husky whisper, 'that this ship, well officered and well manned, with several cabin passengers —some fifty Spaniards in all—sailed from Buenos Ayres bound to Lima, with a general cargo, Paraguay tea and the like—and,' pointing forward, 'that parcel of negroes, now not more than a hundred and fifty, as you see, but then numbering over three hundred souls. Off Cape Horn we had heavy gales. In one moment, by night, three of my best officers, with fifteen sailors, were lost, with the main-yard; the spar snapping under them in the slings, as they sought, with heavers, to beat down the icy sail. To lighten the hull, the heavier sacks of mata were thrown into the sea, with most of the water-pipes lashed on deck at the time. And this last necessity it was, combined with the prolonged detentions afterwards experienced, which eventually brought about our chief causes of suffering. When—'

Here there was a sudden fainting attack of his cough, brought on, no doubt, by his mental distress. His servant sustained him, and drawing a cordial from his pocket placed it to his lips. He a little revived. But unwilling to leave him unsupported while yet imperfectly restored, the black with one arm still encircled his master, at the same time keeping his eye fixed on his face, as if to watch for the first sign of complete restoration, or relapse, as the event might prove.

The Spaniard proceeded, but brokenly and obscurely, as one in a dream.

—'Oh, my God! rather than pass through what I have, with joy I would have hailed the most terrible gales; but—'

His cough returned and with increased violence; this subsiding, with reddened lips and closed eyes he fell heavily against his supporter.

'His mind wanders. He was thinking of the plague that followed the gales,' plaintively sighed the servant; 'my poor, poor master!' wringing one hand, and with the other wiping the mouth. 'But be patient, Señor,' again turning to Captain Delano, 'these fits do not last long; master will soon be himself.'

Don Benito reviving, went on; but as this portion of the story was very brokenly delivered, the substance only will here be set down.

It appeared that after the ship had been many days tossed in storms off the Cape, the scurvy broke out, carrying off numbers of the whites and blacks. When at last they had worked round into the Pacific, their spars and sails were so damaged, and so inadequately handled by the surviving mariners, most of whom were become invalids, that, unable to lay her northerly course by the wind, which was powerful, the unmanageable ship for successive days and nights was blown northwestward, where the breeze suddenly deserted her, in unknown waters to sultry calms. The absence of the water-pipes now proved as fatal to life as before their presence had menaced it. Induced, or at least aggravated, by the more than scanty allowance of water, a malignant fever followed the scurvy; with the excessive heat of the lengthened calm, making such short work of it as to sweep away, as by billows, whole familes of the Africans, and a yet larger number, proportionably, of the Spaniards, including, by a luckless fatality, every officer on board. Consequently, in the smart west winds eventually following the calm, the already rent sails having to be simply dropped, not furled, at need, had been gradually reduced to the beggar's rags they were now. To procure substitutes for his lost sailors, as well as supplies of water and sails, the captain at the earliest opportunity had made for Baldivia, the southernmost civilized port of Chili and South America; but upon nearing the coast the thick weather had prevented him from so much as sighting that harbour. Since which period, almost without a crew, and almost without canvas and almost without water, and at intervals giving its added dead to the sea, the *San Dominick* had been battle-dored about by contrary winds, inveigled by currents, or grown weedy in calms. Like a man lost in woods, more than once she had doubled upon her own track.

'But throughout these calamities,' huskily continued Don Benito, painfully turning in the half embrace of his servant, 'I have to thank those negroes you see, who, though to your inexperienced eyes appearing unruly, have, indeed, conducted themselves with less of restlessness than even their owner could have thought possible under such circumstances.'

Here he again fell faintly back. Again his mind wandered: but he rallied, and less obscurely proceeded.

'Yes, their owner was quite right in assuring me that no fetters would be needed with his blacks; so that while, as is wont in this transportation, those negroes have always remained upon deck—not thrust below, as in the Guinea-men—they have, also, from the beginning, been freely permitted to range within given bounds at their pleasure.'

Once more the faintness returned—his mind roved—but, recovering, he resumed:

'But it is Babo here to whom, under God, I owe not only my own preservation, but likewise to him, chiefly, the merit is due, of pacifying his more ignorant brethren, when at intervals tempted to murmurings.'

'Ah, master,' sighed the black, bowing his face, 'don't speak of me; Babo is nothing; what Babo has done was but duty.'

'Faithful fellow!' cried Captain Delano. 'Don Benito, I envy you such a friend; slave I cannot call him.'

As master and man stood before him, the black up-holding the white, Captain Delano could not but bethink him of the beauty of that relationship which could present such a spectacle of fidelity on the one hand and confidence on the other. The scene was heightened by the contrast in dress, denoting their relative positions. The Spaniard wore a loose Chili jacket of dark velvet; white small clothes and stockings, with silver buckles at the knee and instep; a high-crowned sombrero, of fine grass; a slender sword, silver mounted, hung from a knot in his sash; the last being an almost invariable adjunct, more for utility than ornament, of a South American gentleman's dress to this hour. Excepting when his occasional nervous contortions brought about disarray, there was a certain precision in his attire, curiously at variance with the unsightly disorder around; especially in the belittered Ghetto, forward of the main-mast, wholly occupied by the blacks.

The servant wore nothing but wide trousers, apparently, from their coarseness and patches, made out of some old topsail; they were clean, and confined at the waist by a bit of unstranded rope, which, with his composed, deprecatory air at times, made him look something like a begging friar of St. Francis.

However unsuitable for the time and place, at least in the blunt-thinking American's eyes, and however strangely surviving in the midst of all his afflictions, the toilette of Don Benito might not, in fashion at least, have gone beyond the style of the day among South Americans of his class. Though on the present voyage sailing from Buenos Ayres, he had avowed himself a native and resident of Chili, whose inhabitants had not so generally adopted the plain coat and once plebeian pantaloons; but, with a becoming modification, adhered to their provincial costume, picturesque as any in the world. Still, relatively to the pale history of the voyage, and his own pale face, there seemed something so incongruous in the Spaniard's apparel, as almost to suggest the image of an invalid courtier tottering about London streets in the time of the plague.

The portion of the narrative which, perhaps, most excited interest, as well as some surprise, considering the latitudes in question, was the long calms spoken of, and more particularly the ship's so long drifting about. Without communicating the opinion, of course, the American could not but impute at least part of the detentions both to clumsy seamanship and faulty navigation. Eyeing Don

Benito's small, yellow hands, he easily inferred that the young captain had not got into command at the hawse-hole but the cabin-window, and if so, why wonder at incompetence, in youth, sickness, and aristocracy united? Such was his democratic conclusion.

But drowning criticism in compassion, after a fresh repetition of his sympathies, Captain Delano having heard out his story, not only engaged, as in the first place, to see Don Benito and his people supplied in their immediate bodily needs, but, also, now further promised to assist him in procuring a large permanent supply of water, as well as some sails and rigging; and, though it would involve no small embarrassment to himself, yet he would spare three of his best seamen for temporary deck officers; so that without delay the ship might proceed to Concepcion, there fully to refit for Lima, her destined port.

Such generosity was not without its effect, even upon the invalid. His face lighted up; eager and hectic, he met the honest glance of his visitor. With gratitude he seemed overcome.

'This excitement is bad for master,' whispered the servant, taking his arm, and with soothing words gently drawing him aside.

When Don Benito returned, the American was pained to observe that his hopefulness, like the sudden kindling in his cheek, was but febrile and transient.

Ere long, with a joyless mien, looking up toward the poop, the host invited his guest to accompany him there, for the benefit of what little breath of wind might be stirring.

As during the telling of the story, Captain Delano had once or twice started at the occasional cymballing of the hatchet-polishers, wondering why such an interruption should be allowed, especially in that part of the ship, and in the ears of an invalid; and, moreover, as the hatchets had anything but an attractive look, and the handlers of them still less so, it was, therefore, to tell the truth, not without some lurking reluctance, or even shrinking, it may be, that Captain Delano, with apparent complaisance, acquiesced in his host's invitation. The more so, since with an untimely caprice of punctilio, rendered distressing by his cadaverous aspect, Don Benito, with Castilian bows, solemnly insisted upon his guest's preceding him up the ladder leading to the elevation; where, one on each side of the last step, sat four armorial supporters and sentries, two of the ominous file. Gingerly enough stepped good Captain Delano between them, and in the instant of leaving them behind, like one running the gauntlet, he felt an apprehensive twitch in the calves of his legs.

But when, facing about, he saw the whole file, like so many organ-grinders, still stupidly intent on their work, unmindful of everything beside, he could not but smile at his late fidgeting panic.

Presently, while standing with Don Benito, looking forward upon the decks below, he was struck by one of those instances of insubordination previously alluded to. Three black boys, with two Spanish boys, were sitting together on the hatches, scraping a rude wooden platter, in which some scanty mess had recently been cooked. Suddenly, one of the black boys, enraged at a word dropped by one of his white companions, seized a knife, and though called to forbear by one of the oakum-pickers, struck the lad over the head, inflicting a gash from which blood flowed.

In amazement, Captain Delano inquired what this meant. To which the pale Benito dully muttered, that it was merely the sport of the lad.

'Pretty serious sport, truly,' rejoined Captain Delano.

'Had such a thing happened on board the *Bachelor's Delight*, instant punishment would have followed.'

At these words the Spaniard turned upon the American one of his sudden, staring, half-lunatic looks; then, relapsing into his torpor, answered, 'Doubtless, doubtless, Señor.'

Is it, thought Captain Delano, that this helpless man is one of those paper captains I've known, who by policy wink at what by power they cannot put down? I know no sadder sight than a commander who has little of command but the name.

'I should think, Don Benito,' he now said, glancing toward the oakum-picker who had sought to interfere with the boys, 'that you would find it advantageous to keep all your blacks employed, especially the younger ones, no matter at what useless task, and no matter what happens to the ship. Why, even with my little band, I find such a course indispensable. I once kept a crew on my quarterdeck thrumming mats for my cabin, when, for three days, I had given up my ship—mats, men, and all—for a speedy loss, owing to the violence of a gale in which we could do nothing but helplessly drive before it.'

'Doubtless, doubtless,' muttered Don Benito.

'But,' continued Captain Delano, again glancing upon the oakum-pickers and then at the hatchet-polishers, near by, 'I see you keep some at least of your host employed.'

'Yes,' was again the vacant response.

'Those old men there, shaking their pows from their pulpits,' continued Captain Delano, pointing to the oakum-pickers, 'seem to act the part of old dominies to the rest, little heeded as their admonitions are at times. Is this voluntary on their part, Don Benito, or have you appointed them shepherds to your flock of black sheep?'

'What posts they fill, I appointed them,' rejoined the

Spaniard in acrid tone, as if resenting some supposed satiric reflection.

'And these others, these Ashantee conjurors here,' continued Captain Delano, rather uneasily eyeing the brandished steel of the hatchet-polishers, where in spots it had been brought to a shine, 'this seems a curious business they are at, Don Benito?'

'In the gales we met,' answered the Spaniard, 'what of our general cargo was not thrown overboard was much damaged by the brine. Since coming into calm weather, I have had several cases of knives and hatchets daily brought up for overhauling and cleaning.'

'A prudent idea, Don Benito. You are part owner of ship and cargo, I presume; but not of the slaves, perhaps?'

'I am owner of all you see,' impatiently returned Don Benito, 'except the main company of blacks, who belonged to my late friend, Alexandro Aranda.'

As he mentioned this name, his air was heart-broken, his knees shook; his servant supported him.

Thinking he divined the cause of such unusual emotion, to confirm his surmise, Captain Delano, after a pause, said, 'And may I ask, Don Benito, whether—since awhile ago you spoke of some cabin passengers—the friend, whose loss so afflicts you, at the outset of the voyage accompanied his blacks?'

'Yes.'

'But died of the fever?'

'Died of the fever.—Oh, could I but—'

Again quivering, the Spaniard paused.

'Pardon me,' said Captain Delano slowly, 'but I think that, by a sympathetic experience, I conjecture, Don Benito, what it is that gives the keener edge to your grief. It was once my hard fortune to lose at sea a dear friend, my own brother, then supercargo. Assured of the welfare of his spirit, its departure I could have borne like a man; but that honest eye, that honest hand—both of which had so often met mine—and that warm heart; all, all—like scraps to the dogs—to throw all to the sharks! It was then I vowed never to have for fellow-voyager a man I loved, unless, unbeknown to him, I had provided every requisite, in case of a fatality, for embalming his mortal part for interment on shore. Were your friend's remains now on board this ship, Don Benito, not thus strangely would the mention of his name affect you.'

'On board this ship?' echoed the Spaniard. Then, with horrified gestures, as directed against some spectre, he unconsciously fell into the ready arms of his attendant, who, with a silent appeal toward Captain Delano, seemed beseeching him not again to broach a theme so unspeakably distressing to his master.

This poor fellow now, thought the pained American, is the victim of that sad superstition which associates goblins with the deserted body of man, as ghosts with an abandoned house. How unlike are we made! What to me, in like case, would have been a solemn satisfaction, the bare suggestion, even, terrifies the Spaniard into this trance. Poor Alexandro Aranda! what would you say could you here see your friend—who, on former voyages, when you for months were left behind, has, I dare say, often longed, and longed, for one peep at you—now transported with terror at the least thought of having you anyway nigh him.

At this moment, with a dreary graveyard toll, betokening a flaw, the ship's forecastle bell, smote by one of the grizzled oakum-pickers, proclaimed ten o'clock through the leaden calm; when Captain Delano's attention was caught by the moving figure of a gigantic black, emerging from the general crowd below, and slowly advancing toward the elevated poop. An iron collar was about his neck, from which depended a chain, thrice wound round his body; the terminating links padlocked together at a broad band of iron, his girdle.

'How like a mute Atufal moves,' murmured the servant.

The black mounted the steps of the poop, and, like a brave prisoner, brought up to receive sentence, stood in unquailing muteness before Don Benito, now recovered from his attack.

At the first glimpse of his approach, Don Benito had started, a resentful shadow swept over his face; and, as with the sudden memory of bootless rage, his white lips glued together.

This is some mulish mutineer, thought Captain Delano, surveying, not without a mixture of admiration, the colossal form of the negro.

'See, he waits your question, master,' said the servant.

Thus reminded, Don Benito, nervously averting his glance, as if shunning, by anticipation, some rebellious response, in a disconcerted voice, thus spoke:

'Atufal, will you ask my pardon now?'

The black was silent.

'Again, master,' murmured the servant, with bitter upbraiding eyeing his countryman; 'Again, master; he will bend to master yet.'

'Answer,' said Don Benito, still averting his glance, 'say but the one word *pardon*, and your chains shall be off.'

Upon this, the black, slowly raising both arms, let them lifelessly fall, his links clanking, his head bowed; as much as to say, 'No, I am content.'

'Go,' said Don Benito, with inkept and unknown emotion.

Deliberately as he had come, the black obeyed.

'Excuse me, Don Benito,' said Captain Delano, 'but this scene surprises me; what means it, pray?'

'It means that that negro alone, of all the band, has given me peculiar cause of offence. I have put him in chains; I—'

Here he paused; his hand to his head, as if there were a swimming there, or a sudden bewilderment of memory had come over him; but meeting his servant's kindly glance seemed reassured, and proceeded:

'I could not scourge such a form. But I told him he must ask my pardon. As yet he has not. At my command, every two hours he stands before me.'

'And how long has this been?'

'Some sixty days.'

'And obedient in all else? And respectful?'

'Yes.'

'Upon my conscience, then,' exclaimed Captain Delano, impulsively, 'he has a royal spirit in him, this fellow.'

'He may have some right to it,' bitterly returned Don Benito; 'he says he was king in his own land.'

'Yes,' said the servant, entering a word, 'those slits in Atufal's ears once held wedges of gold; but poor Babo here, in his own land, was only a poor slave; a black man's slave was Babo, who now is the white's.'

Somewhat annoyed by these conversational familiarities, Captain Delano turned curiously upon the attendant, then glanced inquiringly at his master; but, as if long wonted to these little informalities, neither master nor man seemed to understand him.

'What, pray, was Atufal's offence, Don Benito?' asked Captain Delano; 'if it was not something very serious, take a fool's advice, and, in view of his general docility, as well as in some natural respect for his spirit, remit his penalty.'

'No, no, master never will do that,' here murmured the servant to himself, 'proud Atufal must first ask master's pardon. The slave there carries the padlock, but master here carries the key.'

His attention thus directed, Captain Delano now noticed for the first time that, suspended by a slender silken cord, from Don Benito's neck hung a key. At once, from the servant's muttered syllables divining the key's purpose, he smiled and said: 'So, Don Benito—padlock and key—significant symbols, truly.'

Biting his lip, Don Benito faltered.

Though the remark of Captain Delano, a man of such native simplicity as to be incapable of satire or irony, had been dropped in playful allusion to the Spaniard's singularly evidenced lordship over the black; yet the hypochondriac seemed in some way to have taken it as a malicious reflection upon his confessed inability thus far to break down, at least, on a verbal summons, the entrenched will of the slave. Deploring this supposed misconception, yet despairing of correcting it, Captain Delano shifted the subject; but finding his companion more than ever withdrawn, as if still slowly digesting the lees of the presumed affront above-mentioned, by-and-by Captain Delano likewise became less talkative, oppressed, against his own will, by what seemed the secret vindictiveness of the morbidly sensitive Spaniard. But the good sailor himself, of a quite contrary disposition, refrained, on his part, alike from the appearance as from the feeling of resentment, and if silent, was only so from contagion.

Presently the Spaniard, assisted by his servant, somewhat discourteously crossed over from Captain Delano;

a procedure which, sensibly enough, might have been allowed to pass for idle caprice of ill-humour, had not master and man, lingering round the corner of the elevated skylight, begun whispering together in low voices. This was unpleasing. And more: the moody air of the Spaniard, which at times had not been without a sort of vale-tudinarian stateliness, now seemed anything but digni-fied; while the menial familiarity of the servant lost its original charm of simple-hearted attachment.

In his embarrassment, the visitor turned his face to the other side of the ship. By so doing, his glance accidentally fell on a young Spanish sailor, a coil of rope in his hand, just stepped from the deck to the first round of the mizzen-rigging. Perhaps the man would not have been parti-cularly noticed, were it not that, during his ascent to one of the yards, he, with a sort of covert intentness, kept his eye fixed on Captain Delano, from whom, presently, it passed, as if by a natural sequence, to the two whisperers.

His own attention thus redirected to that quarter, Captain Delano gave a slight start. From something in Don Benito's manner just then, it seemed as if the visitor had, at least partly, been the subject of the withdrawn consultation going on—a conjecture as little agreeable to the guest as it was little flattering to the host.

The singular alternations of courtesy and ill-breeding in the Spanish captain were unaccountable, except on one of two suppositions—innocent lunacy, or wicked im-posture.

But the first idea, though it might naturally have occurred to an indifferent observer, and, in some respect, had not hitherto been wholly a stranger to Captain Delano's mind, yet, now that, in an incipient way, he began to regard the stranger's conduct something in the light of an intentional affront, of course the idea of lunacy was virtually vacated. But if not a lunatic, what then? Under the circumstances, would a gentleman, nay, any honest boor, act the part now acted by his host? The man was an impostor. Some low-born adventurer, masquerading as an oceanic grandee; yet so ignorant of the first requisites of mere gentlemanhood as to be betrayed into the present remarkable indecorum. That strange ceremoniousness, too, at other times evinced, seemed not uncharacteristic of one playing a part above his real level. Benito Cereno—Don Benito Cereno—a sounding name. One, too, at that period, not unknown, in the surname, to supercargoes and sea captains trading along the Spanish Main, as belonging to one of the most enterprising and extensive mercantile families in all those provinces; several members of it having titles; a sort of Castilian Rothschild, with a noble brother, or cousin, in every great trading town of South America. The alleged Don Benito was in early manhood, about twenty-nine or thirty. To assume a sort of roving cadetship in the maritime affairs of such a house, what more likely scheme for a young knave of talent and spirit? But the Spaniard was a pale invalid. Never mind. For even to the degree of simulating mortal disease, the craft of some tricksters had been known to attain. To think that, under the aspect of infantile weakness, the most savage energies might be couched—those velvets of the Spaniard but the velvet paw to his fangs.

From no train of thought did these fancies come; not from within, but from without; suddenly, too, and in one throng, like hoar frost; yet as soon to vanish as the mild sun of Captain Delano's good-nature regained its meridian.

Glancing over once again toward Don Benito—whose side-face, revealed above the skylight, was now turned toward him—Captain Delano was struck by the profile, whose clearness of cut was refined by the thinness incident to ill-health, as well as ennobled about the chin by the beard. Away with suspicion. He was a true off-shoot of a true hidalgo Cereno.

Relieved by these and other better thoughts, the visitor, lightly humming a tune, now began indifferently pacing the poop, so as not to betray to Don Benito that he had at all mistrusted incivility, much less duplicity; for such mistrust would yet be proved illusory, and by the event; though, for the present, the circumstance which had provoked that distrust remained unexplained. But when that little mystery should have been cleared up, Captain Delano thought he might extremely regret it, did he allow Don Benito to become aware that he had indulged in ungenerous surmises. In short, to the Spaniard's black-letter text, it was best, for a while, to leave open margin.

Presently, his pale face twitching and overcast, the Spaniard, still supported by his attendant, moved over toward his guest, when, with even more than his usual embarrassment, and a strange sort of intriguing intonation in his husky whisper, the following conversation began:

'Señor, may I ask how long you have lain at this isle?'

'Oh, but a day or two, Don Benito.'

'And from what port are you last?'

'Canton.'

'And there, Señor, you exchanged your seal-skins for teas and silks, I think you said?'

'Yes. Silks, mostly.'

'And the balance you took in specie, perhaps?'

Captain Delano, fidgeting a little, answered—

'Yes; some silver; not a very great deal, though.'

'Ah—well. May I ask how many men have you on board, Señor?'

Captain Delano slightly started, but answered:

'About five-and-twenty, all told.'

'And at present, Señor, all on board, I suppose?'

'All on board, Don Benito,' replied the captain now with satisfaction.

'And will be tonight, Señor?'

At this last question, following so many pertinacious ones, for the soul of him Captain Delano could not but look very earnestly at the questioner, who, instead of meeting the glance, with every token of craven discomposure dropped his eyes to the deck; presenting an unworthy contrast to his servant, who, just then, was kneeling at his feet adjusting a loose shoe-buckle; his disengaged face meantime, with humble curiosity, turned openly up into his master's downcast one.

The Spaniard, still with a guilty shuffle, repeated his question:

'And—and will be tonight, Señor?'

'Yes, for aught I know,' returned Captain Delano,— 'but nay,' rallying himself into fearless truth, 'some of them talked of going off on another fishing party about midnight.'

'Your ships generally go—go more or less armed, I believe, Señor?'

'Oh, a six-pounder or two, in case of emergency,' was the intrepidly indifferent reply, 'with a small stock of muskets, sealing-spears, and cutlasses, you know.'

As he thus responded, Captain Delano again glanced at Don Benito, but the latter's eyes were averted; while abruptly and awkwardly shifting the subject, he made some peevish allusion to the calm, and then, without apology, once more, with his attendant, withdrew to the opposite bulwarks, where the whispering was resumed.

At this moment, and ere Captain Delano could cast a cool thought upon what had just passed, the young Spanish sailor before mentioned was seen descending from the rigging. In act of stooping over to spring inboard to the deck, his voluminous, unconfined frock, or shirt, of coarse wollen, much spotted with tar, opened out far down the chest, revealing a soiled under-garment of what seemed the finest linen, edged, about the neck, with a narrow blue ribbon, sadly faded and worn. At this moment the young sailor's eye was again fixed on the whisperers, and Captain Delano thought he observed a lurking significance in it, as if silent sighs of some free-mason sort had that instant been interchanged.

This once more impelled his own glance in the direction of Don Benito, and, as before, he could not but infer that himself formed the subject of the conference. He paused. The sound of the hatchet-polishing fell on his ears. He cast another swift side-look at the two. They had the air of conspirators. In connection with the late questionings, and the incident of the young sailor, these things now begat such return of involuntary suspicion, that the singular guilelessness of the American could not endure it. Plucking up a gay and humorous expression, he crossed over to the two rapidly, saying: 'Ha, Don Benito, your black here seems high in your trust; a sort of privy-counsellor, in fact.'

Upon this, the servant looked up with a good-natured grin, but the master started as from a venomous bite. It was a moment or two before the Spaniard sufficiently recovered himself to reply; which he did, at last, with cold constraint: 'Yes, Señor, I have trust in Babo.'

Here Babo, changing his previous grin of mere animal

humour into an intelligent smile, not ungratefully eyed his master.

Finding that the Spaniard now stood silent and reserved, as if involuntarily, or purposely giving hint that his guest's proximity was inconvenient just then, Captain Delano, unwilling to appear uncivil even to incivility itself, made some trivial remark and moved off; again and again turning over in his mind the mysterious demeanour of Don Benito Cereno.

He had descended from the poop, and, wrapped in thought, was passing near a dark hatchway, leading down into the steerage, when, perceiving motion there, he looked to see what moved. The same instant there was a sparkle in the shadowy hatchway, and he saw one of the Spanish sailors, prowling there, hurriedly placing his hand in the bosom of his frock, as if hiding something. Before the man could have been certain who it was that was passing, he slunk below out of sight. But enough was seen of him to make it sure that he was the same young sailor before noticed in the rigging.

What was that which so sparkled? thought Captain Delano. It was no lamp—no match—no live coal. Could it have been a jewel? But how come sailors with jewels?— or with silk-trimmed under-shirts either? Has he been robbing the trunks of the dead cabin passengers? But if so, he would hardly wear one of the stolen articles on board ship here. Ah, ah—if now that was, indeed, a secret sign I saw passing between this suspicious fellow and his captain awhile since; if I could only be certain that in my uneasiness my senses did not deceive me, then—

Here, passing from one suspicious thing to another, his mind revolved the point of the strange questions put to him concerning his ship.

By a curious coincidence, as each point was recalled,

the black wizards of Ashantee would strike up with their hatchets, as in ominous comment on the white stranger's thoughts. Pressed by such enigmas and portents, it would have been almost against nature, had not, even into the least distrustful heart, some ugly misgivings obtruded.

Observing the ship now helplessly fallen into a current, with enchanted sails, drifting with increased rapidity seaward; and noting that, from a lately intercepted projection of the land, the sealer was hidden, the stout mariner began to quake at thoughts which he barely durst confess to himself. Above all, he began to feel a ghostly dread of Don Benito. And yet when he roused himself, dilated his chest, felt himself strong on his legs, and coolly considered it—what did all these phantoms amount to?

Had the Spaniard any sinister scheme, it must have reference not so much to him (Captain Delano) as to his ship (the *Bachelor's Delight*). Hence the present drifting away of the one ship from the other, instead of favouring any such possible scheme, was, for the time at least, opposed to it. Clearly any suspicion, combining such contradictions, must need be delusive. Beside, was it not absurd to think of a vessel in distress—a vessel by sickness almost dismanned of her crew—a vessel whose inmates were parched for water—was it not a thousand times absurd that such a craft should, at present, be of a piratical character; or her commander, either for himself or those under him, cherish any desire but for speedy relief and refreshment? But then, might not general distress, and thirst in particular, be affected? And might not that same undiminished Spanish crew, alleged to have perished off to a remnant, be at that very moment lurking in the hold? On heart-broken pretence of entreating a cup of cold water, fiends in human form had got into lonely dwellings, nor retired until a dark deed had been done. And among the Malay pirates, it was no unusual thing to lure ships after them into their treacherous harbours, or entice boarders from a declared enemy at sea, by the spectacle of thinly manned or vacant decks, beneath which prowled a hundred spears with yellow arms ready to upthrust them through the mats. Not that Captain Delano had entirely credited such things. He had heard of them—and now, as stories, they recurred. The present destination of the ship was the anchorage. There she would be near his own vessel. Upon gaining that vicinity, might not the *San Dominick*, like a slumbering volcano, suddenly let loose energies now hid?

He recalled the Spaniard's manner while telling his story. There was a gloomy hesitancy and subterfuge about it. It was just the manner of one making up his tale for evil purposes, as he goes. But if that story was not true, what was the truth? That the ship had unlawfully come into the Spaniard's possession? But in many of its details, especially in reference to the more calamitous parts, such as the fatalities among the seamen, the consequent prolonged beating about, the past sufferings from obstinate calms, and still continued suffering from thirst; in all these points, as well as others, Don Benito's story had corroborated not only the wailing ejaculations of the indiscriminate multitude, white and black, but likewise— what seemed impossible to be counterfeit—by the very expression and play of every human feature, which Captain Delano saw. If Don Benito's story was throughout an invention, then every soul on board, down to the youngest negress, was his carefully drilled recruit in the plot: an incredible inference. And yet, if there was ground for mistrusting the Spanish captain's veracity, that inference was a legitimate one.

In short, scarce an uneasiness entered the honest sailor's mind but, by a subsequent spontaneous act of good sense, it was ejected. At last he began to laugh at these forebodings; and laugh at the strange ship for, in its aspect someway siding with them, as it were; and laugh, too, at the odd-looking blacks, particularly those old scissors-grinders, the Ashantees; and those bed-ridden old knitting-women, the oakum-pickers; and, in a human way, he almost began to laugh at the dark Spaniard himself, the central hobgoblin of all.

For the rest, whatever in a serious way seemed enigmatical, was now good-naturedly explained away by the thought that, for the most part, the poor invalid scarcely knew what he was about; either sulking in black vapours, or putting random questions without sense or object. Evidently, for the present, the man was not fit to be entrusted with the ship. On some benevolent plea withdrawing the command from him, Captain Delano would yet have to send her to Concepcion in charge of his second mate, a worthy person and good navigator—a plan which would prove no wiser for the *San Dominick* than for Don Benito; for—relieved from all anxiety, keeping wholly to his cabin—the sick man, under the good nursing of his servant, would probably, by the end of the passage, be in a measure restored to health and with that he should also be restored to authority.

Such were the American's thoughts. They were tranquillizing. There was a difference between the idea of Don Benito's darky preordaining Captain Delano's fate, and Captain Delano's lightly arranging Don Benito's. Nevertheless, it was not without something of relief that the good seaman presently perceived his whale-boat in the distance. Its absence had been prolonged by unexpected detention at the sealer's side, as well as its returning trip lengthened by the continual recession of the goal.

The advancing speck was observed by the blacks. Their shouts attracted the attention of Don Benito, who, with a return of courtesy, approaching Captain Delano, expressed satisfaction at the coming of some supplies, slight and temporary as they must necessarily prove.

Captain Delano responded; but while doing so, his attention was drawn to something passing on the deck below: among the crowd climbing the landward bulwarks, anxiously watching the coming boat, two blacks, to all appearances accidentally incommoded by one of the sailors, flew out against him with horrible curses, which the sailor someway resenting, the two blacks dashed him to the deck and jumped upon him, despite the earnest cries of the oakum-pickers.

'Don Benito,' said Captain Delano quickly, 'do you see what is going on there? Look!'

But, seized by his cough, the Spaniard staggered, with both hands to his face, on the point of falling. Captain Delano would have supported him, but the servant was more alert, who, with one hand sustaining his master, with the other applied the cordial. Don Benito, restored, the black withdrew his support, slipping aside a little, but dutifully remaining within call of a whisper. Such discretion was here evinced as quite wiped away, in the visitor's eyes, any blemish of impropriety which might have attached to the attendant, from the indecorous conferences before mentioned; showing, too, that if the servant were to blame, it might be more the master's fault than his own, since when left to himself he could conduct thus well.

His glance thus called away from the spectacle or disorder to the more pleasing one before him, Captain

Delano could not avoid again congratulating Don Benito upon possessing such a servant, who, though perhaps a little too forward now and then, must upon the whole be invaluable to one in the invalid's situation.

'Tell me, Don Benito,' he added, with a smile—'I should like to have your man here myself—what will you take for him? Would fifty doubloons be any object?'

'Master wouldn't part with Babo for a thousand doubloons,' murmured the black, overhearing the offer, and taking it in earnest, and, with the strange vanity of a faithful slave appreciated by his master, scorning to hear so paltry a valuation put upon him by a stranger. But Don Benito, apparently hardly yet completely restored, and again interrupted by his cough, made but some broken reply.

Soon his physical distress became so great, affecting his mind, too, apparently, that, as if to screen the sad spectacle, the servant gently conducted his master below.

Left to himself, the American, to while away the time till his boat should arrive, would have pleasantly accosted some one of the few Spanish seamen he saw; but recalling something that Don Benito had said touching their ill conduct, he refrained, as a ship-master indisposed to countenance cowardice or unfaithfulness in seamen.

While, with these thoughts, standing with eye directed forward toward that handful of sailors—suddenly he thought that some of them returned the glance and with a sort of meaning. He rubbed his eyes, and looked again; but again seemed to see the same thing. Under a new form, but more obscure than any previous one, the old suspicions recurred, but, in the absence of Don Benito, with less of panic than before. Despite the bad account given of the sailors, Captain Delano resolved forthwith to accost one of them. Descending the poop, he made his

way through the blacks, his movement drawing a queer
cry from the oakum-pickers, prompted by whom the
negroes, twitching each other aside, divided before him;
but, as if curious to see what was the object of this deliberate visit to their Ghetto, closing in behind, in tolerable
order, followed the white stranger up. His progress thus
proclaimed as by mounted kings-at-arms, and escorted
as by a Caffre guard of honour, Captain Delano, assuming
a good-humoured, off-hand air, continued to advance;
now and then saying a blithe word to the negroes, and his
eye curiously surveying the white faces, here and there
sparsely mixed in with the blacks, like stray white pawns
venturously involved in the ranks of the chessmen opposed.

While thinking which of them to select for his purpose,
he chanced to observe a sailor seated on the deck engaged
in tarring the strap of a large block, with a circle of blacks
squatted round him inquisitively eyeing the process.

The mean employment of the man was in contrast with
something superior in his figure. His hand, black with
continually thrusting it into the tar-pot held for him by
a negro, seemed not naturally allied to his face, a face
which would have been a very fine one but for its haggardness. Whether this haggardness had aught to do with
criminality, could not be determined; since, as intense
heat and cold, though unlike, produce like sensations, so
innocence and guilt, when, through casual association
with mental pain, stamping any visible impress, use one
seal—a hacked one.

Not again that this reflection occurred to Captain
Delano at the time, charitable man as he was. Rather
another idea. Because observing so singular a haggardness
to be combined with a dark eye, averted as in trouble and
shame, and then, however illogically, uniting in his mind

his own private suspicions of the crew with the confessed ill-opinion on the part of their captain, he was insensibly operated upon by certain general notions, which, while disconnecting pain and abashment from virtue, as invariably link them with vice.

If, indeed, there be any wickedness on board this ship, thought Captain Delano, be sure that man there has fouled his hand in it, even as now he fouls it in the pitch. I don't like to accost him. I will speak to this other, this old Jack here on the windlass.

He advanced to an old Barcelona tar, in ragged red breeches and dirty night-cap, cheeks trenched and bronzed, whiskers dense as thorn hedges. Seated between two sleepy-looking Africans, this mariner, like his younger shipmate, was employed upon some rigging— splicing a cable—the sleepy-looking blacks performing the inferior function of holding the outer parts of the ropes for him.

Upon Captain Delano's approach, the man at once hung his head below its previous level; the one necessary for business. It appeared as if he desired to be thought absorbed, with more than common fidelity, in his task. Being addressed, he glanced up, but with what seemed a furtive, diffident air, which sat strangely enough on his weather-beaten visage, much as if a grizzly bear, instead of growling and biting, should simper and cast sheep's eyes. He was asked several questions concerning the voyage—questions purposely referring to several particulars in Don Benito's narrative—not previously corroborated by those impulsive cries greeting the visitor on first coming on board. The questions were briefly answered, confirming all that remained to be confirmed of the story. The negroes about the windlass joined in with the old sailor, but, as they became talkative, he by degrees became mute, and at length quite glum, seemed morosely unwilling to answer more questions, and yet, all the while, this ursine air was somehow mixed with his sheepish one.

Despairing of getting into unembarrassed talk with such a centaur, Captain Delano, after glancing round for a more promising countenance, but seeing none, spoke pleasantly to the blacks to make way for him; and so, amid various grins and grimaces, returned to the poop, feeling a little strange at first, he could hardly tell why, but upon the whole with regained confidence in Benito Cereno.

How plainly, thought he, did that old whiskerando yonder betray a consciousness of ill-desert. No doubt, when he saw me coming, he dreaded lest I, apprised by his captain of the crew's general misbehaviour, came with sharp words for him, and so down with his head. And yet—and yet, now that I think of it, that very old fellow, if I err not, was one of those who seemed so earnestly eyeing me here awhile since. Ah, these currents spin one's head round almost as much as they do the ship. Ha, there now's a pleasant sort of sunny sight; quite sociable, too.

His attention had been drawn to a slumbering negress, partly disclosed through the lace-work of some rigging, lying, with youthful limbs carelessly disposed, under the lee of the bulwarks, like a doe in the shade of a woodland rock. Sprawling at her lapped breasts was her wide-awake fawn, stark naked, its black little body half lifted from the deck, crosswise with its dam's; its hands, like two paws, clambering upon her; its mouth and nose ineffectually rooting to get at the mark; and meantime giving a vexatious half-grunt, blending with the composed snore of the negress.

The uncommon vigour of the child at length roused the mother. She started up, at distance facing Captain

Delano. But, as if not at all concerned at the attitude in which she had been caught, delightedly she caught the child up, with maternal transports, covering it with kisses.

There's naked nature, now; pure tenderness and love, thought Captain Delano, well pleased.

This incident prompted him to remark the other negresses more particularly than before. He was gratified with their manners; like most uncivilized women, they seemed at once tender of heart and tough of constitution; equally ready to die for their infants or fight for them. Unsophisticated as leopardesses; loving as doves. Ah! thought Captain Delano, these perhaps are some of the very women whom Mungo Park saw in Africa, and gave such a noble account of.

These natural sights somehow insensibly deepened his confidence and ease. At last he looked to see how his boat was getting on; but it was still pretty remote. He turned to see if Don Benito had returned; but he had not.

To change the scene, as well as to please himself with a leisurely observation of the coming boat, stepping over into the mizzen-chains he clambered his way into the starboard quarter-gallery; one of those abandoned Venetian-looking water-balconies previously mentioned; retreats cut off from the deck. As his foot pressed the half-damp, half-dry sea-mosses matting the place, and a chance phantom cats-paw—an islet of breeze, unheralded, un-followed—as this ghostly cats-paw came fanning his cheek, as his glance fell upon the row of small, round dead-lights, all closed like coppered eyes of the coffined, and the state-cabin door, once connecting with the gallery, even as the dead-lights had once looked out upon it, but now caulked fast like a sarcophagus lid; to a purple-black, tarred-over panel, threshold, and post; and he bethought him of the time, when that state-cabin and this state-balcony had heard the voices of the Spanish king's officers, and the forms of the Lima viceroy's daughters had per-haps leaned where he stood—as these and other images flitted through his mind, as the cats-paw through the calm, gradually he felt rising a dreamy inquietude, like that of one who alone on the prairie feels unrest from the repose of the noon.

He leaned against the carved balustrade, again looking off toward his boat; but found his eye falling upon the ribboned grass, trailing along the ship's water-line, straight as a border of green box; and parterres of sea-weed, broad ovals and crescents, floating nigh and far, with what seemed long formal alleys between, crossing the terraces of swells, and sweeping round as if leading to the grottoes below. And overhanging all was the balustrade by his arm, which, partly stained with pitch and partly embossed with moss, seemed the charred ruin of some summer-house in a grand garden long running to waste.

Trying to break one charm, he was but becharmed anew. Though upon the wide sea, he seemed in some far inland country; prisoner in some deserted château, left to stare at empty grounds, and peer out at vague roads, where never wagon or wayfarer passed.

But these enchantments were a little disenchanted as his eye fell on the corroded main-chains. Of an ancient style, massy and rusty in link, shackle and bolt, they seemed even more fit for the ship's present business than the one for which probably she had been built.

Presently he thought something moved nigh the chains. He rubbed his eyes, and looked hard. Groves of rigging were about the chains; and there, peering from behind a great stay, like an Indian from behind a hemlock, a Spanish sailor, a marlingspike in his hand, was seen, who made what seemed an imperfect gesture toward the balcony—but immediately, as if alarmed by some advancing step along the deck within, vanished into the recesses of the hempen forest, like a poacher.

What meant this? Something the man had sought to communicate, unbeknown to anyone, even to his captain. Did the secret involve aught unfavourable to his captain? Were those previous misgivings of Captain Delano's about to be verified? Or, in his haunted mood at the moment, had some random, unintentional motion of the man, while busy with the stay, as if repairing it, been mistaken for a significant beckoning?

Not unbewildered, again he gazed off for his boat. But it was temporarily hidden by a rocky spur of the isle. As with some eagerness he bent forward, watching for the first shooting view of its beak, the balustrade gave way before him like charcoal. Had he not clutched an outreaching rope he would have fallen into the sea. The crash, though feeble, and the fall, though hollow, of the rotten fragments, must have been overheard. He glanced up. With sober curiosity peering down upon him was one of the old oakum-pickers, slipped from his perch to an outside boom; while below the old negro—and, invisible to him, reconnoitring from a port-hole like a fox from the mouth of its den—crouched the Spanish sailor again. From something suddenly suggested by the man's air, the mad idea now darted into Captain Delano's mind; that Don Benito's plea of indisposition, in withdrawing below, was but a pretence: that he was engaged there maturing some plot, of which the sailor, by some means gaining an inkling, had a mind to warn the stranger against; incited, it may be, by gratitude for a kind word on first boarding the ship. Was it from foreseeing some possible interference like this, that Don Benito had, beforehand, given such a bad character of his sailors, while praising the negroes; though, indeed, the former seemed as docile as the latter the contrary? The whites, too, by nature, were the shrewder race. A man with some evil design, would not he be likely to speak well of that stupidity which was blind to his depravity, and malign that intelligence from which it might not be hidden? Not unlikely, perhaps. But if the whites had dark secrets concerning Don Benito, could then Don Benito be any way in complicity with the blacks? But they were too stupid. Besides, who ever heard of a white so far a renegade as to apostatize from his very species almost, by leaguing in against it with negroes? These difficulties recalled former ones. Lost in their mazes, Captain Delano, who had now regained the deck, was uneasily advancing along it, when he observed a new face: an aged sailor seated cross-legged near the main hatchway. His skin was shrunk up with wrinkles like a pelican's empty pouch; his hair frosted; his countenance grave and composed. His hands were full of ropes, which he was working into a large knot. Some blacks were about him obligingly dipping the strands for him, here and there, as the exigencies of the operation demanded.

Captain Delano crossed over to him, and stood in silence surveying the knot; his mind, by a not uncongenial transition, passing from its own entanglements to those of the hemp. For intricacy such a knot he had never seen in an American ship, or indeed any other. The old man looked like an Egyptian priest, making gordian knots for the temple of Ammon. The knot seemed a combination of double-bow-line-knot, treble-crown-knot, back-handed-well-knot, knot-in-and-out-knot, and jamming-knot.

At last, puzzled to comprehend the meaning of such a knot, Captain Delano, addressed the knotter:—

'What are you knotting there, my man?'

'The knot,' was the brief reply, without looking up.

'So it seems; but what is it for?'

'For someone else to undo,' muttered back the old man, plying his fingers harder than ever, the knot being now nearly completed.

While Captain Delano stood watching him, suddenly the old man threw the knot toward him, and said in broken English,—the first heard in the ship,—something to this effect—'Undo it, cut it, quick.' It was said lowly, but with such condensation of rapidity, that the long, slow words in Spanish, which had preceded and followed, almost operated as covers to the brief English between.

For a moment, knot in hand, and knot in head, Captain Delano stood mute; while, without further heeding him, the old man was now intent upon other ropes. Presently there was a slight stir behind Captain Delano. Turning, he saw the chained negro, Atufal, standing quietly there. The next moment the old sailor rose, muttering, and, followed by his subordinate negroes, removed to the forward part of the ship, where in the crowd he disappeared.

An elderly negro, in a clout like an infant's, and with a pepper and salt head, and a kind of attorney air, now approached Captain Delano. In tolerable Spanish, and with a good-natured, knowing wink, he informed him that the old knotter was simple-witted, but harmless; often playing his old tricks. The negro concluded by begging the knot, for of course the stranger would not care to be troubled with it. Unconsciously, it was handed to him. With a sort of congé, the negro received it, and turning his back ferreted into it like a detective Custom House officer after smuggled laces. Soon, with some African

word, equivalent to pshaw, he tossed the knot overboard.

All this is very queer now, thought Captain Delano,
with a qualmish sort of emotion; but as one feeling incipient seasickness, he strove, by ignoring the symptoms,
to get rid of the malady. Once more he looked off for his
boat. To his delight, it was now again in view, leaving the
rocky spur astern.

The sensation here experienced, after at first relieving
his uneasiness, with unforeseen efficiency, soon began to
remove it. The less distant sight of that well-known boat—
showing it, not as before, half blended with the haze, but
with outline defined, so that its individuality, like a man's,
was manifest; that boat, *Rover* by name, which, though now
in strange seas, had often pressed the beach of Captain
Delano's home, and brought to its threshold for repairs,
had familiarly lain there, as a Newfoundland dog; the sight
of that household boat evoked a thousand trustful associations, which, contrasted with previous suspicions, filled
him not only with lightsome confidence, but somehow
with half humorous self-reproaches at his former lack of it.

'What, I, Amasa Delano—Jack of the Beach, as they
called me when a lad—I, Amasa; the same that, duck-
satchel in hand, used to paddle along the waterside to the
schoolhouse made from the old hulk;—I, little Jack of
the Beach, that used to go berrying with cousin Nat and
the rest; I to be murdered here at the ends of the earth,
on board a haunted pirate-ship by a horrible Spaniard?—
Too nonsensical to think of! Who would murder Amasa
Delano? His conscience is clean. There is someone above.
Fie, fie, Jack of the Beach! you are a child indeed; a child
of the second childhood, old boy; you are beginning to
dote and drool, I'm afraid.'

Light of heart and foot, he stepped aft, and there was

met by Don Benito's servant, who, with a pleasing expression, responsive to his own present feelings, informed him that his master had recovered from the effects of his coughing fit, and had just ordered him to go present his compliments to his good guest, Don Amasa, and say that he (Don Benito) would soon have the happiness to rejoin him.

There now, do you mark that? again thought Captain Delano, walking the poop. What a donkey I was. This kind gentleman who here sends me his kind compliments, he, but ten minutes ago, dark-lantern in hand, was dodging round some old grind-stone in the hold, sharpening a hatchet for me, I thought. Well, well; these long calms have a morbid effect on the mind, I've often heard, though I never believed it before. Ha! glancing toward the boat; there's *Rover*; a good dog; a white bone in her mouth. A pretty big bone though, seems to me.—What? Yes, she has fallen afoul of the bubbling tide-rip there. It sets her the other way, too, for the time. Patience.

It was now about noon, though, from the greyness of everything, it seemed to be getting toward dusk.

The calm was confirmed. In the far distance, away from the influence of land, the leaden ocean seemed laid out and leaded up, its course finished, soul gone, defunct. But the current from landward, where the ship was, increased; silently sweeping her further and further toward the tranced waters beyond.

Still, from his knowledge of those latitudes, cherishing hopes of a breeze, and a fair and fresh one, at any moment, Captain Delano, despite present prospects, buoyantly counted upon bringing the *San Dominick* safely to anchor ere night. The distance swept over was nothing; since, with a good wind, ten minutes' sailing would retrace more than sixty minutes' drifting. Meantime, one moment turning to mark *Rover* fighting the tide-rip, and the next to see Don Benito approaching, he continued walking the poop.

Gradually he felt a vexation arising from the delay of his boat; this soon merged into uneasiness; and at last, his eye falling continually, as from a stage-box into the pit, upon the strange crowd before and below him, and by-and-by recognizing there the face—now composed to indifference—of the Spanish sailor who had seemed to beckon from the main chains, something of his old trepidations returned.

Ah, thought he—gravely enough—this is like the ague: because it went off, it follows not that it won't come back.

Though ashamed of the relapse, he could not altogether subdue it; and so, exerting his good nature to the utmost, insensibly he came to a compromise.

Yes, this is a strange craft; a strange history, too, and strange folks on board. But—nothing more.

By way of keeping his mind out of mischief till the boat should arrive, he tried to occupy it with turning over and over, in a purely speculative sort of way, some lesser peculiarities of the captain and crew. Among others, four curious points recurred.

First, the affair of the Spanish lad assailed with a knife by the slave boy; an act winked at by Don Benito. Second, the tyranny in Don Benito's treatment of Atufal, the black; as if a child should lead a bull of the Nile by the ring in his nose. Third, the trampling of the sailor by the two negroes; a piece of insolence passed over without so much as a reprimand. Fourth, the cringing submission to their master of all the ship's underlings, mostly blacks; as if by the least inadvertence they feared to draw down his despotic displeasure.

Coupling these points, they seemed somewhat contradictory. But what then, thought Captain Delano, glancing

toward his now nearing boat,—what then? Why, this
Don Benito is a very capricious commander. But he is
not the first of the sort I have seen; though it's true he
rather exceeds any other. But as a nation—continued he
in his reveries—these Spaniards are all an odd set; the
very word Spaniard has a curious, conspirator, Guy-
Fawkish twang to it. And yet, I dare say, Spaniards in the
main are as good folks as any in Duxbury, Massachusetts.
Ah, good! At last *Rover* has come.

As, with its welcome freight, the boat touched the side,
the oakum-pickers, with venerable gestures, sought to
restrain the blacks, who, at the sight of three gurried
water-casks in its bottom, and a pile of wilted pumpkins
in its bow, hung over the bulwarks in disorderly raptures.

Don Benito with his servant now appeared; his coming,
perhaps, hastened by hearing the noise. Of him Captain
Delano sought permission to serve out the water, so that
all might share alike, and none injure themselves by unfair excess. But sensible, and, on Don Benito's account,
kind as this offer was, it was received with what seemed
impatience; as if aware that he lacked energy as a commander, Don Benito, with the true jealousy of weakness,
resented as an affront any interference. So, at least,
Captain Delano inferred.

In another moment the casks were being hoisted in,
when some of the eager negroes accidentally jostled
Captain Delano, where he stood by the gangway; so that,
unmindful of Don Benito, yielding to the impulse of the
moment, with good-natured authority he bade the blacks
stand back; to enforce his words making use of a half-
mirthful, half-menacing gesture. Instantly the blacks
paused, just where they were, each negro and negress
suspended in his or her posture, exactly as the word had
found them—for a few seconds continuing so—while, as

between the responsive posts of a telegraph, an unknown syllable ran from man to man among the perched oakum-pickers. While Captain Delano's attention was fixed by this scene, suddenly the hatchet-polishers half rose, and a rapid cry came from Don Benito.

Thinking that at the signal of the Spaniard he was about to be massacred, Captain Delano would have sprung for his boat, but paused, as the oakum-pickers, dropping down into the crowd with earnest exclamations, forced every white and every negro back, at the same moment, with gestures friendly and familiar, almost jocose, bidding him, in substance, not be a fool. Simultaneously the hatchet-polishers resumed their seats, quietly as so many tailors, and at once, as if nothing had happened, the work of hoisting in the casks was resumed, whites and blacks singing at the tackle.

Captain Delano glanced toward Don Benito. As he saw his meagre form in the act of recovering itself from reclining in the servant's arms, into which the agitated invalid had fallen, he could not but marvel at the panic by which himself had been surprised on the darting supposition that such a commander, who upon a legitimate occasion, so trivial, too, as it now appeared, could lose all self-command, was, with energetic iniquity, going to bring about his murder.

The casks being on deck, Captain Delano was handed a number of jars and cups by one of the steward's aides, who, in the name of Don Benito, entreated him to do as he had proposed: dole out the water. He complied, with republican impartiality as to this republican element, which always seeks one level, serving the oldest white no better than the youngest black; excepting, indeed, poor Don Benito, whose condition, if not rank, demanded an extra allowance. To him, in the first place, Captain

Delano presented a fair pitcher of the fluid; but, thirsting as he was for fresh water, Don Benito quaffed not a
drop until after several grave bows and salutes: a recipro-
cation of courtesies which the sight-loving Africans hailed
with clapping of hands.

Two of the less wilted pumpkins being reserved for the
cabin table, the residue were minced up on the spot for
the general regalement. But the soft bread, sugar, and
bottled cider, Captain Delano would have given the
Spaniards alone, and in chief Don Benito; but the latter
objected; which disinterestedness, on his part, not a little
pleased the American; and so mouthfuls all around were
given alike to whites and blacks; excepting one bottle of
cider, which Babo insisted upon setting aside for his
master.

Here it may be observed that as, on the first visit of the
boat, the American had not permitted his men to board
the ship, neither did he now; being unwilling to add to
the confusion of the decks.

Not uninfluenced by the peculiar good humour at
present prevailing, and for the time oblivious of any but
benevolent thoughts, Captain Delano, who from recent
indications counted upon a breeze within an hour or two
at furthest, despatched the boat back to the sealer with
orders for all the hands that could be spared immediately
to set about rafting casks to the watering-place and filling
them. Likewise he bade word be carried to his chief officer,
that if against present expectation the ship was not
brought to anchor by sunset, he need be under no concern, for as there was to be a full moon that night, he
(Captain Delano) would remain on board ready to play
the pilot, should the wind come soon or late.

As the two captains stood together, observing the
departing boat—the servant as it happened having just

spied a spot on his master's velvet sleeve, and silently engaged rubbing it out—the American expressed his regrets that the *San Dominick* had not boats; none, at least, but the unseaworthy old hulk of the long-boat, which, warped as a camel's skeleton in the desert, and almost as bleached, lay potwise inverted amidships, one side a little tipped, furnishing a subterranean sort of den for family groups of the blacks, mostly women and small children; who, squatting on old mats below, or perched above in the dark dome, on the elevated seats, were described, some distance within, like a social circle of bats, sheltering in some friendly cave; at intervals, ebon flights of naked boys and girls, three or four years old, darting in and out of the den's mouth.

'Had you three or four boats now, Don Benito,' said Captain Delano, 'I think that, by tugging at the oars, your negroes here might help along matters some.—Did you sail from port without boats, Don Benito?'

'They were stove in the gales, Señor.'

'That was bad. Many men, too, you lost then. Boats and men.—Those must have been hard gales, Don Benito.'

'Past all speech,' cringed the Spaniard.

'Tell me, Don Benito,' continued his companion with increased interest, 'tell me, were these gales immediately off the pitch of Cape Horn?'

'Cape Horn?—who spoke of Cape Horn?'

'Yourself did, when giving me an account of your voyage,' answered Captain Delano with almost equal astonishment at this eating of his own words, even as he ever seemed eating his own heart, on the part of the Spaniard. 'You yourself, Don Benito, spoke of Cape Horn,' he emphatically repeated.

The Spaniard turned, in a sort of stooping posture,

pausing an instant, as one about to make a plunging exchange of elements, as from air to water.

At this moment a messenger-boy, a white, hurried by, in the regular performance of his function carrying the last expired half-hour forward to the forecastle, from the cabin time-piece, to have it struck at the ship's large bell.

'Master,' said the servant, discontinuing his work on the coat sleeve, and addressing the rapt Spaniard with a sort of timid apprehensiveness, as one charged with a duty, the discharge of which, it was foreseen, would prove irksome to the very person who had imposed it, and for whose benefit it was intended, 'master told me never mind where he was, or how engaged, always to remind him, to a minute, when shaving-time comes. Miguel has gone to strike the half-hour afternoon. It is *now*, master. Will master go into the cuddy?'

'Ah—yes,' answered the Spaniard, starting, somewhat as from dreams into realities; then turning upon Captain Delano, he said that ere long he would resume the conversation.

'Then if master means to talk more to Don Amasa,' said the servant, 'why not let Don Amasa sit by master in the cuddy, and master can talk, and Don Amasa can listen, while Babo here lathers and strops.'

'Yes,' said Captain Delano, not unpleased with this sociable plan, 'yes, Don Benito, unless you had rather not, I will go with you.'

'Be it so, Señor.'

As the three passed aft, the American could not but think it another strange instance of his host's capriciousness, this being shaved with such uncommon punctuality in the middle of the day. But he deemed it more than likely that the servant's anxious fidelity had something to do with the matter; inasmuch as the timely interruption

served to rally his master from the mood which had
evidently been coming upon him.

The place called the cuddy was a light deck-cabin
formed by the poop, a sort of attic to the large cabin
below. Part of it had formerly been the quarters of the
officers; but since their death all the partitionings had
been thrown down, and the whole interior converted into
one spacious and airy marine hall; for absence of fine
furniture and picturesque disarray, of odd appurtenances,
somewhat answering to the wide, cluttered hall of some
eccentric bachelor-squire in the country, who hangs his
shooting-jacket and tobacco-pouch on deer antlers, and
keeps his fishing-rod, tongs, and walking-stick in the
same corner.

The similitude was heightened, if not originally suggested, by glimpses of the surrounding sea; since, in one
aspect, the country and the ocean seem cousins-german.

The floor of the cuddy was matted. Overhead, four or
five old muskets were stuck into horizontal holes along
the beams. One one side was a claw-footed old table lashed
to the deck; a thumbed missal on it, and over it a small,
meagre crucifix attached to the bulkhead. Under the table
lay a dented cutlass or two, with a hacked harpoon, among
some melancholy old rigging, like a heap of poor friar's
girdles. There were also two long, sharp-ribbed settees
of malacca cane, black with age, and uncomfortable to
look at as inquisitors' racks, with a large, misshapen arm-
chair, which, furnished with a rude barber's crotch at the
back, working with a screw, seemed some grotesque
Middle Ages engine of torment. A flag locker was in one
corner, exposing various coloured bunting, some rolled
up, others half unrolled, still others tumbled. Opposite
was a cumbrous washstand, of black mahogany, all of one
block, with a pedestal, like a font, and over it a railed shelf,

containing combs, brushes and other implements of the toilet. A torn hammock of stained grass swung near; the sheets tossed, and the pillow wrinkled up like a brow, as if whoever slept here slept but illy, with alternate visitations of sad thoughts and bad dreams.

The further extremity of the cuddy, overhanging the ship's stern, was pierced with three openings, windows or port holes, according as men or cannon might peer, socially or unsocially, out of them. At present neither men nor cannon were seen, though huge ring-bolts and other rusty iron fixtures of the wood-work hinted of twenty-four-pounders.

Glancing toward the hammock as he entered, Captain Delano said, 'You sleep here, Don Benito?'

'Yes, Señor, since we got into mild weather.'

'This seems a sort of dormitory, sitting-room, sail-loft, chapel, armoury, and private closet together, Don Benito,' added Captain Delano, looking round.

'Yes, Señor; events have not been favourable to much order in my arrangements.'

Here the servant, napkin on arm, made a motion as if waiting his master's good pleasure. Don Benito signified his readiness, when, seating him in the malacca arm-chair, and for the guest's convenience drawing opposite it one of the settees, the servant commenced operations by throwing back his master's collar and loosening his cravat.

There is something in the negro which, in a peculiar way, fits him for avocations about one's person. Most negroes are natural valets and hair-dressers; taking to the comb and brush congenially as to the castanets, and flourishing them apparently with almost equal satisfaction. There is, too, a smooth tact about them in this employment, with a marvellous, noiseless, gliding briskness, not ungraceful in its way, singularly pleasing to behold, and still more so to be the manipulated subject of. And above all is the great gift of good humour. Not the mere grin or laugh is here meant. Those were unsuitable. But a certain easy cheerfulness, harmonious in every glance and gesture; as though God had set the whole negro to some pleasant tune.

When to all this is added the docility arising from the unaspiring contentment of a limited mind, and that susceptibility of blind attachment sometimes inhering in indisputable inferiors, one readily perceives why those hypochondriacs, Johnson and Byron—it may be something like the hypochondriac, Benito Cereno—took to their hearts, almost to the exclusion of the entire white race, their serving men, the negroes, Barber and Fletcher. But if there be that in the negro which exempts him from the inflicted sourness of the morbid or cynical mind, how, in his most prepossessing aspects, must he appear to a benevolent one? When at ease with respect to exterior things, Captain Delano's nature was not only benign, but familiarly and humorously so. At home, he had often taken rare satisfaction in sitting in his door, watching some free man of colour at his work or play. If on a voyage he chanced to have a black sailor, invariably he was on chatty, and half-gamesome terms with him. In fact, like most men of a good, blithe heart, Captain Delano took to negroes, not philanthropically, but genially, just as other men to Newfoundland dogs.

Hitherto the circumstances in which he found the *San Dominick* had repressed the tendency. But in the cuddy, relieved from his former uneasiness, and, for various reasons, more sociably inclined than at any previous period of the day, and seeing the coloured servant, napkin on arm, so debonair about his master, in a business so familiar as that of shaving, too, all his old weakness for negroes returned.

Among other things, he was amused with an odd instance of the African love of bright colours and fine shows, in the black's informally taking from the flag-locker a great piece of bunting of all hues, and lavishly tucking it under his master's chin for an apron.

The mode of shaving among the Spaniards is a little different from what it is with other nations. They have a basin, specially called a barber's basin, which on one side is scooped out, so as accurately to receive the chin, against which it is closely held in lathering; which is done, not with a brush, but with soap dipped in the water of the basin and rubbed on the face.

In the present instance salt-water was used for lack of better; and the parts lathered were only the upper lip, and low down under the throat, all the rest being cultivated beard.

These preliminaries being somewhat novel to Captain Delano he sat curiously eyeing them, so that no conversation took place, nor for the present did Don Benito appear disposed to renew any.

Setting down his basin, the negro searched among the razors, as for the sharpest, and having found it, gave it an additional edge by expertly stropping it on the firm, smooth, oily skin of his open palm; he then made a gesture as if to begin, but midway stood suspended for an instant, one hand elevating the razor, the other professionally dabbling among the bubbling suds on the Spaniard's lank neck. Not unaffected by the close sight of the gleaming steel, Don Benito nervously shuddered, his usual ghastliness was heightened by the lather, which later, again, was intensified in its hue by the contrasting sootiness of the negro's body. Altogether the scene was

somewhat peculiar, at least to Captain Delano, nor, as he
saw the two thus postured, could he resist the vagary, that
in the black he saw a headsman, and in the white, a man
at the block. But this was one of those antic conceits,
appearing and vanishing in a breath, from which, perhaps,
the best regulated mind is not free.

Meantime the agitation of the Spaniard had a little
loosened the bunting from around him, so that one
broad fold swept curtain-like over the chair-arm to the
floor, revealing, amid a profusion of armorial bars and
ground-colours—black, blue and yellow—a closed castle
in a blood-red field diagonal with a lion rampant in a
white.

'The castle and the lion,' exclaimed Captain Delano—
'why, Don Benito, this is the flag of Spain you use here.
It's well it's only I, and not the King, that sees this,' he
added with a smile, 'but'—turning toward the black,—
'it's all one, I suppose, so the colours be gay,' which playful remark did not fail somewhat to tickle the negro.

'Now, master,' he said, readjusting the flag, and pressing the head gently further back into the crotch of the
chair; 'now, master,' and the steel glanced nigh the throat.

Again Don Benito faintly shuddered.

'You must not shake so, master.—See, Don Amasa,
master always shakes when I shave him. And yet master
knows I never yet have drawn blood, though it's true, if
master will shake so, I may some of these times. Now,
master,' he continued. 'And now, Don Amasa, please go
on with your talk about the gale, and all that, master can
hear, and between times master can answer.'

'Ah yes, these gales,' said Captain Delano; 'but the
more I think of your voyage, Don Benito, the more I
wonder, not at the gales, terrible as they must have been,
but at the disastrous interval following them. For here,

by your account, have you been these two months and more getting from Cape Horn to St. Maria, a distance which I myself, with a good wind, have sailed in a few days. True, you had calms, and long ones, but to be becalmed for two months, that is, at least, unusual. Why, Don Benito, had almost any other gentleman told me such a story, I should have been half disposed to a little incredulity.'

Here an involuntary expression came over the Spaniard, similar to that just before on the deck, and whether it was the start he gave, or a sudden gawky roll of the hull in the calm, or a momentary unsteadiness of the servant's hand; however it was, just then the razor drew blood, spots of which stained the creamy lather under the throat; immediately the black barber drew back his steel, and remaining in his professional attitude, back to Captain Delano, and face to Don Benito, held up the trickling razor, saying, with a sort of half humorous sorrow, 'See, master,—you shook so—here's Babo's first blood.'

No sword drawn before James the First of England, no assassination in that timid King's presence, could have produced a more terrified aspect than was now presented by Don Benito.

Poor fellow, thought Captain Delano, so nervous he can't even bear the sight of barber's blood; and this unstrung, sick man, is it credible that I should have imagined he meant to spill all my blood, who can't endure the sight of one little drop of his own? Surely, Amasa Delano, you have been beside yourself this day. Tell it not when you get home, sappy Amasa. Well, well, he looks like a murderer, doesn't he? More like as if himself were to be done for. Well, well, this day's experience shall be a good lesson.

Meantime, while these things were running through

the honest seaman's mind, the servant had taken the napkin from his arm, and to Don Benito had said: 'But answer Don Amasa, please, master, while I wipe this ugly stuff off the razor, and strop it again.'

As he said the words, his face was turned half round, so as to be alike visible to the Spaniard and the American, and seemed by its expression to hint, that he was desirous, by getting his master to go on with the conversation, considerately to withdraw his attention from the recent annoying accident. As if glad to snatch the offered relief, Don Benito resumed, rehearsing to Captain Delano, that not only were the calms of unusual duration, but the ship had fallen in with obstinate currents and other things he added, some of which were but repetitions of former statements, to explain how it came to pass that the passage from Cape Horn to St. Maria had been so exceedingly long, now and then mingling with his words, incidental praises, less qualified than before, to the blacks, for their general good conduct.

These particulars were not given consecutively, the servant now and then using his razor, and so, between the intervals of shaving, the story and panegyric went on with more than usual huskiness.

To Captain Delano's imagination, now again not wholly at rest, there was something so hollow in the Spaniard's manner, with apparently some reciprocal hollowness in the servant's dusky comment of silence, that the idea flashed across him, that possibly master and man, for some unknown purpose, were acting out, both in word and deed, nay, to the very tremor of Don Benito's limbs, some juggling play before him. Neither did the suspicion of collusion lack apparent support, from the fact of those whispered conferences before mentioned. But then, what could be the object of enacting this play of the barber before him? At last, regarding the notion as a whimsy, insensibly suggested, perhaps, by the theatrical aspect of Don Benito in his harlequin ensign, Captain Delano speedily banished it.

The shaving over, the servant bestirred himself with a small bottle of scented waters, pouring a few drops on the head, and then diligently rubbing; the vehemence of the exercise causing the muscles of his face to twitch rather strangely.

His next operation was with comb, scissors, and brush; going round and round, smoothing a curl here, clipping an unruly whisker-hair there, giving a graceful sweep to the temple-lock, with other impromptu touches evincing the hand of a master; while, like any resigned gentleman in barber's hands, Don Benito bore all, much less uneasily, at least, than he had done the razoring; indeed, he sat so pale and rigid now, that the negro seemed a Nubian sculptor finishing off a white statue-head.

All being over at last, the standard of Spain removed, tumbled up, and tossed back into the flag-locker, the negro's warm breath blowing away any stray hair which might have lodged down his master's neck; collar and cravat readjusted; a speck of lint whisked off the velvet lapel; all this being done; backing off a little space, and pausing with an expression of subdued self-complacency, the servant for a moment surveyed his master, as, in toilet at least, the creature of his own tasteful hands.

Captain Delano playfully complimented him upon his achievement; at the same time congratulating Don Benito.

But neither sweet waters, nor shampooing, nor fidelity, nor sociality, delighted the Spaniard. Seeing him relapsing into forbidding gloom, and still remaining seated, Captain Delano, thinking that his presence was undesired just then, withdrew, on pretence of seeing whether, as he had prophesied, any signs of a breeze were visible.

Walking forward to the mainmast, he stood awhile thinking over the scene, and not without some undefined misgivings, when he heard a noise near the cuddy, and turning, saw the negro, his hand to his cheek. Advancing, Captain Delano perceived that the cheek was bleeding. He was about to ask the cause, when the negro's wailing soliloquy enlightened him.

'Ah, when will master get better from his sickness; only the sour heart that sour sickness breeds made him serve Babo so; cutting Babo with the razor, because, only by accident, Babo had given master one little scratch; and for the first time in so many a day, too. Ah, ah, ah,' holding his hand to his face.

Is it possible, thought Captain Delano; was it to wreak in private his Spanish spite against this poor friend of his, that Don Benito, by his sullen manner, impelled me to withdraw? Ah, this slavery breeds ugly passions in man! Poor fellow!

He was about to speak in sympathy to the negro, but with a timid reluctance he now re-entered the cuddy.

Presently master and man came forth; Don Benito leaning on his servant as if nothing had happened.

But a sort of love-quarrel, after all, thought Captain Delano.

He accosted Don Benito, and they slowly walked together. They had gone but a few paces, when the steward —a tall, rajah-looking mulatto, orientally set off with a pagoda turban formed by three or four Madras handkerchiefs wound about his head, tier on tier—approaching with a salaam, announced lunch in the cabin.

On their way thither, the two captains were preceded by the mulatto, who, turning round as he advanced, with continual smiles and bows, ushered them in, a display of elegance which quite completed the insignificance of the small bare-headed Babo, who, as if not unconscious of inferiority, eyed askance the graceful steward. But in part, Captain Delano imputed his jealous watchfulness to that peculiar feeling which the full-blooded African entertains for the adulterated one. As for the steward, his manner, if not bespeaking much dignity of self-respect, yet evidenced his extreme desire to please; which is doubly meritorious, as at once Christian and Chesterfieldian.

Captain Delano observed with interest that while the complexion of the mulatto was hybrid, his physiognomy was European; classically so.

'Don Benito,' whispered he, 'I am glad to see this usher-of-the-golden-rod of yours; the sight refutes an ugly remark once made to me by a Barbados planter that when a mulatto has a regular European face, look out for him; he is a devil. But see, your steward here has features more regular than King George's of England; and yet there he nods, and bows, and smiles; a king, indeed—the king of kind hearts and polite fellows. What a pleasant voice he has, too?'

'He has, Señor.'

'But, tell me, has he not, so far as you have known him, always proved 'a good, worthy fellow?' said Captain Delano, pausing, while with a final genuflexion the steward disappeared into the cabin; 'come, for the reason just mentioned, I am curious to know.'

'Francesco is a good man,' rather sluggishly responded Don Benito, like a phlegmatic appreciator, who would neither find fault nor flatter.

'Ah, I thought so. For it were strange indeed, and not very creditable to us white-skins, if a little of our blood mixed with the African's, should, far from improving the latter's quality, have the sad effect of pouring vitriolic acid into black broth; improving the hue, perhaps, but not the wholesomeness.'

'Doubtless, doubtless, Señor, but'—glancing at Babo 'not to speak of negroes, your planter's remark I have heard applied to the Spanish and Indian intermixtures in our provinces. But I know nothing about the matter,' he listlessly added.

And here they entered the cabin.

The lunch was a frugal one. Some of Captain Delano's fresh fish and pumpkins, biscuit and salt beef, the reserved bottle of cider, and the *San Dominick's* last bottle of Canary.

As they entered, Francesco, with two or three coloured aides, was hovering over the table giving the last adjustments. Upon perceiving their master they withdrew, Francesco making a smiling congé, and the Spaniard, without condescending to notice it, fastidiously remarking to his companion that he relished not superfluous attendance.

Without companions, host and guest sat down, like a childless married couple, at opposite ends of the table, Don Benito waving Captain Delano to his place, and, weak as he was, insisting upon that gentleman being seated before himself.

The negro placed a rug under Don Benito's feet, and a cushion behind his back, and then stood behind, not his master's chair, but Captain Delano's. At first, this a little surprised the latter. But it was soon evident that, in taking his position, the black was still true to his master; since by facing him he could the more readily anticipate his slightest want.

'This is an uncommonly intelligent fellow of yours, Don Benito,' whispered Captain Delano across the table.

'You say true, Señor.'

During the repast, the guest again reverted to parts of Don Benito's story, begging further particulars here and there. He inquired how it was that the scurvy and fever should have committed such wholesale havoc upon the whites, while destroying less than half of the blacks. As if this question reproduced the whole scene of plague before the Spaniard's eyes, miserably reminding him of his solitude in a cabin where before he had had so many friends and officers round him, his hand shook, his face became hueless, broken words escaped; but directly the sane memory of the past seemed replaced by insane terrors of the present. With starting eyes he stared before him at vacancy. For nothing was to be seen but the hand of his servant pushing the Canary over towards him. At length a few sips served partially to restore him. He made random reference to the different constitutions of races, enabling one to offer more resistance to certain maladies than another. The thought was new to his companion.

Presently Captain Delano, intending to say something to his host concerning the pecuniary part of the business he had undertaken for him, especially—since he was strictly accountable to his owners—with reference to the new suit of sails, and other things of that sort; and naturally preferring to conduct such affairs in private, was desirous that the servant should withdraw, imagining that Don Benito for a few minutes could dispense with his attendance. He, however, waited awhile; thinking that, as the conversation proceeded, Don Benito, without being prompted, would perceive the propriety of the step.

But it was otherwise. At last catching his host's eye, Captain Delano, with a slight backward gesture of his thumb, whispered, 'Don Benito, pardon me, but there is an interference with the full expression of what I have to say to you.'

Upon this the Spaniard changed countenance; which was imputed to his resenting the hint, as in some way a reflection upon his servant. After a moment's pause, he assured his guest that the black's remaining with them could be of no disservice; because since losing his officers he had made Babo (whose original office, it now appeared, had been captain of the slaves) not only his constant attendant and companion, but in all things his confidant.

After this, nothing more could be said; though, indeed, Captain Delano could hardly avoid some little tinge of irritation upon being left ungratified in so inconsiderable a wish, by one, too, for whom he intended such solid services. But it is only his querulousness, thought he; and so filling his glass he proceeded to business.

The price of the sails and other matters was fixed upon. But while this was being done, the American observed that, though his original offer of assistance had been hailed with hectic animation, yet now when it was reduced to a business transaction, indifference and apathy were betrayed. Don Benito, in fact, appeared to submit to hearing the details more out of regard to common propriety, than from any impression that weighty benefit to himself and his voyage was involved.

Soon, this manner became still more reserved. The effort was vain to seek to draw him into social talk. Gnawed by his splenetic mood, he sat twitching his beard, while to little purpose the hand of his servant, mute as that on the wall, slowly pushed over the Canary.

Lunch being over, they sat down on the cushioned transom; the servant placing a pillow behind his master. The long continuance of the calm had now affected the atmosphere. Don Benito sighed heavily, as if for breath.

'Why not adjourn to the cuddy,' said Captain Delano; 'there is more air there.' But the host sat silent and motionless.

Meantime his servant knelt before him, with a large fan of feathers. And Francesco, coming in on tiptoes, handed the negro a little cup of aromatic waters, with which at intervals he chafed his master's brow, smoothing the hair along the temples as a nurse does a child's. He spoke no word. He only rested his eye on his master's, as if, amid all Don Benito's distress, a little to refresh his spirit by the silent sight of fidelity.

Presently the ship's bell sounded two o'clock; and through the cabin-windows a slight rippling of the sea was discerned; and from the desired direction.

'There,' exclaimed Captain Delano, 'I told you so, Don Benito, look!'

He had risen to his feet, speaking in a very animated tone, with a view the more to rouse his companion. But though the crimson curtain of the stern-window near him that moment fluttered against his pale cheek, Don Benito seemed to have even less welcome for the breeze than the calm.

Poor fellow, thought Captain Delano, bitter experience has taught him that one ripple does not make a wind, any more than one swallow a summer. But he is mistaken for once. I will get his ship in for him, and prove it.

Briefly alluding to his weak condition, he urged his host to remain quietly where he was, since he (Captain Delano) would with pleasure take upon himself the responsibility of making the best use of the wind.

Upon gaining the deck, Captain Delano started at the unexpected figure of Atufal, monumentally fixed at the threshold, like one of those sculptured porters of black marble guarding the porches of Egyptian tombs.

But this time the start was, perhaps, purely physical. Atufal's presence, singularly attesting docility even in sullenness, was contrasted with that of the hatchet-polishers, who in patience evinced their industry; while both spectacles showed, that lax as Don Benito's general authority might be, still, whenever he chose to exert it, no man so savage or colossal but must, more or less, bow.

Snatching a trumpet which hung from the bulwarks, with a free step Captain Delano advanced to the forward edge of the poop, issuing his orders in his best Spanish. The few sailors and many negroes, all equally pleased, obediently set about heading the ship toward the harbour.

While giving some directions about setting a lower stu'n-sail, suddenly Captain Delano heard a voice faithfully repeating his orders. Turning, he saw Babo, now for the time acting, under the pilot, his original part of captain of the slaves. This assistance proved valuable. Tattered sails and warped yards were soon brought into some trim. And no brace or halyard was pulled but to the blithe songs of the inspirited negroes.

Good fellows, thought Captain Delano, a little training would make fine sailors of them. Why, see, the very women pull and sing, too. These must be some of those Ashantee negresses that make such capital soldiers, I've heard. But who's at the helm? I must have a good hand there.

He went to see.

The *San Dominick* steered with a cumbrous tiller, with large horizontal pullies attached. At each pulley-end stood a subordinate black, and between them, at the tiller-head, the responsible post, a Spanish seaman, whose countenance evinced his due share in the general hope-fulness and confidence at the coming of the breeze.

He proved the same man who had behaved with so shame-faced an air on the windlass.

'Ah,—it is you, my man,' exclaimed Captain Delano— 'well, no more sheep's-eyes now;—look straightforward and keep the ship so. Good hand, I trust? And want to get into the harbour, don't you?'

'Sí, Señor,' assented the man with an inward chuckle, grasping the tiller-head firmly. Upon this, unperceived by the American, the two blacks eyed the sailor askance.

Finding all right at the helm, the pilot went forward to the forecastle, to see how matters stood there.

The ship now had way enough to breast the current. With the approach of evening, the breeze would be sure to freshen.

Having done all that was needed for the present, Captain Delano, giving his last orders to the sailors, turned aft to report affairs to Don Benito in the cabin; perhaps additionally incited to rejoin him by the hope of snatching a moment's private chat while his servant was engaged upon deck.

From opposite sides, there were, beneath the poop, two approaches to the cabin; one further forward than the other, and consequently communicating with a longer passage. Marking the servant still above, Captain Delano, taking the nighest entrance—the one last named, and at whose porch Atufal still stood—hurried on his way, till, arrived at the cabin threshold, he paused an instant, a little to recover from his eagerness. Then, with the words of his intended business upon his lips, he entered. As he advanced toward the Spaniard, on the transom, he heard another footstep, keeping time with his. From the opposite door, a salver in hand, the servant was likewise advancing.

'Confound the faithful fellow,' thought Captain Delano; 'what a vexatious coincidence.'

Possibly, the vexation might have been something
different, were it not for the buoyant confidence inspired
by the breeze. But even as it was, he felt a slight twinge,
from a sudden involuntary association in his mind of
Babo with Atufal.

'Don Benito,' said he, 'I give you joy; the breeze will
hold, and will increase. By the way, your tall man and
time-piece, Atufal, stands without. By your order, of
course?'

Don Benito recoiled, as if at some bland satirical touch,
delivered with such adroit garnish of apparent good-
breeding as to present no handle for retort.

He is like one flayed alive, thought Captain Delano;
where may one touch him without causing a shrink?

The servant moved before his master, adjusting a
cushion; recalled to civility, the Spaniard stiffly replied:
'You are right. The slave appears where you saw him,
according to my command; which is, that if at the given
hour I am below, he must take his stand and abide my
coming.'

'Ah now, pardon me, but that is treating the poor
fellow like an ex-king denied. Ah, Don Benito,' smiling,
'for all the license you permit in some things, I fear lest,
at bottom, you are a bitter hard master.'

Again Don Benito shrank; and this time, as the good
sailor thought, from a genuine twinge of his conscience.

Conversation now became constrained. In vain Captain
Delano called attention to the now perceptible motion of
the keel gently cleaving the sea; with lack-lustre eye,
Don Benito returned words few and reserved.

By-and-by, the wind having steadily risen, and still
blowing right into the harbour, bore the *San Dominick*

swiftly on. Rounding a point of land, the sealer at distance
came into open view.

Meantime Captain Delano had again repaired to the
deck, remaining there some time. Having at last altered
the ship's course, so as to give the reef a wide berth, he
returned for a few moments below.

I will cheer up my poor friend, this time, thought he.

'Better and better, Don Benito,' he cried as he blithely
re-entered; 'there will soon be an end to your cares, at
least for awhile. For when, after a long, sad voyage, you
know, the anchor drops into the haven, all its vast weight
seems lifted from the captain's heart. We are getting on
famously, Don Benito. My ship is in sight. Look through
this sidelight here; there she is; all a-taunt-o! The
Bachelor's Delight, my good friend. Ah, how this wind
braces one up. Come, you must take a cup of coffee with
me this evening. My old steward will give you as fine
a cup as ever any sultan tasted. What say you, Don
Benito, will you?'

At first, the Spaniard glanced feverishly up, casting
a longing look toward the sealer, while with mute concern
his servant gazed into his face. Suddenly the old ague of
coldness returned, and dropping back to his cushions he
was silent.

'You do not answer. Come, all day you have been my
host; would you have hospitality all on one side?'

'I cannot go,' was the response.

'What? it will not fatigue you. The ships will lie together as near as they can, without swinging foul. It will
be little more than stepping from deck to deck; which is
but as from room to room. Come, come, you must not
refuse me.'

'I cannot go,' decisively and repulsively repeated Don
Benito.

Renouncing all but the last appearance of courtesy, with a sort of cadaverous sullenness, and biting his thin nails to the quick, he glanced, almost glared, at his guest; as if impatient that a stranger's presence should interfere with the full indulgence of his morbid hour. Meantime the sound of the parted waters came more and more gurglingly and merrily in at the windows; as reproaching him for his dark spleen; as telling him that, sulk as he might, and go mad with it, nature cared not a jot; since, whose fault was it, pray?

But the foul mood was now at its depth, as the fair wind at its height.

There was something in the man so far beyond any mere unsociality or sourness previously evinced, that even the forbearing good-nature of his guest could no longer endure it. Wholly at a loss to account for such demeanour, and deeming sickness with eccentricity, however extreme, no adequate excuse, well satisfied, too, that nothing in his own conduct could justify it, Captain Delano's pride began to be roused. Himself became reserved. But all seemed one to the Spaniard. Quitting him, therefore, Captain Delano once more went to the deck.

The ship was now within less than two miles of the sealer. The whale-boat was seen darting over the interval.

To be brief, the two vessels, thanks to the pilot's skill, ere long in neighbourly style lay anchored together.

Before returning to his own vessel, Captain Delano had intended communicating to Don Benito the practical details of the proposed services to be rendered. But, as it was, unwilling anew to subject himself to rebuffs, he resolved, now that he had seen the *San Dominick* safely moored, immediately to quit her, without further allusion to hospitality or business. Indefinitely postponing his ulterior plans, he would regulate his future actions according to future circumstances. His boat was ready to receive him; but his host still tarried below. Well, thought Captain Delano, if he has little breeding, the more need to show mine. He descended to the cabin to bid a ceremonious, and, it may be, tacitly rebukeful adieu. But to his great satisfaction, Don Benito, as if he began to feel the weight of that treatment with which his slighted guest had, not indecorously, retaliated upon him, now supported by his servant, rose to his feet, and grasping Captain Delano's hand, stood tremulous; too much agitated to speak. But the good augury hence drawn was suddenly dashed, by his resuming all his previous reserve, with augmented gloom, as, with half-averted eyes, he silently reseated himself on his cushions. With a corresponding return of his own chilled feelings, Captain Delano bowed and withdrew.

He was hardly midway in the narrow corridor, dim as a tunnel, leading from the cabin to the stairs, when a sound, as of the tolling for execution in some jail-yard, fell on his ears. It was the echo of the ship's flawed bell, striking the hour, drearily reverberated in this subterranean vault. Instantly, by a fatality not to be withstood, his mind, responsive to the portent, swarmed with superstitious suspicions. He paused. In images far swifter than these sentences, the minutest details of all his former distrusts swept through him.

Hitherto, credulous good-nature had been too ready to furnish excuses for reasonable fears. Why was the Spaniard, so superfluously punctilious at times, now heedless of common propriety in not accompanying to the side his departing guest? Did indisposition forbid? Indisposition had not forbidden more irksome exertion that day. His last equivocal demeanour recurred. He had risen to his feet, grasped his guest's hand, motioned toward his hat; then, in an instant, all was eclipsed in sinister muteness and gloom. Did this imply one brief, repentant relenting at the final moment, from some iniquitous plot, followed by remorseless return to it? His last glance seemed to express a calamitous, yet acquiescent farewell to Captain Delano for ever. Why decline the invitation to visit the sealer that evening? Or was the Spaniard less hardened than the Jew, who refrained not from supping at the board of Him whom the same night he meant to betray? What imported all those day-long enigmas and contradictions, except they were intended to mystify, preliminary to some stealthy blow? Atufal, the pretended rebel, but punctual shadow, that moment lurked by the threshold without. He seemed a sentry, and more. Who, by his own confession, had stationed him there? Was the negro now lying in wait?

The Spaniard behind—his creature before: to rush from darkness to light was the involuntary choice.

The next moment, with clenched jaw and hand, he passed Atufal, and stood unarmed in the light. As he saw his trim ship lying peacefully at her anchor, and almost within ordinary call; as he saw his household boat, with familiar faces in it, patiently rising and falling on the short waves by the *San Dominick*'s side; and then, glancing about the decks where he stood, saw the oakum-pickers still gravely plying their fingers; and heard the low, buzzing whistle and industrious hum of the hatchet-polishers, still bestirring themselves over their endless occupation; and more than all, as he saw the benign aspect of Nature, taking her innocent repose in the evening; the screened sun in the quiet camp of the west shining out like the mild light from Abraham's tent; as his charmed eye and ear took in all these, with the chained figure of the black, the clenched jaw and hand relaxed. Once again he smiled at the phantoms which had mocked him, and felt something like a tinge of remorse, that, by indulging them even for a moment, he should, by implication, have betrayed an almost atheist doubt of the ever-watchful Providence above.

There was a few minutes' delay, while, in obedience to his orders, the boat was being hooked along to the gangway. During this interval, a sort of saddened satisfaction stole over Captain Delano, at thinking of the kindly offices he had that day discharged for a stranger. Ah, thought he, after good actions one's conscience is never ungrateful, however much so the benefited party may be.

Presently, his foot, in the first act of descent into the boat, pressed the first round of the side-ladder, his face presented inward upon the deck. In the same moment, he heard his name courteously sounded; and, to his pleased surprise, saw Don Benito advancing—an unwonted energy in his air, as if, at the last moment, intent upon making amends for his recent discourtesy. With instinctive good feeling, Captain Delano, revoking his foot, turned and reciprocally advanced. As he did so, the Spaniard's nervous eagerness increased, but his vital energy failed; so that, the better to support him, the servant, placing his master's hand on his naked shoulder, and gently holding it there, formed himself into a sort of crutch.

When the two captains met, the Spaniard again fervently took the hand of the American, at the same time casting an earnest glance into his eyes, but, as before, too much overcome to speak.

I have done him wrong, self-reproachfully thought Captain Delano; his apparent coldness has deceived me; in no instance has he meant to offend.

Meantime, as if fearful that the continuance of the scene might too much unstring his master, the servant seemed anxious to terminate it. And so, still presenting himself as a crutch, and walking between the two captains, he advanced with them toward the gangway; while still, as if full of kindly contrition, Don Benito would not let go the hand of Captain Delano, but retained it in his, across the black's body.

Soon they were standing by the side, looking over into the boat, whose crew turned up their curious eyes. Waiting a moment for the Spaniard to relinquish his hold, the now embarrassed Captain Delano lifted his foot, to overstep the threshold of the open gangway; but still Don Benito would not let go his hand. And yet, with an agitated tone, he said, 'I can go no further; here I must bid you adieu. Adieu, my dear, dear Don Amasa. Go—go!' suddenly tearing his hand loose, 'go, and God guard you better than me, my best friend.'

Not unaffected, Captain Delano would now have lingered; but catching the meekly admonitory eye of the servant, with a hasty farewell he descended into his boat, followed by the continual adieus of Don Benito, standing rooted in the gangway.

Seating himself in the stern, Captain Delano, making a last salute, ordered the boat shoved off. The crew had their oars on end. The bowsman pushed the boat a sufficient distance for the oars to be lengthwise dropped. The instant that was done, Don Benito sprang over the bulwarks, falling at the feet of Captain Delano; at the same time, calling towards his ship, but in tones so frenzied, that none in the boat could understand him. But, as if not equally obtuse, three Spanish sailors, from three different and distant parts of the ship, splashed into the sea, swimming after their captain, as if intent upon his rescue.

The dismayed officer of the boat eagerly asked what this meant. To which, Captain Delano, turning a disdainful smile upon the unaccountable Benito Cereno, answered that, for his part, he neither knew nor cared; but it seemed as if the Spaniard had taken it into his head to produce the impression among his people that the boat wanted to kidnap him. 'Or else—give way for your lives,' he wildly added, starting at a clattering hubbub in the ship, above which rang the tocsin of the hatchet-polishers; and seizing Don Benito by the throat he added, 'this plotting pirate means murder!' Here, in apparent verification of the words, the servant, a dagger in his hand, was seen on the rail overhead, poised, in the act of leaping, as if with desperate fidelity to befriend his master to the last; while, seemingly to aid the black, the three Spanish sailors were trying to clamber into the hampered bow. Meantime, the whole host of negroes, as if inflamed at the sight of their jeopardized captain, impended in one sooty avalanch over the bulwarks.

All this, with what preceded, and what followed, occurred with such involutions of rapidity, that past, present, and future seemed one.

Seeing the negro coming, Captain Delano had flung the Spaniard aside, almost in the very act of clutching him, and, by the unconscious recoil, shifting his place, with arms thrown up, so promptly grappled the servant in his descent, that with dagger presented at Captain Delano's heart, the black seemed of purpose to have leaped there as to his mark. But the weapon was wrenched away, and the assailant dashed down into the bottom of the boat, which now, with disentangled oars, began to speed through the sea.

At this juncture, the left hand of Captain Delano, on one side, again clutched the half-reclined Don Benito, heedless that he was in a speechless faint, while his right foot, on the other side, ground the prostrate negro; and his right arm pressed for added speed on the after oar, his eye bent forward, encouraging his men to their utmost.

But here, the officer of the boat, who had at last succeeded in beating off the towing Spanish sailors, and was now, with face turned aft, assisting the bowsman at his oar, suddenly called to Captain Delano, to see what the black was about; while a Portuguese oarsman shouted to him to give heed to what the Spaniard was saying.

Glancing down at his feet, Captain Delano saw the freed hand of the servant aiming with a second dagger— a small one, before concealed in his wool—with this he was snakishly writhing up from the boat's bottom, at the heart of his master, his countenance lividly vindictive, expressing the centred purpose of his soul; while the Spaniard, half-choked, was vainly shrinking away, with husky words, incoherent to all but the Portuguese.

That moment, across the long benighted mind of Captain Delano, a flash of revelation swept, illuminating in unanticipated clearness Benito Cereno's whole mysterious demeanour, with every enigmatic event of the day, as well as the entire past voyage of the *San Dominick*. He smote Babo's hand down, but his own heart smote him harder. With infinite pity he withdrew his hold from Don Benito. Not Captain Delano, but Don Benito, the black, in leaping into the boat, had intended to stab.

Both the black's hands were held, as, glancing up toward the *San Dominick*, Captain Delano, now with the scales dropped from his eyes, saw the negroes, not in misrule, not in tumult, not as if frantically concerned for Don Benito, but with mask torn away, flourishing hatchets and knives, in ferocious piratical revolt. Like delirious black dervishes, the six Ashantees danced on the poop. Prevented by their foes from springing into the water, the Spanish boys were hurrying up to the topmost spars, while such of the few Spanish sailors, not already in the sea, less alert, were descried, helplessly mixed in, on deck, with the blacks.

Meantime Captain Delano hailed his own vessel, ordering the ports up, and the guns run out. But by this time the cable of the *San Dominick* had been cut; and the fagend, in lashing out, whipped away the canvas shroud about the beak, suddenly revealing, as the bleached hull swung round toward the open ocean, death for the figurehead, in a human skeleton; chalky comment on the chalked words below, '*Follow your leader.*'

At the sight, Don Benito, covering his face, wailed out: ' 'Tis he, Aranda! my murdered, unburied friend!'

Upon reaching the sealer, calling for ropes, Captain Delano bound the negro, who made no resistance, and had him hoisted to the deck. He would then have assisted the now almost helpless Don Benito up the side; but Don Benito, wan as he was, refused to move, or be moved, until the negro should have been first put below out of view. When, presently assured that it was done, he no more shrank from the ascent.

The boat was immediately despatched back to pick up the three swimming sailors. Meantime, the guns were in readiness, though, owing to the *San Dominick* having glided somewhat astern of the sealer, only the aftermost one could be brought to bear. With this, they fired six times; thinking to cripple the fugitive ship by bringing down her spars. But only a few inconsiderable ropes were shot away. Soon the ship was beyond the guns' range, steering broad out of the bay; the blacks thickly clustering round the bowsprit, one moment with taunting cries toward the whites, the next with upthrown gestures hailing the now dusky expanse of ocean—cawing crows escaped from the hand of the fowler.

The first impulse was to slip the cables and give chase. But, upon second thought, to pursue with whale-boat and yawl seemed more promising.

Upon inquiring of Don Benito what firearms they had on board the *San Dominick*, Captain Delano was answered that they had none that could be used; because, in the earlier stages of the mutiny, a cabin-passenger, since dead, had secretly put out of order the locks of what few muskets there were. But with all his remaining strength, Don Benito entreated the American not to give chase, either with ship or boat; for the negroes had already proved themselves such desperadoes, that, in case of a present assault, nothing but a total massacre of the whites could be looked for. But, regarding this warning as coming from one whose spirit had been crushed by misery, the American did not give up his design.

The boats were got ready and armed. Captain Delano ordered twenty-five men into them. He was going himself when Don Benito grasped his arm.

'What! have you saved my life, Señor, and are you now going to throw away your own?'

The officers also, for reasons connected with their interests and those of the voyage, and a duty owing to the owners, strongly objected against their commander's going. Weighing their remonstrances a moment, Captain Delano felt bound to remain; appointing his chief mate— an athletic and resolute man, who had been a privateer's man, and, as his enemies whispered, a pirate—to head the party. The more to encourage the sailors, they were told, that the Spanish captain considered his ship as good as lost; that she and her cargo, including some gold and silver, were worth upwards of ten thousand doubloons. Take her, and no small part should be theirs. The sailors replied with a shout.

The fugitives had now almost gained an offing. It was nearly night; but the moon was rising. After hard, prolonged pulling, the boats came up on the ship's quarters, at a suitable distance laying upon their oars to discharge their muskets. Having no bullets to return, the negroes sent their yells. But, upon the second volley, Indian-like, they hurtled their hatchets. One took off a sailor's fingers. Another struck the whale-boat's bow, cutting off the rope there, and remaining stuck in the gunwale, like a woodman's axe. Snatching it, quivering from its lodgement, the mate hurled it back. The returned gauntlet now stuck in the ship's broken quarter-gallery, and so remained.

The negroes giving too hot a reception, the whites kept a more respectful distance. Hovering now just out of reach of the hurtling hatchets, they, with a view to the close encounter which must soon come, sought to decoy the blacks into entirely disarming themselves of their most murderous weapons in a hand-to-hand fight, by foolishly flinging them, as missiles, short of the mark, into the sea. But ere long perceiving the stratagem, the negroes desisted, though not before many of them had to replace their lost hatchets with hand-spikes; an exchange which, as counted upon, proved in the end favourable to the assailants.

Meantime, with a strong wind, the ship still clove the water; the boats alternately falling behind, and pulling up, to discharge fresh volleys.

The fire was mostly directed toward the stern, since there, chiefly, the negroes, at present, were clustering. But to kill or maim the negroes was not the object. To take them, with the ship, was the object. To do it, the ship must be boarded; which could not be done by boats while she was sailing so fast.

A thought now struck the mate. Observing the Spanish boys still aloft, high as they could get, he called to them to descend to the yards, and cut adrift the sails. It was done. About this time, owing to causes hereafter to be shown, two Spaniards, in the dress of sailors and conspicuously showing themselves, were killed; not by volleys, but by deliberate marksman's shots; while, as it afterwards appeared, during one of the general discharges, Atufal, the black, and the Spaniard at the helm likewise were killed. What now, with the loss of the sails, and loss of leaders, the ship became unmanageable to the negroes.

With creaking masts she came heavily round to the wind; the prow slowly swinging into view of the boats, its skeleton gleaming in the horizontal moonlight, and casting a gigantic ribbed shadow upon the water. One extended arm of the ghost seemed beckoning the whites to avenge it.

'Follow your leader!' cried the mate; and, one on each bow, the boats boarded. Scaling-spears and cutlasses crossed hatchets and handspikes. Huddled upon the long-boat amidships, the negresses raised a wailing chant, whose chorus was the clash of the steel.

For a time, the attack wavered; the negroes wedging themselves to beat it back; the half-repelled sailors, as yet unable to gain a footing, fighting as troopers in the saddle, one leg sideways flung over the bulwarks, and one without, plying their cutlasses like carters' whips. But in vain. They were almost overborne, when, rallying themselves into a squad as one man, with a huzza, they sprang inboard; where, entangled, they involuntarily separated again. For a few breaths' space there was a vague, muffled, inner sound as of submerged sword-fish rushing hither

and thither through shoals of black-fish. Soon, in a re-
united band, and joined by the Spanish seamen, the whites
came to the surface, irresistibly driving the negroes toward
the stern. But a barricade of casks and sacks, from side to
side, had been thrown up by the mainmast. Here the
negroes faced about, and though scorning peace or truce,
yet fain would have had a respite. But, without pause,
overleaping the barrier, the unflagging sailors again
closed. Exhausted, the blacks now fought in despair. Their
red tongues lolled, wolf-like, from their black mouths.
But the pale sailors' teeth were set; not a word was
spoken; and, in five minutes more, the ship was won.

Nearly a score of the negroes were killed. Exclusive of
those by the balls, many were mangled; their wounds—
mostly inflicted by the long-edged scaling-spears—resembling those shaven ones of the English at Preston
Pans, made by the poled scythes of the Highlanders. On
the other side, none were killed, though several were
wounded; some severely, including the mate. The surviving negroes were temporarily secured, and the ship,
towed back into the harbour at midnight, once more lay
anchored.

Omitting the incidents and arrangements ensuing,
suffice it that, after two days spent in refitting, the two
ships sailed in company for Concepcion in Chili, and
thence for Lima in Peru; where, before the vice-regal
courts, the whole affair, from the beginning, underwent
investigation.

Though midway on the passage, the ill-fated Spaniard,
relaxed from constraint, showed some signs of regaining
health with free-will; yet, agreeably to his own foreboding,
shortly before arriving at Lima, he relapsed, finally
becoming so reduced as to be carried ashore in arms.
Hearing of his story and plight, one of the many religious

institutions of the City of Kings opened an hospitable refuge to him, where both physician and priest were his nurses, and a member of the order volunteered to be his one special guardian and consoler, by night and by day.

The following extracts, translated from one of the official Spanish documents, will, it is hoped, shed light on the preceding narrative, as well as, in the first place, reveal the true port of departure and true history of the *San Dominick*'s voyage, down to the time of her touching at the island of Santa Maria.

But, ere the extracts come, it may be well to preface them with a remark.

The document selected, from among many others, for partial translation, contains the deposition of Benito Cereno, the first taken in the case. Some disclosures therein were, at the time, held dubious for both learned and natural reasons. The tribunal inclined to the opinion that the deponent, not undisturbed in his mind by recent events, raved of some things which could never have happened. But subsequent depositions of the surviving sailors, bearing out the revelations of their captain in several of the strangest particulars, gave credence to the rest. So that the tribunal, in its final decision, rested its capital sentences upon statements which, had they lacked confirmation, it would have deemed it but duty to reject.

. . . . .

I, Don José de Abos and Padilla, His Majesty's Notary for the Royal Revenue, and Register of this Province, and Notary Public of the Holy Crusade of this Bishopric, etc.

Do certify and declare, as much as is requisite in law, that, in the criminal cause commenced the twenty-fourth of the month of September, in the year seventeen hundred and ninety-nine, against the Senegal negroes of the ship *San Dominick*, the following declaration before me was made.

Declaration of the first witness, DON BENITO CERENO.

The same day, and month, and year, His Honour, Doctor Juan Martinez de Dozas, Councillor of the Royal Audience of this Kingdom, and learned in the law of this Intendancy, ordered the captain of the ship *San Dominick*, Don Benito Cereno, to appear; which he did in his litter, attended by the monk Infelez; of whom he received, before Don José de Abos and Padilla, Notary Public of the Holy Crusade, the oath, which he took by God, our Lord, and a sign of the Cross; under which he promised to tell the truth of whatever he should know and should be asked;—and being interrogated agreeably to the tenor of the act commencing the process, he said, that on the twentieth of May last, he set sail with his ship from the port of Valparaiso, bound to that of Callao; loaded with the produce of the country and one hundred and sixty blacks, of both sexes, mostly belonging to Don Alexandro Aranda, gentleman, of the city of Mendoza; that the crew of the ship consisted of thirty-six men, beside the persons who went as passengers; that the negroes were in part as follows:

Here, in the original, follows a list of some fifty names, descriptions, and ages, compiled from certain recovered documents of Aranda's and also from recollections of the deponent, from which portions only are extracted.

—One, from about eighteen to nineteen years, named José, and this was the man that waited upon his master, Don Alexandro, and who speaks well the Spanish, having served him four or five years; . . . a mulatto, named

Francesco, the cabin steward, of a good person and voice, having sung in the Valparaiso churches, native of the province of Buenos Ayres, aged about thirty-five years. . . . A smart negro, named Dago, who had been for many years a grave-digger among the Spaniards, aged forty-six years. . . . Four old negroes, born in Africa, from sixty to seventy, but sound, caulkers by trade, whose names are as follows:—the first was named Muri, and he was killed (as was also his son named Diamelo); the second, Nacta; the third, Yola, likewise killed; the fourth, Ghofan; and six full-grown negroes, aged from thirty to forty-five, all raw, and born among the Ashantees—Martinqui, Yan, Lecbe, Mapenda, Yambaio, Akim; four of whom were killed; . . . a powerful negro named Atufal, who, being supposed to have been a chief in Africa, his owners set great store by him. . . . And a small negro of Senegal, but some years among the Spaniards, aged about thirty, which negro's name was Babo; . . . that he does not remember the names of the others, but that still expecting the residue of Don Alexandro's papers will be found, will then take due account of them all, and remit to the court; . . . and thirty-nine women and children of all ages.

After the catalogue, the deposition goes on as follows:

. . . That all the negroes slept upon deck, as is customary in this navigation, and none wore fetters, because the owner, his friend Aranda, told him that they were all tractable; . . . that on the seventh day after leaving port, at three o'clock in the morning, all the Spaniards being asleep except the two officers on the watch, who were the boatswain, Juan Robles, and the carpenter, Juan Bautista Gayete, and the helmsman and his boy, the negroes revolted suddenly, wounded dangerously the boatswain and the carpenter, and successively killed eighteen men

of those who were sleeping upon deck, some with hand-
spikes and hatchets, and others by throwing them alive
overboard, after tying them; that of the Spaniards upon
deck, they left about seven, as he thinks, alive and tied, to
manœuvre the ship and three or four more who hid themselves, remained also alive. Although in the act of revolt
the negroes made themselves masters of the hatchway,
six or seven wounded went through it to the cockpit,
without any hindrance on their part; that in the act of
revolt, the mate and another person, whose name he
does not recollect, attempted to come up through the
hatchway, but having been wounded at the onset, they
were obliged to return to the cabin; that the deponent
resolved at break of day to come up the companionway,
where the negro Babo was, being the ringleader, and
Atufal, who assisted him, and having spoken to them,
exhorted them to cease committing such atrocities, asking
them, at the same time, what they wanted and intended
to do, offering, himself, to obey their commands; that,
notwithstanding this, they threw, in his presence, three
men, alive and tied, overboard; that they told the deponent to come up, and that they would not kill him;
which having done, the negro Babo asked him whether
there were in those seas any negro countries where they
might be carried, and he answered them, no; that the
negro Babo afterwards told him to carry them to Senegal,
or to the neighbouring islands of St. Nicholas; and he
answered, that this was impossible, on account of the
great distance, the necessity involved of rounding Cape
Horn, the bad condition of the vessel, the want of provisions, sails, and water; but that the negro Babo replied
to him he must carry them in any way; that they would do
and conform themselves to everything the deponent
should require as to eating and drinking; that after a long

conference, being absolutely compelled to please them, for they threatened him to kill all the whites if they were not, at all events, carried to Senegal, he told them that what was most wanting for the voyage was water; that they would go near the coast to take it, and hence they would proceed on their course; that the negro Babo agreed to it; and the deponent steered toward the intermediate ports, hoping to meet some Spanish or foreign vessel that would save them; that within ten or eleven days they saw the land, and continued their course by it in the vicinity of Nasca; that the deponent observed that the negroes were now restless and mutinous, because he did not effect the taking in of water, the negro Babo having required, with threats, that it should be done, without fail, the following day; he told him he saw plainly that the coast was steep, and the rivers designated in the maps were not to be found, with other reasons suitable to the circumstances; that the best way would be to go to the island of Santa Maria, where they might water and victual easily, it being a desert island, as the foreigners did; that the deponent did not go to Pisco, that was near, nor make any other port of the coast, because the negro Babo had intimated to him several times, that he would kill all the whites the very moment he should perceive any city, town, or settlement of any kind on the shores to which they should be carried: that having determined to go to the island of Santa Maria, as the deponent had planned, for the purpose of trying whether, in the passage or in the island itself, they could find any vessel that should favour them, or whether he could escape from it in a boat to the neighbouring coast of Arruco; to adopt the necessary means he immediately changed his course, steering for the island; that the negroes Babo and Atufal held daily conferences, in which they discussed what was necessary

for their design of returning to Senegal, whether they
were to kill all the Spaniards, and particularly the deponent; that eight days after parting from the coast of
Nasca, the deponent being on the watch a little after day-
break, and soon after the negroes had their meeting, the
negro Babo came to the place where the deponent was,
and told him that he had determined to kill his master,
Don Alexandro Aranda, both because he and his companions could not otherwise be sure of their liberty, and
that, to keep the seamen in subjection, he wanted to pre-
pare a warning of what road they should be made to take
did they or any of them oppose him; and that, by means
of the death of Don Alexandro, that warning would best
be given; but, that what this last meant, the deponent
did not at the time comprehend, nor could not, further
than that the death of Don Alexandro was intended; and
moreover, the negro Babo proposed to the deponent to
call the mate Raneds, who was sleeping in the cabin, before
the thing was done, for fear, as the deponent understood
it, that the mate, who was a good navigator, should be
killed with Don Alexandro and the rest; that the deponent, who was the friend, from youth of Don Alexandro,
prayed and conjured, but all was useless; for the negro
Babo answered him that the thing could not be prevented,
and that all the Spaniards risked their death if they should
attempt to frustrate his will in this matter, or any other;
that, in this conflict, the deponent called the mate,
Raneds, who was forced to go apart, and immediately the
negro Babo commanded the Ashantee Martinqui and
the Ashantee Lecbe to go and commit the murder; that
those two went down with hatchets to the berth of Don
Alexandro; that, yet half alive and mangled, they dragged
him on deck; that they were going to throw him overboard
in that state, but the negro Babo stopped them, bidding

the murder be completed on the deck before him, which was done, when, by his orders, the body was carried below, forward; that nothing more was seen of it by the deponent for three days; . . . that Don Alonzo Sidonia, an old man, long resident at Valparaiso, and lately appointed to a civil office in Peru, whither he had taken passage, was at the time sleeping in the berth opposite Don Alexandro's; that, awakening at his cries, surprised by them, and at the sight of the negroes with their bloody hatchets in their hands, he threw himself into the sea through a window which was near him, and was drowned, without it being in the power of the deponent to assist or take him up; . . . that, a short time after killing Aranda, they brought upon deck his german-cousin, of middle-age, Don Francisco Masa, of Mendoza, and the young Don Joaquin, Marques de Aramboalaza, then lately from Spain, with his Spanish servant Ponce, and the three young clerks of Aranda, José Mozairi, Lorenzo Bargas, and Hermenegildo Gandix, all of Cadiz; that Don Joaquin and Hermenegildo Gandix, the negro Babo for purposes hereafter to appear, preserved alive; but Don Francisco Masa, José Mozairi, and Lorenzo Bargas, with Ponce, the servant, beside the boatswain, Juan Robles, the boatswain's mates, Manuel Viscaya and Roderigo Hurta, and four of the sailors, the negro Babo ordered to be thrown alive into the sea, although they made no resistance, nor begged for anything else but mercy; that the boatswain, Juan Robles, who knew how to swim, kept the longest above water, making acts of contrition, and, in the last words he uttered, charged this deponent to cause mass to be said for his soul to our Lady of Succour: . . . that, during the three days which followed, the deponent, uncertain what fate had befallen the remains of Don Alexandro, frequently asked the negro Babo where they were, and, if still on board, whether they were to be preserved for interment ashore, entreating him so to order it; that the negro Babo answered nothing till the fourth day, when at sunrise, the deponent coming on deck, the negro Babo showed him a skeleton, which had been substituted for the ship's proper figurehead, the image of Christopher Colon, the discoverer of the New World; that the negro Babo asked him whose skeleton that was, and whether, from its whiteness, he should not think it a white's; that, upon his covering his face, the negro Babo, coming close, said words to this effect: 'Keep faith with the blacks from here to Senegal, or you shall in spirit, as now in body, follow your leader,' pointing to the prow; . . . that the same morning the negro Babo took by succession each Spaniard forward, and asked him whose skeleton that was, and whether, from its whiteness, he should not think it a white's; that each Spaniard covered his face; that then to each the negro Babo repeated the words in the first place said to the deponent; . . . that they (the Spaniards), being then assembled aft, the negro Babo harangued them, saying that he had now done all; that the deponent (as navigator for the negroes) might pursue his course, warning him and all of them that they should, soul and body, go the way of Don Alexandro if he saw them (the Spaniards) speak or plot anything against them (the negroes)— a threat which was repeated every day; that, before the events last mentioned, they had tied the cook to throw him overboard, for it is not known what thing they heard him speak, but finally the negro Babo spared his life, at the request of the deponent; that a few days after, the deponent, endeavouring not to omit any means to preserve the lives of the remaining whites, spoke to the negroes peace and tranquillity, and agreed to draw up a paper, signed by the deponent and the sailors who could write, as also by the negro Babo, for himself and all the blacks, in which the deponent obliged himself to carry them to Senegal, and they not to kill any more, and he formally to make over to them the ship, with the cargo, with which they were for that time satisfied and quieted. . . . But the next day, the more surely to guard against the sailors' escape, the negro Babo commanded all the boats to be destroyed but the long-boat, which was unseaworthy, and another, a cutter in good condition, which, knowing it would yet be wanted for lowering the water casks, he had it lowered down into the hold.

.   .   .   .

Various particulars of the prolonged and perplexed navigation ensuing here follow, with incidents of a calamitous calm, from which portion one passage is extracted, to wit :

—That on the fifth day of the calm, all on board suffering much from the heat, and want of water, and five having died in fits, and mad, the negroes became irritable, and for a chance gesture, which they deemed suspicious— though it was harmless—made by the mate, Raneds, to the deponent, in the act of handing a quadrant, they killed him; but that for this they afterwards were sorry, the mate being the only remaining navigator on board, except the deponent.

.   .   .   .

—That omitting other events, which daily happened, and which can only serve uselessly to recall past misfortunes and conflicts, after seventy-three days' navigation, reckoned from the time they sailed from Nasca, during which they navigated under a scanty allowance of water, and were afflicted with the calms before mentioned, they at last arrived at the island of Santa Maria, on the seventeenth of the month of August, at about six

o'clock in the afternoon, at which hour they cast anchor
very near the American ship, *Bachelor's Delight*, which
lay in the same bay, commanded by the generous Captain
Amasa Delano; but at six o'clock in the morning, they
had already descried the port, and the negroes became
uneasy, as soon as at distance they saw the ship, not having
expected to see one there; that the negro Babo pacified
them, assuring them that no fear need be had; that
straightway he ordered the figure on the bow to be covered
with canvas, as for repairs, and had the decks a little set
in order; that for a time the negro Babo and the negro
Atufal conferred; that the negro Atufal was for sailing
away, but the negro Babo would not, and, by himself,
cast about what to do; that at last he came to the deponent,
proposing to him to say and do all that the deponent
declares to have said and done to the American captain;
. . . that the negro Babo warned him that if he varied in
the least, or uttered any word, or gave any look that
should give the least intimation of the past events or
present state, he would instantly kill him, with all his
companions, showing a dagger, which he carried hid,
saying something which, as he understood it, meant
that that dagger would be alert as his eye; that the negro
Babo then announced the plan to all his companions,
which pleased them; that he then, the better to disguise
the truth, devised many expedients, in some of them
uniting deceit and defence; that of this sort was the device
of the six Ashantees before named, who were his bravos;
that them he stationed on the break of the poop, as if to
clean certain hatchets (in cases, which were part of the
cargo), but in reality to use them, and distribute them at
need, and at a given word he told them that, among other
devices, was the device of presenting Atufal, his right-
hand man, as chained, though in a moment the chains

could be dropped; that in every particular he informed the deponent what part he was expected to enact in every device, and what story he was to tell on every occasion, always threatening him with instant death if he varied in the least: that, conscious that many of the negroes would be turbulent, the negro Babo appointed the four aged negroes, who were caulkers, to keep what domestic order they could on the decks; that again and again he harangued the Spaniards and his companions, informing them of his intent, and of his devices, and of the invented story that this deponent was to tell, charging them lest any of them varied from that story; that these arrangements were made and matured during the interval of two or three hours, between their first sighting the ship and the arrival on board of Captain Amasa Delano; that this happened at about half-past seven in the morning, Captain Amasa Delano coming in his boat, and all gladly receiving him; that the deponent, as well as he could force himself, acting then the part of principal owner, and a free captain of the ship, told Captain Amasa Delano, when called upon, that he came from Buenos Ayres, bound to Lima, with three hundred negroes; that off Cape Horn, and in a subsequent fever, many negroes had died; that also, by similar casualties, all the sea officers and the greatest part of the crew had died.

.   .   .   .

And so the deposition goes on, circumstantially recounting the fictitious story dictated to the deponent by Babo, and through the deponent imposed upon Captain Delano; and also recounting the friendly offers of Captain Delano, with other things, but all of which is here omitted. After the fictitious, strange story, etc., the deposition proceeds:

—That the generous Captain Amasa Delano remained

on board all the day, till he left the ship anchored at six
o'clock in the evening, deponent speaking to him always
of his pretended misfortunes, under the fore-mentioned
principles, without having had it in his power to tell a
single word, or give him the least hint, that he might know
the truth and state of things; because the negro Babo,
performing the office of an officious servant with all the
appearance of submission of the humble slave, did not
leave the deponent one moment; that this was in order to
observe the deponent's actions and words, for the negro
Babo understands well the Spanish; and besides, there
were thereabout some others who were constantly on
the watch, and likewise understood the Spanish; . . .
that upon one occasion, while deponent was standing on
the deck conversing with Amasa Delano, by a secret sign
the negro Babo drew him (the deponent) aside, the act
appearing as if originating with the deponent; that then,
he being drawn aside, the negro Babo proposed to him to
gain from Amasa Delano full particulars about his ship,
and crew, and arms; that the deponent asked 'For what?'
that the negro Babo answered he might conceive; that,
grieved at the prospect of what might overtake the
generous Captain Amasa Delano, the deponent at first
refused to ask the desired questions, and used every argument to induce the negro Babo to give up this new design;
that the negro Babo showed the point of his dagger; that,
after the information had been obtained, the negro Babo
again drew him aside, telling him that that very night he
(the deponent) would be captain of two ships instead of
one, for that, great part of the American's ship's crew
being to be absent fishing, the six Ashantees, without
any one else, would easily take it; that at this time he said
other things to the same purpose; that no entreaties
availed; that before Amasa Delano's coming on board, no

hint had been given touching the capture of the American
ship: that to prevent this project the deponent was powerless; . . . —that in some things his memory is confused,
he cannot distinctly recall every event; . . . —that as soon
as they had cast anchor at six of the clock in the evening,
as has before been stated, the American captain took leave
to return to his vessel; that upon a sudden impulse, which
the deponent believes to have come from God and his
angels, he, after the farewell had been said, followed the
generous Captain Amasa Delano as far as the gunwale,
where he stayed, under the pretence of taking leave, until
Amasa Delano should have been seated in his boat; that
on shoving off, the deponent sprang from the gunwale,
into the boat, and fell into it, he knows not how, God
guarding him; that—

*Here, in the original, follows the account of what further
happened at the escape, and how the 'San Dominick' was
retaken, and of the passage to the coast; including in the
recital many expressions of 'eternal gratitude' to the 'generous Captain Amasa Delano.' The deposition then proceeds
with recapitulatory remarks, and a partial renumeration of
the negroes, making record of their individual part in the
past events, with a view to furnishing, according to command
of the court, the data whereon to found the criminal sentences
to be pronounced. From this portion is the following:*

—That he believes that all the negroes, though not in
the first place knowing to the design of revolt, when it was
accomplished, approved it. . . . That the negro, José,
eighteen years old, and in the personal service of Don
Alexandro, was the one who communicated the information to the negro Babo, about the state of things in the
cabin, before the revolt; that this is known, because, in the
preceding midnight, he used to come from his berth,

which was under his master's, in the cabin, to the deck
where the ringleader and his associates were, and had
secret conversations with the negro Babo, in which he was
several times seen by the mate; that, one night, the mate
drove him away twice; . . . that this same negro José, was
the one who, without being commanded to do so by the
negro Babo, as Lecbe and Martinqui were, stabbed his
master, Don Alexandro, after he had been dragged half-
lifeless to the deck; . . . that the mulatto steward, Francesco, was of the first band of revolters, that he was, in all
things, the creature and tool of the negro Babo; that, to
make his court, he, just before a repast in the cabin,
proposed, to the negro Babo, poisoning a dish for the
generous Captain Amasa Delano; this is known and
believed, because the negroes have said it; but that the
negro Babo, having another design, forbade Francesco;
. . . that the Ashantee Lecbe was one of the worst of them;
for that, on the day the ship was retaken, he assisted in
the defence of her, with a hatchet in each hand, with one of
which he wounded, in the breast, the chief mate of Amasa
Delano, in the first act of boarding; this all knew; that,
in sight of the deponent, Lecbe struck, with a hatchet,
Don Francisco Masa when, by the negro Babo's orders,
he was carrying him to throw him overboard, alive;
beside participating in the murder, before mentioned, of
Don Alexandro Aranda, and others of the cabin-pas-
sengers; that, owing to the fury with which the Ashantees
fought in the engagement with the boats, but this Lecbe
and Yan survived; that Yan was as bad as Lecbe; that Yan
was the man who, by Babo's command, willingly prepared
the skeleton of Don Alexandro, in a way the negroes
afterwards told the deponent, but which he, so long as
reason is left him, can never divulge; that Yan and Lecbe
were the two who, in a calm by night, riveted the skeleton

to the bow; this also the negroes told him; that the negro Babo was he who traced the inscription below it; that the negro Babo was the plotter from first to last; he ordered every murder, and was the helm and keel of the revolt; that Atufal was his lieutenant in all; but Atufal, with his own hand, committed no murder; nor did the negro Babo; . . . that Atufal was shot, being killed in the fight with the boats, ere boarding; . . . that the negresses, of age, were knowing to the revolt, and testified themselves satisfied at the death of their master, Don Alexandro; that, had the negroes not restrained them, they would have tortured to death, instead of simply killing, the Spaniards slain by command of the negro Babo; that the negresses used their utmost influence to have the deponent made away with; that, in the various acts of murder, they sang songs and danced—not gaily, but solemnly; and before the engagement with the boats, as well as during the action, they sang melancholy songs to the negroes, and that this melancholy tone was more inflaming than a different one would have been, and was so intended; that all this is believed, because the negroes have said it.

—That of the thirty-six men of the crew—exclusive of the passengers (all of whom are now dead), which the deponent had knowledge of—six only remained alive, with four cabin-boys and ship-boys, not included with the crew; . . . —that the negroes broke an arm of one of the cabin-boys and gave him strokes with hatchets.

Then follow various random disclosures referring to various periods of time. The following are extracted :

—That during the presence of Captain Amasa Delano on board, some attempts were made by the sailors, and one by Hermenegildo Gandix, to convey hints to him of the true state of affairs; but that these attempts were ineffectual, owing to fear of incurring death, and furthermore owing to the devices which offered contradictions to the true state of affairs; as well as owing to the generosity and piety of Amasa Delano, incapable of sounding such wickedness; . . . that Luys Galgo, a sailor about sixty years of age, and formerly of the king's navy, was one of those who sought to convey tokens to Captain Amasa Delano; but his intent, though undiscovered, being suspected, he was, on a pretence, made to retire out of sight, and at last into the hold, and there was made away with. This the negroes have since said; . . . that one of the ship-boys feeling, from Captain Amasa Delano's presence, some hopes of release, and not having enough prudence, dropped some chance-word respecting his expectations, which being overheard and understood by a slave-boy with whom he was eating at the time, the latter struck him on the head with a knife, inflicting a bad wound, but of which the boy is now healing; that likewise, not long before the ship was brought to anchor, one of the seamen, steering at the time, endangered himself by letting the blacks remark a certain unconscious hopeful expression in his countenance, arising from some cause similar to the above; but this sailor, by his heedful after conduct, escaped; . . . that these statements are made to show the court that from the beginning to the end of the revolt, it was impossible for the deponent and his men to act otherwise than they did; . . . —that the third clerk, Hermenegildo Gandix, who before had been forced to live among the seamen, wearing a seaman's habit, and in all respects appearing to be one for the time; he, Gandix, was killed by a musket-ball fired through a mistake from the American boats before boarding; having in his fright ran up the mizzen-rigging, calling to the boats—'don't board,' lest upon their boarding the negroes should kill him; that this inducing the Americans to believe he some way favoured the cause of the negroes, they fired two balls at him, so that he fell wounded from the rigging, and was drowned in the sea; . . . —that the young Don Joaquin, Marques de Arambaolaza, like Hermenegildo Gandix, the third clerk, was degraded to the office and appearance of a common seaman; that upon one occasion, when Don Joaquin shrank, the negro Babo commanded the Ashantee Lecbe to take tar and heat it, and pour it upon Don Joaquin's hands; . . . —that Don Joaquin was killed owing to another mistake of the Americans, but one impossible to be avoided, as upon the approach of the boats, Don Joaquin, with a hatchet tied edge out and upright to his hand, was made by the negroes to appear on the bulwarks; whereupon, seen with arms in his hands and in a question-able attitude, he was shot for a renegade seaman; . . . —that on the person of Don Joaquin was found secreted a jewel, which, by papers that were discovered, proved to have been meant for the shrine of our Lady of Mercy in Lima; a votive offering, beforehand prepared and guarded, to attest his gratitude, when he should have landed in Peru, his last destination, for the safe conclusion of his entire voyage from Spain; . . . —that the jewel, with the other effects of the late Don Joaquin, is in the custody of the brethren of the Hospital de Sacerdotes, awaiting the decision of the honourable court; . . . —that, owing to the condition of the deponent, as well as the haste in which the boats departed for the attack, the Americans were not forewarned that there were, among the apparent crew, a passenger and one of the clerks dis-guised by the negro Babo; . . . —that, beside the negroes killed in the action, some were killed after the capture and reanchoring at night, when shackled to the ring-bolts on deck; that these deaths were committed by the sailors, ere they could be prevented. That so soon as informed of it, Captain Amasa Delano used all his authority, and, in particular with his own hand, struck down Martinez Gola, who, having found a razor in the pocket of an old jacket of his, which one of the shackled negroes had on, was aiming it at the negro's throat; that the noble Captain Amasa Delano also wrenched from the hand of Bartholomew Barlo, a dagger secreted at the time of the massacre of the whites, with which he was in the act of stabbing a shackled negro, who, the same day, with another negro, had thrown him down and jumped upon him; . . . —that, for all the events, befalling through so long a time, during which the ship was in the hands of the negro Babo, he cannot here give account; but that, what he has said is the most substantial of what occurs to him at present, and is the truth under the oath which he has taken; which declaration he affirmed and ratified, after hearing it read to him.

He said that he is twenty-nine years of age, and broken in body and mind; that when finally dismissed by the court, he shall not return home to Chili, but betake himself to the monastery on Mount Agonia without; and signed with his honour, and crossed himself, and, for the time, departed as he came, in his litter, with the monk Infelez, to the Hospital de Sacerdotes.

                                   BENITO CERENO.
DOCTOR ROZAS.

If the deposition of Benito Cereno has served as the key to fit into the lock of the complications which preceded it, then, as a vault whose door has been flung back, the *San Dominick*'s hull lies open today.

Hitherto the nature of this narrative, besides rendering

the intricacies in the beginning unavoidable, has more or less required that many things, instead of being set down in the order of occurrence, should be retrospectively, or irregularly given; this last is the case with the following passages, which will conclude the account:

During the long, mild voyage to Lima, there was, as before hinted, a period during which Don Benito a little recovered his health, or, at least in some degree, his tranquillity. Ere the decided relapse which came, the two captains had many cordial conversations—their fraternal unreserve in singular contrast with former withdrawments.

Again and again, it was repeated, how hard it had been to enact the part forced on the Spaniard by Babo.

'Ah, my dear Don Amasa,' Don Benito once said, 'at those very times when you thought me so morose and ungrateful—nay when, as you now admit, you half thought me plotting your murder—at those very times my heart was frozen; I could not look at you, thinking of what, both on board this ship and your own, hung, from other hands, over my kind benefactor. And as God lives, Don Amasa, I know not whether desire for my own safety alone could have nerved me to that leap into your boat, had it not been for the thought that, did you, unenlightened, return to your ship, you, my best friend, with all who might be with you, stolen upon, that night, in your hammocks, would never in this world have wakened again. Do but think how you walked this deck, how you sat in this cabin, every inch of ground mined into honey-combs under you. Had I dropped the least hint, made the least advance toward an understanding between us, death, explosive death—yours as mine— would have ended the scene.'

'True, true,' cried Captain Delano, starting, 'you saved

my life, Don Benito, more than I yours; saved it, too, against my knowledge and will.'

'Nay, my friend,' rejoined the Spaniard, courteous even to the point of religion, 'God charmed your life, but you saved mine. To think of some things you did— those smilings and chattings, rash pointings and gesturings. For less than these, they slew my mate, Raneds; but you had the Prince of Heaven's safe conduct through all ambuscades.'

'Yes, all is owing to Providence, I know; but the temper of my mind that morning was more than commonly pleasant, while the sight of so much suffering—more apparent than real—added to my good nature, compassion, and charity, happily interweaving the three. Had it been otherwise, doubtless, as you hint, some of my interferences with the blacks might have ended unhappily enough. Besides that, those feelings I spoke of enabled me to get the better of momentary distrust, at times when acuteness might have cost me my life, without saving another's. Only at the end did my suspicions get the better of me, and you know how wide of the mark they then proved.'

'Wide, indeed,' said Don Benito, sadly; 'you were with me all day; stood with me, sat with me, talked with me, looked at me, ate with me, drank with me; and yet, your last act was to clutch for a villain, not only an innocent man, but the most pitiable of all men. To such degree may malign machinations and deceptions impose. So far may even the best men err, in judging the conduct of one with the recesses of whose condition he is not acquainted. But you were forced to it; and you were in time undeceived. Would that, in both respects, it was so ever, and with all men.'

'I think I understand you; you generalize, Don Benito;

and mournfully enough. But the past is passed; why moralize upon it? Forget it. See, yon bright sun has forgotten it all, and the blue sea, and the blue sky; these have turned over new leaves.'

'Because they have no memory,' he dejectedly replied; 'because they are not human.'

'But these mild trades that now fan your cheek, Don Benito, do they not come with a human-like healing to you? Warm friends, steadfast friends are the trades.'

'With their steadfastness they but waft me to my tomb, Señor,' was the foreboding response.

'You are saved, Don Benito,' cried Captain Delano, more and more astonished and pained; 'you are saved; what has cast such a shadow upon you?'

'The negro.'

There was silence, while the moody man sat, slowly and unconsciously gathering his mantle about him, as if it were a pall.

There was no more conversation that day.

But if the Spaniard's melancholy sometimes ended in muteness upon topics like the above, there were others upon which he never spoke at all; on which, indeed, all his old reserves were piled. Pass over the worst and, only to elucidate, let an item or two of these be cited. The dress so precise and costly, worn by him on the day whose events have been narrated, had not willingly been put on. And that silver-mounted sword, apparent symbol of despotic command, was not, indeed, a sword, but the ghost of one. The scabbard, artificially stiffened, was empty.

As for the black—whose brain, not body, had schemed and led the revolt, with the plot—his slight frame, inadequate to that which it held, had at once yielded to the superior muscular strength of his captor, in the boat. Seeing all was over, he uttered no sound, and could not be forced to. His aspect seemed to say: since I cannot do deeds, I will not speak words. Put in irons in the hold, with the rest, he was carried to Lima. During the passage Don Benito did not visit him. Nor then, nor at any time after, would he look at him. Before the tribunal he refused. When pressed by the judges he fainted. On the testimony of the sailors alone rested the legal identity of Babo. And yet the Spaniard would, upon occasion, verbally refer to the negro, as has been shown; but look on him he would not, or could not.

Some months after, dragged to the gibbet at the tail of a mule, the black met his voiceless end. The body was burned to ashes; but for many days, the head, that hive of subtlety, fixed on a pole in the Plaza, met, unabashed, the gaze of the whites; and across the Plaza looked toward St. Bartholomew's church, in whose vaults slept then, as now, the recovered bones of Aranda; and across the Rimac bridge looked toward the monastery, on Mount Agonia without; where, three months after being dismissed by the court, Benito Cereno, borne on the bier, did, indeed, follow his leader.

Baker's Bluejay Yarn

MARK TWAIN

(1835-1910)

ANIMALS talk to each other, of course. There can be no question about that; but I suppose there are very few people who can understand them. I never knew but one man who could. I knew he could, however, because he told me so himself. He was a middle-aged, simple-hearted miner who had lived in a lonely corner of California, among the woods and mountains, a good many years, and had studied the ways of his only neighbours, the beasts and the birds, until he believed he could accurately translate any remark which they made. This was Jim Baker. According to Jim Baker, some animals have only a limited education, and use only very simple words, and scarcely ever a comparison or a flowery figure, whereas, certain other animals have a large vocabulary, a fine command of language and a ready and fluent delivery; consequently these latter talk a great deal; they like it; they are conscious of their talent, and they enjoy 'showing off'. Baker said, that after long and careful observation, he had come to the conclusion that the bluejays were the best talkers he had found among birds and beasts. Said he:

'There's more *to* a bluejay than any other creature. He has got more moods, and more different kinds of feelings than other creatures; and, mind you, whatever a bluejay feels, he can put into language. And no mere commonplace language, either, but rattling, out-and-out book-talk—bristling with metaphor, too—just bristling! And as for command of language—why *you* never see a bluejay get stuck for a word. No man ever did. They just boil out of him! And another thing: I've noticed a good deal, and there's no bird, or cow, or anything that uses as good grammar as a bluejay. You can say a cat uses good grammar. Well, a cat does—but you let a cat get excited once; you let a cat get to pulling fur with another cat on a shed, nights, and you'll hear grammar that will give you the lockjaw. Ignorant people think it's the *noise* which fighting cats make that is so aggravating, but it ain't so; it's the sickening grammar they use. Now I've never heard a jay use bad grammar but very seldom;

and when they do, they are as ashamed as a human; they shut right down and leave.

'You may call a jay a bird. Well, so he is, in a measure —because he's got feathers on him, and don't belong to no church, perhaps; but otherwise he is just as much a human as you be. And I'll tell you for why. A jay's gifts, and instincts, and feelings, and interests, cover the whole ground. A jay hasn't got any more principle than a Congressman. A jay will lie, a jay will steal, a jay will deceive, a jay will betray; and four times out of five, a jay will go back on his solemnest promise. The sacredness of an obligation is a thing which you can't cram into no bluejay's head. Now, on top of all this, there's another thing; a jay can outswear any gentleman in the mines. You think a cat can swear. Well, a cat can; but you give a bluejay a subject that calls for his reserve-powers, and where is your cat? Don't talk to *me*—I know too much about this thing. And there's yet another thing; in the one little particular of scolding—just good, clean, out-and-out scolding—a bluejay can lay over anything, human or divine. Yes, sir, a jay is everything that a man is. A jay can cry, a jay can laugh, a jay can feel shame, a jay can reason and plan and discuss, a jay likes gossip and scandal, a jay has got a sense of humour, a jay knows when he is an ass just as well as you do—maybe better. If a jay ain't human, he better take in his sign, that's all. Now I'm going to tell you a perfectly true fact about some bluejays.

'When I first begun to understand jay language correctly, there was a little incident happened here. Seven years ago, the last man in this region but me moved away. There stands his house,—been empty ever since; a log house, with a plank roof—just one big room, and no more; no ceiling—nothing between the rafters and the floor. Well, one Sunday morning I was sitting out here in front of my cabin, with my cat, taking the sun, and looking at the blue hills, and listening to the leaves rustling so lonely in the trees, and thinking of the home away yonder in the states, that I hadn't heard from in thirteen years, when a bluejay lit on that house, with an acorn in his mouth, and says, "Hello, I reckon I've struck something." When he spoke, the acorn dropped out of his mouth and rolled down the roof, of course, but he didn't care; his mind was all on the thing he had struck. It was a knot-hole in the roof. He cocked his head to one side, shut one eye and put the other one to the hole, like a 'possum looking down a jug; then he glanced up with his bright eyes, gave a wink or two with his wings—which signifies gratification, you understand,—and says, "It looks like a hole, it's located like a hole,—blamed if I don't believe it *is* a hole!"

'Then he cocked his head down and took another look; he glances up perfectly joyful, this time; winks his wings and his tail both, and says, "Oh, no, this ain't no fat thing, I reckon! If I ain't in luck!—why it's a perfectly elegant hole!" So he flew down and got that acorn, and fetched it up and dropped it in, and was just tilting his head back, with the heavenliest smile on his face, when all of a sudden he was paralysed into a listening attitude and that smile faded gradually out of his countenance like breath off'n a razor, and the queerest look of surprise took its place. Then he says, "Why, I didn't hear it fall!" He cocked his eye at the hole again, and took a long look; raised up and shook his head; stepped around to the other side of the hole and took another look from that side; shook his head again. He studied a while, then he just went into the *de*tails—walked round and round the hole and spied into it from every point of the compass.

No use. Now he took a thinking attitude on the comb of the roof and scratched the back of his head with his right foot a minute, and finally says, "Well, it's too many for *me*, that's certain; must be a mighty long hole; however, I ain't got no time to fool around here, I got to 'tend to business; I reckon it's all right—chance it, anyway."

'So he flew off and fetched another acorn and dropped it in, and tried to flirt his eye to the hole quick enough to see what become of it, but he was too late. He held his eye there as much as a minute; then he raised up and sighed, and says, "Confound it, I don't seem to understand this thing, no way; however, I'll tackle her again." He fetched another acorn, and done his level best to see what become of it, but he couldn't. He says, "Well, *I* never struck no such a hole as this before; I'm of the opinion it's a totally new kind of a hole." Then he begun to get mad. He held in for a spell, walking up and down the comb of the roof and shaking his head and muttering to himself; but his feelings got the upper hand of him, presently, and he broke loose and cussed himself black in the face. I never see a bird take on so about a little thing. When he got through he walks to the hole and looks in again for half a minute; then he says, "Well, you're a long hole, and a deep hole, and a mighty singular hole altogether—but I've started in to fill you, and I'm d—d if I *don't* fill you, if it takes a hundred years!"

'And with that, away he went. You never see a bird work so since you was born. He laid into his work like a nigger, and the way he hove acorns into that hole for about two hours and a half was one of the most exciting and astonishing spectacles I ever struck. He never stopped to take a look any more—he just hove 'em in and went for more. Well, at last he could hardly flop his wings, he was so tuckered out. He comes a-drooping down, once more, sweating like an ice-pitcher, drops his acorn in and says, "*Now* I guess I've got the bulge on you by this time!" So he bent down for a look. If you'll believe me, when his head come up again he was just pale with rage. He says, "I've shovelled acorns enough in there to keep the family thirty years, and if I can see a sign of one of 'em I wish I may land in a museum with a belly full of sawdust in two minutes!"

'He just had strength enough to crawl up on to the comb and lean his back agin the chimbly, and then he collected his impressions and begun to free his mind. I see in a second that what I had mistook for profanity in the mines was only just the rudiments, as you may say.

'Another jay was going by, and heard him doing his devotions, and stops to inquire what was up. The sufferer told him the whole circumstance, and says, "Now yonder's the hole, and if you don't believe me, go and look for yourself." So this fellow went and looked, and comes back and says, "How many did you say you put in there?" "Not any less than two tons," says the sufferer. The other jay went and looked again. He couldn't seem to make it out, so he raised a yell, and three more jays came. They all examined the hole, they all made the sufferer tell it over again, then they all discussed it, and got off as many leather-headed opinions about it as an average crowd of humans could have done.

'They called in more jays; then more and more, till pretty soon this whole region 'peared to have a blue flush about it. There must have been five thousand of them; and such another jawing and disputing and ripping and cussing, you never heard. Every jay in the whole lot put his eye to the hole and delivered a more chuckle-headed opinion about the mystery than the jay that went there before him. They examined the house all over, too. The door was standing half open, and at last one old jay happened to go and light on it and look in. Of course, that knocked the mystery galley-west in a second. There lay the acorns, scattered all over the floor. He flopped his wings and raised a whoop. "Come here!" he says, "Come here, everybody; hang'd if this fool hasn't been trying to fill up a house with acorns!" They all came a-swooping down like a blue cloud, and as each fellow lit on the door and took a glance, the whole absurdity of the contract that that first jay had tackled hit him home and he fell over backwards suffocating with laughter, and the next jay took his place and done the same.

'Well, sir, they roosted around here on the housetop and the trees for an hour, and guffawed over that thing like human beings. It ain't any use to tell me a bluejay hasn't got a sense of humour, because I know better. And memory, too. They brought jays here from all over the United States to look down that hole, every summer for three years. Other birds, too. And they could all see the point, except an owl that come from Nova Scotia to visit the Yo Semite, and he took this thing in on his way back. He said he couldn't see anything funny in it. But then he was a good deal disappointed about Yo Semite, too.'

The Coup de Grâce

AMBROSE BIERCE

(1842-1914)

THE fighting had been hard and continuous, that was attested by all the senses. The very taste of battle was in the air. All was now over; it remained only to succour the wounded and bury the dead—to 'tidy up a bit,' as the humorist of a burying squad put it. A good deal of 'tidying up' was required. As far as one could see through the forest, between the splintered trees, lay wrecks of men and horses. Among them moved the stretcher-bearers, gathering and carrying away the few who showed signs of life. Most of the wounded had died of exposure while the right to minister to their wants was in dispute. It is an army regulation that the wounded must wait; the best way to care for them is to win the battle. It must be confessed that victory is a distinct advantage to a man requiring attention, but many do not live to avail themselves of it.

The dead were collected in groups of a dozen or a score, and laid side by side in rows while the trenches were dug to receive them. Some, found at too great a distance from these rallying points, were buried where they lay. There was little attempt at identification, though in most cases, the burying parties being detailed to glean the same ground which they had assisted to reap, the names of the victorious dead were known and listed. The enemy's fallen had to be content with counting. But of that they got enough; many of them were counted several times, and the total, as given in the official report of the victorious commander, denoted rather a hope than a result.

At some little distance from the spot where one of the burying parties had established its 'bivouac of the dead,' a man in the uniform of a Federal officer stood leaning against a tree. From his feet upward to his neck his attitude was that of weariness reposing; but he turned his head uneasily from side to side; his mind was apparently not at rest. He was perhaps uncertain in what direction to go; he was not likely to remain long where he was, for already the level rays of the setting sun struggled redly through the open spaces of the wood, and the weary soldiers were quitting their task for the day. He would hardly make a night of it alone there among the dead. Nine men in ten whom you meet after a battle inquire the way to some fraction of the army—as if anyone could know. Doubtless this officer was lost. After resting himself a moment, he would follow one of the retiring burial squads.

When all were gone, he walked straight away into the forest toward the red west, its light staining his face like blood. The air of confidence with which he now strode along showed that he was on familiar ground; he had recovered his bearings. The dead on his right and on his left were unregarded as he passed. An occasional low moan from some sorely-stricken wretch whom the relief parties had not reached, and who would have to pass a comfortless night beneath the stars with his thirst to keep him company, was equally unheeded. What, indeed, could the officer have done, being no surgeon and having no water?

At the head of a shallow ravine, a mere depression of the ground, lay a small group of bodies. He saw, and, swerving suddenly from his course, walked rapidly toward them. Scanning each one sharply as he passed, he stopped at last above one which lay at a slight remove from the others, near a clump of small trees. He looked at it narrowly. It seemed to stir. He stooped and laid his hand upon its face. It screamed.

The officer was Captain Downing Madwell, of a Massachusetts regiment of infantry, a daring and intelligent soldier, an honourable man.

In the regiment were two brothers named Halcrow— Caffal and Creede Halcrow. Caffal Halcrow was a sergeant in Captain Madwell's company, and these two men, the sergeant and the captain, were devoted friends. In so far as disparity of rank, difference in duties, and considerations of military discipline would permit, they were commonly together. They had, indeed, grown up together from childhood. A habit of the heart is not easily broken off. Caffal Halcrow had nothing military in his taste or disposition, but the thought of separation from his friend was disagreeable; he enlisted in the company in which Madwell was second lieutenant. Each had taken two steps upward in rank, but between the highest non-commissioned and the lowest commissioned officer the social gulf is deep and wide, and the old relation was maintained with difficulty and a difference.

Creede Halcrow, the brother of Caffal, was the major of the regiment—a cynical, saturnine man, between whom and Captain Madwell there was a natural antipathy which circumstances had nourished and strengthened to an active animosity. But for the restraining influence of their mutual relation to Caffal, these two patriots would doubtless have endeavoured to deprive their country of one another's services.

At the opening of the battle that morning, the regiment

was performing outpost duty a mile away from the main army. It was attacked and nearly surrounded in the forest, but stubbornly held its ground. During a lull in the fighting, Major Halcrow came to Captain Madwell. The two exchanged formal salutes, and the major said: 'Captain, the colonel directs that you push your company to the head of this ravine and hold your place there until recalled. I need hardly apprise you of the dangerous character of the movement, but if you wish, you can, I suppose, turn over the command to your first lieutenant. I was not, however, directed to authorize the substitution; it is merely a suggestion of my own, unofficially made.'

To this deadly insult Captain Madwell coolly replied:—

'Sir, I invite you to accompany the movement. A mounted officer would be a conspicuous mark, and I have long held the opinion that it would be better if you were dead.'

The art of repartee was cultivated in military circles as early as 1862.

A half hour later Captain Madwell's company was driven from its position at the head of the ravine, with a loss of one-third its number. Among the fallen was Sergeant Halcrow. The regiment was soon afterward forced back to the main line, and at the close of the battle was miles away. The captain was now standing at the side of his subordinate and friend.

Sergeant Halcrow was mortally hurt. His clothing was deranged; it seemed to have been violently torn apart, exposing the abdomen. Some of the buttons of his jacket had been pulled off and lay on the ground beside him, and fragments of his other garments were strewn about. His leather belt was parted, and had apparently been dragged from beneath him as he lay. There had been no

very great effusion of blood. The only visible wound was
a wide, ragged opening in the abdomen. It was defiled
with earth and dead leaves. Protruding from it was a
lacerated end of the small intestine. In all his experience
Captain Madwell had not seen a wound like this. He
could neither conjecture how it was made nor explain
the attendant circumstances—the strangely torn clothing, the parted belt, the besmirching of the white skin.
He knelt and made a closer examination. When he rose
to his feet, he turned his eyes in various directions as if
looking for an enemy. Fifty yards away, on the crest of
a low, thinly-wooded hill, he saw several dark objects
moving about among the fallen men—a herd of swine.
One stood with its back to him, its shoulders sharply
elevated. Its forefeet were upon a human body, its head
was depressed and invisible. The bristly ridge of its
chine showed black against the red west. Captain Madwell drew away his eyes and fixed them again upon the
thing which had been his friend.

The man who had suffered these monstrous mutila-
tions was alive. At intervals he moved his limbs; he
moaned at every breath. He stared blankly into the face
of his friend, and if touched screamed. In his giant agony
he had torn up the ground on which he lay; his clenched
hands were full of leaves and twigs and earth. Articulate
speech was beyond his power; it was impossible to know
if he were sensible to anything but pain. The expression
of his face was an appeal; his eyes were full of prayer.
For what?

There was no misreading that look; the captain had
too frequently seen it in eyes of those whose lips had
still the power to formulate it by an entreaty for death.
Consciously or unconsciously, this writhing fragment of
humanity, this type and example of acute sensation, this

handiwork of man and beast, this humble, unheroic Prometheus, was imploring everything, all, the whole non-*ego*, for the boon of oblivion. To the earth and the sky alike, to the trees, to the man, to whatever took form in sense or consciousness, this incarnate suffering addressed its silent plea.

For what, indeed?—For that which we accord to even the meanest creature without sense to demand it, denying it only to the wretched of our own race: for the blessed release, the rite of uttermost compassion, the *coup de grâce*.

Captain Madwell spoke the name of his friend. He repeated it over and over without effect until emotion choked his utterance. His tears plashed upon the livid face beneath his own and blinded himself. He saw nothing but a blurred and moving object, but the moans were more distinct than ever, interrupted at briefer intervals by sharper shrieks. He turned away, struck his hand upon his forehead, and strode from the spot. The swine, catching sight of him, threw up their crimson muzzles, regarding him suspiciously a second, and then, with a gruff, concerted grunt, raced away out of sight. A horse, its foreleg splintered horribly by a cannon shot, lifted its head sidewise from the ground and neighed piteously. Madwell stepped forward, drew his revolver and shot the poor beast between the eyes, narrowly observing its death struggle, which, contrary to his expectation, was violent and long; but at last it lay still. The tense muscles of its lips, which had uncovered the teeth in a horrible grin, relaxed; the sharp, clean-cut profile took on a look of profound peace and rest.

Along the distant thinly-wooded crest to westward the fringe of sunset fire had now nearly burned itself out. The light upon the trunks of the trees had faded to a tender grey; the shadows were in their tops, like great dark birds aperch. The night was coming and there were miles of haunted forest between Captain Madwell and camp. Yet he stood there at the side of the dead animal, apparently lost to all sense of his surroundings. His eyes were bent upon the earth at his feet; his left hand hung loosely at his side, his right still held the pistol. Suddenly he lifted his face, turned it toward his dying friend, and walked rapidly back to his side. He knelt upon one knee, cocked the weapon, placed the muzzle against the man's forehead, turned away his eyes and pulled the trigger. There was no report. He had used his last cartridge for the horse. The sufferer moaned and his lips moved convulsively. The froth that ran from them had a tinge of blood.

Captain Madwell rose to his feet and drew his sword from the scabbard. He passed the fingers of his left hand along the edge from hilt to point. He held it out straight before him as if to test his nerves. There was no visible tremor of the blade; the ray of bleak skylight that it reflected was steady and true. He stooped, and with his left hand tore away the dying man's shirt, rose, and placed the point of the sword just over the heart. This time he did not withdraw his eyes. Grasping the hilt with both hands, he thrust downward with all his strength and weight. The blade sank into the man's body —through his body into the earth; Captain Madwell came near falling forward upon his work. The dying man drew up his knees and at the same time threw his right arm across his breast and grasped the steel so tightly that the knuckles of the hand visibly whitened. By a violent but vain effort to withdraw the blade, the wound was enlarged; a rill of blood escaped, running sinuously down into the deranged clothing. At that moment three men stepped silently forward from behind the clump of young trees which had concealed their approach. Two were hospital attendants and carried a stretcher.

The third was Major Creede Halcrow.

The Beast in the Jungle

HENRY JAMES

(1843-1916)

I

WHAT determined the speech that startled him in the course of their encounter scarcely matters, being probably but some words spoken by himself quite without intention—spoken as they lingered and slowly moved together after their renewal of acquaintance. He had been conveyed by friends, an hour or two before, to the house at which she was staying; the party of visitors at the other house, of whom he was one, and thanks to whom it was his theory, as always, that he was lost in the crowd, had been invited over to luncheon. There had been after luncheon much dispersal, all in the interest of the original motive, a view of Weatherend itself and the fine things, intrinsic features, pictures, heirlooms, treasures of all the arts, that made the place almost famous; and the great rooms were so numerous that guests could wander at their will, hang back from the principal group, and, in cases where they took such matters with the last seriousness, give themselves up to mysterious appreciations and measurements. There were persons to be observed, singly or in couples, bending toward objects in out-of-the-way corners with their hands on their knees and their heads nodding quite as with the emphasis of an excited sense of smell. When they were two they either mingled their sounds of ecstasy or melted into silences of even deeper import, so that there were aspects of the occasion that gave it for Marcher much the air of the 'look round,' previous to a sale highly advertised, that excites or quenches, as may be, the dream of acquisition. The dream of acquisition at Weatherend would have had to be wild indeed, and John Marcher found himself, among such suggestions, disconcerted almost equally by the presence of those who knew too much and by that of those who knew nothing. The great rooms caused so much poetry and history to press upon him that he needed to wander apart to feel in a proper relation with them, though his doing so was not, as happened, like the gloating of some of his companions, to be compared to the movements of a dog sniffing a cupboard. It had an issue promptly enough in a direction that was not to have been calculated.

It led, in short, in the course of the October afternoon, to his closer meeting with May Bartram, whose face, a reminder, yet not quite a remembrance, as they sat, much separated, at a very long table, had begun merely by troubling him rather pleasantly. It affected him as the sequel of something of which he had lost the beginning. He knew it, and for the time quite welcomed it, as a continuation, but didn't know what it continued, which was an interest, or an amusement, the greater as he was also somehow aware—yet without a direct sign from her—that the young woman herself had not lost the thread. She had not lost it, but she wouldn't give it back to him, he saw, without some putting forth of his hand for it; and he not only saw that, but saw several things more, things odd enough in the light of the fact that at the moment some accident of grouping brought them face to face he was still merely fumbling with the idea that any contact between them in the past would have had no importance. If it had had no importance he scarcely knew why his actual impression of her should so seem to have so much; the answer to which, however, was that in such a life as they all appeared to be leading for the moment one could but take things as they came. He was satisfied, without in the least being able to say why, that this young lady might roughly have ranked in the house as a poor relation; satisfied also that she was not there on a brief visit, but was more or less a part of the establishment—almost a working, a remunerated part. Didn't she enjoy at periods a protection that she paid for by helping, among other services, to show the place and explain it, deal with the tiresome people, answer questions about the dates of the buildings, the styles of the furniture, the authorship of the pictures, the favourite haunts of the ghost? It wasn't that she looked as if you could have given her shillings—it was impossible to look less so. Yet when she finally drifted toward him, distinctly handsome, though ever so much older— older than when he had seen her before—it might have been as an effect of her guessing that he had, within the couple of hours, devoted more imagination to her than to all the others put together, and had thereby penetrated to a kind of truth that the others were too stupid for. She *was* there on harder terms than anyone; she was there as a consequence of things suffered, in one way and another, in the interval of years; and she remembered him very much as she was remembered—only a good deal better.

By the time they at last thus came to speech they were alone in one of the rooms—remarkable for a fine portrait over the chimney-place—out of which their friends had passed, and the charm of it was that even before they had spoken they had practically arranged with each other to stay behind for talk. The charm, happily, was in other things too; it was partly in there being scarce a spot at Weatherend without something to stay behind for. It was in the way the autumn day looked into the high windows as it waned; in the way the red light, breaking at the close from under a low, sombre sky, reached out in a long shaft and played over old wainscots, old tapestry, old gold, old colour. It was most of all perhaps in the way she came to him as if, since she had been turned on to deal with the simpler sort, he might, should he choose to keep the whole thing down, just take her mild attention for a part of her general business. As soon as he heard her voice, however, the gap was filled up and the missing link supplied; the slight irony he divined in her attitude lost its advantage. He almost jumped at it to get there before her. 'I met you years and years ago in Rome. I remember all about it.' She confessed to disappointment—she had been so sure he didn't; and to prove how well he did he began to pour forth the particular recollections that popped up as he called for them. Her face and her voice, all at his service now, worked the miracle—the impression operating like the torch of a lamplighter who touches into flame, one by one, a long row of gas jets. Marcher flattered himself that the illumination was brilliant, yet he was really still more pleased on her showing him, with amusement, that in his haste to make everything right he had got most things rather wrong. It hadn't been at Rome—it had been at Naples; and it hadn't been seven years before—it had been more nearly ten. She hadn't been either with her uncle and aunt, but with her mother and her brother; in addition to which it was not with the Pembles that *he* had been, but with the Boyers, coming down in their company from Rome—a point on which she insisted, a little to his confusion, and as to which she had her evidence in hand. The Boyers she had known, but she didn't know the Pembles, though she had heard of them, and it was the people he was with who had made them acquainted. The incident of the thunderstorm that had raged round them with such violence as to drive them for refuge into an excavation—this incident had not occurred at the Palace of the Cæsars, but at Pompeii, on an occasion when they had been present there at an important find.

He accepted her amendments, he enjoyed her corrections, though the moral of them was, she pointed out, that he *really* didn't remember the least thing about her; and he only felt it as a drawback that when all was made comformable to the truth there didn't appear much of anything left. They lingered together still, she neglecting her office—for from the moment he was so clever she had no proper right to him—and both neglecting the house, just waiting as to see if a memory or two more wouldn't again breathe upon them. It had not taken them many minutes, after all, to put down on the table, like the cards of a pack, those that constituted their respective hands; only what came out was that the pack was unfortunately not perfect—that the past, invoked, invited, encouraged, could give them, naturally, no more than it had. It had made them meet—her at twenty, him at twenty-five; but nothing was so strange, they seemed to say to each other, as that, while so occupied, it hadn't done a little more for them. They looked at each other as with the feeling of an occasion missed; the present one

would have been so much better if the other, in the far
distance, in the foreign land, hadn't been so stupidly
meagre. There weren't, apparently, all counted, more
than a dozen little old things that had succeeded in
coming to pass between them; trivialities of youth,
simplicities of freshness, stupidities of ignorance, small
possible germs, but too deeply buried—too deeply
(didn't it seem?) to sprout after so many years. Marcher
said to himself that he ought to have rendered her some
service—saved her from a capsized boat in the Bay, or at
least recovered her dressing-bag, filched from her cab,
in the streets of Naples, by a lazzarone with a stiletto.
Or it would have been nice if he could have been taken
with fever, alone at his hotel, and she could have come
to look after him, to write to his people, to drive him out
in convalescence. *Then* they would be in possession of
the something or other that their actual show seemed to
lack. It yet somehow presented itself, this show, as too
good to be spoiled; so that they were reduced for a few
minutes more to wondering a little helplessly why—
since they seemed to know a certain number of the same
people—their reunion had been so long averted. They
didn't use that name for it, but their delay from minute
to minute to join the others was a kind of confession that
they didn't quite want it to be a failure. Their attempted
supposition of reasons for their not having met but
showed how little they knew of each other. There came
in fact a moment when Marcher felt a positive pang.
It was vain to pretend she was an old friend, for all the
communities were wanting, in spite of which it was as an
old friend that he saw she would have suited him. He
had new ones enough—was surrounded with them, for
instance, at that hour at the other house; as a new one
he probably wouldn't have so much as noticed her. He

would have liked to invent something, get her to make-believe with him that some passage of a romantic or critical kind *had* originally occurred. He was really almost reaching out in imagination—as against time—for something that would do, and saying to himself that if it didn't come this new incident would simply and rather awkwardly close. They would separate, and now for no second or for no third chance. They would have tried and not succeeded. Then it was, just at the turn, as he afterwards made it out to himself, that, everything else failing, she herself decided to take up the case and, as it were, save the situation. He felt as soon as she spoke that she had been consciously keeping back what she said and hoping to get on without it; a scruple in her that immensely touched him when, by the end of three or four minutes more, he was able to measure it. What she brought out, at any rate, quite cleared the air and supplied the link—the link it was such a mystery he should frivolously have managed to lose.

'You know you told me something that I've never forgotten and that again and again has made me think of you since; it was that tremendously hot day when we went to Sorrento, across the bay, for the breeze. What I allude to was what you said to me, on the way back, as we sat, under the awning of the boat, enjoying the cool. Have you forgotten?'

He had forgotten, and he was even more surprised than ashamed. But the great thing was that he saw it was no vulgar reminder of any 'sweet' speech. The vanity of women had long memories, but she was making no claim on him of a compliment or a mistake. With another woman, a totally different one, he might have feared the recall possibly even some imbecile 'offer'. So, in having to say that he had indeed forgotten, he was conscious rather of a loss than of a gain; he already saw an interest in the matter of her reference. 'I try to think—but I give it up. Yet I remember the Sorrento day.'

'I'm not very sure you do,' May Bartram after a moment said; 'and I'm not very sure I ought to want you to. It's dreadful to bring a person back, at any time, to what he was ten years before. If you've lived away from it,' she smiled, 'so much the better.'

'Ah, if *you* haven't why should I?' he asked.

'Lived away, you mean, from what I myself was?'

'From what *I* was. I was of course an ass,' Marcher went on; 'but I would rather know from you just the sort of ass I was than—from the moment you have something in your mind—not know anything.'

Still, however, she hesitated. 'But if you've completely ceased to be that sort——?'

'Why, I can then just so all the more bear to know. Besides, perhaps I haven't.'

'Perhaps. Yet if you haven't,' she added, 'I should suppose you would remember. Not indeed that *I* in the least connect with my impression the invidious name you use. If I had only thought you foolish,' she explained, 'the thing I speak of wouldn't so have remained with me. It was about yourself.' She waited, as if it might come to him; but as, only meeting her eyes in wonder, he gave no sign, she burnt her ships. 'Has it ever happened?'

Then it was that, while he continued to stare, a light broke for him and the blood slowly came to his face, which began to burn with recognition. 'Do you mean I told you——?' But he faltered, lest what came to him shouldn't be right, lest he should only give himself away.

'It was something about yourself that it was natural

one shouldn't forget—that is if one remembered you at all. That's why I ask you,' she smiled, 'if the thing you then spoke of has ever come to pass?'

Oh, then he saw, but he was lost in wonder and found himself embarrassed. This, he also saw, made her sorry for him, as if her allusion had been a mistake. It took him but a moment, however, to feel that it had not been, much as it had been a surprise. After the first little shock of it her knowledge on the contrary began, even if rather strangely, to taste sweet to him. She was the only other person in the world, then who would have it, and she had had it all these years, while the fact of his having so breathed his secret had unaccountably faded from him. No wonder they couldn't have met as if nothing had happened. 'I judge,' he finally said, 'that I know what you mean. Only I had strangely enough lost the consciousness of having taken you so far into my confidence.'

'Is it because you've taken so many others as well?'

'I've taken nobody. Not a creature since then.'

'So that I'm the only person who knows?'

'The only person in the world.'

'Well,' she quickly replied, 'I myself have never spoken. I've never, never repeated of you what you told me.' She looked at him so that he perfectly believed her. Their eyes met over it in such a way that he was without a doubt. 'And I never will.'

She spoke with an earnestness that, as if almost excessive, put him at ease about her possible derision. Somehow the whole question was a new luxury to him—that is, from the moment she was in possession. If she didn't take the ironic view she clearly took the sympathetic, and that was what he had had, in all the long time, from no one whomsoever. What he felt was that he couldn't at

present have begun to tell her and yet could profit perhaps exquisitely by the accident of having done so of old.
'Please don't then. We're just right as it is.'

'Oh, I am,' she laughed, 'if you are!' To which she
added: 'Then you do still feel in the same way?'

It was impossible to him not to take to himself that she
was really interested, and it all kept coming as a sort of
revelation. He had thought of himself so long as abomi-
nably alone, and, lo, he wasn't alone a bit. He hadn't
been, it appeared, for an hour—since those moments on
the Sorrento boat. It was *she* who had been, he seemed to
see as he looked at her—she who had been made so by
the graceless fact of his lapse of fidelity. To tell her what
he had told her—what had it been but to ask something
of her? something that she had given, in her charity,
without his having, by a remembrance, by a return of
the spirit, failing another encounter, so much as thanked
her. What he had asked of her had been simply at first
not to laugh at him. She had beautifully not done so for
ten years, and she was not doing so now. So he had
endless gratitude to make up. Only for that he must see
just how he had figured to her. 'What, exactly, was the
account I gave——?'

'Of the way you did feel? Well, it was very simple.
You said you had had from your earliest time, as the
deepest thing within you, the sense of being kept for
something rare and strange, possibly prodigious and
terrible, that was sooner or later to happen to you, that
you had in your bones the foreboding and the conviction
of, and that would perhaps overwhelm you.'

'Do you call that very simple?' John Marcher asked.

She thought a moment. 'It was perhaps because I
seemed, as you spoke, to understand it.'

'You do understand it?' he eagerly asked.

Again she kept her kind eyes on him. 'You still have the belief?'

'Oh!' he exclaimed helplessly. There was too much to say.

'Whatever it is to be,' she clearly made out, 'it hasn't yet come.'

He shook his head in complete surrender now. 'It hasn't yet come. Only, you know, it isn't anything I'm to *do*, to achieve in the world, to be distinguished or admired for. I'm not such an ass as *that*. It would be much better, no doubt, if I were.'

'It's to be something you're merely to suffer?'

'Well, say to wait for—to have to meet, to face, to see suddenly break out in my life; possibly destroying all further consciousness, possibly annihilating me; possibly, on the other hand, only altering everything, striking at the root of all my world and leaving me to the consequences, however they shape themselves.'

She took this in, but the light in her eyes continued for him not to be that of mockery. 'Isn't what you describe perhaps but the expectation—or, at any rate, the sense of danger, familiar to so many people—of falling in love?'

John Marcher thought. 'Did you ask me that before?'

'No—I wasn't so free-and-easy then. But it's what strikes me now.'

'Of course,' he said after a moment, 'it strikes you. Of course it strikes *me*. Of course what's in store for me may be no more than that. The only thing is,' he went on, 'that I think that if it had been that, I should by this time know.'

'Do you mean because you've *been* in love?' And then as he but looked at her in silence: 'You've been in love, and it hasn't meant such a cataclysm, hasn't proved the great affair?'

'Here I am, you see. It hasn't been overwhelming.'

'Then it hasn't been love,' said May Bartram.

'Well, I at least thought it was. I took it for that—I've taken it till now. It was agreeable, it was delightful, it was miserable,' he explained. 'But it wasn't strange. It wasn't what *my* affair's to be.'

'You want something all to yourself—something that nobody else knows or *has* known?'

'It isn't a question of what I "want"—God knows I don't want anything. It's only a question of the apprehension that haunts me—that I live with day by day.'

He said this so lucidly and consistently that, visibly, it further imposed itself. If she had not been interested before she would have been interested now. 'Is it a sense of coming violence?'

Evidently now too, again, he liked to talk of it. 'I don't think of it as—when it does come—necessarily violent. I only think of it as natural and as of course, above all, unmistakable. I think of it simply as *the* thing. *The* thing will of itself appear natural.'

'Then how will it appear strange?'

Marcher bethought himself. 'It won't—to *me*.'

'To whom then?'

'Well,' he replied, smiling at last, 'say to you.'

'Oh then, I'm to be present?'

'Why, you *are* present—since you know.'

'I see.' She turned it over. 'But I mean at the catastrophe.'

At this, for a minute, their lightness gave way to their gravity; it was as if the long look they exchanged held them together. 'It will only depend on yourself—if you'll watch with me.'

'Are you afraid?' she asked.

'Don't leave me *now*,' he went on.

'Are you afraid?' she repeated.

'Do you think me simply out of my mind?' he pursued instead of answering. 'Do I merely strike you as a harmless lunatic?'

'No,' said May Bartram. 'I understand you. I believe you.'

'You mean you feel how my obsession—poor old thing!—may correspond to some possible reality?'

'To some possible reality.'

'Then you *will* watch with me?'

She hesitated, then for the third time put her question. 'Are you afraid?'

'Did I tell you I was—at Naples?'

'No, you said nothing about it.'

'Then I don't know. And I should *like* to know,' said John Marcher. 'You'll tell me yourself whether you think so. If you'll watch with me you'll see.'

'Very good then.' They had been moving by this time across the room, and at the door, before passing out, they paused as if for the full wind-up of their understanding. 'I'll watch with you,' said May Bartram.

II

The fact that she 'knew'—knew and yet neither chaffed him nor betrayed him—had in a short time begun to constitute between them a sensible bond, which became more marked when, within the year that followed their afternoon at Weatherend, the opportunities for meeting multiplied. The event that thus promoted these occasions was the death of the ancient lady, her great-aunt, under whose wing, since losing her mother, she had to such an extent found shelter, and who, though but the widowed

mother of the new successor to the property, had succeeded—thanks to a high tone and a high temper—in not
forfeiting the supreme position at the great house. The
deposition of this personage arrived but with her death,
which, followed by many changes, made in particular a
difference for the young woman in whom Marcher's
expert attention had recognized from the first a dependent with a pride that might ache though it didn't bristle.
Nothing for a long time had made him easier than the
thought that the aching must have been much soothed
by Miss Bartram's now finding herself able to set up a
small home in London. She had acquired property, to
an amount that made that luxury just possible, under her
aunt's extremely complicated will, and when the whole
matter began to be straightened out, which indeed took
time, she let him know that the happy issue was at last
in view. He had seen her again before that day, both
because she had more than once accompanied the ancient
lady to town and because he had paid another visit to
the friends who so conveniently made of Weatherend
one of the charms of their own hospitality. These friends
had taken him back there; he had achieved there again
with Miss Bartram some quiet detachment; and he had
in London succeeded in persuading her to more than
one brief absence from her aunt. They went together, on
these latter occasions, to the National Gallery and the
South Kensington Museum, where, among vivid re-
minders, they talked of Italy at large—not now attempting to recover, as at first, the taste of their youth and their
ignorance. That recovery, the first day at Weatherend,
had served its purpose well, had given them quite
enough; so that they were, to Marcher's sense, no longer
hovering about the head-waters of their stream, but had
felt their boat pushed sharply off and down the current.

They were literally afloat together; for our gentleman
this was marked, quite as marked as that the fortunate
cause of it was just the buried treasure of her knowledge.
He had with his own hands dug up this little hoard,
brought to light—that is to within reach of the dim day
constituted by their discretions and privacies—the object
of value the hiding-place of which he had, after putting
it into the ground himself, so strangely, so long forgotten. The exquisite luck of having again just stumbled
on the spot made him indifferent to any other question;
he would doubtless have devoted more time to the odd
accident of his lapse of memory if he had not been moved
to devote so much to the sweetness, the comfort, as he
felt, for the future, that this accident itself had helped to
keep fresh. It had never entered into his plan that anyone
should 'know', and mainly for the reason that it was not
in him to tell anyone. That would have been impossible,
since nothing but the amusement of a cold world would
have waited on it. Since, however, a mysterious fate had
opened his mouth in youth, in spite of him, he would
count that a compensation and profit by it to the utmost.
That the right person *should* know tempered the asperity
of his secret more even than his shyness had permitted
him to imagine; and May Bartram was clearly right,
because—well, because there she was. Her knowledge
simply settled it; he would have been sure enough by
this time had she been wrong. There was that in his
situation, no doubt, that disposed him too much to see
her as a mere confidant, taking all her light for him from
the fact—the fact only—of her interest in his predica-
ment, from her mercy, sympathy, seriousness, her con-
sent not to regard him as the funniest of the funny.
Aware, in fine, that her price for him was just in her
giving him this constant sense of his being admirably

spared, he was careful to remember that she had, after all, also a life of her own, with things that might happen to *her*, things that in friendship one should likewise take account of. Something fairly remarkable came to pass with him, for that matter, in this connexion—something represented by a certain passage of his consciousness, in the suddenest way, from one extreme to the other.

He had thought himself, so long as nobody knew, the most disinterested person in the world, carrying his concentrated burden, his perpetual suspense, ever so quietly, holding his tongue about it, giving others no glimpse of it nor of its effect upon his life, asking of them no allowance and only making on his side all those that were asked. He had disturbed nobody with the queerness of having to know a haunted man, though he had had moments of rather special temptation on hearing people say that they were 'unsettled'. If they were as unsettled as he was—he who had never been settled for an hour in his life—they would know what it meant. Yet it wasn't, all the same, for him to make them, and he listened to them civilly enough. This was why he had such good— though possibly such rather colourless—manners; this was why, above all, he could regard himself, in a greedy world, as decently—as, in fact, perhaps even a little sublimely—unselfish. Our point is accordingly that he valued this character quite sufficiently to measure his present danger of letting it lapse, against which he promised himself to be much on his guard. He was quite ready, none the less, to be selfish just a little, since, surely, no more charming occasion for it had come to him. 'Just a little,' in a word, was just as much as Miss Bartram, taking one day with another, would let him. He never would be in the least coercive, and he would keep well before him the lines on which consideration for her—the

very highest—ought to proceed. He would thoroughly
establish the heads under which her affairs, her require-
ments, her peculiarities—he went so far as to give them
the latitude of that name—would come into their intercourse. All this naturally was a sign of how much he took
the intercourse itself for granted. There was nothing
more to be done about *that*. It simply existed; had sprung
into being with her first penetrating question to him in
the autumn light there at Weatherend. The real form it
should have taken on the basis that stood out large was
the form of their marrying. But the devil in this was that
the very basis itself put marrying out of the question.
His conviction, his apprehension, his obsession, in short,
was not a condition he could invite a woman to share;
and that consequence of it was precisely what was the
matter with him. Something or other lay in wait for him,
amid the twists and the turns of the months and the years,
like a crouching beast in the jungle. It signified little
whether the crouching beast were destined to slay him or
to be slain. The definite point was the inevitable spring
of the creature; and the definite lesson from that was that
a man of feeling didn't cause himself to be accompanied
by a lady on a tiger-hunt. Such was the image under
which he had ended by figuring his life.

They had at first, none the less, in the scattered hours
spent together, made no allusion to that view of it;
which was a sign he was handsomely ready to give that
he didn't expect, that he in fact didn't care always to be
talking about it. Such a feature in one's outlook was really
like a hump on one's back. The difference it made every
minute of the day existed quite independently of discus-
sion. One discussed, of course, *like* a hunchback, for
there was always, if nothing else, the hunchback face.
That remained, and she was watching him; but people

watched best, as a general thing, in silence, so that such
would be predominantly the manner of their vigil. Yet
he didn't want, at the same time, to be solemn; solemn
was what he imagined he too much tended to be with
other people. The thing to be, with the one person who
knew, was easy and natural—to make the reference
rather than be seeming to avoid it, to avoid it rather
than be seeming to make it, and to keep it, in any case,
familiar, facetious even, rather than pedantic and por-
tentous. Some such consideration as the latter was doubtless in his mind, for instance, when he wrote pleasantly
to Miss Bartram that perhaps the great thing he had so
long felt as in the lap of the gods was no more than this
circumstance, which touched him so nearly, of her
acquiring a house in London. It was the first allusion
they had yet again made, needing any other hitherto so
little; but when she replied, after having given him the
news, that she was by no means satisfied with such a
trifle, as the climax to so special a suspense, she almost
set him wondering if she hadn't even a larger conception
of singularity for him than he had for himself. He was
at all events destined to become aware little by little, as
time went by, that she was all the while looking at his life,
judging it, measuring it, in the light of the thing she
knew, which grew to be at last, with the consecration of
the years, never mentioned between them save as 'the
real truth' about him. That had always been his own
form of reference to it, but she adopted the form so
quietly that, looking back at the end of a period, he knew
there was no moment at which it was traceable that she
had, as he might say, got inside his condition, or exchanged the attitude of beautifully indulging for that of
still more beautifully believing him.

It was always open to him to accuse her of seeing him

but as the most harmless of maniacs, and this, in the long run—since it covered so much ground—was his easiest description of their friendship. He had a screw loose for her, but she liked him in spite of it, and was practically, against the rest of the world, his kind, wise keeper, unremunerated, but fairly amused and, in the absence of other near ties, not disreputably occupied. The rest of the world of course thought him queer, but she, she only, knew how, and above all why, queer; which was precisely what enabled her to dispose the concealing veil in the right folds. She took his gaiety from him—since it had to pass with them for gaiety—as she took everything else; but she certainly so far justified by her unerring touch his finer sense of the degree to which he had ended by convincing her. *She* at least never spoke of the secret of his life except as 'the real truth about you,' and she had in fact a wonderful way of making it seem, as such, the secret of her own life too. That was in fine how he so constantly felt her as allowing for him; he couldn't on the whole call it anything else. He allowed for himself, but she, exactly, allowed still more; partly because, better placed for a sight of the matter, she traced his unhappy perversion through portions of its course into which he could scarce follow it. He knew how he felt, but, besides knowing that, she knew how he *looked* as well; he knew each of the things of importance he was insidiously kept from doing, but she could add up the amount they made, understand how much, with a lighter weight on his spirit, he might have done, and thereby establish how, clever as he was, he fell short. Above all she was in the secret of the difference between the forms he went through—those of his little office under Government, those of caring for his modest patrimony, for his library, for his garden in the country, for the people in

London whose invitations he accepted and repaid—and
the detachment that reigned beneath them and that made
of all behaviour, all that could in the least be called behaviour, a long act of dissimulation. What it had come to
was that he wore a mask painted with the social simper,
out of the eye-holes of which there looked eyes of an expression not in the least matching the other features. This
the stupid world, even after years, had never more than
half discovered. It was only May Bartram who had, and
she achieved, by an art indescribable, the feat of at once—
or perhaps it was only alternately—meeting the eyes from
in front and mingling her own vision, as from over his
shoulder, with their peep through the apertures.

So, while they grew older together, she did watch with
him, and so she let this association give shape and colour
to her own existence. Beneath *her* forms as well detachment had learned to sit, and behaviour had become for
her, in the social sense, a false account of herself. There
was but one account of her that would have been true
all the while, and that she could give, directly, to nobody,
least of all to John Marcher. Her whole attitude was a
virtual statement, but the perception of that only seemed
destined to take its place for him as one of the many
things necessarily crowded out of his consciousness. If
she had, moreover, like himself, to make sacrifices to
their real truth, it was to be granted that her compensation might have affected her as more prompt and more
natural. They had long periods, in this London time,
during which, when they were together, a stranger might
have listened to them without in the least pricking up his
ears; on the other hand, the real truth was equally liable
at any moment to rise to the surface, and the auditor
would then have wondered indeed what they were talking
about. They had from an early time made up their mind

that society was, luckily, unintelligent, and the margin that this gave them had fairly become one of their commonplaces. Yet there were still moments when the situation turned almost fresh—usually under the effect of some expression drawn from herself. Her expressions doubtless repeated themselves, but her intervals were generous. 'What saves us, you know, is that we answer so completely to so usual an appearance: that of the man and woman whose friendship has become such a daily habit, or almost, as to be at last indispensable.' That, for instance, was a remark she had frequently enough had occasion to make, though she had given it at different times different developments. What we are especially concerned with is the turn it happened to take from her one afternoon when he had come to see her in honour of her birthday. This anniversary had fallen on a Sunday, at a season of thick fog and general outward gloom; but he had brought her his customary offering, having known her now long enough to have established a hundred little customs. It was one of his proofs to himself, the present he made her on her birthday, that he had not sunk into real selfishness. It was mostly nothing more than a small trinket, but it was always fine of its kind, and he was regularly careful to pay for it more than he thought he could afford. 'Our habit saves you, at least, don't you see? because it makes you, after all, for the vulgar, indistinguishable from other men. What's the most inveterate mark of men in general? Why, the capacity to spend endless time with dull women—to spend it, I won't say without being bored, but without minding that they are, without being driven off at a tangent by it; which comes to the same thing. I'm your dull woman, a part of the daily bread for which you pray at church. That covers your tracks more than anything.'

'And what covers yours?' asked Marcher, whom his
dull woman could mostly to this extent amuse. 'I see of
course what you mean by your saving me, in one way
and another, so far as other people are concerned—I've
seen it all along. Only, what is it that saves *you*? I often
think, you know, of that.'

She looked as if she sometimes thought of that too,
but in rather a different way. 'Where other people, you
mean, are concerned?'

'Well, you're really so in with me, you know—as a sort
of result of my being so in with yourself. I mean of my
having such an immense regard for you, being so
tremendously grateful for all you've done for me. I sometimes ask myself if it's quite fair. Fair I mean to have so
involved and—since one may say it—interested you.
I almost feel as if you hadn't really had time to do anything else.'

'Anything else but be interested?' she asked. 'Ah,
what else does one ever want to be? If I've been "watching" with you, as we long ago agreed that I was to do,
watching is always in itself an absorption.'

'Oh, certainly,' John Marcher said, 'if you hadn't had
your curiosity——! Only, doesn't it sometimes come to
you, as time goes on, that your curiosity is not being particularly repaid?'

May Bartram had a pause. 'Do you ask that, by any
chance, because you feel at all that yours isn't? I mean
because you have to wait so long.'

Oh, he understood what she meant. 'For the thing to
happen that never does happen? For the beast to jump
out? No, I'm just where I was about it. It isn't a matter
as to which I can *choose*, I can decide for a change. It
isn't one as to which there *can* be a change. It's in the lap
of the gods. One's in the hands of one's law—there

one is. As to the form the law will take, the way it will operate, that's its own affair.'

'Yes,' Miss Bartram replied: 'of course one's fate is coming, of course it *has* come, in its own form and its own way, all the while. Only, you know, the form and the way in your case were to have been—well, something so exceptional and, as one may say, so particularly *your* own.'

Something in this made him look at her with suspicion. 'You say "were to *have* been", as if in your heart you had begun to doubt.'

'Oh!' she vaguely protested.

'As if you believed,' he went on, 'that nothing will now take place.'

She shook her head slowly, but rather inscrutably. 'You're far from my thought.'

He continued to look at her. 'What then is the matter with you?'

'Well,' she said after another wait, 'the matter with me is simply that I'm more sure than ever my curiosity, as you call it, will be but too well repaid.'

They were frankly grave now; he had got up from his seat, had turned once more about the little drawing-room to which, year after year, he brought his inevitable topic; in which he had, as he might have said, tasted their intimate community with every sauce, where every object was as familiar to him as the things of his own house and the very carpets were worn with his fitful walk very much as the desks in old counting-houses are worn by the elbows of generations of clerks. The generations of his nervous moods had been at work there, and the place was the written history of his whole middle life. Under the impression of what his friend had just said he knew himself, for some reason, more aware of these things, which made him, after a moment, stop again before her. 'Is it, possibly, that you've grown afraid?'

'Afraid?' He thought, as she repeated the word, that his question had made her, a little, change colour; so that, lest he should have touched on a truth, he explained very kindly, 'You remember that that was what you asked *me* long ago—that first day at Weatherend.'

'Oh yes, and you told me you didn't know—that I was to see for myself. We've said little about it since, even in so long a time.'

'Precisely,' Marcher interposed—'quite as if it were too delicate a matter for us to make free with. Quite as if we might find, on pressure, that I *am* afraid. For then,' he said, 'we shouldn't, should we? quite know what to do.'

She had for the time no answer to this question. 'There have been days when I thought you were. Only, of course,' she added, 'there have been days when we have thought almost anything.'

'Everything. Oh!' Marcher softly groaned as with a gasp, half spent, at the face, more uncovered just then than it had been for a long while, of the imagination always with them. It had always had its incalculable moments of glaring out, quite as with the very eyes of the very Beast, and, used as he was to them, they could still draw from him the tribute of a sigh that rose from the depths of his being. All that they had thought, first and last, rolled over him; the past seemed to have been reduced to mere barren speculation. This in fact was what the place had just struck him as so full of—the simplification of everything but the state of suspense. That remained only by seeming to hang in the void surrounding it. Even his original fear, if fear it had been, had lost itself in the desert. 'I judge, however,' he continued, 'that you see I'm not afraid now.'

'What I see is, as I make it out, that you've achieved something almost unprecedented in the way of getting used to danger. Living with it so long and so closely, you've lost your sense of it; you know it's there, but you're indifferent, and you cease even, as of old, to have to whistle in the dark. Considering what the danger is,' May Bartram wound up, 'I'm bound to say that I don't think your attitude could well be surpassed.'

John Marcher faintly smiled. 'It's heroic?'

'Certainly—call it that.'

He considered. 'I *am*, then, a man of courage?'

'That's what you were to show me.'

He still, however, wondered. 'But doesn't the man of courage know what he's afraid of—or *not* afraid of? I don't know *that*, you see. I don't focus it. I can't name it. I only know I'm exposed.'

'Yes, but exposed—how shall I say?—so directly. So intimately. That's surely enough.'

'Enough to make you feel, then—as what we may call the end of our watch—that I'm not afraid?'

'You're not afraid. But it isn't,' she said, 'the end of our watch. That is it isn't the end of yours. You've everything still to see.'

'Then why haven't *you*?' he asked. He had had, all along, today, the sense of her keeping something back, and he still had it. As this was his first impression of that, it made a kind of date. The case was the more marked as she didn't at first answer; which in turn made him go on. 'You know something I don't.' Then his voice, for that of a man of courage, trembled a little. 'You know what's to happen.' Her silence, with the face she showed, was almost a confession—it made him sure. 'You know, and you're afraid to tell me. It's so bad that you're afraid I'll find out.'

All this might be true, for she did look as if, un-expectedly to her, he had crossed some mystic line that she had secretly drawn round her. Yet she might, after all, not have worried; and the real upshot was that he himself at all events, needn't. 'You'll never find out.'

III

It was all to have made, none the less, as I have said, a date; as came out in the fact that again and again, even after long intervals, other things that passed between them wore, in relation to this hour, but the character of recalls and results. Its immediate effect had been indeed rather to lighten insistence—almost to provoke a reaction; as if their topic had dropped by its own weight and as if moreover, for that matter, Marcher had been visited by one of his occasional warnings against egotism. He had kept up, he felt, and very decently on the whole his consciousness of the importance of not being selfish, and it was true that he had never sinned in that direction without promptly enough trying to press the scales the other way. He often repaired his fault, the season per-mitting, by inviting his friend to accompany him to the opera; and it not infrequently thus happened that, to show he didn't wish her to have but one sort of food for her mind, he was the cause of her appearing there with him a dozen nights in the month. It even happened that, seeing her home at such times, he occasionally went in with her to finish, as he called it, the evening, and, the better to make his point, sat down to the frugal but always careful little supper that awaited his pleasure. His point was made, he thought, by his not eternally insisting with her on himself; made for instance, at such hours, when it befell that, her piano at hand and each of them familiar with it, they went over passages of the opera together. It chanced to be on one of these occasions, however, that he reminded her of her not having answered a certain question he had put to her during the talk that had taken place between them on her last birthday. 'What is it that saves *you*?'—saved her, he meant, from that appearance of variation from the usual human type. If he had practically escaped remark, as she pretended, by doing, in the most important particular, what most men do—find the answer to life in patching up an alliance of a sort with a woman no better than himself—how had she escaped it, and how could the alliance, such as it was, since they must suppose it had been more or less noticed, have failed to make her rather positively talked about?

'I never said,' May Bartram replied, 'that it hadn't made me talked about.'

'Ah well then, you're not "saved".'

'It has not been a question for me. If you've had your woman, I've had,' she said, 'my man.'

'And you mean that makes you all right?'

She hesitated. 'I don't know why it shouldn't make me—humanly, which is what we're speaking of—as right as it makes you.'

'I see,' Marcher returned. ' "Humanly", no doubt, as showing that you're living for something. Not, that is, just for me and my secret.'

May Bartram smiled. 'I don't pretend it exactly shows that I'm not living for you. It's my intimacy with you that's in question.'

He laughed as he saw what she meant. 'Yes, but since, as you say, I'm only, so far as people make out, ordinary, you're—aren't you?—no more than ordinary either. You help me to pass for a man like another. So if I

G

am, as I understand you, you're not compromised. Is
that it?'

She had another hesitation, but she spoke clearly
enough. 'That's it. It's all that concerns me—to help you
to pass for a man like another.'

He was careful to acknowledge the remark handsomely. 'How kind, how beautiful, you are to me! How
shall I ever repay you?'

She had her last grave pause, as if there might be a
choice of ways. But she chose. 'By going on as you are.'

It was into this going on as he was that they relapsed,
and really for so long a time that the day inevitably came
for a further sounding of their depths. It was as if these
depths, constantly bridged over by a structure that was
firm enough in spite of its lightness and of its occasional
oscillation in the somewhat vertiginous air, invited on
occasion, in the interest of their nerves, a dropping of
the plummet and a measurement of the abyss. A difference had been made moreover, once for all, by the fact
that she had, all the while, not appeared to feel the need
of rebutting his charge of an idea within her that she
didn't dare to express, uttered just before one of the
fullest of their later discussions ended. It had come up
for him then that she 'knew' something and that what
she knew was bad—too bad to tell him. When he had
spoken of it as visibly so bad that she was afraid he might
find it out, her reply had left the matter too equivocal
to be let alone and yet, for Marcher's special sensibility,
almost too formidable again to touch. He circled about it
at a distance that alternately narrowed and widened and
that yet was not much affected by the consciousness in
him that there was nothing she could 'know', after all,
any better than he did. She had no source of knowledge
that he hadn't equally—except of course that she might

have finer nerves. That was what women had where they were interested; they made out things, where people were concerned, that the people often couldn't have made out for themselves. Their nerves, their sensibility, their imagination, were conductors and revealers, and the beauty of May Bartram was in particular that she had given herself so to his case. He felt in these days what, oddly enough, he had never felt before, the growth of a dread of losing her by some catastrophe—some catastrophe that yet wouldn't at all be *the* catastrophe: partly because she had, almost of a sudden, begun to strike him as useful to him as never yet, and partly by reason of an appearance of uncertainty in her health, coincident and equally new. It was characteristic of the inner detachment he had hitherto so successfully cultivated and to which our whole account of him is a reference, it was characteristic that his complications, such as they were, had never yet seemed so as at this crisis to thicken about him, even to the point of making him ask himself if he were, by any chance, of a truth, within sight or sound, within touch or reach, within the immediate jurisdiction of the thing that waited.

When the day came, as come it had to, that his friend confessed to him her fear of a deep disorder in her blood, he felt somehow the shadow of a change and the chill of a shock. He immediately began to imagine aggravations and disasters, and above all to think of her peril as the direct menace for himself of personal privation. This indeed gave him one of those partial recoveries of equanimity that were agreeable to him—it showed him that what was still first in his mind was the loss she herself might suffer. 'What if she should have to die before knowing, before seeing——?' It would have been brutal, in the early stages of her trouble, to put that question to her; but it had immediately sounded for him to his own concern, and the possibility was what most made him sorry for her. If she did 'know', moreover, in the sense of her having had some—what should he think?—mystical, irresistible light, this would make the matter not better, but worse, inasmuch as her original adoption of his own curiosity had quite become the basis of her life. She had been living to see what would *be* to be seen, and it would be cruel to her to have to give up before the accomplishment of the vision. These reflections, as I say, refreshed his generosity; yet, make them as he might, he saw himself, with the lapse of the period, more and more disconcerted. It lapsed for him with a strange, steady sweep, and the oddest oddity was that it gave him, independently of the threat of much inconvenience, almost the only positive surprise his career, if career it could be called, had yet offered him. She kept the house as she had never done; he had to go to her to see her—she could meet him nowhere now, though there was scarce a corner of their loved old London in which she had not in the past, at one time or another, done so; and he found her always seated by her fire in the deep, old-fashioned chair she was less and less able to leave. He had been struck one day, after an absence exceeding his usual measure, with her suddenly looking much older to him than he had ever thought of her being; then he recognized that the suddenness was all on his side—he had just been suddenly struck. She looked older because inevitably, after so many years, she *was* old, or almost; which was of course true in still greater measure of her companion. If she was old, or almost, John Marcher assuredly was, and yet it was her showing of the lesson, not his own, that brought the truth home to him. His surprises began here; when once they had begun they multiplied; they came rather with a rush: it was as if, in the oddest way in the world, they had all been kept back, sown in a thick cluster, for the late afternoon of life, the time at which, for people in general, the unexpected has died out.

One of them was that he should have caught himself— for he *had* so done—*really* wondering if the great accident would take form now as nothing more than his being condemned to see this charming woman, this admirable friend, pass away from him. He had never so unreservedly qualified her as while confronted in thought with such a possibility; in spite of which there was small doubt for him that as an answer to his long riddle the mere effacement of even so fine a feature of his situation would be an abject anticlimax. It would represent, as connected with his past attitude, a drop of dignity under the shadow of which his existence could only become the most grotesque of failures. He had been far from holding it a failure—long as he had waited for the appearance that was to make it a success. He had waited for a quite other thing, not for such a one as that. The breath of his good faith came short, however, as he recognized how long he had waited, or how long, at least, his companion had. That she, at all events, might be recorded as having waited in vain—this affected him sharply, and all the more because of his at first having done little more than amuse himself with the idea. It grew more grave as the gravity of her condition grew, and the state of mind it produced in him, which he ended by watching, himself, as if it had been some definite disfigurement of his outer person, may pass for another of his surprises. This conjoined itself still with another, the really stupefying consciousness of a question that he would have allowed to shape itself had he dared. What did everything mean— what, that is, did *she* mean, she and her vain waiting and her probable death and the soundless admonition of it all—unless that, at this time of day, it was simply, it was overwhelmingly too late? He had never, at any stage of his queer consciousness, admitted the whisper of such a correction; he had never, till within these last few months, been so false to his conviction as not to hold that what was to come to him had time, whether *he* struck himself as having it or not. That at last, at last, he certainly hadn't it, to speak of, or had it but in the scantiest measure—such, soon enough, as things went with him, became the inference with which his old obsession had to reckon: and this it was not helped to do by the more and more confirmed appearance that the great vagueness casting the long shadow in which he had lived had, to attest itself, almost no margin left. Since it was in Time that he was to have met his fate, so it was in Time that his fate was to have acted; and as he waked up to the sense of no longer being young, which was exactly the sense of being stale, just as that, in turn, was the sense of being weak, he waked up to another matter beside. It all hung together; they were subject, he and the great vagueness, to an equal and indivisible law. When the possibilities themselves had, accordingly, turned stale, when the secret of the gods had grown faint, had perhaps even quite evaporated, that, and that only, was failure. It wouldn't have been failure to be bankrupt, dishonoured, pilloried, hanged; it was failure not to be anything. And so, in the dark valley into which his path had taken its unlooked-for twist, he wondered not a little as he groped. He didn't care what awful crash might overtake him, with what ignominy or what monstrosity he might yet be associated—since he wasn't, after all, too utterly old to suffer—if it would only be decently proportionate to the posture he had kept, all his life, in the

promised presence of it. He had but one desire left—that
he shouldn't have been 'sold'.

IV

Then it was that one afternoon, while the spring of the
year was young and new, she met, all in her own way,
his frankest betrayal of these alarms. He had gone in late
to see her, but evening had not settled, and she was
presented to him in that long, fresh light of waning April
days which affects us often with a sadness sharper than
the greyest hours of autumn. The week had been warm,
the spring was supposed to have begun early, and May
Bartram sat, for the first time in the year, without a fire,
a fact that, to Marcher's sense, gave the scene of which
she formed part a smooth and ultimate look, an air of
knowing, in its immaculate order and its cold, meaning-
less cheer, that it would never see a fire again. Her own
aspect—he could scarce have said why—intensified this
note. Almost as white as wax, with the marks and signs
in her face as numerous and as fine as if they had been
etched by a needle, with soft white draperies relieved by
a faded green scarf, the delicate tone of which had been
consecrated by the years, she was the picture of a serene,
exquisite, but impenetrable sphinx, whose head, or
indeed all whose person, might have been powdered with
silver. She was a sphinx, yet with her white petals and
green fronds she might have been a lily too—only an
artificial lily, wonderfully imitated and constantly kept,
without dust or stain, though not exempt from a slight
droop and a complexity of faint creases, under some clear
glass bell. The perfection of household care, of high
polish and finish, always reigned in her rooms, but they
especially looked to Marcher at present as if everything

had been wound up, tucked in, put away, so that she might sit with folded hands and with nothing more to do. She was 'out of it', to his vision; her work was over; she communicated with him as across some gulf, or from some island of rest that she had already reached, and it made him feel strangely abandoned. Was it—or, rather, wasn't it—that if for so long she had been watching with him the answer to their question had swum into her ken and taken on its name, so that her occupation was verily gone? He had as much as charged her with this in saying to her, many months before, that she even then knew something she was keeping from him. It was a point he had never since ventured to press, vaguely fearing, as he did, that it might become a difference, perhaps a disagreement, between them. He had in short, in this later time, turned nervous, which was what, in all the other years, he had never been; and the oddity was that his nervousness should have waited till he had begun to doubt, should have held off so long as he was sure. There was something, it seemed to him, that the wrong word would bring down on his head, something that would so at least put an end to his suspense. But he wanted not to speak the wrong word; that would make everything ugly. He wanted the knowledge he lacked to drop on him, if drop it could, by its own august weight. If she was to forsake him it was surely for her to take leave. This was why he didn't ask her again, directly, what she knew; but it was also why, approaching the matter from another side, he said to her in the course of his visit: 'What do you regard as the very worst that, at this time of day, *can* happen to me?'

He had asked her that in the past often enough; they had, with the odd, irregular rhythm of their intensities and avoidances, exchanged ideas about it and then had seen the ideas washed away by cool intervals, washed like figures traced in sea-sand. It had ever been the mark of their talk that the oldest allusions in it required but a little dismissal and reaction to come out again, sounding for the hour as new. She could thus at present meet his inquiry quite freshly and patiently. 'Oh yes, I've repeatedly thought, only it always seemed to me of old that I couldn't quite make up my mind. I thought of dreadful things, between which it was difficult to choose; and so must you have done.'

'Rather! I feel now as if I had scarce done anything else. I appear to myself to have spent my life in thinking of nothing *but* dreadful things. A great many of them I've at different times named to you, but there were others I couldn't name.'

'They were too, too dreadful?'

'Too, too dreadful—some of them.'

She looked at him a minute, and there came to him as he met it an inconsequent sense that her eyes, when one got their full clearness, were still as beautiful as they had been in youth, only beautiful with a strange, cold light—a light that somehow was a part of the effect, if it wasn't rather a part of the cause, of the pale, hard sweetness of the season and the hour. 'And yet,' she said at last, 'there are horrors we have mentioned.'

It deepened the strangeness to see her, as such a figure in such a picture, talk of 'horrors', but she was to do, in a few minutes, something stranger yet—though even of this he was to take the full measure but afterwards—and the note of it was already in the air. It was, for the matter of that, one of the signs that her eyes were having again such a high flicker of their prime. He had to admit, however, what she said. 'Oh yes, there were times when we did go far.' He caught himself in the act of speaking as if it all were over. Well, he wished it were; and the consummation depended, for him, clearly, more and more on his companion.

But she had now a soft smile. 'Oh, far——!'

It was oddly ironic. 'Do you mean you're prepared to go further?'

She was frail and ancient and charming as she continued to look at him, yet it was rather as if she had lost the thread. 'Do you consider that we went so far?'

'Why, I thought it the point you were just making—that we *had* looked most things in the face.'

'Including each other?' She still smiled. 'But you're quite right. We've had together great imaginations, often great fears; but some of them have been unspoken.'

'Then the worst—we haven't faced that. I *could* face it, I believe, if I knew what you think it. I feel,' he explained, 'as if I had lost my power to conceive such things.' And he wondered if he looked as blank as he sounded. 'It's spent.'

'Then why do you assume,' she asked, 'that mine isn't?'

'Because you've given me signs to the contrary. It isn't a question for you of conceiving, imagining, comparing. It isn't a question now of choosing.' At last he came out with it. 'You know something that I don't. You've shown me that before.'

These last words affected her, he could see in a moment, remarkably, and she spoke with firmness. 'I've shown you, my dear, nothing.'

He shook his head. 'You can't hide it.'

'Oh, oh!' May Bartram murmured over what she couldn't hide. It was almost a smothered groan.

'You admitted it months ago, when I spoke of it to you as of something you were afraid I would find out. Your answer was that I couldn't, that I wouldn't, and I don't pretend I have. But you had something therefore in mind, and I see now that it must have been, that it still is, the possibility that, of all possibilities, has settled itself for you as the worst. This,' he went on, 'is why I appeal to you. I'm only afraid of ignorance now—I'm not afraid of knowledge.' And then as for a while she said nothing: 'What makes me sure is that I see in your face and feel here, in this air and amid these appearances, that you're out of it. You've done. You've had your experience. You leave me to my fate.'

Well, she listened, motionless and white in her chair, as if she had in fact a decision to make, so that her whole manner was a virtual confession, though still with a small, fine, inner stiffness, an imperfect surrender. 'It *would* be the worst,' she finally let herself say. 'I mean the thing that I've never said.'

It hushed him a moment. 'More monstrous than all the monstrosities we've named?'

'More monstrous. Isn't that what you sufficiently express,' she asked, 'in calling it the worst?'

Marcher thought. 'Assuredly—if you mean, as I do, something that includes all the loss and all the shame that are thinkable.'

'It would if it *should* happen,' said May Bartram. 'What we're speaking of, remember, is only my idea.'

'It's your belief,' Marcher returned. 'That's enough for me. I feel your beliefs are right. Therefore if, having this one, you give me no more light on it, you abandon me.'

'No, no!' she repeated. 'I'm with you—don't you see?—still.' And as if to make it more vivid to him she rose from her chair—a movement she seldom made in these days—and showed herself, all draped and all soft, in her fairness and slimness. 'I haven't forsaken you.'

It was really, in its effort against weakness, a generous assurance, and had the success of the impulse not, happily, been great, it would have touched him to pain more than to pleasure. But the cold charm in her eyes had spread, as she hovered before him, to all the rest of her person, so that it was, for the minute, almost like a recovery of youth. He couldn't pity her for that; he could only take her as she showed—as capable still of helping him. It was as if, at the same time, her light might at any instant go out; wherefore he must make the most of it. There passed before him with intensity the three or four things he wanted most to know; but the question that came of itself to his lips really covered the others. 'Then tell me if I shall consciously suffer.'

She promptly shook her head. 'Never!'

It confirmed the authority he imputed to her, and it produced on him an extraordinary effect. 'Well, what's better than that? Do you call that the worst?'

'You think nothing is better?' she asked.

She seemed to mean something so special that he again sharply wondered, though still with the dawn of a prospect of relief. 'Why not, if one doesn't *know*?' After which, as their eyes, over his question, met in a silence, the dawn deepened and something to his purpose came, prodigiously, out of her very face. His own, as he took it in, suddenly flushed to the forehead, and he gasped with the force of a perception to which, on the instant, everything fitted. The sound of his gasp filled the air; then he became articulate. 'I see—if I don't suffer!'

In her own look, however, was doubt. 'You see what?'

'Why, what you mean—what you've always meant.'

She again shook her head. 'What I mean isn't what I've always meant. It's different.'

'It's something new?'

She hesitated. 'Something new. It's not what you think. I see what you think.'

His divination drew breath then; only her correction might be wrong. 'It isn't that I *am* a donkey?' he asked between faintness and grimness. 'It isn't that it's all a mistake?'

'A mistake?' she pityingly echoed. *That* possibility, for her, he saw, would be monstrous; and if she guaranteed him the immunity from pain it would accordingly not be what she had in mind. 'Oh, no,' she declared; 'it's nothing of that sort. You've been right.'

Yet he couldn't help asking himself if she weren't, thus pressed, speaking but to save him. It seemed to him he should be most lost if his history should prove all a platitude. 'Are you telling me the truth, so that I sha'n't have been a bigger idiot than I can bear to know? I *haven't* lived with a vain imagination, in the most besotted illusion? I haven't waited but to see the door shut in my face?'

She shook her head again. 'However the case stands *that* isn't the truth. Whatever the reality, it *is* a reality. The door isn't shut. The door's open,' said May Bartram.

'Then something's to come?'

She waited once again, always with her cold, sweet eyes on him. 'It's never too late.' She had, with her gliding step, diminished the distance between them, and she stood nearer to him, close to him, a minute, as if still full of the unspoken. Her movement might have been for some finer emphasis of what she was at once hesitating and deciding to say. He had been standing by the chimney-piece, fireless and sparely adorned, a small, perfect old French clock and two morsels of rosy Dresden constituting all its furniture; and her hand grasped the shelf while she kept him waiting, grasped it a little as for support and encouragement. She only kept him waiting, however; that is he only waited. It had become suddenly, from her movement and attitude, beautiful and vivid to him that she had something more to give him; her wasted face delicately shone with it, and it glittered, almost as with the white lustre of silver, in her expression. She was right, incontestably, for what he saw in her face was the truth, and strangely, without consequence, while their talk of it as dreadful was still in the air, she appeared to present it as inordinately soft. This, prompting bewilderment, made him but gape the more gratefully for her revelation, so that they continued for some minutes silent, her face shining at him, her contact imponderably pressing, and his stare all kind, but all expectant. The end, none the less, was that what he had expected failed to sound. Something else took place instead, which seemed to consist at first in the mere closing of her eyes. She gave way at the same instant to a slow, fine shudder, and though he remained staring—though he stared, in fact, but the harder—she turned off and regained her chair. It was the end of what she had been intending, but it left him thinking only of that.

'Well, you don't say——?'

She had touched in her passage a bell near the chimney and had sunk back, strangely pale. 'I'm afraid I'm too ill.'

'Too ill to tell me?' It sprang up sharp to him, and almost to his lips, the fear that she would die without giving him light. He checked himself in time from so expressing his question, but she answered as if she had heard the words.

'Don't you know—now?'

' "Now"——?' She had spoken as if something that

had made a difference had come up within the moment.
But her maid, quickly obedient to her bell, was already
with them. 'I know nothing.' And he was afterwards to
say to himself that he must have spoken with odious
impatience, such an impatience as to show that, supremely
disconcerted, he washed his hands of the whole question.

'Oh!' said May Bartram.

'Are you in pain?' he asked, as the woman went to her.

'No,' said May Bartram.

Her maid, who had put an arm round her as if to take
her to her room, fixed on him eyes that appealingly con-
tradicted her; in spite of which, however, he showed
once more his mystification. 'What then has happened?'

She was once more, with her companion's help, on
her feet, and, feeling withdrawal imposed on him, he had
found, blankly, his hat and gloves and had reached the
door. Yet he waited for her answer. 'What *was* to,' she
said.

V

He came back the next day, but she was then unable to
see him, and as it was literally the first time this had
occurred in the long stretch of their acquaintance he
turned away, defeated and sore, almost angry—or feeling
at least that such a break in their custom was really the
beginning of the end—and wandered alone with his
thoughts, especially with one of them that he was unable
to keep down. She was dying, and he would lose her;
she was dying, and his life would end. He stopped in
the park, into which he had passed, and stared before
him at his recurrent doubt. Away from her the doubt
pressed again; in her presence he had believed her, but
as he felt his forlornness he threw himself into the

explanation that, nearest at hand, had most of a miserable warmth for him and least of a cold torment. She had deceived him to save him—to put him off with something in which he should be able to rest. What could the thing that was to happen to him be, after all, but just this thing that had begun to happen? Her dying, her death, his consequent solitude—*that* was what he had figured as the beast in the jungle, that was what had been in the lap of the gods. He had had her word for it as he left her; for what else, on earth, could she have meant? It wasn't a thing of a monstrous order; not a fate rare and distinguished; not a stroke of fortune that overwhelmed and immortalized; it had only the stamp of the common doom. But poor Marcher, at this hour, judged the common doom sufficient. It would serve his turn, and even as the consummation of infinite waiting he would bend his pride to accept it. He sat down on a bench in the twilight. He hadn't been a fool. Something had *been*, as she had said, to come. Before he rose indeed it had quite struck him that the final fact really matched with the long avenue through which he had had to reach it. As sharing his suspense, and as giving herself all, giving her life, to bring it to an end, she had come with him every step of the way. He had lived by her aid, and to leave her behind would be cruelly, damnably to miss her. What could be more overwhelming than that?

Well, he was to know within the week, for though she kept him a while at bay, left him restless and wretched during a series of days on each of which he asked about her only again to have to turn away, she ended his trial by receiving him where she had always received him. Yet she had been brought out at some hazard into the presence of so many of the things that were, consciously, vainly, half their past, and there was scant service left in the gentleness of her mere desire, all too visible, to check his obsession and wind up his long trouble. That was clearly what she wanted; the one thing more, for her own peace, while she could still put out her hand. He was so affected by her state that, once seated by her chair, he was moved to let everything go; it was she herself therefore who brought him back, took up again, before she dismissed him, her last word of the other time. She showed how she wished to leave their affair in order. 'I'm not sure you understood. You've nothing to wait for more. It *has* come.'

Oh, how he looked at her! 'Really?'

'Really.'

'The thing that, as you said, *was* to?'

'The thing that we began in our youth to watch for.'

Face to face with her once more he believed her; it was a claim to which he had so abjectly little to oppose. 'You mean that it has come as a positive, definite occurrence, with a name and a date?'

'Positive. Definite. I don't know about the "name", but, oh, with a date!'

He found himself again too helplessly at sea. 'But come in the night—come and passed me by?'

May Bartram had her strange, faint smile. 'Oh no, it hasn't passed you by!'

'But if I haven't been aware of it, and it hasn't touched me——?'

'Ah, your not being aware of it,' and she seemed to hesitate an instant to deal with this—'your not being aware of it is the strangeness *in* the strangeness. It's the wonder *of* the wonder.' She spoke as with the softness almost of a sick child, yet now at last, at the end of all, with the perfect straightness of a sibyl. She visibly knew that she knew, and the effect on him was of something

co-ordinate, in its high character, with the law that had
ruled him. It was the true voice of the law; so on her lips
would the law itself have sounded. 'It *has* touched you,'
she went on. 'It has done its office. It has made you all
its own.'

'So utterly without my knowing it?'

'So utterly without your knowing it.' His hand, as he
leaned to her, was on the arm of her chair, and, dimly
smiling always now, she placed her own on it. 'It's
enough if *I* know it.'

'Oh!' he confusedly sounded, as she herself of late so
often had done.

'What I long ago said is true. You'll never know now,
and I think you ought to be content. You've *had* it,' said
May Bartram.

'But had what?'

'Why, what was to have marked you out. The proof of
your law. It has acted. I'm too glad,' she then bravely
added, 'to have been able to see what it's *not*.'

He continued to attach his eyes to her, and with the
sense that it was all beyond him, and that *she* was too,
he would still have sharply challenged her, had he not
felt it an abuse of her weakness to do more than take
devoutly what she gave him, take it as hushed as to a
revelation. If he did speak, it was out of the foreknowledge
of his loneliness to come. 'If you're glad of what it's
"not", it might then have been worse?'

She turned her eyes away, she looked straight before
her with which, after a moment: 'Well, you know our
fears.'

He wondered. 'It's something then we never feared?'

On this, slowly, she turned to him. 'Did we ever
dream, with all our dreams, that we should sit and talk
of it thus?'

He tried for a little to make out if they had; but it was as if their dreams, numberless enough, were in solution in some thick, cold mist, in which thought lost itself. 'It might have been that we couldn't talk?'

'Well'—she did her best for him—'not from this side. This, you see,' she said, 'is the *other* side.'

'I think,' poor Marcher returned, 'that all sides are the same to me.' Then, however, as she softly shook her head in correction: 'We mightn't, as it were, have got across——?'

'To where we are—no. We're *here*'—she made her weak emphasis.

'And much good does it do us!' was her friend's frank comment.

'It does us the good it can. It does us the good that *it* isn't here. It's past. It's behind,' said May Bartram. 'Before——' but her voice dropped.

He had got up, not to tire her, but it was hard to combat his yearning. She after all told him nothing but that his light had failed—which he knew well enough without her. 'Before——?' he blankly echoed.

'Before, you see, it was always to *come*. That kept it present.'

'Oh, I don't care what comes now! Besides,' Marcher added, 'it seems to me I liked it better present, as you say, than I can like it absent with *your* absence.'

'Oh mine!'—and her pale hands made light of it.

'With the absence of everything.' He had a dreadful sense of standing there before her for—so far as anything but this proved, this bottomless drop was concerned—the last time of their life. It rested on him with a weight he felt he could scarce bear, and this weight it apparently was that still pressed out what remained in him of speakable protest. 'I believe you; but I can't begin to pretend

I understand. *Nothing*, for me, is past; nothing *will* pass
until I pass myself, which I pray my stars may be as soon
as possible. Say, however,' he added, 'that I've eaten my
cake, as you contend, to the last crumb—how can the
thing I've never felt at all be the thing I was marked out
to feel?'

She met him, perhaps, less directly, but she met him
unperturbed. 'You take your "feelings" for granted.
You were to suffer your fate. That was not necessarily
to know it.'

'How in the world—when what is such knowledge
but suffering?'

She looked up at him a while, in silence. 'No—you
don't understand.'

'I suffer,' said John Marcher.

'Don't, don't!'

'How can I help at least *that*?'

'*Don't!*' May Bartram repeated.

She spoke it in a tone so special, in spite of her weakness, that he stared an instant—stared as if some light,
hitherto hidden, had shimmered across his vision. Darkness again closed over it, but the gleam had already
become for him an idea. 'Because I haven't the right——?'

'Don't *know*—when you needn't,' she mercifully
urged. 'You needn't—for we shouldn't.'

'Shouldn't?' If he could but know what she meant!

'No—it's too much.'

'Too much?' he still asked—but with a mystification
that was the next moment, of a sudden, to give way. Her
words, if they meant something, affected him in this
light—the light also of her wasted face—as meaning *all*,
and the sense of what knowledge had been for herself
came over him with a rush which broke through into a
question. 'Is it of that, then, you're dying?'

She but watched him, gravely at first, as if to see, with this, where he was, and she might have seen something, or feared something, that moved her sympathy. 'I would live for you still—if I could.' Her eyes closed for a little, as if, withdrawn into herself, she were, for a last time, trying. 'But I can't!' she said as she raised them again to take leave of him.

She couldn't indeed, as but too promptly and sharply appeared, and he had no vision of her after this that was anything but darkness and doom. They had parted forever in that strange talk; access to her chamber of pain, rigidly guarded, was almost wholly forbidden him; he was feeling now moreover, in the face of doctors, nurses, the two or three relatives attracted doubtless by the presumption of what she had to 'leave', how few were the rights, as they were called in such cases, that he had to put forward, and how odd it might even seem that their intimacy shouldn't have given him more of them. The stupidest fourth cousin had more, even though she had been nothing in such a person's life. She had been a feature of features in *his*, for what else was it to have been so indispensable? Strange beyond saying were the ways of existence, baffling for him the anomaly of his lack, as he felt it to be, of producible claim. A woman might have been, as it were, everything to him, and it might yet present him in no connexion that anyone appeared obliged to recognize. If this was the case in these closing weeks it was the case more sharply on the occasion of the last offices rendered, in the great grey London cemetery, to what had been mortal, to what had been precious, in his friend. The concourse at her grave was not numerous, but he saw himself treated as scarce more nearly concerned with it than if there had been a thousand others. He was in short from this moment face to face with the fact that he was to profit extraordinarily little by the interest May Bartram had taken in him. He couldn't quite have said what he expected, but he had somehow not expected this approach to a double privation. Not only had her interest failed him, but he seemed to feel himself unattended—and for a reason he couldn't sound—by the distinction, the dignity, the propriety, if nothing else, of the man markedly bereaved. It was as if, in the view of society, he had not *been* markedly bereaved, as if there still failed some sign or proof of it, and as if, none the less, his character could never be affirmed, nor the deficiency ever made up. There were moments, as the weeks went by, when he would have liked, by some almost aggressive act, to take his stand on the intimacy of his loss, in order that it *might* be questioned and his retort, to the relief of his spirit, so recorded; but the moments of an irritation more helpless followed fast on these, the moments during which, turning things over with a good conscience but with a bare horizon, he found himself wondering if he oughtn't to have begun, so to speak, further back.

He found himself wondering indeed at many things, and this last speculation had others to keep it company. What could he have done, after all, in her lifetime, without giving them both, as it were, away? He couldn't have made it known she was watching him, for that would have published the superstition of the Beast. This was what closed his mouth now—now that the Jungle had been threshed to vacancy and that the Beast had stolen away. It sounded too foolish and too flat; the difference for him in this particular, the extinction in his life of the element of suspense, was such in fact as to surprise him. He could scarce have said what the effect resembled; the abrupt cessation, the positive prohibition, of music perhaps, more than anything else, in some place all adjusted and all accustomed to sonority and to attention. If he could at any rate have conceived lifting the veil from his image at some moment of the past (what had he done, after all, if not lift it to *her*?), so to do this today, to talk to people at large of the jungle cleared and confide to them that he now felt it as safe, would have been not only to see them listen as to a goodwife's tale, but really to hear himself tell one. What it presently came to in truth was that poor Marcher waded through his beaten grass, where no life stirred, where no breath sounded, where no evil eye seemed to gleam from a possible lair, very much as if vaguely looking for the Beast, and still more as if missing it. He walked about in an existence that had grown strangely more spacious, and, stopping fitfully in places where the undergrowth of life struck him as closer, asked himself yearningly, wondered secretly, and sorely, if it would have lurked here or there. It would have at all events *sprung*; what was at least complete was his belief in the truth itself of the assurance given him. The change from his old sense to his new was absolute and final: what was to happen *had* so absolutely and finally happened that he was as little able to know a fear for his future as to know a hope; so absent in short was any question of anything still to come. He was to live entirely with the other question, that of his unidentified past, that of his having to see his fortune impenetrably muffled and masked.

The torment of this vision became then his occupation; he couldn't perhaps have consented to live but for the possibility of guessing. She had told him, his friend, not to guess; she had forbidden him, so far as he might, to know, and she had even in a sort denied the power in him to learn: which were so many things, precisely, to

deprive him of rest. It wasn't that he wanted, he argued
for fairness, that anything that had happened to him
should happen over again; it was only that he shouldn't,
as an anticlimax, have been taken sleeping so sound as
not to be able to win back by an effort of thought the lost
stuff of consciousness. He declared to himself at moments that he would either win it back or have done with
consciousness for ever; he made this idea his one motive,
in fine, made it so much his passion that none other, to
compare with it, seemed ever to have touched him. The
lost stuff of consciousness became thus for him as a
strayed or stolen child to an unappeasable father; he
hunted it up and down very much as if he were knocking
at doors and inquiring of the police. This was the spirit
in which, inevitably, he set himself to travel; he started
on a journey that was to be as long as he could make it;
it danced before him that, as the other side of the globe
couldn't possibly have less to say to him, it might, by a
possibility of suggestion, have more. Before he quitted
London, however, he made a pilgrimage to May Bartram's
grave, took his way to it through the endless avenues of
the grim suburban metropolis, sought it out in the
wilderness of tombs, and, though he had come but for
the renewal of the act of farewell, found himself, when
he had at last stood by it, beguiled into long intensities. He stood for an hour, powerless to turn away
and yet powerless to penetrate the darkness of death;
fixing with his eyes her inscribed name and date, beating
his forehead against the fact of the secret they kept,
drawing his breath, while he waited as if, in pity of him,
some sense would rise from the stones. He kneeled on
the stones, however, in vain; they kept what they concealed; and if the face of the tomb did become a face
for him it was because her two names were like a pair of

eyes that didn't know him. He gave them a last long look, but no palest light broke.

VI

He stayed away, after this, for a year; he visited the depths of Asia, spending himself on scenes of romantic interest, of superlative sanctity; but what was present to him everywhere was that for a man who had known what *he* had known the world was vulgar and vain. The state of mind in which he had lived for so many years shone out to him, in reflection, as a light that coloured and refined, a light beside which the glow of the East was garish, cheap and thin. The terrible truth was that he had lost—with everything else—a distinction as well; the things he saw couldn't help being common when he had become common to look at them. He was simply now one of them himself—he was in the dust, without a peg for the sense of difference; and there were hours when, before the temples of gods and the sepulchres of kings, his spirit turned, for nobleness of association, to the barely discriminated slab in the London suburb. That had become for him, and more intensely with time and distance, his one witness of a past glory. It was all that was left to him for proof or pride, yet the past glories of Pharaohs were nothing to him as he thought of it. Small wonder then that he came back to it on the morrow of his return. He was drawn there this time as irresistibly as the other, yet with a confidence, almost, that was doubtless the effect of the many months that had elapsed. He had lived, in spite of himself, into his change of feeling, and in wandering over the earth had wandered, as might be said, from the circumference to the centre of his desert. He had settled to his safety and accepted perforce his extinction; figuring to himself, with some colour, in the likeness of certain little old men he remembered to have seen, of whom, all meagre and wizened as they might look, it was related that they had in their time fought twenty duels or been loved by ten princesses. They indeed had been wondrous for others, while he was but wondrous for himself; which, however, was exactly the cause of his haste to renew the wonder by getting back, as he might put it, into his own presence. That had quickened his steps and checked his delay. If his visit was prompt it was because he had been separated so long from the part of himself that alone he now valued.

It is accordingly not false to say that he reached his goal with a certain elation and stood there again with a certain assurance. The creature beneath the sod *knew* of his rare experience, so that, strangely now, the place had lost for him its mere blankness of expression. It met him in mildness—not, as before, in mockery; it wore for him the air of conscious greeting that we find, after absence, in things that have closely belonged to us and which seem to confess of themselves to the connexion. The plot of ground, the graven tablet, the tended flowers affected him so as belonging to him that he quite felt for the hour like a contented landlord reviewing a piece of property. Whatever had happened—well, had happened. He had not come back this time with the vanity of that question, his former worrying, 'What, *what?*' now practically so spent. Yet he would, none the less, never again so cut himself off from the spot; he would come back to it every month, for if he did nothing else by its aid he at least held up his head. It thus grew for him, in the oddest way, a positive resource; he carried out his idea of periodical returns, which took their place at last among the most inveterate of his habits. What it all amounted to, oddly enough, was that, in his now so simplified world, this garden of death gave him the few square feet of earth on which he could still most live. It was as if, being nothing anywhere else for anyone, nothing even for himself, he were just everything here, and if not for a crowd of witnesses, or indeed for any witness but John Marcher, then by clear right of the register that he could scan like an open page. The open page was the tomb of his friend, and *there* were the facts of the past, there the truth of his life, there the backward reaches in which he could lose himself. He did this, from time to time, with such effect that he seemed to wander through the old years with his hand in the arm of a companion who was, in the most extraordinary manner, his other, his younger self; and to wander, which was more extraordinary yet, round and round a third presence— not wandering she, but stationary, still, whose eyes, turning with his revolution, never ceased to follow him, and whose seat was his point, so to speak, of orientation. Thus in short he settled to live—feeding only on the sense that he once *had* lived, and dependent on it not only for a support but for an identity.

It sufficed him, in its way, for months, and the year elapsed; it would doubtless even have carried him further but for an accident, superficially slight, which moved him, in a quite other direction, with a force beyond any of his impressions of Egypt or of India. It was a thing of the merest chance—the turn, as he afterwards felt, of a hair, though he was indeed to live to believe that if light hadn't come to him in this particular fashion it would still have come in another. He was to live to believe this, I say, though he was not to live, I may not less definitely mention, to do much else. We allow him at any rate the benefit of the conviction, struggling up

for him at the end, that, whatever might have happened
or not happened, he would have come round of himself
to the light. The incident of an autumn day had put the
match to the train laid from of old by his misery. With
the light before him he knew that even of late his ache
had only been smothered. It was strangely drugged, but
it throbbed; at the touch it began to bleed. And the
touch, in the event, was the face of a fellow-mortal. This
face, one grey afternoon when the leaves were thick in the
alleys, looked into Marcher's own, at the cemetery, with
an expression like the cut of a blade. He felt it, that is,
so deep down that he winced at the steady thrust. The
person who so mutely assaulted him was a figure he had
noticed, on reaching his own goal, absorbed by a grave
a short distance away, a grave apparently fresh, so that
the emotion of the visitor would probably match it for
frankness. This fact alone forbade further attention,
though during the time he stayed he remained vaguely
conscious of his neighbour, a middle-aged man apparently, in mourning, whose bowed back, among the
clustered monuments and mortuary yews, was constantly
presented. Marcher's theory that these were elements in
contact with which he himself revived, had suffered, on
this occasion, it may be granted, a sensible though inscrutable check. The autumn day was dire for him as
none had recently been, and he rested with a heaviness
he had not yet known on the low stone table that bore
May Bartram's name. He rested without power to move,
as if some spring in him, some spell vouchsafed, had
suddenly been broken forever. If he could have done
that moment as he wanted he would simply have
stretched himself on the slab that was ready to take him,
treating it as a place prepared to receive his last sleep.
What in all the wide world had he now to keep awake

for? He stared before him with the question, and it was
then that, as one of the cemetery walks passed near him,
he caught the shock of the face.

His neighbour at the other grave had withdrawn, as he
himself, with force in him to move, would have done by
now, and was advancing along the path on his way to
one of the gates. This brought him near, and his pace
was slow, so that—and all the more as there was a kind of
hunger in his look—the two men were for a minute
directly confronted. Marcher felt him on the spot as one
of the deeply stricken—a perception so sharp that
nothing else in the picture lived for it, neither his dress,
his age, nor his presumable character and class; nothing
lived but the deep ravage of the features that he showed.
He *showed* them—that was the point; he was moved, as
he passed, by some impulse that was either a signal for
sympathy or, more possibly, a challenge to another
sorrow. He might already have been aware of our friend,
might, at some previous hour, have noticed in him the
smooth habit of the scene, with which the state of his
own senses so scantly consorted, and might thereby
have been stirred as by a kind of overt discord. What
Marcher was at all events conscious of was, in the first
place, that the image of scarred passion presented to
him was conscious too—of something that profaned the
air; and, in the second, that, roused, startled, shocked,
he was yet the next moment looking after it, as it went,
with envy. The most extraordinary thing that had happened to him—though he had given that name to other
matters as well—took place, after his immediate vague
stare, as a consequence of this impression. The stranger
passed, but the raw glare of his grief remained, making
our friend wonder in pity what wrong, what wound it
expressed, what injury not to be healed. What had the

man *had* to make him, by the loss of it, so bleed and yet live?

Something—and this reached him with a pang—that *he*, John Marcher, hadn't; the proof of which was precisely John Marcher's arid end. No passion had ever touched him, for this was what passion meant; he had survived and maundered and pined, but where had been *his* deep ravage? The extraordinary thing we speak of was the sudden rush of the result of this question. The sight that had just met his eyes named to him, as in letters of quick flame, something he had utterly, insanely missed, and what he had missed made these things a train of fire, made them mark themselves in an anguish of inward throbs. He had seen *outside* of his life, not learned it within, the way a woman was mourned when she had been loved for herself; such was the force of his conviction of the meaning of the stranger's face, which still flared for him like a smoky torch. It had not come to him, the knowledge, on the wings of experience; it had brushed him, jostled him, upset him, with the disrespect of chance, the insolence of an accident. Now that the illumination had begun, however, it blazed to the zenith, and what he presently stood there gazing at was the sounded void of his life. He gazed, he drew breath, in pain; he turned in his dismay, and, turning, he had before him in sharper incision than ever the open page of his story. The name on the table smote him as the passage of his neighbour had done, and what it said to him, full in the face, was that *she* was what he had missed. This was the awful thought, the answer to all the past, the vision at the dread clearness of which he turned as cold as the stone beneath him. Everything fell together, confessed, explained, overwhelmed; leaving him most of all stupefied at the blindness he had cherished. The fate he had been marked for he had met with a vengeance—. he had emptied the cup to the lees; he had been the man of his time, *the* man, to whom nothing on earth was to have happened. That was the rare stroke—that was his visitation. So he saw it, as we say, in pale horror, while the pieces fitted and fitted. So *she* had seen it, while he didn't, and so she served at this hour to drive the truth home. It was the truth, vivid and monstrous, that all the while he had waited the wait was itself his portion. This the companion of his vigil had at a given moment perceived, and she had then offered him the chance to baffle his doom. One's doom, however, was never baffled, and on the day she had told him that his own had come down she had seen him but stupidly stare at the escape she offered him.

The escape would have been to love her; then, *then* he would have lived. *She* had lived—who could say now with what passion?—since she had loved him for himself; whereas he had never thought of her (ah, how it hugely glared at him!) but in the chill of his egotism and the light of her use. Her spoken words came back to him, and the chain stretched and stretched. The beast had lurked indeed, and the beast, at its hour, had sprung; it had sprung in that twilight of the cold April when, pale, ill, wasted, but all beautiful, and perhaps even then recoverable, she had risen from her chair to stand before him and let him imaginably guess. It had sprung as he didn't guess; it had sprung as she hopelessly turned from him, and the mark, by the time he left her, had fallen where it *was* to fall. He had justified his fear and achieved his fate; he had failed, with the last exactitude, of all he was to fail of; and a moan now rose to his lips as he remembered she had prayed he mightn't know. This horror of waking—*this* was knowledge, knowledge under the breath of which the very tears in his eyes seemed to freeze. Through them, none the less, he tried to fix it and hold it; he kept it there before him so that he might feel the pain. That at least, belated and bitter, had something of the taste of life. But the bitterness suddenly sickened him, and it was as if, horribly, he saw, in the truth, in the cruelty of his image, what had been appointed and done. He saw the Jungle of his life and saw the lurking Beast; then, while he looked, perceived it, as by a stir of the air, rise, huge and hideous, for the leap that was to settle him. His eyes darkened—it was close; and, instinctively turning, in his hallucination, to avoid it, he flung himself, on his face, on the tomb.

The Return of a Private

HAMLIN GARLAND

(1860-1940)

THE nearer the train drew toward La Crosse, the soberer the little group of 'vets' became. On the long way from New Orleans they had beguiled tedium with jokes and friendly chaff; or with planning with elaborate detail what they were going to do now, after the war. A long journey, slowly, irregularly, yet persistently pushing northward. When they entered on Wisconsin territory they gave a cheer, and another when they reached Madison, but after that they sank into a dumb expectancy. Comrades dropped off at one or two points beyond, until there were only four or five left who were bound for La Crosse County.

Three of them were gaunt and brown, the fourth was

gaunt and pale, with signs of fever and ague upon him. One had a great scar down his temple, one limped, and they all had unnaturally large, bright eyes, showing emaciation. There were no hands greeting them at the station, no banks of gayly dressed ladies waving handkerchiefs and shouting 'Bravo!' as they came in on the caboose of a freight train into the towns that had cheered and blared at them on their way to war. As they looked out or stepped upon the platform for a moment, while the train stood at the station, the loafers looked at them indifferently. Their blue coats, dusty and grimy, were too familiar now to excite notice, much less a friendly word. They were the last of the army to return, and the loafers were surfeited with such sights.

The train jogged forward so slowly that it seemed likely to be midnight before they should reach La Crosse. The little squad grumbled and swore, but it was no use; the train would not hurry, and, as a matter of fact, it was nearly two o'clock when the engine whistled 'down brakes'.

All of the group were farmers, living in districts several miles out of the town, and all were poor.

'Now, boys,' said Private Smith, he of the fever and ague, 'we are landed in La Crosse in the night. We've got to stay somewhere till mornin'. Now I ain't got no two dollars to waste on a hotel. I've got a wife and children, so I'm goin' to roost on a bench and take the cost of a bed out of my hide.'

'Same here,' put in one of the other men. 'Hide'll grow on again, dollars'll come hard. It's going to be mighty hot skirmishin' to find a dollar these days.'

'Don't think they'll be a deputation of citizens waitin' to 'scort us to a hotel, eh?' said another. His sarcasm was too obvious to require an answer.

Smith went on, 'Then at daybreak we'll start for home
—at least, I will.'

'Well, I'll be dummed if I'll take two dollars out o' *my*
hide,' one of the younger men said. 'I'm goin' to a hotel,
ef I don't never lay up a cent.'

'That'll do f'r you,' said Smith; 'but if you had a wife
an' three young uns dependin' on yeh—'

'Which I ain't, thank the Lord! and don't intend
havin' while the court knows itself.'

The station was deserted, chill, and dark, as they came
into it at exactly a quarter to two in the morning. Lit by
the oil lamps that flared a dull red light over the dingy
benches, the waiting room was not an inviting place.
The younger man went off to look up a hotel, while the
rest remained and prepared to camp down on the floor
and benches. Smith was attended to tenderly by the
other men, who spread their blankets on the bench for
him, and, by robbing themselves, made quite a comfortable bed, though the narrowness of the bench made his
sleeping precarious.

It was chill, though August, and the two men, sitting
with bowed heads, grew stiff with cold and weariness,
and were forced to rise now and again and walk about to
warm their stiffened limbs. It did not occur to them,
probably, to contrast their coming home with their going
forth, or with the coming home of the generals, colonels,
or even captains——but to Private Smith, at any rate,
there came a sickness at heart almost deadly as he lay
there on his hard bed and went over his situation.

In the deep of the night, lying on a board in the town
where he had enlisted three years ago, all elation and
enthusiasm gone out of him, he faced the fact that with
the joy of home-coming was already mingled the bitter
juice of care. He saw himself sick, worn out, taking up

the work on his half-cleared farm, the inevitable mortgage standing ready with open jaw to swallow half his
earnings. He had given three years of his life for a mere
pittance of pay, and now!—

Morning dawned at last, slowly, with a pale yellow
dome of light rising silently above the bluffs, which
stand like some huge storm-devastated castle, just east
of the city. Out to the left the great river swept on its
massive yet silent way to the south. Blue-jays called
across the water from hillside to hillside through the
clear, beautiful air, and hawks began to skim the tops of
the hills. The older men were astir early, but Private
Smith had fallen at last into a sleep, and they went out
without waking him. He lay on his knapsack, his gaunt
face turned toward the ceiling, his hands clasped on his
breast, with a curious pathetic effect of weakness and
appeal.

An engine switching near woke him at last, and he
slowly sat up and stared about. He looked out of the
window and saw that the sun was lightening the hills
across the river. He rose and brushed his hair as well as
he could, folded his blankets up, and went out to find his
companions. They stood gazing silently at the river and
at the hills.

'Looks natcher'l, don't it?' they said, as he came out.

'That's what it does,' he replied. 'An' it looks good.
D' yeh see that peak?' He pointed at a beautiful sym-
metrical peak, rising like a slightly truncated cone, so
high that it seemed the very highest of them all. It was
touched by the morning sun and it glowed like a beacon,
and a light scarf of gray morning fog was rolling up its
shadowed side.

'My farm's just beyond that. Now, if I can only ketch
a ride, we'll be home by dinner-time.'

'I'm talkin' about breakfast,' said one of the others.

'I guess it's one more meal o' hardtack f'r me,' said Smith.

They foraged around, and finally found a restaurant with a sleepy old German behind the counter, and procured some coffee, which they drank to wash down their hardtack.

'Time'll come,' said Smith, holding up a piece by the corner, 'when this'll be a curiosity.'

'I hope to God it will! I bet I've chawed hardtack enough to shingle every house in the coolly. I've chawed it when my lampers was down, and when they wasn't. I've took it dry, soaked, and mashed. I've had it wormy, musty, sour, and blue-mouldy. I've had it in little bits and big bits; 'fore coffee an' after coffee. I'm ready f'r a change. I'd like t' git holt jest about now o' some of the hot biscuits my wife c'n make when she lays herself out f'r company.'

'Well, if you set there gabblin', you'll never *see* yer wife.'

'Come on,' said Private Smith. 'Wait a moment, boys; less take suthin'. It's on me.' He led them to the rusty tin dipper which hung on a nail beside the wooden water-pail, and they grinned and drank. Then shouldering their blankets and muskets, which they were 'takin' home to the boys,' they struck out on their last march.

'They called that coffee Jayvy,' grumbled one of them, 'but it never went by the road where government Jayvy resides. I reckon I know coffee from peas.'

They kept together on the road along the turnpike, and up the winding road by the river, which they followed for some miles. The river was very lovely, curving down along its sandy beds, pausing now and then under broad basswood trees, or running in dark, swift, silent currents under tangles of wild grapevines, and drooping alders, and haw trees. At one of these lovely spots the three vets sat down on the thick green sward to rest, 'on Smith's account'. The leaves of the trees were as fresh and green as in June, the jays called cheery greetings to them, and kingfishers darted to and fro with swooping, noiseless flight.

'I tell yeh, boys, this knocks the swamps of Loueesiana into kingdom come.'

'You bet. All they c'n raise down there is snakes, niggers, and p'rticler hell.'

'An' fighting men,' put in the older man.

'An' fightin' men. If I had a good hook an' line I'd sneak a pick'rel out o' that pond. Say, remember that time I shot that alligator——'

'I guess we'd better be crawlin' along,' interrupted Smith, rising and shouldering his knapsack, with considerable effort, which he tried to hide.

'Say, Smith, lemme give you a lift on that.'

'I guess I c'n manage,' said Smith, grimly.

'Course. But, yo' see, I may not have a chance right off to pay yeh back for the times you've carried my gun and hull caboodle. Say, now, gimme that gun, anyway.'

'All right, if yeh feel like it, Jim,' Smith replied, and they trudged along doggedly in the sun, which was getting higher and hotter each half-mile.

'Ain't it queer there ain't no teams comin' along,' said Smith, after a long silence.

'Well, no, seein's it's Sunday.'

'By jinks, that's a fact. It *is* Sunday. I'll git home in time f'r dinner, sure!' he exulted. 'She don't hev dinner usially till about *one* on Sundays.' And he fell into a muse, in which he smiled.

'Well, I'll git home jest about six o'clock, jest about

when the boys are milkin' the cows,' said old Jim Cranby. 'I'll step into the barn, an' then I'll say: "*Heah*! why ain't this milkin' done before this time o' day?" An' then won't they yell!' he added, slapping his thigh in great glee.

Smith went on. 'I'll jest go up the path. Old Rover'll come down the road to meet me. He won't bark; he'll know me, an' he'll come down waggin' his tail an' showin' his teeth. That's his way of laughin'. An' so I'll walk up to the kitchen door, an' I'll say, "*Dinner* f'r a hungry man!" An' then she'll jump up, an'——'

He couldn't go on. His voice choked at the thought of it. Saunders, the third man, hardly uttered a word, but walked silently behind the others. He had lost his wife the first year he was in the army. She died of pneumonia, caught in the autumn rains while working in the fields in his place.

They plodded along till at last they came to a parting of the ways. To the right the road continued up the main valley; to the left it went over the big ridge.

'Well, boys,' began Smith, as they grounded their muskets and looked away up the valley, 'here's where we shake hands. We've marched together a good many miles, an' now I s'pose we're done.'

'Yes, I don't think we'll do any more of it f'r a while. I don't want to, I know.'

'I hope I'll see yeh once in a while, boys, to talk over old times.'

'Of course,' said Saunders, whose voice trembled a little, too. 'It ain't *exactly* like dyin'.' They all found it hard to look at each other.

'But we'd ought'r go home with you,' said Cranby. 'You'll never climb that ridge with all them things on yer back.'

'Oh, I'm all right! Don't worry about me. Every step takes me nearer home, yeh see. Well, good-by, boys.'

They shook hands. 'Good-by. Good luck!'

'Same to you. Lemme know how you find things at home.'

'Good-by.'

'Good-by.'

He turned once before they passed out of sight, and waved his cap, and they did the same, and all yelled. Then all marched away with their long, steady, loping, veteran step. The solitary climber in blue walked on for a time, with his mind filled with the kindness of his comrades, and musing upon the many wonderful days they had had together in camp and field.

He thought of his chum, Billy Tripp. Poor Billy! A 'minie' ball fell into his breast one day, fell wailing like a cat, and tore a great ragged hole in his heart. He looked forward to a sad scene with Billy's mother and sweet-heart. They would want to know all about it. He tried to recall all that Billy had said, and the particulars of it, but there was little to remember, just that wild wailing sound high in the air, a dull slap, a short, quick, expulsive groan, and the boy lay with his face in the dirt in the ploughed field they were marching across.

That was all. But all the scenes he had since been through had not dimmed the horror, the terror of that moment, when his boy comrade fell, with only a breath between a laugh and a death-groan. Poor handsome Billy! Worth millions of dollars was his young life.

These sombre recollections gave way at length to more cheerful feelings as he began to approach his home coolly. The fields and houses grew familiar, and in one or two he was greeted by people seated in the doorways. But he was in no mood to talk, and pushed on steadily, though he stopped and accepted a drink of milk once at the well-side of a neighbour.

The sun was burning hot on that slope, and his step grew slower, in spite of his iron resolution. He sat down several times to rest. Slowly he crawled up the rough, reddish-brown road, which wound along the hillside, under great trees, through dense groves of jack oaks, with tree-tops far below him on his left hand, and the hills far above him on his right. He crawled along like some minute, wingless variety of fly.

He ate some hardtack, sauced with wild berries, when he reached the summit of the ridge, and sat there for some time, looking down into his home coolly.

Sombre, pathetic figure! His wide, round, gray eyes gazing down into the beautiful valley, seeing and not seeing, the splendid cloud-shadows sweeping over the western hills and across the green and yellow wheat far below. His head drooped forward on his palm, his shoulders took on a tired stoop, his cheek-bones showed painfully. An observer might have said, 'He is looking down upon his own grave.'

II

Sunday comes in a Western wheat harvest with such sweet and sudden relaxation to man and beast that it would be holy for thát reason, if for no other, and Sundays are usually fair in harvest-time. As one goes out into the field in the hot morning sunshine, with no sound abroad save the crickets and the indescribably pleasant silken rustling of the ripened grain, the reaper and the very sheaves in the stubble seem to be resting, dreaming.

Around the house, in the shade of the trees, the men sit, smoking, dozing, or reading the papers, while the women, never resting, move about at the housework. The men eat on Sundays about the same as on other days, and breakfast is no sooner over and out of the way than dinner begins.

But at the Smith farm there were no men dozing or reading. Mrs. Smith was alone with her three children, Mary, nine, Tommy, six, and little Ted, just past four. Her farm, rented to a neighbour, lay at the head of a coolly or narrow gully, made at some far-off post-glacial period by the vast and angry floods of water which gullied these tremendous furrows in the level prairie— furrows so deep that undisturbed portions of the original level rose like hills on either side, rose to quite considerable mountains.

The chickens wakened her as usual that Sabbath morning from dreams of her absent husband, from whom she had not heard for weeks. The shadows drifted over the hills, down the slopes, across the wheat, and up the opposite wall in leisurely way, as if, being Sunday, they could take it easy also. The fowls clustered about the housewife as she went out into the yard. Fuzzy little chickens swarmed out from the coops, where their clucking and perpetually disgruntled mothers tramped about, petulantly thrusting their heads through the spaces between the slats.

A cow called in a deep, musical bass, and a calf answered from a little pen near by, and a pig scurried guiltily out of the cabbages. Seeing all this, seeing the pig in the cabbages, the tangle of grass in the garden, the broken fence which she had mended again and again —the little woman, hardly more than a girl, sat down and cried. The bright Sabbath morning was only a mockery without him!

A few years ago they had bought this farm, paying

part, mortgaging the rest in the usual way. Edward Smith was a man of terrible energy. He worked 'nights and Sundays', as the saying goes, to clear the farm of its brush and of its insatiate mortgage! In the midst of his Herculean struggle came the call for volunteers, and with the grim and unselfish devotion to his country which made the Eagle Brigade able to 'whip its weight in wild-cats', he threw down his scythe and grub-axe, turned his cattle loose, and became a blue-coated cog in a vast machine for killing men, and not thistles. While the millionaire sent his money to England for safe-keeping, this man, with his girl-wife and three babies, left them on a mortgaged farm, and went away to fight for an idea. It was foolish, but it was sublime for all that.

That was three years before, and the young wife, sitting on the well-curb on this bright Sabbath harvest morning, was righteously rebellious. It seemed to her that she had borne her share of the country's sorrow. Two brothers had been killed, the renter in whose hands her husband had left the farm had proved a villain; one year the farm had been without crops, and now the overripe grain was waiting the tardy hand of the neigh-bour who had rented it, and who was cutting his own grain first.

About six weeks before, she had received a letter say-ing, 'We'll be discharged in a little while.' But no other word had come from him. She had seen by the papers that his army was being discharged, and from day to day other soldiers slowly percolated in blue streams back into the State and county, but still *her* hero did not return.

Each week she had told the children that he was coming, and she had watched the road so long that it had become unconscious; and as she stood at the well, or by the kitchen door, her eyes were fixed unthinkingly on the road that wound down the coolly.

Nothing wears on the human soul like waiting. If the stranded mariner, searching the sun-bright seas, could once give up hope of a ship, that horrible grinding on his brain would cease. It was this waiting, hoping, on the edge of despair, that gave Emma Smith no rest.

Neighbours said, with kind intentions: 'He's sick, maybe, an' can't start north just yet. He'll come along one o' these days.'

'Why don't he write?' was her question, which silenced them all. This Sunday morning it seemed to her as if she could not stand it longer. The house seemed intolerably lonely. So she dressed the little ones in their best calico dresses and home-made jackets, and, closing up the house, set off down the coolly to old Mother Gray's.

'Old Widder Gray' lived at the 'mouth of the coolly'. She was a widow woman with a large family of stalwart boys and laughing girls. She was the visible incarnation of hospitality and optimistic poverty. With Western open-heartedness she fed every mouth that asked food of her, and worked herself to death as cheerfully as her girls danced in the neighbourhood harvest dances.

She waddled down the path to meet Mrs. Smith with a broad smile on her face.

'Oh, you little dears! Come right to your granny. Gimme me a kiss! Come right in, Mis' Smith. How are yeh, anyway? Nice mornin', ain't it? Come in an' set down. Everything's in a clutter, but that won't scare you any.'

She led the way into the best room, a sunny, square room, carpeted with a faded and patched rag carpet, and papered with white-and-green wall-paper, where a few faded effigies of dead members of the family hung in variously sized oval walnut frames. The house resounded with singing, laughter, whistling, tramping of heavy boots, and riotous scufflings. Half-grown boys came to the door and crooked their fingers at the children, who ran out, and were soon heard in the midst of the fun.

'Don't s'pose you've heard from Ed?' Mrs. Smith shook her head. 'He'll turn up some day, when you ain't lookin' for 'm.' The good old soul had said that so many times that poor Mrs. Smith derived no comfort from it any longer.

'Liz heard from Al the other day. He's comin' some day this week. Anyhow, they expect him.'

'Did he say anything of——'

'No, he didn't,' Mrs. Gray admitted. 'But then it was only a short letter, anyhow. Al ain't much for writin', anyhow.—But come out and see my new cheese. I tell yeh, I don't believe I ever had better luck in my life. If Ed should come, I want you should take him up a piece of this cheese.'

It was beyond human nature to resist the influence of that noisy, hearty, loving household, and in the midst of the singing and laughing the wife forgot her anxiety, for the time at least, and laughed and sang with the rest.

About eleven o'clock a wagon-load more drove up to the door, and Bill Gray, the widow's oldest son, and his whole family, from Sand Lake Coolly, piled out amid a good-natured uproar. Every one talked at once, except Bill, who sat in the wagon with his wrists on his knees, a straw in his mouth, and an amused twinkle in his blue eyes.

'Ain't heard nothin' o' Ed, I s'pose?' he asked in a kind of bellow. Mrs. Smith shook her head. Bill, with a delicacy very striking in such a great giant, rolled his quid in his mouth, and said:

'Didn't know but you had. I hear two or three of the Sand Lake boys are comin'. Left New Orleenes some time this week. Didn't write nothin' about Ed, but no news is good news in such cases, mother always says.'

'Well, go put out yer team,' said Mrs. Gray, 'an' go'n bring me in some taters, an', Sim, you go see if you c'n find some corn. Sadie, you put on the water to bile. Come now, hustle yer boots, all o' yeh. If I feed this yer crowd, we've got to have some raw materials. If y' think I'm goin' to feed yeh on pie—you're just mightily mistaken.'

The children went off into the field, the girls put dinner on to boil, and then went to change their dresses and fix their hair. 'Somebody might come,' they said.

'Land sakes, *I hope* not! I don't know where in time I'd set 'em, 'less they'd eat at the second table,' Mrs. Gray laughed, in pretended dismay.

The two elder boys, who had served their time in the army, lay out on the grass before the house, and whittled and talked desultorily about the war and the crops, and planned buying a threshing-machine. The older girls and Mrs. Smith helped enlarge the table and put on the dishes, talking all the time in that cheery, incoherent, and meaningful way a group of such women have,—a conversation to be taken for its spirit rather than for its letter, though Mrs. Gray at last got the ear of them all and dissertated at length on girls.

'Girls in love ain' no use in the whole blessed week,' she said. 'Sundays they're a-lookin' down the road, expectin' he'll *come*. Sunday afternoons they can't think o' nothin' else, 'cause he's *here*. Monday mornin's they're sleepy and kind o' dreamy and slimpsy, and good f'r nothin' on Tuesday and Wednesday. Thursday they git absent-minded, an' begin to look off toward Sunday agin, an' mope aroun' and let the dishwater git cold, right under their noses. Friday they break dishes, an' go off in the best room an' snivel, an' look out o' the winder. Saturdays they have queer spurts o' workin' like all p'ssessed, an' spurts o' frizzin' their hair. An' Sunday they begin it all over agin.'

The girls giggled and blushed, all through this tirade from their mother, their broad faces and powerful frames anything but suggestive of lackadaisical sentiment. But Mrs. Smith said:

'Now, Mrs. Gray, I hadn't ought to stay to dinner. You've got——'

'Now you set right down! If any of them girls' beaus comes, they'll have to take what's left, that's all. They ain't s'posed to have much appetite, nohow. No, you're goin' to stay if they starve, an' they ain't no danger o' that.'

At one o'clock the long table was piled with boiled potatoes, cords of boiled corn on the cob, squash and pumpkin pies, hot biscuit, sweet pickles, bread and butter, and honey. Then one of the girls took down a conch-shell from a nail, and going to the door, blew a long, fine, free blast, that showed there was no weakness of lungs in her ample chest.

Then the children came out of the forest of corn, out of the creek, out of the loft of the barn, and out of the garden.

'They come to their feed f'r all the world jest like the pigs when y' holler "poo-ee!" See 'em scoot!' laughed Mrs. Gray, every wrinkle on her face shining with delight.

The men shut up their jack-knives, and surrounded the horse-trough to souse their faces in the cold, hard water, and in a few moments the table was filled with a merry crowd, and a row of wistful-eyed youngsters circled the kitchen wall, where they stood first on one leg and then on the other, in impatient hunger.

'Now pitch in, Mrs. Smith,' said Mrs. Gray, presiding over the table. 'You know these men critters. They'll eat every grain of it, if yeh give 'em a chance. I swan, they're made o' India-rubber, their stomachs is, I know it.'

'Haf to eat to work,' said Bill, gnawing a cob with a swift, circular motion that rivalled a corn-sheller in results.

'More like workin' to eat,' put in one of the girls, with a giggle. 'More eat 'n work with you.'

'*You* needn't say anything, Net. Any one that'll eat seven ears——'

'I didn't, no such thing. You piled your cobs on my plate.'

'That'll do to tell Ed Varney. It won't go down here where we know yeh.'

'Good land! Eat all yeh want! They's plenty more in the fiel's, but I can't afford to give you young uns tea. The tea is for us women-folks, and 'specially f'r Mis' Smith an' Bill's wife. We're a-goin' to tell fortunes by it.'

One by one the men filled up and shoved back, and one by one the children slipped into their places, and by two o'clock the women alone remained around the debris-covered table, sipping their tea and telling fortunes.

As they got well down to the grounds in the cup, they shook them with a circular motion in the hand, and then turned them bottom-side-up quickly in the saucer, then twirled them three or four times one way, and three or four times the other, during a breathless pause. Then Mrs. Gray lifted the cup, and, gazing into it with profound gravity, pronounced the impending fate.

It must be admitted that, to a critical observer, she had abundant preparation for hitting close to the mark, as when she told the girls that 'somebody was comin'.' 'It's a man,' she went on gravely. 'He is cross-eyed——'

'Oh, you hush!' cried Nettie.

'He has red hair, and is death on b'iled corn and hot biscuit.'

The others shrieked with delight.

'But he's goin' to get the mitten, that red-headed feller is, for I see another feller comin' up behind him.'

'Oh, lemme see, lemme see!' cried Nettie.

'Keep off,' said the priestess, with a lofty gesture. 'His hair is black. He don't eat so much, and he works more.'

The girls exploded in a shriek of laughter, and pounded their sister on the back.

At last came Mrs. Smith's turn, and she was trembling with excitement as Mrs. Gray again composed her jolly face to what she considered a proper solemnity of expression.

'Somebody is comin' to *you*,' she said, after a long pause. 'He's got a musket on his back. He's a soldier. He's almost here. See?'

She pointed at two little tea-stems, which really formed a faint suggestion of a man with a musket on his back. He had climbed nearly to the edge of the cup. Mrs. Smith grew pale with excitement. She trembled so she could hardly hold the cup in her hand as she gazed into it.

'It's Ed,' cried the old woman. 'He's on the way home. Heavens an' earth! There he is now!' She turned and waved her hand out toward the road. They rushed to the door to look where she pointed.

A man in a blue coat, with a musket on his back, was toiling slowly up the hill on the sun-bright, dusty road, toiling slowly, with bent head half hidden by a heavy knapsack. So tired it seemed that walking was indeed a process of falling. So eager to get home he would not stop, would not look aside, but plodded on, amid the cries of the locusts, the welcome of the crickets, and the rustle of the yellow wheat. Getting back to God's country, and his wife and babies!

Laughing, crying, trying to call him and the children at the same time, the little wife, almost hysterical, snatched her hat and ran out into the yard. But the soldier had disappeared over the hill into the hollow beyond, and, by the time she had found the children, he was too far away for her voice to reach him. And, besides, she was not sure it was her husband, for he had not turned his head at their shouts. This seemed so strange. Why didn't he stop to rest at his old neighbour's house? Tortured by hope and doubt, she hurried up the coolly as fast as she could push the baby wagon, the blue-coated figure just ahead pushing steadily, silently forward up the coolly.

When the excited, panting little group came in sight of the gate they saw the blue-coated figure standing, leaning upon the rough rail fence, his chin on his palms, gazing at the empty house. His knapsack, canteen, blankets, and musket lay upon the dusty grass at his feet.

He was like a man lost in a dream. His wide, hungry eyes devoured the scene. The rough lawn, the little unpainted house, the field of clear yellow wheat behind it, down across which streamed the sun, now almost ready to touch the high hill to the west, the crickets crying merrily, a cat on the fence near by, dreaming, unmindful of the stranger in blue——

How peaceful it all was. O God! How far removed from all camps, hospitals, battle lines. A little cabin in a Wisconsin coolly, but it was majestic in its peace. How did he ever leave it for those years of tramping, thirsting, killing?

Trembling, weak with emotion, her eyes on the silent figure, Mrs. Smith hurried up to the fence. Her feet made no noise in the dust and grass, and they were close upon him before he knew of them. The oldest boy ran a little ahead. He will never forget that figure, that face. It will always remain as something epic, that return of the private. He fixed his eyes on the pale face covered with a ragged beard.

'Who *are* you, sir?' asked the wife, or, rather, started to ask, for he turned, stood a moment, and then cried:

'Emma!'

'Edward!'

The children stood in a curious row to see their mother kiss this bearded, strange man, the elder girl sobbing sympathetically with her mother. Illness had left the soldier partly deaf, and this added to the strangeness of his manner.

But the youngest child stood away, even after the girl had recognized her father and kissed him. The man turned then to the baby, and said in a curiously un-paternal tone:

'Come here, my little man; don't you know me?' But the baby backed away under the fence and stood peering at him critically.

'My little man!' What meaning in those words! This baby seemed like some other woman's child, and not the infant he had left in his wife's arms. The war had come between him and his baby—he was only a strange man to him, with big eyes; a soldier, with mother hanging to his arm, and talking in a loud voice.

'And this is Tom,' the private said, drawing the oldest

boy to him. '*He'll* come and see me. *He* knows his poor old pap when he comes home from the war.'

The mother heard the pain and reproach in his voice and hastened to apologize.

'You've changed so, Ed. He can't know yeh. This is papa, Teddy; come and kiss him—Tom and Mary do. Come, won't you?' But Teddy still peered through the fence with solemn eyes, well out of reach. He resembled a half-wild kitten that hesitates, studying the tones of one's voice.

'I'll fix him,' said the soldier, and sat down to undo his knapsack, out of which he drew three enormous and very red apples. After giving one to each of the older children, he said:

'*Now* I guess he'll come. Eh, my little man? Now come see your pap.'

Teddy crept slowly under the fence, assisted by the overzealous Tommy, and a moment later was kicking and squalling in his father's arms. Then they entered the house, into the sitting room, poor, bare, art-forsaken little room, too, with its rag carpet, its square clock, and its two or three chromos and pictures from *Harper's Weekly* pinned about.

'Emma, I'm all tired out,' said Private Smith, as he flung himself down on the carpet as he used to do, while his wife brought a pillow to put under his head, and the children stood about munching their apples.

'Tommy, you run and get me a pan of chips, and Mary, you get the tea-kettle on, and I'll go and make some biscuit.'

And the soldier talked. Question after question he poured forth about the crops, the cattle, the renter, the neighbours. He slipped his heavy government brogan shoes off his poor, tired, blistered feet, and lay out with utter, sweet relaxation. He was a free man again, no longer a soldier under a command. At supper he stopped once, listened and smiled. 'That's old Spot. I know her voice. I s'pose that's her calf out there in the pen. I can't milk her to-night, though. I'm too tired. But I tell you, I'd like a drink of her milk. What's become of old Rove?'

'He died last winter. Poisoned, I guess.' There was a moment of sadness for them all. It was some time before the husband spoke again, in a voice that trembled a little.

'Poor old feller! He'd 'a' known me half a mile away. I expected him to come down the hill to meet me. It 'ud 'a' been more like comin' home if I could 'a' seen him comin' down the road an' waggin' his tail, an' laughin' that way he has. I tell yeh, it kind o' took hold o' me to see the blinds down an' the house shut up.'

'But, yeh see, we—we expected you'd write again 'fore you started. And then we thought we'd see you if you *did* come,' she hastened to explain.

'Well, I ain't worth a cent on writin'. Besides, it's just as well yeh didn't know when I was comin'. I tell you, it sounds good to hear them chickens out there, an' turkeys, an' the crickets. Do you know they don't have just the same kind o' crickets down South? Who's Sam hired t' help cut yer grain?'

'The Ramsey boys.'

'Looks like a good crop; but I'm afraid I won't do much gettin' it cut. This cussed fever an' ague has got me down pretty low. I don't know when I'll get rid of it. I'll bet I've took twenty-five pounds of quinine if I've taken a bit. Gimme another biscuit. I tell yeh, they taste good, Emma. I ain't had anything like it——Say, if you'd 'a' hear'd me braggin' to th' boys about your butter 'n' biscuits I'll bet your ears 'ud 'a' burnt.'

The private's wife coloured with pleasure. 'Oh, you're always a-braggin' about your things. Everybody makes good butter.'

'Yes; old lady Snyder, for instance.'

'Oh, well, she ain't to be mentioned. She's Dutch.'

'Or old Mis' Snively. One more cup o' tea, Mary. That's my girl! I'm feeling better already. I just b'lieve the matter with me is, I'm *starved*.'

This was a delicious hour, one long to be remembered. They were like lovers again. But their tenderness, like that of a typical American family, found utterance in tones, rather than in words. He was praising her when praising her biscuit, and she knew it. They grew soberer when he showed where he had been struck, one ball burning the back of his hand, one cutting away a lock of hair from his temple, and one passing through the calf of his leg. The wife shuddered to think how near she had come to being a soldier's widow. Her waiting no longer seemed hard. This sweet, glorious hour effaced it all.

Then they rose, and all went out into the garden and down to the barn. He stood beside her while she milked old Spot. They began to plan fields and crops for next year.

His farm was weedy and encumbered, a rascally renter had run away with his machinery (departing between two days), his children needed clothing, the years were coming upon him, he was sick and emaciated, but his heroic soul did not quail. With the same courage with which he had faced his Southern march he entered upon a still more hazardous future.

Oh, that mystic hour! The pale man with big eyes standing there by the well, with his young wife by his side. The vast moon swinging above the eastern peaks, the cattle winding down the pasture slopes with jangling bells, the crickets singing, the stars blooming out sweet and far and serene; the katydids rhythmically calling, the little turkeys crying querulously, as they settled to roost in the poplar tree near the open gate. The voices at the well drop lower, the little ones nestle in their father's arms at last, and Teddy falls asleep there.

The common soldier of the American volunteer army had returned. His war with the South was over, and his fight, his daily running fight with nature and against the injustice of his fellow-men, was begun again.

Roman Fever

EDITH WHARTON

(1862–1937)

I

FROM the table át which they had been lunching two American ladies of ripe but well-cared-for middle age moved across the lofty terrace of the Roman restaurant and, leaning on its parapet, looked first at each other, and then down on the outspread glories of the Palatine and the Forum, with the same expression of vague but benevolent approval.

As they leaned there a girlish voice echoed up gaily from the stairs leading to the court below. 'Well, come along, then,' it cried, not to them but to an invisible companion, 'and let's leave the young things to their knitting'; and a voice as fresh laughed back: 'Oh, look here, Babs, not actually *knitting*—' 'Well, I mean figuratively,' rejoined the first. 'After all, we haven't left our poor

parents much else to do. . . .' and at that point the turn
of the stairs engulfed the dialogue.

The two ladies looked at each other again, this time
with a tinge of smiling embarrassment, and the smaller
and paler one shook her head and coloured slightly.

'Barbara!' she murmured, sending an unheard rebuke
after the mocking voice in the stairway.

The other lady, who was fuller, and higher in colour,
with a small determined nose supported by vigorous
black eyebrows, gave a good-humoured laugh. 'That's
what our daughters think of us!'

Her companion replied by a deprecating gesture. 'Not
of us individually. We must remember that. It's just the
collective modern idea of Mothers. And you see—' Half
guiltily she drew from her handsomely mounted black
hand-bag a twist of crimson silk run through by two fine
knitting needles. 'One never knows,' she murmured.
'The new system has certainly given us a good deal of
time to kill; and sometimes I get tired just looking—even
at this.' Her gesture was now addressed to the stupen-
dous scene at their feet.

The dark lady laughed again, and they both relapsed
upon the view, contemplating it in silence, with a sort of
diffused serenity which might have been borrowed from
the spring effulgence of the Roman skies. The luncheon-
hour was long past, and the two had their end of the vast
terrace to themselves. At its opposite extremity a few
groups, detained by a lingering look at the outspread
city, were gathering up guide-books and fumbling for
tips. The last of them scattered, and the two ladies were
alone on the air-washed height.

'Well, I don't see why we shouldn't just stay here,'
said Mrs. Slade, the lady of the high colour and energetic
brows. Two derelict basket-chairs stood near, and she

pushed them into the angle of the parapet, and settled herself in one, her gaze upon the Palatine. 'After all, it's still the most beautiful view in the world.'

'It always will be, to me,' assented her friend Mrs. Ansley, with so slight a stress on the 'me' that Mrs. Slade, though she noticed it, wondered if it were not merely accidental, like the random underlinings of old-fashioned letter-writers.

'Grace Ansley was always old-fashioned,' she thought; and added aloud, with a retrospective smile: 'It's a view we've both been familiar with for a good many years. When we first met here we were younger than our girls are now. You remember?'

'Oh, yes, I remember,' murmured Mrs. Ansley, with the same undefinable stress.— 'There's that head-waiter wondering,' she interpolated. She was evidently far less sure than her companion of herself and of her rights in the world.

'I'll cure him of wondering,' said Mrs. Slade, stretching her hand toward a bag as discreetly opulent-looking as Mrs. Ansley's. Signing to the head-waiter, she explained that she and her friend were old lovers of Rome, and would like to spend the end of the afternoon looking down on the view—that is, if it did not disturb the service? The head-waiter, bowing over her gratuity, assured her that the ladies were most welcome, and would be still more so if they would condescend to remain for dinner. A full moon night, they would remember. . . .

Mrs. Slade's black brows drew together, as though references to the moon were out-of-place and even unwelcome. But she smiled away her frown as the head-waiter retreated. 'Well, why not? We might do worse. There's no knowing, I suppose, when the girls will

be back. Do you even know back from *where*? I
don't!'

Mrs. Ansley again coloured slightly. 'I think those
young Italian aviators we met at the Embassy invited
them to fly to Tarquinia for tea. I suppose they'll want
to wait and fly back by moonlight.'

'Moonlight—moonlight! What a part it still plays. Do
you suppose they're as sentimental as we were?'

'I've come to the conclusion that I don't in the least
know what they are,' said Mrs. Ansley. 'And perhaps we
didn't know much more about each other.'

'No; perhaps we didn't.'

Her friend gave her a shy glance. 'I never should have
supposed you were sentimental, Alida.'

'Well, perhaps I wasn't.' Mrs. Slade drew her lids
together in retrospect; and for a few moments the two
ladies, who had been intimate since childhood, reflected
how little they knew each other. Each one, of course,
had a label ready to attach to the other's name; Mrs.
Delphin Slade, for instance, would have told herself,
or any one who asked her, that Mrs. Horace Ansley,
twenty-five years ago, had been exquisitely lovely—no,
you wouldn't believe it, would you? . . . though, of
course, still charming, distinguished. . . . Well, as a girl
she had been exquisite; far more beautiful than her
daughter Barbara, though certainly Babs, according to
the new standards at any rate, was more effective—had
more *edge*, as they say. Funny where she got it, with those
two nullities as parents. Yes; Horace Ansley was—well,
just the duplicate of his wife. Museum specimens of old
New York. Good-looking, irreproachable, exemplary.
Mrs. Slade and Mrs. Ansley had lived opposite each
other—actually as well as figuratively—for years. When
the drawing-room curtains in No. 20 East 73rd Street

were renewed, No. 23, across the way, was always aware
of it. And of all the movings, buyings, travels, anniver-
saries, illnesses—the tame chronicle of an estimable pair.
Little of it escaped Mrs. Slade. But she had grown
bored with it by the time her husband made his big *coup*
in Wall Street, and when they bought in upper Park
Avenue had already begun to think: 'I'd rather live
opposite a speak-easy for a change; at least one might see
it raided.' The idea of seeing Grace raided was so
amusing that (before the move) she launched it at a
woman's lunch. It made a hit, and went the rounds—she
sometimes wondered if it had crossed the street, and
reached Mrs. Ansley. She hoped not, but didn't much
mind. Those were the days when respectability was at a
discount, and it did the irreproachable no harm to laugh
at them a little.

A few years later, and not many months apart, both
ladies lost their husbands. There was an appropriate
exchange of wreaths and condolences, and a brief renewal
of intimacy in the half-shadow of their mourning; and
now, after another interval, they had run across each
other in Rome, at the same hotel, each of them the
modest appendage of a salient daughter. The similarity
of their lot had again drawn them together, lending
itself to mild jokes, and the mutual confession that, if in
old days it must have been tiring to 'keep up' with
daughters, it was now, at times, a little dull not to.

No doubt, Mrs. Slade reflected, she felt her unem-
ployment more than poor Grace ever would. It was a big
drop from being the wife of Delphin Slade to being his
widow. She had always regarded herself (with a certain
conjugal pride) as his equal in social gifts, as contributing
her full share to the making of the exceptional couple
they were: but the difference after his death was ir-

remediable. As the wife of the famous corporation lawyer, always with an international case or two on hand, every day brought its exciting and unexpected obligation: the impromptu entertaining of eminent colleagues from abroad, the hurried dashes on legal business to London, Paris, or Rome, where the entertaining was so handsomely reciprocated; the amusement of hearing in her wake: 'What, that handsome woman with the good clothes and the eyes is Mrs. Slade—*the* Slade's wife? Really? Generally the wives of celebrities are such frumps.'

Yes; being *the* Slade's widow was a dullish business after that. In living up to such a husband all her faculties had been engaged; now she had only her daughter to live up to, for the son who seemed to have inherited his father's gifts had died suddenly in boyhood. She had fought through that agony because her husband was there, to be helped and to help; now, after the father's death, the thought of the boy had become unbearable. There was nothing left but to mother her daughter; and dear Jenny was such a perfect daughter that she needed no excessive mothering. 'Now with Babs Ansley I don't know that I *should* be so quiet,' Mrs. Slade sometimes half-enviously reflected; but Jenny, who was younger than her brilliant friend, was that rare accident, an extremely pretty girl who somehow made youth and prettiness seem as safe as their absence. It was all perplexing—and to Mrs. Slade a little boring. She wished that Jenny would fall in love—with the wrong man, even; that she might have to be watched, out-manœuvred, rescued. And instead, it was Jenny who watched her mother, kept her out of draughts, made sure that she had taken her tonic. . . .

Mrs. Ansley was much less articulate than her friend,

and her mental portrait of Mrs. Slade was slighter, and drawn with fainter touches. 'Alida Slade's awfully brilliant; but not as brilliant as she thinks,' would have summed it up; though she would have added, for the enlightenment of strangers, that Mrs. Slade had been an extremely dashing girl; much more so than her daughter, who was pretty, of course, and clever in a way, but had none of her mother's—well, 'vividness', some one had once called it. Mrs. Ansley would take up current words like this, and cite them in quotation marks, as unheard-of audacities. No; Jenny was not like her mother. Sometimes Mrs. Ansley thought Alida Slade was disappointed; on the whole she had had a sad life. Full of failures and mistakes; Mrs. Ansley had always been rather sorry for her. . . .

So these two ladies visualized each other, each through the wrong end of her little telescope.

II

For a long time they continued to sit side by side without speaking. It seemed as though, to both, there was a relief in laying down their somewhat futile activities in the presence of the vast Memento Mori which faced them. Mrs. Slade sat quite still, her eyes fixed on the golden slope of the Palace of the Cæsars, and after a while Mrs. Ansley ceased to fidget with her bag, and she too sank into meditation. Like many intimate friends, the two ladies had never before had occasion to be silent together, and Mrs. Ansley was slightly embarrassed by what seemed, after so many years, a new stage in their intimacy, and one with which she did not yet know how to deal.

Suddenly the air was full of that deep clangour of bells which periodically covers Rome with a roof of silver.

Mrs. Slade glanced at her wrist-watch. 'Five o'clock already,' she said, as though surprised.

Mrs. Ansley suggested interrogatively: 'There's bridge at the Embassy at five.' For a long time Mrs. Slade did not answer. She appeared to be lost in contemplation, and Mrs. Ansley thought the remark had escaped her. But after a while she said, as if speaking out of a dream: 'Bridge, did you say? Not unless you want to. . . . But I don't think I will, you know.'

'Oh, no,' Mrs. Ansley hastened to assure her. 'I don't care to at all. It's so lovely here; and so full of old memories, as you say.' She settled herself in her chair, and almost furtively drew forth her knitting. Mrs. Slade took sideway note of this activity, but her own beautifully cared-for hands remained motionless on her knee.

'I was just thinking,' she said slowly, 'what different things Rome stands for to each generation of travellers. To our grandmothers, Roman fever; to our mothers, sentimental dangers—how we used to be guarded!—to our daughters, no more dangers than the middle of Main Street. They don't know it—but how much they're missing!'

The long golden light was beginning to pale, and Mrs. Ansley lifted her knitting a little closer to her eyes. 'Yes; how we were guarded!'

'I always used to think,' Mrs. Slade continued, 'that our mothers had a much more difficult job than our grandmothers. When Roman fever stalked the streets it must have been comparatively easy to gather in the girls at the danger hour; but when you and I were young, with such beauty calling us, and the spice of disobedience thrown in, and no worse risk than catching cold during the cool hour after sunset, the mothers used to be put to it to keep us in—didn't they?'

She turned again toward Mrs. Ansley, but the latter had reached a delicate point in her knitting. 'One, two, three—slip two; yes, they must have been,' she assented, without looking up.

Mrs. Slade's eyes rested on her with a deepened attention. 'She can knit—in the face of *this*! How like her. . . .'

Mrs. Slade leaned back, brooding, her eyes ranging from the ruins which faced her to the long green hollow of the Forum, the fading glow of the church fronts beyond it, and the outlying immensity of the Colosseum. Suddenly she thought: 'It's all very well to say that our girls have done away with sentiment and moonlight. But if Babs Ansley isn't out to catch that young aviator—the one who's a Marchese—then I don't know anything. And Jenny has no chance beside her. I know that too. I wonder if that's why Grace Ansley likes the two girls to go everywhere together? My poor Jenny as a foil—!' Mrs. Slade gave a hardly audible laugh, and at the sound Mrs. Ansley dropped her knitting.

'Yes—?'

'I—oh, nothing. I was only thinking how your Babs carries everything before her. That Campolieri boy is one of the best matches in Rome. Don't look so innocent, my dear—you know he is. And I was wondering, ever so respectfully, you understand . . . wondering how two such exemplary characters as you and Horace had managed to produce anything quite so dynamic.' Mrs. Slade laughed again, with a touch of asperity.

Mrs. Ansley's hands lay inert across her needles. She looked straight out at the great accumulated wreckage of passion and splendour at her feet. But her small profile was almost expressionless. At length she said: 'I think you overrate Babs, my dear.'

Mrs. Slade's tone grew easier. 'No; I don't. I appreci-
ate her. And perhaps envy you. Oh, my girl's perfect;
if I were a chronic invalid I'd—well, I think I'd rather
be in Jenny's hands. There must be times . . . but there!
I always wanted a brilliant daughter . . . and never quite
understood why I got an angel instead.'

Mrs. Ansley echoed her laugh in a faint murmur.
'Babs is an angel too.'

'Of course—of course! But she's got rainbow wings.
Well, they're wandering by the sea with their young men;
and here we sit . . . and it all brings back the past a little
too acutely.'

Mrs. Ansley had resumed her knitting. One might
almost have imagined (if one had known her less well,
Mrs. Slade reflected) that, for her also, too many
memories rose from the lengthening shadows of those
august ruins. But no; she was simply absorbed in her
work. What was there for her to worry about? She knew
that Babs would almost certainly come back engaged to
the extremely eligible Campolieri. 'And she'll sell the
New York house, and settle down near them in Rome,
and never be in their way . . . she's much too tactful.
But she'll have an excellent cook, and just the right
people in for bridge and cocktails . . . and a perfectly
peaceful old age among her grandchildren.'

Mrs. Slade broke off this prophetic flight with a recoil
of self-disgust. There was no one of whom she had less
right to think unkindly than of Grace Ansley. Would she
never cure herself of envying her? Perhaps she had
begun too long ago.

She stood up and leaned against the parapet, filling
her troubled eyes with the tranquillizing magic of the
hour. But instead of tranquillizing her the sight seemed
to increase her exasperation. Her gaze turned toward the

Colosseum. Already its golden flank was drowned in purple shadow, and above it the sky curved crystal clear, without light or colour. It was the moment when afternoon and evening hang balanced in mid-heaven.

Mrs. Slade turned back and laid her hand on her friend's arm. The gesture was so abrupt that Mrs. Ansley looked up, startled.

'The sun's set. You're not afraid, my dear?'

'Afraid—?'

'Of Roman fever or pneumonia? I remember how ill you were that winter. As a girl you had a very delicate throat, hadn't you?'

'Oh, we're all right up here. Down below, in the Forum, it does get deathly cold, all of a sudden . . . but not here.'

'Ah, of course you know because you had to be so careful.' Mrs. Slade turned back to the parapet. She thought: 'I must make one more effort not to hate her.' Aloud she said: 'Whenever I look at the Forum from up here, I remember that story about a great-aunt of yours, wasn't she? A dreadfully wicked great-aunt?'

'Oh, yes; Great-aunt Harriet. The one who was supposed to have sent her young sister out to the Forum after sunset to gather a night-blooming flower for her album. All our great-aunts and grandmothers used to have albums of dried flowers.'

Mrs. Slade nodded. 'But she really sent her because they were in love with the same man—'

'Well, that was the family tradition. They said Aunt Harriet confessed it years afterward. At any rate, the poor little sister caught the fever and died. Mother used to frighten us with the story when we were children.'

'And you frightened *me* with it, that winter when you

and I were here as girls. The winter I was engaged to Delphin.'

Mrs. Ansley gave a faint laugh. 'Oh, did I? Really frightened you? I don't believe you're easily frightened.'

'Not often; but I was then. I was easily frightened because I was too happy. I wonder if you know what that means?'

'I—yes . . .' Mrs. Ansley faltered.

'Well, I suppose that was why the story of your wicked aunt made such an impression on me. And I thought: "There's no more Roman fever, but the Forum is deathly cold after sunset—especially after a hot day. And the Colosseum's even colder and damper".'

'The Colosseum—?'

'Yes. It wasn't easy to get in, after the gates were locked for the night. Far from easy. Still, in those days it could be managed; it *was* managed, often. Lovers met there who couldn't meet elsewhere. You knew that?'

'I—I daresay. I don't remember.'

'You don't remember? You don't remember going to visit some ruins or other one evening, just after dark, and catching a bad chill? You were supposed to have gone to see the moon rise. People always said that expedition was what caused your illness.'

There was a moment's silence; then Mrs. Ansley rejoined: 'Did they? It was all so long ago.'

'Yes. And you got well again—so it didn't matter. But I suppose it struck your friends—the reason given for your illness, I mean—because everybody knew you were so prudent on account of your throat, and your mother took such care of you. . . . You *had* been out late sightseeing, hadn't you, that night?'

'Perhaps I had. The most prudent girls aren't always prudent. What made you think of it now?'

Mrs. Slade seemed to have no answer ready. But after a moment she broke out: 'Because I simply can't bear it any longer—!'

Mrs. Ansley lifted her head quickly. Her eyes were wide and very pale. 'Can't bear what?'

'Why—your not knowing that I've always known why you went.'

'Why I went—?'

'Yes. You think I'm bluffing, don't you? Well, you went to meet the man I was engaged to—and I can repeat every word of the letter that took you there.'

While Mrs. Slade spoke Mrs. Ansley had risen unsteadily to her feet. Her bag, her knitting and gloves, slid in a panic-stricken heap to the ground. She looked at Mrs. Slade as though she were looking at a ghost.

'No, no—don't,' she faltered out.

'Why not? Listen, if you don't believe me. "My one darling, things can't go on like this. I must see you alone. Come to the Colosseum immediately after dark tomorrow. There will be somebody to let you in. No one whom you need fear will suspect"—but perhaps you've forgotten what the letter said?'

Mrs. Ansley met the challenge with an unexpected composure. Steadying herself against the chair she looked at her friend, and replied: 'No; I know it by heart too.'

'And the signature? "Only *your* D.S." Was that it? I'm right, am I? That was the letter that took you out that evening after dark?'

Mrs. Ansley was still looking at her. It seemed to Mrs. Slade that a slow struggle was going on behind the voluntarily controlled mask of her small quiet face. 'I shouldn't have thought she had herself so well in hand,' Mrs. Slade reflected, almost resentfully. But at this moment Mrs. Ansley spoke. 'I don't know how you knew. I burnt that letter at once.'

'Yes; you would, naturally—you're so prudent!' The sneer was open now. 'And if you burnt the letter you're wondering how on earth I know what was in it. That's it, isn't it?'

Mrs. Slade waited, but Mrs. Ansley did not speak.

'Well, my dear, I know what was in that letter because I wrote it!'

'You wrote it?'

'Yes.'

The two women stood for a minute staring at each other in the last golden light. Then Mrs. Ansley dropped back into her chair. 'Oh,' she murmured, and covered her face with her hands.

Mrs. Slade waited nervously for another word or movement. None came, and at length she broke out: 'I horrify you.'

Mrs. Ansley's hands dropped to her knee. The face they uncovered was streaked with tears. 'I wasn't thinking of you. I was thinking—it was the only letter I ever had from him!'

'And I wrote it. Yes; I wrote it! But I was the girl he was engaged to. Did you happen to remember that?'

Mrs. Ansley's head drooped again. 'I'm not trying to excuse myself. . . . I remembered. . . .'

'And still you went?'

'Still I went.'

Mrs. Slade stood looking down on the small bowed figure at her side. The flame of her wrath had already sunk, and she wondered why she had ever thought there would be any satisfaction in inflicting so purposeless a wound on her friend. But she had to justify herself.

'You do understand? I'd found out—and I hated you,

hated you. I knew you were in love with Delphin—and I was afraid; afraid of you, of your quiet ways, your sweetness . . . your . . . well, I wanted you out of the way, that's all. Just for a few weeks; just till I was sure of him. So in a blind fury I wrote that letter. . . . I don't know why I'm telling you now.'

'I suppose,' said Mrs. Ansley slowly, 'it's because you've always gone on hating me.'

'Perhaps. Or because I wanted to get the whole thing off my mind.' She paused. 'I'm glad you destroyed the letter. Of course I never thought you'd die.'

Mrs. Ansley relapsed into silence, and Mrs. Slade, leaning above her, was conscious of a strange sense of isolation, of being cut off from the warm current of human communion. 'You think me a monster!'

'I don't know. . . . It was the only letter I had, and you say he didn't write it?'

'Ah, how you care for him still!'

'I cared for that memory,' said Mrs. Ansley.

Mrs. Slade continued to look down on her. She seemed physically reduced by the blow—as if, when she got up, the wind might scatter her like a puff of dust. Mrs. Slade's jealousy suddenly leapt up again at the sight. All these years the woman had been living on that letter. How she must have loved him, to treasure the mere memory of its ashes! The letter of the man her friend was engaged to. Wasn't it she who was the monster?

'You tried your best to get him away from me, didn't you? But you failed; and I kept him. That's all.'

'Yes. That's all.'

'I wish now I hadn't told you. I'd no idea you'd feel about it as you do; I thought you'd be amused. It all happened so long ago, as you say; and you must do me the justice to remember that I had no reason to think you'd ever taken it seriously. How could I, when you were married to Horace Ansley two months afterward? As soon as you could get out of bed your mother rushed you off to Florence and married you. People were rather surprised—they wondered at its being done so quickly; but I thought I knew. I had an idea you did it out of *pique*—to be able to say you'd got ahead of Delphin and me. Girls have such silly reasons for doing the most serious things. And your marrying so soon convinced me that you'd never really cared.'

'Yes. I suppose it would,' Mrs. Ansley assented.

The clear heaven overhead was emptied of all its gold. Dusk spread over it, abruptly darkening the Seven Hills. Here and there lights began to twinkle through the foliage at their feet. Steps were coming and going on the deserted terrace—waiters looking out of the doorway at the head of the stairs, then reappearing with trays and napkins and flasks of wine. Tables were moved, chairs straightened. A feeble string of electric lights flickered out. Some vases of faded flowers were carried away, and brought back replenished. A stout lady in a dust-coat suddenly appeared, asking in broken Italian if any one had seen the elastic band which held together her tattered Baedeker. She poked with her stick under the table at which she had lunched, the waiters assisting.

The corner where Mrs. Slade and Mrs. Ansley sat was still shadowy and deserted. For a long time neither of them spoke. At length Mrs. Slade began again: 'I suppose I did it as a sort of joke—'

'A joke?'

'Well, girls are ferocious sometimes, you know. Girls in love especially. And I remember laughing to myself all that evening at the idea that you were waiting around

there in the dark, dodging out of sight, listening for every
sound, trying to get in—. Of course I was upset when
I heard you were so ill afterward.'

Mrs. Ansley had not moved for a long time. But now
she turned slowly toward her companion. 'But I didn't
wait. He'd arranged everything. He was there. We were
let in at once,' she said.

Mrs. Slade sprang up from her leaning position.
'Delphin there? They let you in?—Ah, now you're
lying!' she burst out with violence.

Mrs. Ansley's voice grew clearer, and full of surprise.
'But of course he was there. Naturally he came—'

'Came? How did he know he'd find you there? You
must be raving!'

Mrs. Ansley hesitated, as though reflecting. 'But I
answered the letter. I told him I'd be there. So he came.'

Mrs. Slade flung her hands up to her face. 'Oh, God—
you answered! I never thought of your answering. . . .'

'It's odd you never thought of it, if you wrote the
letter.'

'Yes. I was blind with rage.'

Mrs. Ansley rose, and drew her fur scarf about her.
'It is cold here. We'd better go. . . . I'm sorry for you,'
she said, as she clasped the fur about her throat.

The unexpected words sent a pang through Mrs.
Slade. 'Yes; we'd better go.' She gathered up her bag and
cloak. 'I don't know why you should be sorry for me,'
she muttered.

Mrs. Ansley stood looking away from her toward the
dusky secret mass of the Colosseum. 'Well—because I
didn't have to wait that night.'

Mrs. Slade gave an unquiet laugh. 'Yes; I was beaten
there. But I oughtn't to begrudge it to you, I suppose.
At the end of all these years. After all, I had everything;

I had him for twenty-five years. And you had nothing but that one letter that he didn't write.'

Mrs. Ansley was again silent. At length she turned toward the door of the terrace. She took a step, and turned back, facing her companion.

'I had Barbara,' she said, and began to move ahead of Mrs. Slade toward the stairway.

The Open Boat

STEPHEN CRANE

(1871–1900)

A Tale intended to be after the fact: being the experience of four men from the sunk steamer 'Commodore'

I

NONE of them knew the colour of the sky. Their eyes glanced level, and were fastened upon the waves that swept toward them. These waves were of the hue of slate, save for the tops, which were of foaming white, and all of the men knew the colours of the sea. The horizon narrowed and widened, and dipped and rose, and at all times its edge was jagged with waves that seemed thrust up in points like rocks.

Many a man ought to have a bathtub larger than the boat which here rode upon the sea. These waves were most wrongfully and barbarously abrupt and tall, and each froth-top was a problem in small-boat navigation.

The cook squatted in the bottom, and looked with both eyes at the six inches of gunwale which separated him from the ocean. His sleeves were rolled over his fat forearms, and the two flaps of his unbuttoned vest dangled as he bent to bail out the boat. Often he said, 'Gawd! that was a narrow clip.' As he remarked it he invariably gazed eastward over the broken sea.

The oiler, steering with one of the two oars in the boat, sometimes raised himself suddenly to keep clear of water that swirled in over the stern. It was a thin little oar, and it seemed often ready to snap.

The correspondent, pulling at the other oar, watched the waves and wondered why he was there.

The injured captain, lying in the bow, was at this time buried in that profound dejection and indifference which comes, temporarily at least, to even the bravest and most enduring when, willy-nilly, the firm fails, the army loses, the ship goes down. The mind of the master of a vessel is rooted deep in the timbers of her, though he command for a day or a decade; and this captain had on him the stern impression of a scene in the greys of dawn of seven turned faces, and later a stump of a topmast with a white ball on it, that slashed to and fro at the waves, went low and lower, and down. Thereafter there was something strange in his voice. Although steady, it was deep with mourning, and of a quality beyond oration or tears.

'Keep 'er a little more south, Billie,' said he.

'A little more south, sir,' said the oiler in the stern.

A seat in his boat was not unlike a seat upon a bucking broncho, and by the same token a broncho is not much smaller. The craft pranced and reared and plunged like an animal. As each wave came, and she rose for it, she seemed like a horse making at a fence outrageously high. The manner of her scramble over these walls of water is a mystic thing, and, moreover, at the top of them were ordinarily these problems in white water, the foam racing down from the summit of each wave requiring a new leap, and a leap from the air. Then, after scornfully bumping a crest she would slide and race and splash down a long incline, and arrive bobbing and nodding in front of the next menace.

A singular disadvantage of the sea lies in the fact that after successfully surmounting one wave you discover that there is another behind it just as important and just as nervously anxious to do something effective in the way of swamping boats. In a ten-foot dinghy one can get an idea of the resources of the sea in the line of waves that is not probable to the average experience which is never at sea in a dinghy. As each slaty wall of water approached, it shut all else from the view of the men in the boat, and it was not difficult to imagine that this particular wave was the final outburst of the ocean, the last effort of the grim water. There was a terrible grace in the move of the waves, and they came in silence, save for the snarling of the crests.

In the wan light the faces of the men must have been grey. Their eyes must have glinted in strange ways as they gazed steadily astern. Viewed from a balcony, the whole thing would doubtless have been weirdly pictur-esque. But the men in the boat had no time to see it, and if they had had leisure, there were other things to occupy their minds. The sun swung steadily up the sky, and they knew it was broad day because the colour of the sea changed from slate to emerald green streaked with amber lights, and the foam was like tumbling snow. The process of the breaking day was unknown to them. They were aware only of this effect upon the colour of the waves that rolled toward them.

In disjointed sentences the cook and the correspondent argued as to the difference between a life-saving station and a house of refuge. The cook had said: 'There's a house of refuge just north of the Mosquito Inlet Light, and as soon as they see us they'll come off in their boat and pick us up.'

'As soon as who see us?' said the correspondent.

'The crew,' said the cook.

'Houses of refuge don't have crews,' said the correspondent. 'As I understand them, they are only places where clothes and grub are stored for the benefit of shipwrecked people. They don't carry crews.'

'Oh, yes, they do,' said the cook.

'No, they don't,' said the correspondent.

'Well, we're not there yet, anyhow,' said the oiler, in the stern.

'Well,' said the cook, 'perhaps it's not a house of refuge that I'm thinking of as being near Mosquito Inlet Light; perhaps it's a life-saving station.'

'We're not there yet,' said the oiler in the stern.

II

As the boat bounced from the top of each wave the wind tore through the hair of the hatless men, and as the craft plopped her stern down again the spray slashed past them. The crest of each of these waves was a hill, from the top of which the men surveyed for a moment a broad tumultuous expanse, shining and wind-riven. It was probably splendid, it was probably glorious, this play of the free sea, wild with lights of emerald and white and amber.

'Bully good thing it's an on-shore wind,' said the cook. 'If not, where would we be? Wouldn't have a show.'

'That's right,' said the correspondent.

The busy oiler nodded his assent.

Then the captain, in the bow, chuckled in a way that

expressed humour, contempt, tragedy, all in one. 'Do you think we've got much of a show now, boys?' said he.

Whereupon the three were silent, save for a trifle of hemming and hawing. To express any particular optimism at this time they felt to be childish and stupid, but they all doubtless possessed this sense of the situation in their minds. A young man thinks doggedly at such times. On the other hand, the ethics of their condition was decidedly against any open suggestion of hopelessness. So they were silent.

'Oh, well,' said the captain, soothing his children, 'we'll get ashore all right.'

But there was that in his tone which made them think; so the oiler quoth, 'Yes! if this wind holds.'

The cook was bailing. 'Yes! if we don't catch hell in the surf.'

Canton-flannel gulls flew near and far. Sometimes they sat down on the sea, near patches of brown seaweed that rolled over the waves with a movement like carpets on a line in a gale. The birds sat comfortably in groups, and they were envied by some in the dinghy, for the wrath of the sea was no more to them than it was to a covey of prairie chickens a thousand miles inland. Often they came very close and stared at the men with black bead-like eyes. At these times they were uncanny and sinister in their unblinking scrutiny, and the men hooted angrily at them, telling them to be gone. One came, and evidently decided to alight on the top of the captain's head. The bird flew parallel to the boat and did not circle, but made short sidelong jumps in the air in chicken-fashion. His black eyes were wistfully fixed upon the captain's head. 'Ugly brute,' said the oiler to the bird. 'You look as if you were made with a jackknife.' The cook and the correspondent swore darkly at the creature. The captain naturally wished to knock it away with the end of the heavy painter, but he did not dare do it, because anything resembling an emphatic gesture would have capsized this freighted boat; and so, with his open hand, the captain gently and carefully waved the gull away. After it had been discouraged from the pursuit the captain breathed easier on account of his hair, and others breathed easier because the bird struck their minds at this time as being somehow gruesome and ominous.

In the meantime the oiler and the correspondent rowed. And also they rowed. They sat together in the same seat, and each rowed an oar. Then the oiler took both oars; then the correspondent took both oars; then the oiler; then the correspondent. They rowed and they rowed. The very ticklish part of the business was when the time came for the reclining one in the stern to take his turn at the oars. By the very last star of truth, it is easier to steal eggs from under a hen than it was to change seats in the dinghy. First the man in the stern slid his hand along the thwart and moved with care, as if he were of Sèvres. Then the man in the rowing-seat slid his hand along the other thwart. It was all done with the most extraordinary care. As the two sidled past each other, the whole party kept watchful eyes on the coming wave, and the captain cried: 'Look out, now! Steady, there!'

The brown mats of seaweed that appeared from time to time were like islands, bits of earth. They were travelling, apparently, neither one way nor the other. They were, to all intents, stationary. They informed the men in the boat that it was making progress slowly toward the land.

The captain, rearing cautiously in the bow after the dinghy soared on a great swell, said that he had seen the

lighthouse at Mosquito Inlet. Presently the cook remarked that he had seen it. The correspondent was at
the oars then, and for some reason he too wished to look
at the lighthouse but his back was toward the far shore,
and the waves were important, and for some time he
could not seize an opportunity to turn his head. But at
last there came a wave more gentle than the others, and
when at the crest of it he swiftly scoured the western
horizon.

'See it?' said the captain.

'No,' said the correspondent, slowly; 'I didn't see
anything.'

'Look again,' said the captain. He pointed. 'It's
exactly in that direction.'

At the top of another wave the correspondent did as
he was bid, and this time his eyes chanced on a small, still
thing on the edge of the swaying horizon. It was precisely like the point of a pin. It took an anxious eye to
find a lighthouse so tiny.

'Think we'll make it, Captain?'

'If this wind holds and the boat don't swamp, we can't
do much else,' said the captain.

The little boat, lifted by each towering sea and
splashed viciously by the crests, made progress that in
the absence of seaweed was not apparent to those in her.
She seemed just a wee thing wallowing, miraculously top
up, at the mercy of five oceans. Occasionally a great
spread of water, like white flames, swarmed into her.

'Bail her, cook,' said the captain, serenely.

'All right, Captain,' said the cheerful cook.

III

It would be difficult to describe the subtle brotherhood of men that was here established on the seas. No one said that it was so. No one mentioned it. But it dwelt in the boat, and each man felt it warm him. They were a captain, an oiler, a cook, and a correspondent, and they were friends—friends in a more curiously iron-bound degree than may be common. The hurt captain, lying against the water-jar in the bow, spoke always in a low voice and calmly; but he could never command a more ready and swiftly obedient crew than the motley three of the dinghy. It was more than a mere recognition of what was best for the common safety. There was surely in it a quality that was personal and heart-felt. And after this devotion to the commander of the boat, there was this comradeship, that the correspondent, for instance, who had been taught to be cynical of men, knew even at the time was the best experience of his life. But no one said that it was so. No one mentioned it.

'I wish we had a sail,' remarked the captain. 'We might try my overcoat on the end of an oar, and give you two boys a chance to rest.' So the cook and the correspondent held the mast and spread wide the overcoat; the oiler steered; and the little boat made good way with her new rig. Sometimes the oiler had to scull sharply to keep a sea from breaking into the boat, but otherwise sailing was a success.

Meanwhile the lighthouse had been growing slowly larger. It had now almost assumed colour, and appeared like a little grey shadow on the sky. The man at the oars could not be prevented from turning his head rather often to try for a glimpse of this little grey shadow.

At last, from the top of each wave, the men in the tossing boat could see land. Even as the lighthouse was an upright shadow on the sky, this land seemed but a long black shadow on the sea. It certainly was thinner than paper. 'We must be about opposite New Smyrna,' said the cook, who had coasted this shore often in schooners. 'Captain, by the way, I believe they abandoned that life-saving station there about a year ago.'

'Did they?' said the captain.

The wind slowly died away. The cook and the correspondent were not now obliged to slave in order to hold high the oar. But the waves continued their old impetuous swooping at the dinghy, and the little craft, no longer under way, struggled woundily over them. The oiler or the correspondent took the oars again.

Shipwrecks are apropos of nothing. If men could only train for them and have them occur when the men had reached pink condition, there would be less drowning at sea. Of the four in the dinghy none had slept any time worth mentioning for two days and two nights previous to embarking in the dinghy, and in the excitement of clambering about the deck of a foundering ship they had also forgotten to eat heartily.

For these reasons, and for others, neither the oiler nor the correspondent was fond of rowing at this time. The correspondent wondered ingenuously how in the name of all that was sane could there be people who thought it amusing to row a boat. It was not an amusement; it was a diabolical punishment, and even a genius of mental aberrations could never conclude that it was anything but a horror to the muscles and a crime against the back. He mentioned to the boat in general how the amusement of rowing struck him, and the weary-faced oiler smiled in full sympathy. Previously to the foundering, by the way, the oiler had worked a double watch in the engine-room of the ship.

'Take her easy now, boys,' said the captain. 'Don't spend yourselves. If we have to run a surf you'll need all your strength, because we'll sure have to swim for it. Take your time.'

Slowly the land arose from the sea. From a black line it became a line of black and a line of white—trees and sand. Finally the captain said that he could make out a house on the shore. 'That's the house of refuge, sure,' said the cook. 'They'll see us before long, and come out after us.'

The distant lighthouse reared high. 'The keeper ought to be able to make us out now, if he's looking through a glass,' said the captain. 'He'll notify the life-saving people.'

'None of those other boats could have got ashore to give word of this wreck,' said the oiler, in a low voice, 'else the life-boat would be out hunting us.'

Slowly and beautifully the land loomed out of the sea. The wind came again. It had veered from the north-east to the south-east. Finally a new sound struck the ears of the men in the boat. It was the low thunder of the surf on the shore. 'We'll never be able to make the lighthouse now,' said the captain. 'Swing her head a little more north, Billie.'

'A little more north, sir,' said the oiler.

Whereupon the little boat turned her nose once more down the wind, and all but the oarsman watched the shore grow. Under the influence of this expansion doubt and direful apprehension were leaving the minds of the men. The management of the boat was still most absorbing, but it could not prevent a quiet cheerfulness. In an hour, perhaps, they would be ashore.

Their backbones had become thoroughly used to balancing in the boat, and they now rode this wild colt of a dinghy like circus men. The correspondent thought that he had been drenched to the skin, but happening to feel in the top pocket of his coat, he found therein eight cigars. Four of them were soaked with sea-water; four were perfectly scatheless. After a search, somebody produced three dry matches; and thereupon the four waifs rode impudently in their little boat and, with an assurance of an impending rescue shining in their eyes, puffed at the big cigars, and judged well and ill of all men. Everybody took a drink of water.

IV

'Cook,' remarked the captain, 'there don't seem to be any signs of life about your house of refuge.'

'No,' replied the cook. 'Funny they don't see us!'

A broad stretch of lowly coast lay before the eyes of the men. It was of low dunes topped with dark vegetation. The roar of the surf was plain, and sometimes they could see the white lip of a wave as it spun up the beach. A tiny house was blocked out black upon the sky. Southward, the slim lighthouse lifted its little grey length.

Tide, wind, and waves were swinging the dinghy northward. 'Funny they don't see us,' said the men.

The surf's roar was here dulled, but its tone was nevertheless thunderous and mighty. As the boat swam over the great rollers the men sat listening to this roar. 'We'll swamp sure,' said everybody.

It is fair to say here that there was not a life-saving station within twenty miles in either direction; but the men did not know this fact, and in consequence they made dark and opprobrious remarks concerning the eyesight of the nation's life-savers. Four scowling men sat in the dinghy and surpassed records in the invention of epithets.

'Funny they don't see us.'

The light-heartedness of a former time had completely faded. To their sharpened minds it was easy to conjure pictures of all kinds of incompetency and blindness and, indeed, cowardice. There was the shore of the populous land, and it was bitter and bitter to them that from it came no sign.

'Well,' said the captain, ultimately, 'I suppose we'll have to make a try for ourselves. If we stay out here too long, we'll none of us have strength left to swim after the boat swamps.'

And so the oiler, who was at the oars, turned the boat straight for the shore. There was a sudden tightening of muscles. There was some thinking.

'If we don't all get ashore,' said the captain—'if we don't all get ashore, I suppose you fellows know where to send news of my finish?'

They then briefly exchanged some addresses and admonitions. As for the reflections of the men, there was a great deal of rage in them. Perchance they might be formulated thus: 'If I am going to be drowned—if I am going to be drowned—if I am going to be drowned, why, in the name of the seven mad gods who rule the sea, was I allowed to come thus far and contemplate sand and trees? Was I brought here merely to have my nose dragged away as I was about to nibble the sacred cheese of life? It is preposterous. If this old ninny-woman, Fate, cannot do better than this, she should be deprived of the management of men's fortunes. She is an old hen who knows not her intention. If she has decided to drown me, why did she not do it in the beginning and save me all this trouble? The whole affair is absurd.—But no; she cannot mean to drown me. She dare not drown me. She cannot drown me. Not after all this work.' Afterward the man might have had an impulse to shake his fist at the clouds. 'Just you drown me, now, and then hear what I call you!'

The billows that came at this time were more formidable. They seemed always just about to break and roll over the little boat in a turmoil of foam. There was a preparatory and long growl in the speech of them. No mind unused to the sea would have concluded that the dinghy could ascend these sheer heights in time. The shore was still afar. The oiler was a wily surfman. 'Boys,' he said swiftly, 'she won't live three minutes more, and we're too far out to swim. Shall I take her to sea again, Captain?'

'Yes; go ahead!' said the captain.

This oiler, by a series of quick miracles and fast and steady oarsmanship, turned the boat in the middle of the surf and took her safely to sea again.

There was a considerable silence as the boat bumped over the furrowed sea to deeper water. Then somebody in gloom spoke: 'Well, anyhow, they must have seen us from the shore by now.'

The gulls went in slanting flight up the wind toward the grey, desolate east. A squall, marked by dingy clouds and clouds brick-red like smoke from a burning building, appeared from the south-east.

'What do you think of those life-saving people? Ain't they peaches?'

'Funny they haven't seen us.'

'Maybe they think we're out here for sport! Maybe they think we're fishin'. Maybe they think we're damned fools.'

It was a long afternoon. A changed tide tried to force them southward, but wind and wave said northward. Far ahead, where coast-line, sea, and sky formed their mighty angle, there were little dots which seemed to indicate a city on the shore.

'St. Augustine?'

The captain shook his head. 'Too near Mosquito Inlet.'

And the oiler rowed, and then the correspondent rowed; then the oiler rowed. It was a weary business. The human back can become the seat of more aches and pains than are registered in books for the composite anatomy of a regiment. It is a limited area, but it can become the theatre of innumerable muscular conflicts, tangles, wrenches, knots, and other comforts.

'Did you ever like to row, Billie?' asked the correspondent.

'No,' said the oiler; 'hang it!'

When one exchanged the rowing-seat for a place in the bottom of the boat, he suffered a bodily depression that caused him to be careless of everything save an obligation to wiggle one finger. There was cold sea-water swashing to and fro in the boat, and he lay in it. His head, pillowed on a thwart, was within an inch of the swirl of a wave-crest, and sometimes a particularly obstreperous sea came inboard and drenched him once more. But these matters did not annoy him. It is almost certain that if the boat had capsized he would have tumbled comfortably out upon the ocean as if he felt sure that it was a great soft mattress.

'Look! There's a man on the shore!'

'Where?'

'There! See 'im?' See 'im?'

'Yes, sure! He's walking along.'

'Now he's stopped. Look! He's facing us!'

'He's waving at us!'

'So he is! By thunder!'

'Ah, now we're all right! Now we're all right! There'll be a boat out here for us in half an hour.'

'He's going on. He's running. He's going up to that house there.'

The remote beach seemed lower than the sea, and it required a searching glance to discern the little black figure. The captain saw a floating stick, and they rowed to it. A bath towel was by some weird chance in the boat, and, tying this on the stick, the captain waved it. The oarsman did not dare turn his head, so he was obliged to ask questions.

'What's he doing now?'

'He's standing still again. He's looking, I think.— There he goes again—toward the house.—Now he's stopped again.'

'Is he waving at us?'

'No, not now; he was, though.'

'Look! There comes another man!'

'He's running.'

'Look at him go, would you!'

'Why, he's on a bicycle. Now he's met the other man. They're both waving at us. Look!'

'There comes something up the beach.'

'What the devil is that thing?'

'Why, it looks like a boat.'

'Why, certainly, it's a boat.'

'No; it's on wheels.'

'Yes, so it is. Well, that must be the life-boat. They drag them along shore on a wagon.'

'That's the life-boat, sure.'

'No, by God, it's—it's an omnibus.'

'I tell you it's a life-boat.'

'It is not! It's an omnibus. I can see it plain. See? One of these big hotel omnibuses.'

'By thunder, you're right. It's an omnibus, sure as fate. What do you suppose they are doing with an omnibus? Maybe they are going around collecting the life-crew, hey?'

'That's it, likely. Look! There's a fellow waving a little black flag. He's standing on the steps of the omnibus. There come those other two fellows. Now they're all talking together. Look at the fellow with the flag. Maybe he ain't waving it!'

'That ain't a flag, is it? That's his coat. Why, certainly, that's his coat.'

'So it is; it's his coat. He's taken it off and is waving it around his head. But would you look at him swing it!'

'Oh, say, there isn't any life-saving station there. That's just a winter-resort hotel omnibus that has brought over some of the boarders to see us drown.'

'What's that idiot with the coat mean? What's he signalling, anyhow?'

'It looks as if he were trying to tell us to go north. There must be a life-saving station up there.'

'No; he thinks we're fishing. Just giving us a merry hand. See? Ah, there, Willie!'

'Well, I wish I could make something out of those signals. What do you suppose he means?'

'He don't mean anything; he's just playing.'

'Well, if he'd just signal us to try the surf again, or to go to sea and wait, or go north, or go south, or go to hell, there would be some reason in it. But look at him! He just stands there and keeps his coat revolving like a wheel. The ass!'

'There come more people.'

'Now there's quite a mob. Look! Isn't that a boat?'

'Where? Oh, I see where you mean. No, that's no boat.'

'That fellow is still waving his coat.'

'He must think we like to see him do that. Why don't he quit it? It don't mean anything.'

'I don't know. I think he is trying to make us go north. It must be that there's a life-saving station there somewhere.'

'Say, he ain't tired yet. Look at 'im wave!'

'Wonder how long he can keep that up. He's been revolving his coat ever since he caught sight of us. He's an idiot. Why aren't they getting men to bring a boat out? A fishing-boat—one of those big yawls—could come out here all right. Why don't he do something?'

'Oh, it's all right now.'

'They'll have a boat out here for us in less than no time, now that they've seen us.'

A faint yellow tone came into the sky over the low land. The shadows on the sea slowly deepened. The wind bore coldness with it, and the men began to shiver.

'Holy smoke!' said one, allowing his voice to express his impious mood, 'if we keep on monkeying out here! If we've got to flounder out here all night!'

'Oh, we'll never have to stay here all night! Don't you worry. They've seen us now, and it won't be long before they'll come chasing out after us.'

The shore grew dusky. The man waving a coat blended gradually into this gloom, and it swallowed in the same manner the omnibus and the group of people. The spray, when it dashed uproariously over the side, made the voyagers shrink and swear like men who were being branded.

'I'd like to catch the chump who waved the coat. I feel like socking him one, just for luck.'

'Why? What did he do?'

'Oh, nothing, but then he seemed so damned cheerful.'

In the meantime the oiler rowed, and then the correspondent rowed, and then the oiler rowed. Grey-faced and bowed forward, they mechanically, turn by turn, plied the leaden oars. The form of the lighthouse had vanished from the southern horizon, but finally a pale star appeared, just lifting from the sea. The streaked saffron in the west passed before the all-merging darkness, and the sea to the east was black. The land had vanished, and was expressed only by the low and drear thunder of the surf.

'If I am going to be drowned—if I am going to be drowned—if I am going to be drowned, why, in the name of the seven mad gods who rule the sea, was I allowed to come thus far and contemplate sand and trees? Was I brought here merely to have my nose dragged away as I was about to nibble the sacred cheese of life?'

The patient captain, drooped over the water-jar, was sometimes obliged to speak to the oarsman.

'Keep her head up! Keep her head up!'

'Keep her head up, sir.' The voices were weary and low.

This was surely a quiet evening. All save the oarsman lay heavily and listlessly in the boat's bottom. As for him, his eyes were just capable of noting the tall black waves that swept forward in a most sinister silence, save for an occasional subdued growl of a crest.

The cook's head was on a thwart, and he looked without interest at the water under his nose. He was deep in other scenes. Finally he spoke. 'Billie,' he murmured, dreamfully, 'what kind of pie do you like best?'

V

'Pie!' said the oiler and the correspondent, agitatedly.
'Don't talk about those things, blast you!'

'Well,' said the cook, 'I was just thinking about ham
sandwiches and—'

A night on the sea in an open boat is a long night. As
darkness settled finally, the shine of the light, lifting
from the sea in the south, changed to full gold. On the
northern horizon a new light appeared, a small bluish
gleam on the edge of the waters. These two lights were
the furniture of the world. Otherwise there was nothing
but waves.

Two men huddled in the stern, and distances were so
magnificent in the dinghy that the rower was enabled to
keep his feet partly warm by thrusting them under his
companions. Their legs indeed extended far under the
rowing-seat until they touched the feet of the captain
forward. Sometimes, despite the efforts of the tired oarsman, a wave came piling into the boat, an icy wave of the
night, and the chilling water soaked them anew. They
would twist their bodies for a moment and groan, and
sleep the dead sleep once more, while the water in the
boat gurgled about them as the craft rocked.

The plan of the oiler and the correspondent was for
one to row until he lost the ability, and then arouse the
other from his sea-water couch in the bottom of the boat.

The oiler plied the oars until his head drooped forward
and the overpowering sleep blinded him; and he rowed
yet afterward. Then he touched a man in the bottom of
the boat, and called his name. 'Will you spell me for a
little while?' he said, meekly.

'Sure, Billie,' said the correspondent, awaking and

dragging himself to a sitting position. They exchanged places carefully, and the oiler, cuddling down in the sea-water at the cook's side, seemed to go to sleep instantly.

The particular violence of the sea had ceased. The waves came without snarling. The obligation of the man at the oars was to keep the boat headed so that the tilt of the rollers would not capsize her, and to preserve her from filling when the crests rushed past. The black waves were silent and hard to be seen in the darkness. Often one was almost upon the boat before the oarsman was aware.

In a low voice the correspondent addressed the captain. He was not sure that the captain was awake, although this iron man seemed to be always awake. 'Captain, shall I keep her making for that light north, sir?'

The same steady voice answered him. 'Yes. Keep it about two points off the port bow.'

The cook had tied a life-belt around himself in order to get even the warmth which this clumsy cork contrivance could donate, and he seemed almost stove-like when a rower, whose teeth invariably chattered wildly as soon as he ceased his labour, dropped down to sleep.

The correspondent, as he rowed, looked down at the two men sleeping underfoot. The cook's arm was around the oiler's shoulders, and, with their fragmentary clothing and haggard faces, they were the babes of the sea—a grotesque rendering of the old babes in the wood.

Later he must have grown stupid at his work, for suddenly there was a growling of water, and a crest came with a roar and a swash into the boat, and it was a wonder that it did not set the cook afloat in his life-belt. The cook continued to sleep, but the oiler sat up, blinking his eyes and shaking with the new cold.

'Oh, I'm awfully sorry, Billie,' said the correspondent, contritely.

'That's all right, old boy,' said the oiler, and lay down again and was asleep.

Presently it seemed that even the captain dozed, and the correspondent thought that he was the one man afloat on all the oceans. The wind had a voice as it came over the waves, and it was sadder than the end.

There was a long, loud swishing astern of the boat, and a gleaming trail of phosphorescence, like blue flame, was furrowed on the black waters. It might have been made by a monstrous knife.

Then there came a stillness, while the correspondent breathed with open mouth and looked at the sea.

Suddenly there was another swish and another long flash of bluish light, and this time it was alongside the boat, and might almost have been reached with an oar. The correspondent saw an enormous fin speed like a shadow through the water, hurling the crystalline spray and leaving the long glowing trail.

The correspondent looked over his shoulder at the captain. His face was hidden, and he seemed to be asleep. He looked at the babes of the sea. They certainly were asleep. So, being bereft of sympathy, he leaned a little way to one side and swore softly into the sea.

But the thing did not then leave the vicinity of the boat. Ahead or astern, on one side or the other, at intervals long or short, fled the long sparkling streak, and there was to be heard the *whirroo* of the dark fin. The speed and power of the thing was greatly to be admired. It cut the water like a gigantic and keen projectile.

The presence of this biding thing did not affect the man with the same horror that it would if he had been a picnicker. He simply looked at the sea dully and swore in an undertone.

Nevertheless, it is true that he did not wish to be alone

with the thing. He wished one of his companions to awake by chance and keep him company with it. But the captain hung motionless over the water-jar, and the oiler and the cook in the bottom of the boat were plunged in slumber.

VI

'If I am going to be drowned—if I am going to be drowned—if I am going to be drowned, why, in the name of the seven mad gods who rule the sea, was I allowed to come thus far and contemplate sand and trees?'

During this dismal night, it may be remarked that a man would conclude that it was really the intention of the seven mad gods to drown him, despite the abominable injustice of it. For it was certainly an abominable injustice to drown a man who had worked so hard, so hard. The man felt it would be a crime most unnatural. Other people had drowned at sea since galleys swarmed with painted sails, but still—

When it occurs to a man that nature does not regard him as important, and that she feels she would not maim the universe by disposing of him, he at first wishes to throw bricks at the temple, and he hates deeply the fact that there are no bricks and no temples. Any visible expression of nature would surely be pelleted with his jeers.

Then, if there be no tangible thing to hoot, he feels, perhaps, the desire to confront a personification and indulge in pleas, bowed to one knee, and with hands supplicant, saying, 'Yes, but I love myself.'

A high cold star on a winter's night is the word he feels that she says to him. Thereafter he knows the pathos of his situation.

The men in the dinghy had not discussed these matters, but each had, no doubt, reflected upon them in silence and according to his mind. There was seldom any expression upon their faces save the general one of complete weariness. Speech was devoted to the business of the boat.

To chime the notes of his emotion, a verse mysteriously entered the correspondent's head. He had even forgotten that he had forgotten this verse, but it suddenly was in his mind.

A soldier of the Legion lay dying in Algiers;
There was lack of woman's nursing, there was dearth of
*   woman's tears;*
But a comrade stood beside him, and he took that comrade's
*   hand,*
And he said, 'I never more shall see my own, my native
*   land.'*

In his childhood the correspondent had been made acquainted with the fact that a soldier of the Legion lay dying in Algiers, but he had never regarded the fact as important. Myriads of his school-fellows had informed him of the soldier's plight, but the dinning had naturally ended by making him perfectly indifferent. He had never considered it his affair that a soldier of the Legion lay dying in Algiers, nor had it appeared to him as a matter for sorrow. It was less to him than the breaking of a pencil's point.

Now, however, it quaintly came to him as a human, living thing. It was no longer merely a picture of a few throes in the breast of a poet, meanwhile drinking tea and warming his feet at the grate; it was an actuality — stern, mournful, and fine.

The correspondent plainly saw the soldier. He lay

on the sand with his feet out straight and still. While his pale left hand was upon his chest in an attempt to thwart the going of his life, the blood came between his fingers. In the far Algerian distance, a city of low square forms was set against a sky that was faint with the last sunset hues. The correspondent, plying the oars and dreaming of the slow and slower movements of the lips of the soldier, was moved by a profound and perfectly impersonal comprehension. He was sorry for the soldier of the Legion who lay dying in Algiers.

The thing which had followed the boat and waited had evidently grown bored at the delay. There was no longer to be heard the slash of the cutwater, and there was no longer the flame of the long trail. The light in the north still glimmered, but it was apparently no nearer to the boat. Sometimes the boom of the surf rang in the correspondent's ears, and he turned the craft seaward then and rowed harder. Southward, some one had evidently built a watch-fire on the beach. It was too low and too far to be seen, but it made a shimmering, roseate reflection upon the bluff in back of it, and this could be discerned from the boat. The wind came stronger, and sometimes a wave suddenly raged out like a mountain cat, and there was to be seen the sheen and sparkle of a broken crest.

The captain, in the bow, moved on his water-jar and sat erect. 'Pretty long night,' he observed to the correspondent. He looked at the shore. 'Those life-saving people take their time.'

'Did you see that shark playing around?'

'Yes, I saw him. He was a big fellow, all right.'

'Wish I had known you were awake.'

Later the correspondent spoke into the bottom of the boat. 'Billie!' There was a slow and gradual disentanglement. 'Billie, will you spell me?'

'Sure,' said the oiler.

As soon as the correspondent touched the cold, comfortable sea-water in the bottom of the boat and had huddled close to the cook's life-belt he was deep in sleep, despite the fact that his teeth played all the popular airs. This sleep was so good to him that it was but a moment before he heard a voice call his name in a tone that demonstrated the last stages of exhaustion. 'Will you spell me?'

'Sure, Billie.'

The light in the north had mysteriously vanished, but the correspondent took his course from the wide-awake captain.

Later in the night they took the boat farther out to sea, and the captain directed the cook to take one oar at the stern and keep the boat facing the seas. He was to call out if he should hear the thunder of the surf. This plan enabled the oiler and the correspondent to get respite together. 'We'll give those boys a chance to get into shape again,' said the captain. They curled down and, after a few preliminary chatterings and trembles, slept once more the dead sleep. Neither knew they had bequeathed to the cook, the company of another shark, or perhaps the same shark.

As the boat caroused on the waves, spray occasionally bumped over the side and gave them a fresh soaking, but this had no power to break their repose. The ominous slash of the wind and the water affected them as it would have affected mummies.

'Boys,' said the cook, with the notes of every reluctance in his voice, 'she's drifted in pretty close. I guess one of you had better take her to sea again.' The correspondent, aroused, heard the crash of the toppled crests.

As he was rowing, the captain gave him some

whisky-and-water, and this steadied the chills out of him. 'If I ever get ashore and anybody shows me even a photograph of an oar—'

At last there was a short conversation.

'Billie!—Billie, will you spell me?'

'Sure,' said the oiler.

VII

When the correspondent again opened his eyes, the sea and the sky were each of the grey hue of the dawning. Later, carmine and gold was painted upon the waters. The morning appeared finally, in its splendour, with a sky of pure blue, and the sunlight flamed on the tips of the waves.

On the distant dunes were set many little black cottages, and a tall white windmill reared above them. No man, nor dog, nor bicycle appeared on the beach. The cottages might have formed a deserted village.

The voyagers scanned the shore. A conference was held in the boat. 'Well,' said the captain, 'if no help is coming, we might better try a run through the surf right away. If we stay out here much longer we will be too weak to do anything for ourselves at all.' The others silently acquiesced in this reasoning. The boat was headed for the beach. The correspondent wondered if none ever ascended the tall wind-tower, and if then they never looked seaward. This tower was a giant, standing with its back to the plight of the ants. It represented in a degree, to the correspondent, the serenity of nature amid the struggles of the individual—nature in the wind, and nature in the vision of men. She did not seem cruel to him then, nor beneficent, nor treacherous, nor wise. But she was indifferent, flatly indifferent. It is, perhaps,

plausible that a man in this situation, impressed with the
unconcern of the universe, should see the innumerable
flaws of his life, and have them taste wickedly in his
mind, and wish for another chance. A distinction between
right and wrong seems absurdly clear to him, then, in
this new ignorance of the grave-edge, and he understands
that if he were given another opportunity he would mend
his conduct and his words, and be better and brighter
during an introduction or at a tea.

'Now, boys,' said the captain, 'she is going to swamp
sure. All we can do is to work her in as far as possible, and
then when she swamps, pile out and scramble for the
beach. Keep cool now, and don't jump until she swamps
sure.'

The oiler took the oars. Over his shoulders he scanned
the surf. 'Captain,' he said, 'I think I'd better bring her
about and keep her head-on to the seas and back her in.'

'All right, Billie,' said the captain. 'Back her in.' The
oiler swung the boat then, and, seated in the stern, the
cook and the correspondent were obliged to look over
their shoulders to contemplate the lonely and indifferent
shore.

The monstrous inshore rollers heaved the boat high
until the men were again enabled to see the white sheets
of water scudding up the slanted beach. 'We won't get
in very close,' said the captain. Each time a man could
wrest his attention from the rollers, he turned his glance
toward the shore, and in the expression of the eyes during
this contemplation there was a singular quality. The
correspondent, observing the others, knew that they
were not afraid, but the full meaning of their glances was
shrouded.

As for himself, he was too tired to grapple funda-
mentally with the fact. He tried to coerce his mind into

thinking of it, but the mind was dominated at this time by the muscles, and the muscles said they did not care. It merely occurred to him that if he should drown it would be a shame.

There were no hurried words, no pallor, no plain agitation. The men simply looked at the shore. 'Now, remember to get well clear of the boat when you jump,' said the captain.

Seaward the crest of a roller suddenly fell with a thunderous crash, and the long white comber came roaring down upon the boat.

'Steady now,' said the captain. The men were silent. They turned their eyes from the shore to the comber and waited. The boat slid up the incline, leaped at the furious top, bounced over it, and swung down the long back of the wave. Some water had been shipped, and the cook bailed it out.

But the next crest crashed also. The tumbling, boiling flood of white water caught the boat and whirled it almost perpendicular. Water swarmed in from all sides. The correspondent had his hands on the gunwale at this time, and when the water entered at that place he swiftly withdrew his fingers, as if he objected to wetting them.

The little boat, drunken with this weight of water, reeled and snuggled deeper into the sea.

'Bail her out, cook! Bail her out!' said the captain.

'All right, Captain,' said the cook.

'Now, boys, the next one will do for us sure,' said the oiler. 'Mind to jump clear of the boat.'

The third wave moved forward, huge, furious, implacable. It fairly swallowed the dinghy, and almost simultaneously the men tumbled into the sea. A piece of life-belt had lain in the bottom of the boat, and as the correspondent went overboard he held this to his chest with his left hand.

The January water was icy, and he reflected immediately that it was colder than he had expected to find it off the coast of Florida. This appeared to his dazed mind as a fact important enough to be noted at the time. The coldness of the water was sad; it was tragic. This fact was somehow mixed and confused with his opinion of his own situation, so that it seemed almost a proper reason for tears. The water was cold.

When he came to the surface he was conscious of little but the noisy water. Afterward he saw his companions in the sea. The oiler was ahead in the race. He was swimming strongly and rapidly. Off to the correspondent's left, the cook's great white and corked back bulged out of the water; and in the rear the captain was hanging with his one good hand to the keel of the overturned dinghy.

There is a certain immovable quality to a shore, and the correspondent wondered at it amid the confusion of the sea.

It seemed also very attractive; but the correspondent knew that it was a long journey, and he paddled leisurely. The piece of life-preserver lay under him, and sometimes he whirled down the incline of a wave as if he were on a hand-sled.

But finally he arrived at a place in the sea where travel was beset with difficulty. He did not pause swimming to inquire what manner of current had caught him, but there his progress ceased. The shore was set before him like a bit of scenery on a stage, and he looked at it and understood with his eyes each detail of it.

As the cook passed, much farther to the left, the captain was calling to him, 'Turn over on your back, cook! Turn over on your back and use the oar.'

'All right, sir.' The cook turned on his back, and, paddling with an oar, went ahead as if he were a canoe.

Presently the boat also passed to the left of the correspondent, with the captain clinging with one hand to the keel. He would have appeared like a man raising himself to look over a board fence if it were not for the extraordinary gymnastics of the boat. The correspondent marvelled that the captain could still hold to it.

They passed on nearer to shore—the oiler, the cook, the captain—and following them went the water-jar, bouncing gaily over the seas.

The correspondent remained in the grip of this strange new enemy—a current. The shore, with its white slope of sand and its green bluff topped with little silent cottages, was spread like a picture before him. It was very near to him then, but he was impressed as one who, in a gallery, looks at a scene from Brittany or Algiers.

He thought: 'I am going to drown? Can it be possible? Can it be possible? Can it be possible?' Perhaps an individual must consider his own death to be the final phenomenon of nature.

But later a wave perhaps whirled him out of this small deadly current, for he found suddenly that he could again make progress toward the shore. Later still he was aware that the captain, clinging with one hand to the keel of the dinghy, had his face turned away from the shore and toward him, and was calling his name. 'Come to the boat! Come to the boat!'

In his struggle to reach the captain and the boat, he reflected that when one gets properly wearied drowning must really be a comfortable arrangement—a cessation of hostilities accompanied by a large degree of relief; and he was glad of it, for the main thing in his mind for some moments had been horror of the temporary agony. He did not wish to be hurt.

Presently he saw a man running along the shore. He was undressing with most remarkable speed. Coat, trousers, shirt, everything flew magically off him.
'Come to the boat!' called the captain.

'All right, Captain.' As the correspondent paddled, he saw the captain let himself down to bottom and leave the boat. Then the correspondent performed his one little marvel of the voyage. A large wave caught him and flung him with ease and supreme speed completely over the boat and far beyond it. It struck him even then as an event in gymnastics and a true miracle of the sea. An overturned boat in the surf is not a plaything to a swimming man.

The correspondent arrived in water that reached only to his waist, but his condition did not enable him to stand for more than a moment. Each wave knocked him into a heap, and the undertow pulled at him.

Then he saw the man who had been running and undressing, and undressing and running, come bounding into the water. He dragged ashore the cook, and then waded toward the captain; but the captain waved him away and sent him to the correspondent. He was naked— naked as a tree in winter; but a halo was about his head, and he shone like a saint. He gave a strong pull, and a long drag, and a bully heave at the correspondent's hand.

The correspondent, schooled in the minor formulæ, said, 'Thanks, old man.' But suddenly the man cried, 'What's that?' He pointed a swift finger. The correspondent said, 'Go.'

In the shallows, face downward, lay the oiler. His forehead touched sand that was periodically, between each wave, clear of the sea.

The correspondent did not know all that transpired afterward. When he achieved safe ground he fell, striking the sand with each particular part of his body. It was as if he had dropped from a roof, but the thud was grateful to him.

It seemed that instantly the beach was populated with men with blankets, clothes, and flasks, and women with coffee-pots and all the remedies sacred to their minds. The welcome of the land to the men from the sea was warm and generous; but a still and dripping shape was carried slowly up the beach, and the land's welcome for it could only be the different and sinister hospitality of the grave.

When it came night, the white waves paced to and fro in the moonlight, and the wind brought the sound of the great sea's voice to the men on the shore, and they felt that they could then be interpreters.

The Heathen

JACK LONDON

(1876–1916)

I MET him first in a hurricane; and though we had gone through the hurricane on the same schooner, it was not until the schooner had gone to pieces under us that I first laid eyes on him. Without doubt I had seen him with the rest of the Kanaka crew on board, but I had not consciously been aware of his existence, for the *Petite Jeanne* was rather overcrowded. In addition to her eight or ten Kanaka seamen, her white captain, mate, and supercargo, and her six cabin passengers, she sailed from

Rangiroa with something like eighty-five deck passengers—Paumotans and Tahitians, men, women, and children each with a trade box, to say nothing of sleeping mats, blankets, and clothes bundles.

The pearling season in the Paumotus was over, and all hands were returning to Tahiti. The six of us cabin passengers were pearl buyers. Two were Americans, one was Ah Choon (the whitest Chinese I have ever known), one was a German, one was a Polish Jew, and I completed the half dozen.

It had been a prosperous season. Not one of us had cause for complaint, nor one of the eighty-five deck passengers either. All had done well, and all were looking forward to a rest-off and a good time in Papeete.

Of course the *Petite Jeanne* was overloaded. She was only seventy tons, and she had no right to carry a tithe of the mob she had on board. Beneath her hatches she was crammed and jammed with pearl shell and copra. Even the trade room was packed full with shell. It was a miracle that the sailors could work her. There was no moving about the decks. They simply climbed back and forth along the rails.

In the nighttime they walked upon the sleepers, who carpeted the deck, I'll swear, two deep. Oh, and there were pigs and chickens on deck, and sacks of yams, while every conceivable place was festooned with strings of drinking coconuts and bunches of bananas. On both sides, between the fore and main shrouds, guys had been stretched, just low enough for the foreboom to swing clear; and from each of these guys at least fifty bunches of bananas were suspended.

It promised to be a messy passage, even if we did make it in the two or three days that would have been required if the southeast trades had been blowing fresh.

But they weren't blowing fresh. After the first five hours the trade died away in a dozen or so gasping fans. The calm continued all that night and the next day—one of those glaring, glassy calms, when the very thought of opening one's eyes to look at it is sufficient to cause a headache.

The second day a man died—an Easter Islander, one of the best divers that season in the lagoon. Smallpox— that is what it was; though how smallpox could come on board, when there had been no known cases ashore when we left Rangiroa, is beyond me. There it was, though— smallpox, a man dead, and three others down on their backs.

There was nothing to be done. We could not segregate the sick, nor could we care for them. We were packed like sardines. There was nothing to do but rot and die— that is, there was nothing to do after the night that followed the first death. On that night the mate, the supercargo, the Polish Jew, and four native divers sneaked away in the large whaleboat. They were never heard of again. In the morning the captain promptly scuttled the remaining boats, and there we were.

That day there were two deaths; the following day three; then it jumped to eight. It was curious to see how we took it. The natives, for instance, fell into a condition of dumb, stolid fear. The captain—Oudouse, his name was, a Frenchman—became very nervous and voluble. He actually got the twitches. He was a large, fleshy man, weighing at least two hundred pounds, and he quickly became a faithful representation of a quivering jelly mountain of fat.

The German, the two Americans, and myself bought up all the scotch whisky and proceeded to stay drunk. The theory was beautiful—namely, if we kept ourselves soaked in alcohol, every smallpox germ that came into contact with us would immediately be scorched to a cinder. And the theory worked, though I must confess that neither Captain Oudouse nor Ah Choon were attacked by the disease either. The Frenchman did not drink at all, while Ah Choon restricted himself to one drink daily.

It was a pretty time. The sun, going into northern declination, was straight overhead. There was no wind, except for frequent squalls, which blew fiercely for from five minutes to half an hour, and wound up by deluging us with rain. After each squall the awful sun would come out, drawing clouds of steam from the soaked decks.

The steam was not nice. It was the vapour of death, freighted with millions and millions of germs. We always took another drink when we saw it going up from the dead and dying, and usually we took two or three more drinks, mixing them exceptionally stiff. Also we made it a rule to take an additional several each time they hove the dead over to the sharks that swarmed about us.

We had a week of it, and then the whisky gave out. It is just as well, or I shouldn't be alive now. It took a sober man to pull through what followed, as you will agree when I mention the little fact that only two men did pull through. The other man was the heathen—at least, that was what I heard Captain Oudouse call him at the moment I first became aware of the heathen's existence. But to come back.

It was at the end of the week, with the whisky gone and the pearl buyers sober, that I happened to glance at the barometer that hung in the cabin companionway. Its normal register in the Paumotus was 29·90, and it was quite customary to see it vacillate between 29·85 and

30·00, or even 30·05; but to see it as I saw it, down to 29·62, was sufficient to sober the most drunken pearl buyer that ever incinerated smallpox microbes in scotch whisky.

I called Captain Oudouse's attention to it, only to be informed that he had watched it going down for several hours. There was little to do, but that little he did very well, considering the circumstances. He took off the light sails, shortened right down to storm canvas, spread life lines, and waited for the wind. His mistake lay in what he did after the wind came. He hove to on the port tack, which was the right thing to do south of the Equator if—and there was the rub—*if* one were *not* in the direct path of the hurricane.

We were in the direct path. I could see that by the steady increase of the wind and the equally steady fall of the barometer. I wanted him to turn and run with the wind on the port quarter until the barometer ceased falling, and then to heave to. We argued till he was reduced to hysteria, but budge he would not. The worst of it was that I could not get the rest of the pearl buyers to back me up. Who was I, anyway, to know more about the sea and its ways than a properly qualified captain? was what was in their minds, I knew.

Of course the sea rose with the wind frightfully; and I shall never forget the first three seas the *Petite Jeanne* shipped. She had fallen off, as vessels do at times when hove to, and the first sea made a clean breach. The life lines were only for the strong and well, and little good were they even for them when the women and children, the bananas and coconuts, the pigs and trade boxes, the sick and the dying, were swept along in a solid, screeching, groaning mass.

The second sea filled the *Petite Jeanne's* decks flush

with the rails; and as her stern sank down and her bow
tossed skyward, all the miserable dunnage of life and
luggage poured aft. It was a human torrent. They came
head first, feet first, sidewise, rolling over and over,
twisting, squirming, writhing, and crumpling up. Now
and again one caught a grip on a stanchion or a rope;
but the weight of the bodies behind tore such grips
loose.

One man I noticed fetch up, head on and square on,
with the starboard bitt. His head cracked like an egg.
I saw what was coming, sprang on top of the cabin, and
from there into the mainsail itself. Ah Choon and one of
the Americans tried to follow me, but I was one jump
ahead of them. The American was swept away and over
the stern like a piece of chaff. Ah Choon caught a spoke
of the wheel and swung in behind it. But a strapping
Rarotonga *wahine* (woman)—she must have weighed
two hundred and fifty—brought up against him and got
an arm around his neck. He clutched the Kanaka steersman with his other hand; and just at that moment the
schooner flung down to starboard.

The rush of bodies and sea that was coming along the
port runway between the cabin and the rail turned
abruptly and poured to starboard. Away they went—
wahine, Ah Choon, and steersman; and I swear I saw
Ah Choon grin at me with philosophic resignation as he
cleared the rail and went under.

The third sea—the biggest of the three—did not do so
much damage. By the time it arrived nearly everybody
was in the rigging. On deck perhaps a dozen gasping,
half-drowned, and half-stunned wretches were rolling
about or attempting to crawl into safety. They went by
the board, as did the wreckage of the two remaining
boats. The other pearl buyers and myself, between seas,

managed to get about fifteen women and children into the cabin and battened down. Little good it did the poor creatures in the end.

Wind? Out of all my experience I could not have believed it possible for the wind to blow as it did. There is no describing it. How can one describe a nightmare? It was the same way with that wind. It tore the clothes off our bodies. I say *tore them off*, and I mean it. I am not asking you to believe it. I am merely telling something that I saw and felt. There are times when I do not believe it myself. I went through it, and that is enough. One could not face that wind and live. It was a monstrous thing, and the most monstrous thing about it was that it increased and continued to increase.

Imagine countless millions and billions of tons of sand. Imagine this sand tearing along at ninety, a hundred, a hundred and twenty, or any other number of miles per hour. Imagine, further, this sand to be invisible, impalpable, yet to retain all the weight and density of sand. Do all this, and you may get a vague inkling of what that wind was like.

Perhaps sand is not the right comparison. Consider it mud, invisible, impalpable, but heavy as mud. Nay, it goes beyond that. Consider every molecule of air to be a mudbank in itself. Then try to imagine the multitudinous impact of mudbanks. No; it is beyond me. Language may be adequate to express the ordinary conditions of life, but it cannot possibly express any of the conditions of so enormous a blast of wind. It would have been better had I stuck by my original intention of not attempting a description.

I will say this much: the sea, which had risen at first, was beaten down by that wind. More, it seemed as if the whole ocean had been sucked up in the maw of the hurricane, and hurled on through that portion of space which previously had been occupied by the air.

Of course our canvas had gone long before. But Captain Oudouse had on the *Petite Jeanne* something I had never before seen on a South Sea schooner—a sea anchor. It was a conical canvas bag, the mouth of which was kept open by a huge hoop of iron. The sea anchor was bridled something like a kite, so that it bit into the water as a kite bites into the air, but with a difference. The sea anchor remained just under the surface of the ocean in a perpendicular position. A long line, in turn, connected it with the schooner. As a result the *Petite Jeanne* rode bow on to the wind and to what sea there was.

The situation really would have been favourable had we not been in the path of the storm. True, the wind itself tore our canvas out of the gaskets, jerked out our topmasts, and made a raffle of our running gear, but still we would have come through nicely had we not been square in front of the advancing storm centre. That was what fixed us. I was in a state of stunned, numbed, paralysed collapse from enduring the impact of the wind, and I think I was just about ready to give up and die when the centre smote us. The blow we received was an absolute lull. There was not a breath of air. The effect on one was sickening.

Remember that for hours we had been at terrific muscular tension, withstanding the awful pressure of that wind. And then, suddenly, the pressure was removed. I know that I felt as though I was about to expand, to fly apart in all directions. It seemed as if every atom composing my body was repelling every other atom and was on the verge of rushing off irresistibly into space. But that lasted only for a moment. Destruction was upon us.

In the absence of wind and pressure the sea rose. It jumped, it leaped, it soared straight toward the clouds. Remember, from every point of the compass that inconceivable wind was blowing in toward the centre of calm. The result was that the seas sprang up from every point of the compass. There was no wind to check them. They popped up like corks released from the bottom of a pail of water. There was no system to them, no stability. They were hollow, maniacal seas. They were eighty feet high at the least. They were not seas at all. They resembled no sea a man had ever seen.

They were splashes, monstrous splashes—that is all. Splashes that were eighty feet high. Eighty! They were more than eighty. They went over our mastheads. They were spouts, explosions. They were drunken. They fell anywhere, anyhow. They jostled one another; they collided. They rushed together and collapsed upon one another, or fell apart like a thousand waterfalls all at once. It was no ocean any man had ever dreamed of, that hurricane centre. It was confusion thrice confounded. It was anarchy. It was a hell pit of sea water gone mad.

The *Petite Jeanne*? I don't know. The heathen told me afterwards that he did not know. She was literally torn apart, ripped wide open, beaten into a pulp, smashed into kindling wood, annihilated. When I came to I was in the water, swimming automatically, though I was about two thirds drowned. How I got there I had no recollection. I remembered seeing the *Petite Jeanne* fly to pieces at what must have been the instant that my own consciousness was buffeted out of me. But there I was, with nothing to do but make the best of it, and in that best there was little promise. The wind was blowing again, the sea was much smaller and more regular, and I knew that I had passed through the centre. Fortunately there were no sharks about. The hurricane had dissipated the ravenous horde that had surrounded the death ship and fed off the dead.

It was about midday when the *Petite Jeanne* went to pieces, and it must have been two hours afterward when I picked up with one of her hatch covers. Thick rain was driving at the time; and it was the merest chance that flung me and the hatch cover together. A short length of line was trailing from the rope handle; and I knew that I was good for a day, at least, if the sharks did not return. Three hours later, possibly a little longer, sticking close to the cover, and with closed eyes concentrating my whole soul upon the task of breathing in enough air to keep me going and at the same time of avoiding breathing in enough water to drown me, it seemed to me that I heard voices. The rain had ceased, and wind and sea were easing marvellously. Not twenty feet away from me, on another hatch cover, were Captain Oudouse and the heathen. They were fighting over the possession of the cover—at least, the Frenchman was.

'*Païen noir!*' I heard him scream, and at the same time I saw him kick the Kanaka.

Now Captain Oudouse had lost all his clothes except his shoes, and they were heavy brogans. It was a cruel blow, for it caught the heathen on the mouth and the point of the chin, half stunning him. I looked for him to retaliate, but he contented himself with swimming about forlornly a safe ten feet away. Whenever a fling of the sea threw him closer, the Frenchman, hanging on with his hands, kicked out at him with both feet. Also, at the moment of delivering each kick, he called the Kanaka a black heathen.

'For two centimes I'd come over there and drown you, you white beast!' I yelled.

The only reason I did not go was that I felt too tired. The very thought of the effort to swim over was nauseating. So I called to the Kanaka to come to me, and proceeded to share the hatch cover with him. Otoo, he told me his name was (pronounced ō-tō-ō); also he told me that he was a native of Borabora, the most westerly of the Society group. As I learned afterward, he had got the hatch cover first, and, after some time, encountering Captain Oudouse, had offered to share it with him, and had been kicked off for his pains.

And that was how Otoo and I first came together. He was no fighter. He was all sweetness and gentleness, a love creature, though he stood nearly six feet tall and was muscled like a gladiator. He was no fighter, but he was also no coward. He had the heart of a lion; and in the years that followed I have seen him run risks that I would never dream of taking. What I mean is that while he was no fighter, and while he always avoided precipitating a row, he never ran away from trouble when it started. And it was ''Ware shoal!' when once Otoo went into action. I shall never forget what he did to Bill King. It occurred in German Samoa. Bill King was hailed the champion heavyweight of the American Navy. He was a big brute of a man, a veritable gorilla, one of those hard-hitting, roughhousing chaps, and clever with his fists as well. He picked the quarrel, and he kicked Otoo twice and struck him once before Otoo felt it to be necessary to fight. I don't think it lasted four minutes, at the end of which time Bill King was the unhappy possessor of four broken ribs, a broken forearm, and a dislocated shoulder blade. Otoo knew nothing of scientific boxing. He was merely a manhandler; and Bill King was something like three months in recovering from the bit of manhandling he received that afternoon on Apia beach.

But I am running ahead of my yarn. We shared the hatch cover between us. We took turn and turn about, one lying flat on the cover and resting, while the other, submerged to the neck, merely held on with his hands. For two days and nights, spell and spell, on the cover and in the water, we drifted over the ocean. Toward the last I was delirious most of the time; and there were times, too, when I heard Otoo babbling and raving in his native tongue. Our continuous immersion prevented us from dying of thirst, though the sea water and the sunshine gave us the prettiest imaginable combination of salt pickle and sunburn.

In the end Otoo saved my life; for I came to lying on the beach twenty feet from the water, sheltered from the sun by a couple of coconut leaves. No one but Otoo could have dragged me there and stuck up the leaves for shade. He was lying beside me. I went off again; and the next time I came round it was cool and starry night, and Otoo was pressing a drinking coconut to my lips.

We were the sole survivors of the *Petite Jeanne*. Captain Oudouse must have succumbed to exhaustion, for several days later his hatch cover drifted ashore without him. Otoo and I lived with the natives of the atoll for a week, when we were rescued by the French cruiser and taken to Tahiti. In the meantime, however, we had performed the ceremony of exchanging names. In the South Seas such a ceremony binds two men closer together than blood brothership. The initiative had been mine; and Otoo was rapturously delighted when I suggested it.

'It is well,' he said in Tahitian. 'For we have been mates together for two days on the lips of Death.'

'But Death stuttered.' I smiled.

'It was a brave deed you did, master,' he replied, 'and Death was not vile enough to speak.'

'Why do you "master" me?' I demanded with a show of hurt feelings. 'We have exchanged names. To you I am Otoo. To me you are Charley. And between you and me, forever and forever, you shall be Charley, and I shall be Otoo. It is the way of the custom. And when we die, if it does happen that we live again somewhere beyond the stars and the sky, still shall you be Charley to me, and I Otoo to you.'

'Yes, master,' he answered, his eyes luminous and soft with joy.

'There you go!' I cried indignantly.

'What does it matter what my lips utter?' he argued. 'They are only my lips. But I shall think Otoo always. Whenever I think of myself, I shall think of you. Whenever men call me by name, I shall think of you. And beyond the sky and beyond the stars, always and forever, you shall be Otoo to me. Is it well, master?'

I hid my smile and answered that it was well.

We parted at Papeete. I remained ashore to recuperate; and he went on in a cutter to his own island, Borabora. Six weeks later he was back. I was surprised, for he had told me of his wife, and said that he was returning to her, and would give over sailing on far voyages.

'Where do you go, master?' he asked after our first greetings.

I shrugged my shoulders. It was a hard question.

'All the world,' was my answer, 'all the world, all the sea, and all the islands that are in the sea.'

'I will go with you,' he said simply. 'My wife is dead.'

I never had a brother; but from what I have seen of other men's brothers, I doubt if any man ever had a brother that was to him what Otoo was to me. He was brother and father and mother as well. And this I know; I lived a straighter and better man because of Otoo. I cared little for other men, but I had to live straight in Otoo's eyes. Because of him I dared not tarnish myself. He made me his ideal, compounding me, I fear, chiefly out of his own love and worship; and there were times when I stood close to the steep pitch of hell, and would have taken the plunge had not the thought of Otoo restrained me. His pride in me entered into me, until it became one of the major rules in my personal code to do nothing that would diminish that pride of his.

Naturally I did not learn right away what his feelings were toward me. He never criticized, never censured; and slowly the exalted place I held in his eyes dawned upon me, and slowly I grew to comprehend the hurt I could inflict upon him by being anything less than my best.

For seventeen years we were together; for seventeen years he was at my shoulder, watching while I slept, nursing me through fever and wounds—aye, and receiving wounds in fighting for me. He signed on the same ships with me; and together we ranged the Pacific from Hawaii to Sydney Head, and from Torres Straits to the Galapagos. We blackbirded from the New Hebrides and the Line Islands over to the westward clear through the Louisiades, New Britain, New Ireland, and New Hanover. We were wrecked three times—in the Gilberts, in the Santa Cruz group, and in the Fijis. And we traded and salved wherever a dollar promised in the way of pearl and pearl shell, copra, bêche-de-mer, hawkbill turtle shell, and stranded wrecks.

It began in Papeete, immediately after his announce- that he was going with me over all the sea, and the islands in the midst thereof. There was a club in those days in Papeete, where the pearlers, traders, captains, and riff-raff of South Sea adventurers forgathered. The play ran

high, and the drink ran high; and I am very much afraid
that I kept later hours than were becoming or proper. No
matter what the hour was when I left the club, there was
Otoo waiting to see me safely home.

At first I smiled; next I chided him. Then I told him
flatly that I stood in need of no wet-nursing. After that
I did not see him when I came out of the club. Quite by
accident, a week or so later, I discovered that he still
saw me home, lurking across the street among the
shadows of the mango trees. What could I do? I know
what I did do.

Insensibly I began to keep better hours. On wet and
stormy nights, in the thick of the folly and the fun, the
thought would persist in coming to me of Otoo keeping
his dreary vigil under the dripping mangoes. Truly, he
made a better man of me. Yet he was not strait-laced.
And he knew nothing of common Christian morality.
All the people on Borabora were Christians; but he was
a heathen, the only unbeliever on the island, a gross
materialist, who believed that when he died he was dead.
He believed merely in fair play and square dealing. Petty
meanness, in his code, was almost as serious as wanton
homicide; and I do believe that he respected a murderer
more than a man given to small practices.

Concerning me, personally, he objected to my doing
anything that was hurtful to me. Gambling was all right.
He was an ardent gambler himself. But late hours, he
explained, were bad for one's health. He had seen men
who did not take care of themselves die of fever. He was
no teetotaller, and welcomed a stiff nip any time when it
was wet work in the boats. On the other hand, he believed
in liquor in moderation. He had seen many men killed or
disgraced by squareface or scotch.

Otoo had my welfare always at heart. He thought

ahead for me, weighed my plans, and took a greater interest in them than I did myself. At first, when I was unaware of this interest of his in my affairs, he had to divine my intentions, as, for instance, at Papeete, when I contemplated going partners with a knavish fellow countryman on a guana venture. I did not know he was a knave. Nor did any white man in Papeete. Neither did Otoo know, but he saw how thick we were getting, and found out for me, and without my asking him. Native sailors from the ends of the seas knock about on the beach in Tahiti; and Otoo, suspicious merely, went among them till he had gathered sufficient data to justify his suspicions. Oh, it was a nice history, that of Randolph Waters. I couldn't believe it when Otoo first narrated it; but when I sheeted it home to Waters he gave in without a murmur and got away on the first steamer to Auckland.

At first, I am free to confess, I couldn't help resenting Otoo's poking his nose into my business. But I knew that he was wholly unselfish; and soon I had to acknowledge his wisdom and discretion. He had his eyes open always to my main chance, and he was both keen-sighted and farsighted. In time he became my counsellor, until he knew more of my business than I did myself. He really had my interest at heart more than I did. Mine was the magnificent carelessness of youth, for I preferred romance to dollars, and adventure to a comfortable billet with all night in. So it was well that I had someone to look out for me. I know that if it had not been for Otoo I should not be here today.

Of numerous instances, let me give one. I had had some experience in blackbirding before I went pearling in the Paumotus. Otoo and I were on the beach in Samoa—we really were on the beach and hard aground— when my chance came to go as recruiter on a blackbird brig. Otoo signed on before the mast; and for the next half-dozen years, in as many ships, we knocked about the wildest portions of Melanesia. Otoo saw to it that he always pulled stroke oar in my boat. Our custom in recruiting labour was to land the recruiter on the beach. The covering boat always lay on its oars several hundred feet offshore, while the recruiter's boat, also lying on its oars, kept afloat on the edge of the beach. When I landed with my trade goods, leaving my steering sweep apeak, Otoo left his stroke position and came into the stern sheets, where a Winchester lay ready to hand under a flap of canvas. The boat's crew was also armed, the Sniders concealed under canvas flaps that ran the length of the gunwales. While I was busy arguing and per-suading the woolly-headed cannibals to come and labour on the Queensland plantations, Otoo kept watch. And often and often his low voice warned me of suspicious actions and impending treachery. Sometimes it was the quick shot from his rifle that was the first warning I. received. And in my rush to the boat his hand was always there to jerk me flying aboard. Once, I remember, on *Santa Anna*, the boat grounded just as the trouble began. The covering boat was dashing to our assistance, but the several score of savages would have wiped us out before it arrived. Otoo took a flying leap ashore, dug both hands into the trade goods, and scattered tobacco, beads, tomahawks, knives, and calicoes in all directions.

This was too much for the woolly-heads. While they scrambled for the treasures, the boat was shoved clear, and we were aboard and forty feet away. And I got thirty recruits off that very beach in the next four hours.

The particular instance I have in mind was on Malaita, the most savage island in the easterly Solomons. The natives had been remarkably friendly; and how were we to know that the whole village had been taking up a collection for over two years with which to buy a white man's head? The beggars are all head-hunters, and they especially esteem a white man's head. The fellow who captured the head would receive the whole collection. As I say, they appeared very friendly; and on this day I was fully a hundred yards down the beach from the boat. Otoo had cautioned me; and, as usual when I did not heed him, I came to grief.

The first I knew, a cloud of spears sailed out of the mangrove swamp at me. At least a dozen were sticking into me. I started to run, but tripped over one that was fast in my calf, and went down. The woolly-heads made a run for me, each with a long-handled, fantail tomahawk with which to hack off my head. They were so eager for the prize that they got in one another's way. In the confusion I avoided several hacks by throwing myself right and left on the sand.

Then Otoo arrived—Otoo the manhandler. In some way he had got hold of a heavy war club, and at close quarters it was a far more efficient weapon than a rifle. He was right in the thick of them, so that they could not spear him, while their tomahawks seemed worse than useless. He was fighting for me, and he was in a true berserker rage. The way he handled that club was amazing. Their skulls squashed like overripe oranges. It was not until he had driven them back, picked me up in his arms, and started to run that he received his first wounds. He arrived in the boat with four spear thrusts, got his Winchester, and with it got a man for every shot. Then we pulled aboard the schooner and doctored up.

Seventeen years we were together. He made me. I should today be a supercargo, a recruiter, or a memory, if it had not been for him.

'You spend your money, and you go out and get more,' he said one day. 'It is easy to get money now. But when you get old, your money will be spent, and you will not be able to go out and get more. I know, master. I have studied the way of white men. On the beaches are many old men who were young once, and who could get money just like you. Now they are old, and they have nothing, and they wait about for the young men like you to come ashore and buy drinks for them.

'The black boy is a slave on the plantations. He gets twenty dollars a year. He works hard. The overseer does not work hard. He rides a horse and watches the black boy work. He gets twelve hundred dollars a year. I am a sailor on the schooner. I get fifteen dollars a month. That is because I am a good sailor. I work hard. The captain has a double awning and drinks beer out of long bottles. I have never seen him haul a rope or pull an oar. He gets one hundred and fifty dollars a month. I am a sailor. He is a navigator. Master, I think it would be very good for you to know navigation.'

Otoo spurred me on to it. He sailed with me as second mate on my first schooner, and he was far prouder of my command than I was myself. Later on it was:

'The captain is well paid, master; but the ship is in his keeping, and he is never free from the burden. It is the owner who is better paid—and the owner who sits ashore with many servants and turns his money over.'

'True, but a schooner costs five thousand dollars—an old schooner at that,' I objected. 'I should be an old man before I saved five thousand dollars.'

'There be short ways for white men to make money,' he went on, pointing ashore at the coconut-fringed beach.

We were in the Solomons at the time, picking up a

cargo of ivory nuts along the east coast of Guadal-canal.

'Between this river mouth and the next it is two miles,' he said. 'The flat land runs far back. It is worth nothing now. Next year—who knows?—or the year after, men will pay much money for that land. The anchorage is good. Big steamers can lie close up. You can buy the land four miles deep from the old chief for ten thousand sticks of tobacco, ten bottles of squareface, and a Snider, which will cost you, maybe, one hundred dollars. Then you place the deed with the commissioner; and the next year, or the year after, you sell and become the owner of a ship.'

I followed his lead, and his words came true, though in three years instead of two. Next came the grasslands deal on Guadalcanal—twenty thousand acres, on a governmental nine hundred and ninety-nine years' lease at a nominal sum. I owned the lease for precisely ninety days, when I sold it to a company for half a fortune. Always it was Otoo who looked ahead and saw the opportunity. He was responsible for the salving of the *Doncaster*—bought in at auction for a hundred pounds, and clearing three thousand after every expense was paid. He led me into the Savaii plantation and the cocoa venture on Upolu.

We did not go seafaring so much as in the old days. I was too well off. I married, and my standard of living rose; but Otoo remained the same old-time Otoo, moving about the house or trailing through the office, his wooden pipe in his mouth, a shilling undershirt on his back, and a four-shilling lava-lava about his loins. I could not get him to spend money. There was no way of repaying him except with love, and God knows he got that in full measure from all of us. The children worshipped him and if he had been spoilable, my wife would surely have been his undoing.

The children! He really was the one who showed them the way of their feet in the world practical. He began by teaching them to walk. He sat up with them when they were sick. One by one, when they were scarcely toddlers, he took them down to the lagoon and made them into amphibians. He taught them more than I ever knew of the habits of fish and the ways of catching them. In the bush it was the same thing. At seven Tom knew more woodcraft than I ever dreamed existed. At six Mary went over the Sliding Rock without a quiver, and I had seen strong men balk at that feat. And when Frank had just turned six he could bring up shillings from the bottom in three fathoms.

'My people in Borabora do not like heathen—they are all Christians; and I do not like Borabora Christians,' he said one day, when I, with the idea of getting him to spend some of the money that was rightfully his, had been trying to persuade him to make a visit to his own island in one of our schooners—a special voyage which I had hoped to make a record breaker in the matter of prodigal expense.

I say one of *our* schooners, though legally at the time they belonged to me. I struggled long with him to enter into partnership.

'We have been partners from the day the *Petite Jeanne* went down,' he said at last. 'But if your heart so wishes, then shall we become partners by the law. I have no work to do, yet are my expenses large. I drink and eat and smoke in plenty—it costs much, I know. I do not pay for the playing of billiards for I play on your table; but still the money goes. Fishing on the reef is only a rich man's pleasure. It is shocking, the cost of hooks and cotton line. Yes; it is necessary that we be partners by law. I need the money. I shall get it from the head clerk in the office.'

So the papers were made out and recorded. A year later I was compelled to complain.

'Charley,' said I, 'you are a wicked old fraud, a miserly skinflint, a miserable land crab. Behold, your share for the year in all our partnership has been thousands of dollars. The head clerk has given me this paper. It says that in the year you have drawn just eighty-seven dollars and twenty cents.'

'Is there any owing me?' he asked anxiously.

'I tell you thousands and thousands,' I answered.

His face brightened, as with an immense relief.

'It is well,' he said. 'See that the head clerk keeps good account of it. When I want it, I shall want it, and there must not be a cent missing.'

'If there is,' he added fiercely, after a pause, 'it must come out of the clerk's wages.'

And all the time, as I afterward learned, his will, drawn up by Carruthers, and making me sole beneficiary, lay in the American consul's safe.

But the end came, as the end must come to all human associations. It occurred in the Solomons, where our wildest work had been done in the wild young days, and where we were once more—principally on a holiday, incidentally to look after our holdings on Florida Island and to look over the pearling possibilities of the Mboli Pass. We were lying at Savu, having run in to trade for curios.

Now Savu is alive with sharks. The custom of the woolly-heads of burying their dead in the sea did not tend to discourage the sharks from making the adjacent waters a hangout. It was my luck to be coming aboard in a tiny, overloaded, native canoe when the thing capsized.

There were four woolly-heads and myself in it, or, rather, hanging to it. The schooner was a hundred yards away. I was just hailing for a boat when one of the woolly-heads began to scream. Holding on to the end of the canoe, both he and that portion of the canoe were dragged under several times. Then he loosed his clutch and disappeared. A shark had got him.

The three remaining woolly-heads tried to climb out of the water upon the bottom of the canoe. I yelled and cursed and struck at the nearest with my fist, but it was no use. They were in a blind funk. The canoe could barely have supported one of them. Under the three it upended and rolled sidewise, throwing them back into the water.

I abandoned the canoe and started to swim toward the schooner, expecting to be picked up by the boat before I got there. One of the woolly-heads elected to come with me, and we swam along silently, side by side, now and again putting our faces into the water and peering about for sharks. The screams of the man who stayed by the canoe informed us that he was taken. I was peering into the water when I saw a big shark pass directly beneath me. He was fully sixteen feet in length. I saw the whole thing. He got the woolly-head by the middle, and away he went, the poor devil, head, shoulders, and arms out of water all the time, screeching in a heart-rending way. He was carried along in this fashion for several hundred feet, when he was dragged beneath the surface.

I swam doggedly on, hoping that that was the last unattached shark. But there was another. Whether it was one that had attacked the natives earlier, or whether it was one that had made a good meal elsewhere, I do not know. At any rate, he was not in such haste as the others. I could not swim so rapidly now, for a large part of my effort was devoted to keeping track of him. I was watching him when he made his first attack. By good luck I got both hands on his nose, and though his momentum nearly shoved me under, I managed to keep him off. He veered clear and began circling about again. A second time I escaped him by the same manœuvre. The third rush was a miss on both sides. He sheered at the moment my hands should have landed on his nose, but his sandpaper hide (I had on a sleeveless undershirt) scraped the skin off one arm from elbow to shoulder.

By this time I was played out, and gave up hope. The schooner was still two hundred feet away. My face was in the water, and I was watching him manœuvre for another attempt, when I saw a brown body pass between us. It was Otoo.

'Swim for the schooner, master!' he said. And he spoke gaily, as though the affair was a mere lark. 'I know sharks. The shark is my brother.'

I obeyed, swimming slowly on, while Otoo swam about me, keeping always between me and the shark, foiling his rushes and encouraging me.

'The davit tackle carried away, and they are rigging the falls,' he explained a minute or so later, and then went under to head off another attack.

By the time the schooner was thirty feet away I was about done for. I could scarcely move. They were heaving lines at us from on board, but they continually fell short. The shark, finding that it was receiving no hurt, had become bolder. Several times it nearly got me, but each time Otoo was there just the moment before it was too late. Of course Otoo could have saved himself any time. But he stuck by me.

'Good-by, Charley! I'm finished!' I just managed to gasp.

I knew that the end had come, and that the next moment I should throw up my hands and go down.

But Otoo laughed in my face, saying:

'I will show you a new trick. I will make that shark feel sick!'

He dropped in behind me, where the shark was preparing to come at me.

'A little more to the left!' he next called out. 'There is a line there on the water. To the left, master—to the left!'

I changed my course and struck out blindly. I was by that time barely conscious. As my hand closed on the line I heard an exclamation from on board. I turned and looked. There was no sign of Otoo. The next instant he broke surface. Both hands were off at the wrist, the stumps spouting blood.

'Otoo!' he called softly. And I could see in his gaze the love that thrilled in his voice.

Then, and then only, at the very last of all our years, he called me by that name.

'Good-by, Otoo!' he called.

Then he was dragged under, and I was hauled aboard, where I fainted in the captain's arms.

And so passed Otoo, who saved me and made me a man, and who saved me in the end. We met in the maw of a hurricane and parted in the maw of a shark, with seventeen intervening years of comradeship, the like of which I dare to assert has never befallen two men, the one brown and the other white. If Jehovah be from His high place watching every sparrow fall, not least in His kingdom shall be Otoo, the one heathen of Borabora.

I want to know why

SHERWOOD ANDERSON

(1876-1941)

WE got up at four in the morning, that first day in the east. On the evening before we had climbed off a freight train at the edge of town, and with the true instinct of Kentucky boys had found our way across town and to the race track and the stables at once. Then we knew we were all right. Hanley Turner right away found a nigger we knew. It was Bildad Johnson who in the winter works at Ed Becker's livery barn in our home town, Beckersville. Bildad is a good cook as almost all our niggers are and of course he, like everyone in our part of Kentucky who is anyone at all, likes the horses. In the spring Bildad begins to scratch around. A nigger from our country can flatter and wheedle anyone into letting him do most anything he wants. Bildad wheedles the stable men and the trainers from the horse farms in our country around Lexington. The trainers come into town in the evening to stand around and talk and maybe get into a poker game. Bildad gets in with them. He is always doing little favours and telling about things to eat, chicken browned in a pan, and how is the best way to cook sweet potatoes and corn bread. It makes your mouth water to hear him.

When the racing season comes on and the horses go to the races and there is all the talk on the streets in the evenings about the new colts, and everyone says when they are going over to Lexington or to the spring meeting at Churchill Downs or to Latonia, and the horsemen that have been down to New Orleans or maybe at the winter meeting at Havana in Cuba come home to spend a week before they start out again, at such a time when everything talked about in Beckersville is just horses and nothing else and the outfits start out and horse racing is in every breath of air you breathe, Bildad shows up with a job as cook for some outfit. Often when I think about it, his always going all season to the races and working in the livery barn in the winter where horses are and where men like to come and talk about horses, I wish I was a nigger. It's a foolish thing to say, but that's the way I am about being around horses, just crazy. I can't help it.

Well, I must tell you about what we did and let you in on what I'm talking about. Four of us boys from Beckersville, all whites and sons of men who live in Beckersville regular, made up our minds we were going to the races, not just to Lexington or Louisville, I don't mean, but to the big eastern track we were always hearing our Beckersville men talk about, to Saratoga. We were all pretty young then. I was just turned fifteen and I was the oldest of the four. It was my scheme. I admit that and I talked the others into trying it. There was Hanley Turner and Henry Rieback and Tom Tumberton and myself. I had thirty-seven dollars I had earned during the winter working nights and Saturdays in Enoch Myer's grocery. Henry Rieback had eleven dollars and the others, Hanley and Tom had only a dollar or two each. We fixed it all up and laid low until the Kentucky spring meetings were over and some of our men, the sportiest ones, the ones we envied the most, had cut out—then we cut out too.

I won't tell you the trouble we had beating our way on freights and all. We went through Cleveland and

Buffalo and other cities and saw Niagara Falls. We bought things there, souvenirs and spoons and cards and shells with pictures of the falls on them for our sisters and mothers, but thought we had better not send any of the things home. We didn't want to put the folks on our trail and maybe be nabbed.

We got into Saratoga as I said at night and went to the track. Bildad fed us up. He showed us a place to sleep in hay over a shed and promised to keep still. Niggers are all right about things like that. They won't squeal on you. Often a white man you might meet, when you had run away from home like that, might appear to be all right and give you a quarter or a half dollar or something, and then go right and give you away. White men will do that, but not a nigger. You can trust them. They are squarer with kids. I don't know why.

At the Saratoga meeting that year there were a lot of men from home. Dave Williams and Arthur Mulford and Jerry Myers and others. Then there was a lot from Louisville and Lexington Henry Rieback knew but I didn't. They were professional gamblers and Henry Rieback's father is one too. He is what is called a sheet writer and goes away most of the year to tracks. In the winter when he is home in Beckersville he don't stay there much but goes away to cities and deals faro. He is a nice man and generous, is always sending Henry presents, a bicycle and a gold watch and a boy scout suit of clothes and things like that.

My own father is a lawyer. He's all right, but don't make much money and can't buy me things and anyway I'm getting so old now I don't expect it. He never said nothing to me against Henry, but Hanley Turner and Tom Tumberton's fathers did. They said to their boys that money so come by is no good and they didn't want their boys brought up to hear gamblers' talk and be thinking about such things and maybe embrace them.

That's all right and I guess the men know what they are talking about, but I don't see what it's got to do with Henry or with horses either. That's what I'm writing this story about. I'm puzzled. I'm getting to be a man and want to think straight and be O.K., and there's something I saw at the race meeting at the eastern track I can't figure out.

I can't help it, I'm crazy about thoroughbred horses. I've always been that way. When I was ten years old and saw I was growing to be big and couldn't be a rider I was so sorry I nearly died. Harry Hellinfinger in Beckersville, whose father is Postmaster, is grown up and too lazy to work, but likes to stand around in the street and get up jokes on boys like sending them to a hardware store for a gimlet to bore square holes and other jokes like that. He played one on me. He told me that if I would eat a half a cigar I would be stunted and not grow any more and maybe could be a rider. I did it. When father wasn't looking I took a cigar out of his pocket and gagged it down some way. It made me awful sick and the doctor had to be sent for, and then it did no good. I kept right on growing. It was a joke. When I told what I had done and why most fathers would have whipped me but mine didn't.

Well, I didn't get stunted and didn't die. It serves Harry Hellinfinger right. Then I made up my mind I would like to be a stable boy, but had to give that up too. Mostly niggers do that work and I knew father wouldn't let me go into it. No use to ask him.

If you've never been crazy about thoroughbreds it's because you've never been around where they are much and don't know any better. They're beautiful. There isn't anything so lovely and clean and full of spunk and honest and everything as some race horses. On the big horse farms that are all around our town Beckersville there are tracks and the horses run in the early morning. More than a thousand times I've got out of bed before daylight and walked two or three miles to the tracks. Mother wouldn't of let me go but father always says, 'Let him alone'. So I got some bread out of the bread box and some butter and jam, gobbled it and lit out.

At the tracks you sit on the fence with men, whites and niggers, and they chew tobacco and talk, and then the colts are brought out. It's early and the grass is covered with shiny dew and in another field a man is plowing and they are frying things in a shed where the track niggers sleep, and you know how a nigger can giggle and laugh and say things that make you laugh. A white man can't do it and some niggers can't but a track nigger can every time.

And so the colts are brought out and some are just galloped by stable boys, but almost every morning on a big track owned by a rich man who lives maybe in New York, there are always, nearly every morning, a few colts and some of the old race horses and geldings and mares that are cut loose.

It brings a lump up into my throat when a horse runs. I don't mean all horses but some. I can pick them nearly every time. It's in my blood like in the blood of race track niggers and trainers. Even when they just go slop-jogging along with a little nigger on their backs I can tell a winner. If my throat hurts and it's hard for me to swallow, that's him. He'll run like Sam Hill when you let him out. If he don't win every time it'll be a wonder and because they've got him in a pocket behind another or he was pulled or got off bad at the post or something.

If I wanted to be a gambler like Henry Rieback's father I could get rich. I know I could and Henry says so too. All I would have to do is to wait 'til that hurt comes when I see a horse and then bet every cent. That's what I would do if I wanted to be a gambler, but I don't.

When you're at the tracks in the morning—not the race tracks but the training tracks around Beckersville—you don't see a horse, the kind I've been talking about, very often, but it's nice anyway. Any thoroughbred, that is sired right and out of a good mare and trained by a man that knows how, can run. If he couldn't what would he be there for and not pulling a plow?

Well, out of the stables they come and the boys are on their backs and it's lovely to be there. You hunch down on top of the fence and itch inside you. Over in the sheds the niggers giggle and sing. Bacon is being fried and coffee made. Everything smells lovely. Nothing smells better than coffee and manure and horses and niggers and bacon frying and pipes being smoked out of doors on a morning like that. It just gets you, that's what it does.

But about Saratoga. We was there six days and not a soul from home seen us and everything came off just as we wanted it to, fine weather and horses and races and all. We beat our way home and Bildad gave us a basket with fried chicken and bread and other eatables in, and I had eighteen dollars when we got back to Beckersville. Mother jawed and cried but Pop didn't say much. I told everything we done except one thing. I did and saw that alone. That's what I'm writing about. It got me upset. I think about it at night. Here it is.

At Saratoga we laid up nights in the hay in the shed Bildad had showed us and ate with the niggers early and at night when the race people had all gone away. The

men from home stayed mostly in the grandstand and
betting field, and didn't come out around the places
where the horses are kept except to the paddocks just
before a race when the horses are saddled. At Saratoga
they don't have paddocks under an open shed as at
Lexington and Churchill Downs and other tracks down
in our country, but saddle the horses right out in an open
place under trees on a lawn as smooth and nice as
Banker Bohon's front yard here in Beckersville. It's
lovely. The horses are sweaty and nervous and shine
and the men come out and smoke cigars and look at them
and the trainers are there and the owners, and your heart
thumps so you can hardly breathe.

Then the bugle blows for post and the boys that ride
come running out with their silk clothes on and you run
to get a place by the fence with the niggers.

I always am wanting to be a trainer or owner, and at
the risk of being seen and caught and sent home I went
to the paddocks before every race. The other boys
didn't but I did.

We got to Saratoga on a Friday and on Wednesday the
next week the big Mullford Handicap was to be run.
Middlestride was in it and Sunstreak. The weather was
fine and the track fast. I couldn't sleep the night before.

What had happened was that both these horses are the
kind it makes my throat hurt to see. Middlestride is long
and looks awkward and is a gelding. He belongs to Joe
Thompson, a little owner from home who only has a half
dozen horses. The Mullford Handicap is for a mile and
Middlestride can't untrack fast. He goes away slow
and is always way back at the half, then he begins to
run and if the race is a mile and a quarter he'll just eat
up everything and get there.

Sunstreak is different. He is a stallion and nervous

and belongs on the biggest farm we've got in our country, the Van Riddle place that belongs to Mr. Van Riddle of New York. Sunstreak is like a girl you think about sometimes but never see. He is hard all over and lovely too. When you look at his head you want to kiss him. He is trained by Jerry Tillford who knows me and has been good to me lots of times, lets me walk into a horse's stall to look at him close and other things. There isn't anything as sweet as that horse. He stands at the post quiet and not letting on, but he is just burning up inside. Then when the barrier goes up he is off like his name, Sunstreak. It makes you ache to see him. It hurts you. He just lays down and runs like a bird dog. There can't anything I ever see run like him except Middlestride when he gets untracked and stretches himself.

Gee! I ached to see that race and those two horses run, ached and dreaded it too. I didn't want to see either of our horses beaten. We had never sent a pair like that to the races before. Old men in Beckersville said so and the niggers said so. It was a fact.

Before the race I went over to the paddocks to see. I looked a last look at Middlestride, who isn't such a much standing in a paddock that way, then I went to see Sunstreak.

It was his day. I knew when I see him. I forgot all about being seen myself and walked right up. All the men from Beckersville were there and no one noticed me except Jerry Tillford. He saw me and something happened. I'll tell you about that.

I was standing looking at that horse and aching. In some way, I can't tell how, I knew just how Sunstreak felt inside. He was quiet and letting the niggers rub his legs and Mr. Van Riddle himself put the saddle on, but he was just a raging torrent inside. He was like the water in the river at Niagara Falls just before it goes plunk down. That horse wasn't thinking about running. He don't have to think about that. He was just thinking about holding himself back 'til the time for the running came. I knew that. I could just in a way see right inside him. He was going to do some awful running and I knew it. He wasn't bragging or letting on much or prancing or making a fuss, but just waiting. I knew it and Jerry Tillford his trainer knew. I looked up and then that man and I looked into each other's eyes. Something happened to me. I guess I loved the man as much as I did the horse because he knew what I knew. Seemed to me there wasn't anything in the world but that man and the horse and me. I cried and Jerry Tillford had a shine in his eyes. Then I came away to the fence to wait for the race. The horse was better than me, more steadier, and now I know better than Jerry. He was the quietest and he had to do the running.

Sunstreak ran first of course and he busted the world's record for a mile. I've seen that if I never see anything more. Everything came out just as I expected. Middle-stride got left at the post and was way back and closed up to be second, just as I knew he would. He'll get a world's record too some day. They can't skin the Beckersville country on horses.

I watched the race calm because I knew what would happen. I was sure. Hanley Turner and Henry Rieback and Tom Tumberton were all more excited than me.

A funny thing had happened to me. I was thinking about Jerry Tillford the trainer and how happy he was all through the race. I liked him that afternoon even more than I ever liked my own father. I almost forgot the horses thinking that way about him. It was because of what I had seen in his eyes as he stood in the paddocks

beside Sunstreak before the race started. I knew he had
been watching and working with Sunstreak since the
horse was a baby colt, had taught him to run and be
patient and when to let himself out and not to quit,
never. I knew that for him it was like a mother seeing her
child do something brave or wonderful. It was the first
time I ever felt for a man like that.

After the race that night I cut out from Tom and
Hanley and Henry. I wanted to be by myself and I
wanted to be near Jerry Tillford if I could work it. Here
is what happened.

The track in Saratoga is near the edge of town. It
is all polished up and trees around, the evergreen kind,
and grass and everything painted and nice. If you go
past the track you get to a hard road made of asphalt
for automobiles, and if you go along this for a few miles
there is a road turns off to a little rummy-looking farm
house set in a yard.

That night after the race I went along that road
because I had seen Jerry and some other men go that way
in an automobile. I didn't expect to find them. I walked
for a ways and then sat down by a fence to think. It was
the direction they went in. I wanted to be as near Jerry
as I could. I felt close to him. Pretty soon I went up the
side road—I don't know why—and came to the rummy
farm house. I was just lonesome to see Jerry, like wanting
to see your father at night when you are a young kid.
Just then an automobile came along and turned in.
Jerry was in it and Henry Rieback's father, and Arthur
Bedford from home, and Dave Williams and two other
men I didn't know. They got out of the car and went into
the house, all but Henry Rieback's father who quarrelled
with them and said he wouldn't go. It was only about
nine o'clock, but they were all drunk and the rummy

looking farm house was a place for bad women to stay in. That's what it was. I crept up along a fence and looked through a window and saw.

It's what give me the fantods. I can't make it out. The women in the house were all ugly mean-looking women, not nice to look at or be near. They were homely too, except one who was tall and looked a little like the gelding Middlestride, but not clean like him, but with a hard ugly mouth. She had red hair. I saw everything plain. I got up by an old rose bush by an open window and looked. The women had on loose dresses and sat around in chairs. The men came in and some sat on the women's laps. The place smelled rotten and there was rotten talk, the kind a kid hears around a livery stable in a town like Beckersville in the winter but don't ever expect to hear talked when there are women around. It was rotten. A nigger wouldn't go into such a place.

I looked at Jerry Tillford. I've told you how I had been feeling about him on account of his knowing what was going on inside of Sunstreak in the minute before he went to the post for the race in which he made a world's record.

Jerry bragged in that bad woman house as I know Sunstreak wouldn't never have bragged. He said that he made that horse, that it was him that won the race and made the record. He lied and bragged like a fool. I never heard such silly talk.

And then, what do you suppose he did! He looked at the woman in there, the one that was lean and hard-mouthed and looked a little like the gelding Middlestride, but not clean like him, and his eyes began to shine just as they did when he looked at me and at Sunstreak in the paddocks at the track in the afternoon. I stood there by the window—gee!—but I wished I hadn't gone away from the tracks, but had stayed with the boys and the niggers and the horses. The tall rotten looking woman was between us just as Sunstreak was in the paddocks in the afternoon.

Then, all of a sudden, I began to hate that man. I wanted to scream and rush in the room and kill him. I never had such a feeling before. I was so mad clean through that I cried and my fists were doubled up so my finger nails cut my hands.

And Jerry's eyes eyes kept shining and he waved back and forth, and then he went and kissed that woman and I crept away and went back to the tracks and to bed and didn't sleep hardly any, and then next day I got the other kids to start home with me and never told them anything I seen.

I been thinking about it ever since. I can't make it out. Spring has come again and I'm nearly sixteen and go to the tracks mornings same as always, and I see Sunstreak and Middlestride and a new colt named Strident I'll bet will lay them all out, but no one thinks so but me and two or three niggers.

But things are different. At the tracks the air don't taste as good or smell as good. It's because a man like Jerry Tillford, who knows what he does, could see a horse like Sunstreak run, and kiss a woman like that the same day. I can't make it out. Darn him, what did he want to do like that for? I keep thinking about it and it spoils looking at horses and smelling things and hearing niggers laugh and everything. Sometimes I'm so mad about it I want to fight someone. It gives me the fantods. What did he do it for? I want to know why.

A Day's Work

KATHERINE ANNE PORTER

(b. 1890)

THE dull scrambling like a giant rat in the wall meant the dumb-waiter was on its way up, the janitress below hauling on the cable. Mrs. Halloran paused, thumped her iron on the board, and said, 'There it is. Late. You could have put on your shoes and gone around the corner and brought the things an hour ago. I can't do everything.'

Mr. Halloran pulled himself out of the chair, clutching the arms and heaving to his feet slowly, looking around as if he hoped to find crutches standing near. 'Wearing out your socks, too,' added Mrs. Halloran. 'You ought either go barefoot outright or wear your shoes over your socks as God intended,' she said. 'Sock feet. What's the good of it, I'd like to know? Neither one thing nor the other.'

She unrolled a salmon-coloured chiffon nightgown with cream-coloured lace and broad ribbons on it, gave it a light flirt in the air, and spread it on the board. 'God's mercy, look at that indecent thing,' she said. She thumped the iron again and pushed it back and forth over the rumpled cloth. 'You might just set the things in the cupboard,' she said, 'and not leave them around on the floor. You might just.'

Mr. Halloran took a sack of potatoes from the dumb-waiter and started for the cupboard in the corner next the icebox. 'You might as well take a load,' said Mrs. Halloran. 'There's no need on earth making a half-dozen trips back and forth. I'd think the poorest sort of man could well carry more than five pounds of potatoes at one time. But maybe not.'

Her voice tapped on Mr. Halloran's ears like wood on wood. 'Mind your business, will you?' he asked, not speaking to her directly. He carried on the argument with himself. 'Oh, I couldn't do that, Mister Honey,' he answered in a dull falsetto. 'Don't ever ask me to think of such a thing, even. It wouldn't be right,' he said, standing still with his knees bent, glaring bitterly over the potato sack at the scrawny strange woman he had never liked, that one standing there ironing clothes with a dirty look on her whole face like a suffering saint. 'I may not be much good any more,' he told her in his own voice, 'but I still have got wits enough to take groceries off a dumb-waiter, mind you.'

'That's a miracle,' said Mrs. Halloran. 'I'm thankful for that much.'

'There's the telephone,' said Mr. Halloran, sitting in the armchair again and taking his pipe out of his shirt pocket.

'I heard it as well,' said Mrs. Halloran, sliding the iron up and down over the salmon-coloured chiffon.

'It's for you, I've no further business in this world,' said Mr. Halloran. His little greenish eyes glittered; he exposed his two sharp dog-teeth in a grin.

'You could answer it. It could be the wrong number again or for somebody downstairs,' said Mrs. Halloran, her flat voice going flatter, even.

'Let it go in any case,' decided Mr. Halloran, 'for my own part, that is.' He struck a match on the arm of his chair, touched off his pipe, and drew in his first puff while the telephone went on with its nagging.

'It might be Maggie again,' said Mrs. Halloran.

'Let her ring, then,' said Mr. Halloran, settling back and crossing his legs.

'God help a man who won't answer the telephone when his own daughter calls up for a word,' commented Mrs. Halloran to the ceiling. 'And she in deep trouble, too, with her husband treating her like a dog about the money, and sitting out late nights in saloons with that crowd from the Little Tammany Association. He's getting into politics now with the McCorkery gang. No good will come of it, and I told her as much.'

'She's no troubles at all, her man's a sharp fellow who will get ahead if she'll let him alone,' said Mr. Halloran. 'She's nothing to complain of, I could tell her. But what's a father?' Mr. Halloran cocked his head towards the window that opened on the brick-paved areaway and crowed like a rooster, 'What's a father these days and who would heed his advice?'

'You needn't tell the neighbours, there's disgrace enough already,' said Mrs. Halloran. She set the iron back on the gas ring and stepped out to the telephone on the first stair landing. Mr. Halloran leaned forward, his thin, red-haired hands hanging loosely between his knees, his warm pipe sending up its good decent smell right into his nose. The woman hated the pipe and the smell; she was a woman born to make any man miserable. Before the depression, while he still had a good job and prospects of a raise, before he went on relief, before she took in fancy washing and ironing, in the Good Days Before, God's pity, she didn't exactly keep her mouth shut, there wasn't a word known to man she couldn't find an answer for, but she knew which side her bread was buttered on, and put up with it. Now she was, you might say, buttering her own bread and she never forgot it for a minute. And it's her own fault we're not riding round today in a limousine with ash trays and a speaking tube and a cut-glass vase for flowers in it. It's what a man gets for marrying one of these holy women. Gerald McCorkery had told him as much, in the beginning.

'There's a girl will spend her time holding you down,' Gerald had told him. 'You're putting your head in a noose will strangle the life out of you. Heed the advice of one who wishes you well,' said Gerald McCorkery. This was after he had barely set eyes on Lacey Mahaffy one Sunday morning in Coney Island. It was like McCorkery to see that in a flash, born judge of human nature that he was. He could look a man over, size him up, and there was an end to it. And if the man didn't pass muster, McCorkery could ease him out in a way that man would never know how it happened. It was the secret of McCorkery's success in the world.

'This is Rosie, herself,' said Gerald that Sunday in Coney Island. 'Meet the future Mrs. Gerald J. McCorkery.' Lacey Mahaffy's narrow face had gone sour as whey under her big straw hat. She barely nodded to Rosie, who gave Mr. Halloran a look that fairly undressed him right there. Mr. Halloran had thought, too, that McCorkery was picking a strange one; she was good-looking all right, but she had the smell of a regular little Fourteenth Street hustler if Halloran knew anything about women. 'Come on,' said McCorkery, his arm around Rosie's waist, 'let's all go on the roller coaster.' But Lacey would not. She said, 'No, thank you. We didn't plan to stay, and we must go now.' On the way home Mr. Halloran said, 'Lacey, you judge too harshly. Maybe that's a nice girl at heart; hasn't had your opportunities.' Lacey had turned upon him a face ugly as an angry cat's, and said, 'She's a loose, low woman, and 'twas an insult to introduce her to me.' It was a good

while before the pretty fresh face that Mr. Halloran had
fallen in love with returned to her.

Next day in Billy's Place, after three drinks each,
McCorkery said, 'Watch your step, Halloran; think of
your future. There's a straight good girl I don't doubt,
but she's no sort of mixer. A man getting into politics
needs a wife who can meet all kinds. A man needs a
woman knows how to loosen her corsets and sit easy.'

Mrs. Halloran's voice was going on in the hall, a steady
dry rattle like old newspapers blowing on a park bench.
'I told you before it's no good coming to me with your
troubles now. I warned you in time but you wouldn't
listen. . . . I told you just how it would be, I tried my
best. . . . No, you couldn't listen, you always knew better
than your mother. . . . So now all you've got to do is
stand by your married vows and make the best of it. . . .
Now listen to me, if you want himself to do right you
have to do right first. The woman has to do right first,
and then if the man won't do right in turn it's no fault of
hers. You do right whether he does wrong or no, just
because he does wrong is no excuse for you.'

'Ah, will you hear that?' Mr. Halloran asked the areaway in an awed voice. 'There's a holy terror of a saint
for you.'

'. . . the woman has to do right first, I'm telling you,'
said Mrs. Halloran into the telephone, 'and then if he's
a devil in spite of it, why she has to do right without any
help from him.' Her voice rose so the neighbours could
get an earful if they wanted. 'I know you from old, you're
just like your father. You must be doing something
wrong yourself or you wouldn't be in this fix. You're
doing wrong this minute, calling over the telephone
when you ought to be getting your work done. I've got
an iron on, working over the dirty nightgowns of a kind

of woman I wouldn't soil my foot on if I'd had a man to take care of me. So now you do up your housework and dress yourself and take a walk in the fresh air. . . .'

'A little fresh air never hurt anybody,' commented Mr. Halloran loudly through the open window. 'It's the gas gets a man down.'

'Now listen to me, Maggie, that's not the way to talk over the public wires. Now you stop that crying and go and do your duty and don't be worrying me any more. And stop saying you're going to leave your husband, because where will you go, for one thing? Do you want to walk the streets or set up a laundry in your kitchen? You can't come back here, you'll stay with your husband where you belong. Don't be a fool, Maggie. You've got your living, and that's more than many a woman better than you has got. Yes, your father's all right. No, he's just sitting here, the same. God knows what's to become of us. But you know how he is, little he cares. . . . Now remember this, Maggie, if anything goes wrong with your married life it's your own fault and you needn't come here for sympathy. . . . I can't waste any more time on it. Goodbye.'

Mr. Halloran, his ears standing up for fear of missing a word, thought how Gerald J. McCorkery had gone straight on up the ladder with Rosie; and for every step the McCorkerys took upward, he, Michael Halloran, had taken a step downward with Lacey Mahaffy. They had started as greenhorns with the same chances at the same time and the same friends, but McCorkery had seized all his opportunities as they came, getting in steadily with the Big Shots in ward politics, one good thing leading to another. Rosie had known how to back him up and push him onward. The McCorkerys for years had invited him and Lacey to come over to the house and be sociable with the crowd, but Lacey would not.

'You can't run with that fast set and drink and stay out nights and hold your job,' said Lacey, 'and you should know better than to ask your wife to associate with that woman.' Mr. Halloran had got into the habit of dropping around by himself, now and again, for McCorkery still liked him, was still willing to give him a foothold in the right places, still asked him for favours at election time. There was always a good lively crowd at the McCorkerys, wherever they were; for they moved ever so often to a better place, with more furniture. Rosie helped hand around the drinks, taking a few herself with a gay word for everybody. The player piano or the victrola would be going full blast, with everybody dancing, all looking like ready money and a bright future. He would get home late these evenings, back to the same little cold-water walk-up flat, because Lacey would not spend a dollar for show. It must all go into savings against old age, she said. He would be full of good food and drink, and find Lacey, in a bungalow apron, warming up the fried potatoes once more, cross and bitterly silent, hanging her head and frowning at the smell of liquor on his breath. 'You might at least eat the potatoes when I've fried them and waited all this time,' she would say. 'Ah, eat them yourself, they're none of mine,' he would snarl in his disappointment with her, and with the life she was leading him.

He had believed with all his heart for years that he would one day be manager of one of the G. and I. chain grocery stores he worked for, and when that hope gave out there was still his pension when they retired him. But two years before it was due they fired him, on account of the depression, they said. Overnight he was on the sidewalk, with no place to go with the news but home. 'Jesus,' said Mr. Halloran, still remembering that day after nearly seven years of idleness.

The depression hadn't touched McCorkery. He went on and on up the ladder, giving beefsteaks and bean-feasts and beer parties for the boys in Billy's Place, standing in with the right men and never missing a trick. At last the Gerald J. McCorkery Club chartered a whole boat for a big excursion up the river. It was a great day, with Lacey sitting at home sulking. After election Rosie had her picture in the papers, smiling at McCorkery; not fat exactly, just a fine figure of a woman with flowers pinned on her spotted fur coat, her teeth as good as ever. Oh, God, there was a girl for any man's money. Mr. Halloran saw out of his eye-corner the bony stooped back of Lacey Mahaffy, standing on one foot to rest the other like a tired old horse, leaning on her hands waiting for the iron to heat.

'That was Maggie, with her woes,' she said.

'I hope you gave her some good advice,' said Mr. Halloran. 'I hope you told her to take up her hat and walk out on him.'

Mrs. Halloran suspended the iron over a pair of pink satin panties. 'I told her to do right and leave wrong-doing to the men,' she said, in her voice like a phonograph record running down. 'I told her to bear with the trouble God sends as her mother did before her.'

Mr. Halloran gave a loud groan and knocked out his pipe on the chair arm. 'You would ruin the world, woman, if you could, with your wicked soul, treating a new-married girl as if she had no home and no parents to come to. But she's no daughter of mine if she sits there peeling potatoes, letting a man run over her. No daughter of mine and I'll tell her so if she. . . .'

'You know well she's your daughter, so hold your tongue,' said Mrs. Halloran, 'and if she heeded you she'd be walking the streets this minute. I brought her up an honest girl, and an honest woman she's going to be or I'll take her over my knee as I did when she was little. So there you are, Halloran.'

Mr. Halloran leaned far back in his chair and felt along the shelf above his head until his fingers touched a half-dollar he had noticed there. His hand closed over it, he got up instantly and looked about for his hat.

'Keep your daughter, Lacey Mahaffy,' he said, 'she's none of mine but the fruits of your long sinning with the Holy Ghost. And now I'm off for a little round and a couple of beers to keep my mind from dissolving entirely.'

'You can't have that dollar you just now sneaked off the shelf,' said Mrs. Halloran. 'So you think I'm blind besides? Put it back where you found it. That's for our daily bread.'

'I'm sick of bread daily,' said Mr. Halloran, 'I need beer. It was not a dollar, but a half-dollar, as you know well.'

'Whatever it was,' said Mrs. Halloran, 'it stands instead of a dollar to me. So just drop it.'

'You've got tomorrow's potatoes sewed up in your pocket this minute, and God knows what sum's in that black box wherever you hide it, besides the life savings,' said Mr. Halloran. 'I earned this half-dollar on relief, and it's going to be spent properly. And I'll not be back for supper, so you'll save on that, too. So long, Lacey Mahaffy, I'm off.'

'If you never come back, it will be all the same,' said Mrs. Halloran, not looking up.

'If I came back with a pocket full of money, you'd be glad to see me,' said Mr. Halloran.

'It would want to be a great sum,' said Mrs. Halloran. Mr. Halloran shut the door behind him with a fine slam.

He strolled out into the clear fall weather, a late afternoon sun warming his neck and brightening the old red-brick, high-stooped houses of Perry Street. He would go after all these years to Billy's Place, he might find some luck there. He took his time, though, speaking to the neighbours as he went. 'Good afternoon, Mr. Halloran.' 'Good afternoon to you, Missis Caffery. . . .' 'It's fine weather for the time of year, Mr. Gogarty.' 'It is indeed, Mr. Halloran.' Mr. Halloran thrived on these civilities, he loved to flourish his hat and give a hearty good day like a man who has nothing on his mind. Ah, there was the young man from the G. and I. store around the corner. He knew what kind of job Mr. Halloran once held there. 'Good day, Mr. Halloran.' 'Good day to you, Mr. McInerny, how's business holding up with you?' 'Good for the times, Mr. Halloran, that's the best I can say.' 'Things are not getting any better, Mr. McInerny.' 'It's the truth we are all hanging on by the teeth now, Mr. Halloran.'

Soothed by this acknowledgment of man's common misfortune Mr. Halloran greeted the young cop at the corner. The cop, with his quick eyesight, was snatching a read from a newspaper on the stand across the sidewalk. 'How do you do, Young O'Fallon,' asked Mr. Halloran, 'is your business lively these days?'

'Quiet as the tomb itself on this block,' said Young O'Fallon. 'But that's a sad thing about Connolly, now.' His eyes motioned towards the newspaper.

'Is he dead?' asked Mr. Halloran; 'I haven't been out until now, I didn't see the papers.'

'Ah, not yet,' said Young O'Fallon, 'but the G-men are after him, it looks they'll get him surely this time.'

'Connolly in bad with the G-men? Holy Jesus,' said
Mr. Halloran, 'who will they go after next? The medd-
lers.'

'It's that numbers racket,' said the cop. 'What's
the harm, I'd like to know? A man must get his money
from somewhere when he's in politics. They oughta
give him a chance.'

'Connolly's a great fellow, God bless him, I hope he
gives them the slip,' said Mr. Halloran. 'I hope he goes
right through their hands like a greased pig.'

'He's smart,' said the cop. 'That Connolly's a smooth
one. He'll come out of it.'

Ah, will he though? Mr. Halloran asked himself.
Who is safe if Connolly goes under? Wait till I give Lacey
Mahaffy the news about Connolly. I'll like seeing her
face the first time in twenty years. Lacey kept saying,
'A man is a downright fool thinking he must be a crook
to get rich. Plenty of the best people get rich and do no
harm by it. Look at the Connollys now, good practical
Catholics with nine children and more to come if God
sends them, and Mass every day, and they're rolling in
wealth richer than your McCorkerys with all their
wickedness.' So there you are, Lacey Mahaffy, wrong
again, and welcome to your pious Connollys. Still and
all it was Connolly who had given Gerald McCorkery
his start in the world; McCorkery had been publicity
man and then campaign manager for Connolly, in the
days when Connolly had Tammany in the palm of his
hand and the sky was the limit. And McCorkery had
begun at the beginning, God knows. He was running a
little basement place first, rent almost nothing, where the
boys of the Connolly Club and the Little Tammany
Association, just the mere fringe of the district, you
might say, could drop in for quiet evenings for a game

and a drink along with the talk. Nothing low, nothing but what was customary, with the house taking a cut on the winnings and a fine profit on the liquor, and holding the crowd together. Many was the big plan hatched there came out well for everybody. For everybody but myself, and why was that? And when McCorkery says to me, 'You can take over now and run the place for the McCorkery Club,' ah, there was my chance and Lacey Mahaffy wouldn't hear of it, and with Maggie coming on just then it wouldn't do to excite her.

Mr. Halloran went on, following his feet that knew the way to Billy's Place, head down, not speaking to passers-by any more, but talking it out with himself again, again. What a track to go over seeing clearly one by one the crossroads where he might have taken a different turn that would have changed all his fortunes; but no, he had gone the other way and now it was too late. She wouldn't say a thing but 'It's not right and you know it, Halloran,' so what could a man do in all? Ah, you could have gone on with your rightful affairs like any other man, Halloran, it's not the woman's place to decide such things; she'd have come round once she saw the money, or a good whack on the backsides would have put her in her place. Never had mortal woman needed a good walloping worse than Lacey Mahaffy, but he could never find it in his heart to give it to her for her own good. That was just another of your many mistakes, Halloran. But there was always the lifelong job with the G. and I. and peace in the house more or less. Many a man envied me in those days I remember, and I was resting easy on the savings and knowing with that and the pension I could finish out my life with some little business of my own. 'What came of that?' Mr. Halloran inquired in a low voice, looking around him. Nobody answered. You know well what came of it, Halloran. You were fired out like a delivery boy, two years before your time was out. Why did you sit there watching the trick being played on others before you, knowing well it could happen to you and never quite believing what you saw with your own eyes? G. and I. gave me my start, when I was green in this country, and they were my own kind or I thought so. Well, it's done now. Yes, it's done now, but there was all the years you could have cashed in on the numbers game with the best of them, helping collect the protection money and taking your cut. You could have had a fortune by now in Lacey's name, safe in the bank. It was good quiet profit and none the wiser. But they're wiser now, Halloran, don't forget; still it's a lump of grief and disappointment to swallow all the same. The game's up with Connolly, maybe; Lacey Mahaffy had said, 'Numbers is just another way of stealing from the poor, and you weren't born to be a thief like that McCorkery.' Ah, God, no, Halloran, you were born to rot on relief and maybe that's honest enough for her. That Lacey—A fortune in her name would have been no good to me whatever. She's got all the savings tied up, such as they are, she'll pinch and she'll starve, she'll wash dirty clothes first, she won't give up a penny to live on. She has stood in my way, McCorkery, like a skeleton rattling its bones, and you were right about her, she has been my ruin. 'Ah, it's not too late yet, Halloran,' said McCorkery, appearing plain as day inside Mr. Halloran's head with the same old face and way with him. 'Never say die, Halloran. Elections are coming on again, it's a busy time for all, there's work to be done and you're the very man I'm looking for. Why didn't you come to me sooner, you know I never forget an old friend. You don't deserve your ill fortune, Halloran,' McCorkery told him; 'I said so to others and I say it now to your face, never did man deserve more of the world than you, Halloran, but the truth is, there's not always enough good luck to go round; but it's your turn now, and I've got a job for you up to your abilities at last. For a man like you, there's nothing to it at all, you can toss it off with one hand tied, Halloran, and good money in it. Organization work, just among your own neighbours, where you're known and respected for a man of your word and an old friend of Gerald McCorkery. Now look, Halloran,' said Gerald McCorkery, tipping him the wink, 'do I need to say more? It's voters in large numbers we're after, Halloran, and you're to bring them in, alive or dead. Keep your eye on the situation at all times and get in touch with me when necessary. And name your figure in the way of money. And come up to the house sometimes, Halloran, why don't you? Rosie has asked me a hundred times, "Whatever went with Halloran, the life of the party?" That's the way you stand with Rosie, Halloran. We're in a two-storey flat now with green velvet curtains and carpets you can sink to your shoetops in, and there's no reason at all why you shouldn't have the same kind of place if you want it. With your gifts, you were never meant to be a poor man.'

Ah, but Lacey Mahaffy wouldn't have it, maybe. 'Then get yourself another sort of woman, Halloran, you're a good man still, find yourself a woman like Rosie to snuggle down with at night.' Yes, but McCorkery, you forget that Lacey Mahaffy had legs and hair and eyes and a complexion fit for a chorus girl. But would she do anything with them? Never. Would you believe there was a woman wouldn't take off all her clothes at once even to bathe herself? What a hateful thing she was with her evil mind thinking everything was a sin, and never giving a man a chance to show himself a man in any way. But she's faded away now, her mean soul shows out all over her, she's ugly as sin itself now, McCorkery. 'It's what I told you would happen,' said McCorkery, 'but now with the job and the money you can go your ways and let Lacey Mahaffy go hers.' I'll do it, McCorkery. 'And forget about Connolly. Just remember I'm my own man and always was. Connolly's finished, but I'm not. Stronger than ever, Halloran, with Connolly out of the way. I saw this coming long ever ago, Halloran, I got clear of it. They don't catch McCorkery with his pants down, Halloran. And I almost forgot. . . . Here's something for the running expenses to start. Take this for the present, and there's more to come. . . .'

Mr. Halloran stopped short, a familiar smell floated under his nose: the warm beer-and-beefsteak smell of Billy's Place, sawdust and onions, like any other bar maybe, but with something of its own besides. The talk within him stopped also as if a hand had been laid on his mind. He drew his fist out of his pocket almost expecting to find green money in it. The half-dollar was in his palm. 'I'll stay while it lasts and hope McCorkery will come in.'

The moment he stepped inside his eye lighted on McCorkery standing at the bar pouring his own drink from the bottle before him. Billy was mopping the bar before him idly, and his eye, swimming towards Halloran, looked like an oyster in its own juice. McCorkery saw him too. 'Well, blow me down,' he said, in a voice that had almost lost its old County Mayo ring, 'if it ain't my old sidekick from the G. and I. Step right up, Halloran,' he said, his poker-face as good as ever, no man ever saw Gerald McCorkery surprised at anything. 'Step up and name your choice.'

Mr. Halloran glowed suddenly with the warmth around the heart he always had at the sight of McCorkery, he couldn't put a name on it, but there was something about the man. Ah, it was Gerald all right, the same, who never forgot a friend and never seemed to care whether a man was rich or poor, with his face of granite and his eyes like blue agates in his head, a rock of a man surely. There he was, saying 'Step right up', as if they had parted only yesterday; portly and solid in his expensive-looking clothes, as always; his hat a darker grey than his suit, with a devil-may-care roll to the brim, but nothing sporting, mind you. All first-rate, well made, and the right thing for him, more power to him. Mr. Halloran said, 'Ah, McCorkery, you're the one man on this round earth I hoped to see today, but I says to myself, maybe he doesn't come round to Billy's Place so much nowadays.'

'And why not?' asked McCorkery, 'I've been coming around to Billy's Place for twenty-five years now, it's still headquarters for the old guard of the McCorkery Club, Halloran.' He took in Mr. Halloran from head to foot in a flash of a glance and turned towards the bottle.

'I was going to have a beer,' said Mr. Halloran, 'but the smell of that whisky changes my mind for me.' McCorkery poured a second glass, they lifted the drinks with an identical crook of the elbow, a flick of the wrist at each other.

'Here's to crime,' said McCorkery, and 'Here's looking at you,' said Mr. Halloran, merrily. Ah, to hell with it, he was back where he belonged, in good company. He put his foot on the rail and snapped down his whisky, and no sooner was his glass on the bar than McCorkery was filling it again. 'Just time for a few quick ones,' he said, 'before the boys get here.' Mr. Halloran downed that one, too, before he noticed that McCorkery hadn't filled his own glass. 'I'm ahead of you,' said McCorkery, 'I'll skip this one.'

There was a short pause, a silence fell around them that seemed to ooze like a fog from somewhere deep in McCorkery, it was suddenly as if he had not really been there at all, or hadn't uttered a word. Then he said outright: 'Well, Halloran, let's have it. What's on your mind?' And he poured two more drinks. That was McCorkery all over, reading your thoughts and coming straight to the point.

Mr. Halloran closed his hand round his glass and peered into the little pool of whisky. 'Maybe we could sit down,' he said, feeling weak-kneed all at once. McCorkery took the bottle and moved over to the nearest table. He sat facing the door, his look straying there now and then, but he had a set, listening face as if he was ready to hear anything.

'You know what I've had at home all these years,' began Mr. Halloran, solemnly, and paused.

'Oh, God, yes,' said McCorkery, with simple good-fellowship. 'How is herself these days?'

'Worse than ever,' said Mr. Halloran, 'but that's not it.'

'What is it, then, Halloran?' asked McCorkery, pouring drinks. 'You know well you can speak out your mind to me. Is it a loan?'

'No,' said Mr. Halloran. 'It's a job.'

'Now that's a different matter,' said McCorkery. 'What kind of a job?'

Mr. Halloran, his head sunk between his shoulders, saw McCorkery wave a hand and nod at half a dozen men who came in and ranged themselves along the bar. 'Some of the boys,' said McCorkery. 'Go on.' His face was tougher, and quieter, as if the drink gave him a firm hold on himself. Mr. Halloran said what he had planned to say, had said already on the way down, and it still sounded reasonable and right to him. McCorkery waited until he had finished, and got up, putting a hand on Mr. Halloran's shoulder. 'Stay where you are, and help yourself,' he said, giving the bottle a little push, 'and anything else you want, Halloran, order it on me. I'll be back in a few minutes, and you know I'll help you out if I can.'

Halloran understood everything but it was through a soft warm fog, and he hardly noticed when McCorkery passed him again with the men, all in that creepy quiet way like footpads on a dark street. They went into the back room, the door opened on a bright light and closed again, and Mr. Halloran reached for the bottle to help himself wait until McCorkery should come again bringing the good word. He felt comfortable and easy as if he hadn't a bone or muscle in him, but his elbow slipped off the table once or twice and he upset his drink on his sleeve. Ah, McCorkery, is it the whole family you're taking on with the jobs? For my Maggie's husband is in now with the Little Tammany Association. 'There's a bright lad will go far and I've got my eye on him, Halloran,' said the friendly voice of McCorkery in his mind, and the brown face, softer than he remembered it, came up clearly behind his closed eyes.

'Ah, well, it's like myself beginning all over again in him,' said Mr. Halloran, aloud, 'besides my own job that I might have had all this time if I'd just come to see you sooner.'

'True for you,' said McCorkery in a merry County Mayo voice, inside Mr. Halloran's head, 'and now let's drink to the gay future for old times' sake and be damned to Lacey Mahaffy.' Mr. Halloran reached for the bottle but it skipped sideways, rolled out of reach like a creature, and exploded at his feet. When he stood up the chair fell backward from under him. He leaned on the table and it folded up under his hands like cardboard.

'Wait now, take it easy,' said McCorkery, and there he was, real enough, holding Mr. Halloran braced on the one side, motioning with his hand to the boys in the back room, who came out quietly and took hold of Mr. Halloran, some of them, on the other side. Their faces were all Irish, but not an Irishman Mr. Halloran knew in the lot, and he did not like any face he saw. 'Let me be,' he said with dignity, 'I came here to see Gerald J. McCorkery, a friend of mine from old times, and let not a thug among you lay a finger upon me.'

'Come on, Big Shot,' said one of the younger men, in a voice like a file grating, 'come on now, it's time to go.'

'That's a fine low lot you've picked to run with, McCorkery,' said Mr. Halloran, bracing his heels against the slow weight they put upon him towards the door, 'I wouldn't trust one of them far as I could throw him by the tail.'

'All right, all right, Halloran,' said McCorkery. 'Come on with me. Lay off him, Finnegan.' He was leaning over Mr. Halloran and pressing something into his right hand. It was money, a neat little roll of it, good smooth thick money, no other feel like it in the world, you couldn't mistake it. Ah, he'd have an argument to show Lacey Mahaffy would knock her off her feet. Honest money with a job to back it up. 'You'll stand by your given word, McCorkery, as ever?' he asked, peering into the rock-coloured face above him, his feet weaving a dance under him, his heart ready to break with gratitude.

'Ah, sure, sure,' said McCorkery in a loud hearty voice with a kind of curse in it. 'Crisakes, get on with him, do.' Mr. Halloran found himself eased into a taxi-cab at the kerb, with McCorkery speaking to the driver and giving him money. 'So long, Big Shot,' said one of the thug faces, and the taxicab door thumped to. Mr. Halloran bobbed about on the seat for a while, trying to think. He leaned forward and spoke to the driver. 'Take me to my friend Gerald J. McCorkery's house,' he said, 'I've got important business. Don't pay any attention to what he said. Take me to his house.'

'Yeah?' said the driver, without turning his head. 'Well, here's where you get out, see? Right here.' He reached back and opened the door. And sure enough, Mr. Halloran was standing on the sidewalk in front of the flat in Perry Street, alone except for the rows of garbage cans, the taxicab hooting its way around the corner, and a cop coming towards him, plainly to be seen under the street light.

'You should cast your vote for McCorkery, the poor man's friend,' Mr. Halloran told the cop. 'McCorkery's the man who will get us all off the spot. Stands by his old friends like a maniac. Got a wife named Rosie. Vote for McCorkery,' said Mr. Halloran, working hard at his job, 'and you'll be Chief of the Force when Halloran says the word.'

'To hell with McCorkery, that stooge,' said the cop, his mouth square and sour with the things he said and the things he saw and did every night on that beat. 'There you are drunk again, Halloran, shame to you, with Lacey Mahaffy working her heart out over the washboard to buy your beer.'

'It wasn't beer and she didn't buy it, mind you,' said Mr. Halloran, 'and what do you know about Lacey Mahaffy?'

'I knew her from old when I used to run errands for

St. Veronica's Altar Society,' said the cop, 'and she was a great one, even then. Nothing good enough.'

'It's the same today,' said Mr. Halloran, almost sober for a moment.

'Well, go on up now and stay up till you're fit to be seen,' said the cop, censoriously.

'You're Johnny Maginnis,' said Mr. Halloran, 'I know you well.'

'You should know me by now,' said the cop.

Mr. Halloran worked his way upstairs partly on his hands and knees, but once at his own door he stood up, gave a great blow on the panel with his fist, turned the knob and surged in like a wave after the door itself, holding out the money towards Mrs. Halloran, who had finished ironing and was at her mending.

She got up very slowly, her bony hand over her mouth, her eyes starting out at what she saw. 'Ah, did you steal it?' she asked. 'Did you kill somebody for that?' the words grated up from her throat in a dark whisper. Mr. Halloran glared back at her in fear.

'Suffering Saints, Lacey Mahaffy,' he shouted until the whole houseful could hear him, 'haven't ye any mind at all that you can't see your husband has had a turn of fortune and a job and times are changed from tonight? Stealing, is it? That's for your great friends the Connollys with their religion. Connolly steals, but Halloran is an honest man with a job in the McCorkery Club, and money in pocket.'

'McCorkery, is it?' said Mrs. Halloran, loudly too. 'Ah, so there's the whole family, young and old, wicked and innocent, taking their bread from McCorkery, at last. Well, it's no bread of mine, I'll earn my own as I have, you can keep your dirty money to yourself, Halloran, mind you I mean it.'

'Great God, woman,' moaned Mr. Halloran, and he tottered from the door to the table, to the ironing board, and stood there, ready to weep with rage, 'haven't you a soul even that you won't come along with your husband when he's riding to riches and glory on the Tiger's back itself, with everything for the taking and no questions asked?'

'Yes, I have a soul,' cries Mrs. Halloran, clenching her fists, her hair flying. 'Surely I have a soul and I'll save it yet in spite of you. . . .'

She was standing there before him in a kind of faded gingham winding sheet, with her dead hands upraised, her dead eyes blind but fixed upon him, her voice coming up hollow from the deep tomb, her throat thick with grave damp. The ghost of Lacey Mahaffy was threatening him, it came nearer, growing taller as it came, the face changing to a demon's face with a fixed glassy grin. 'It's all that drink on an empty stomach,' said the ghost, in a hoarse growl. Mr. Halloran fetched a yell of horror right out of his very boots, and seized the flatiron from the board. 'Ah, God damn you, Lacey Mahaffy, you devil, keep away, keep away,' he howled, but she advanced on air, grinning and growling. He raised the flatiron and hurled it without aiming, and the spectre, whoever it was, whatever it was, sank and was gone. He did not look, but broke out of the room and was back on the sidewalk before he knew he had meant to go there. Maginnis came up at once. 'Hey there now, Halloran,' he said, 'I mean business this time. You get back upstairs or I'll run you in. Come along now, I'll help you get there this time, and that's the last of it. On relief the way you are, and drinking your head off.'

Mr. Halloran suddenly felt calm, collected; he would take Maginnis up and show him just what had happened.

'I'm not on relief any more, and if you want any trouble, just call on my friend, McCorkery. He'll tell you who I am.'

'McCorkery can't tell me anything about you I don't know already,' said Maginnis. 'Stand up there now.' For Halloran wanted to go up again on his hands and knees.

'Let a man be,' said Mr. Halloran, trying to sit on the cop's feet. 'I killed Lacey Mahaffy at last, you'll be pleased to hear,' he said, looking up into the cop's face. 'It was high time and past. But I did not steal the money.'

'Well, ain't that just too bad,' said the cop, hauling him up under the arms. 'Chees, whyn't you make a good job while you had the chance? Stand up now. Ah, hell with it, stand up or I'll sock you one.'

Mr. Halloran said, 'Well, you don't believe it so wait and see.'

At that moment they both glanced upward and saw Mrs. Halloran coming downstairs. She was holding to the rail, and even in the speckled hall-light they could see a great lumpy clout of flesh standing out on her forehead, all colours. She stopped, and seemed not at all surprised.

'So there you are, Officer Maginnis,' she said. 'Bring him up.'

'That's a fine welt you've got over your eye this time, Mrs. Halloran,' commented Officer Maginnis, politely.

'I fell and hit my head on the ironing board,' said Mrs. Halloran. 'It comes of overwork and worry, day and night. A dead faint, Officer Maginnis. Watch your big feet there, you thriving, natural fool,' she added to Mr. Halloran. 'He's got a job now, you mightn't believe it, Officer Maginnis, but it's true. Bring him on up, and thank you.'

She went ahead of them, opened the door, and led the way to the bedroom through the kitchen, turned back the covers, and Officer Maginnis dumped Mr. Halloran among the quilts and pillows. Mr. Halloran rolled over with a deep groan and shut his eyes.

'Many thanks to you, Officer Maginnis,' said Mrs. Halloran.

'Don't mention it, Mrs. Halloran,' said Officer Maginnis.

When the door was shut and locked, Mrs. Halloran went and dipped a large bath towel under the kitchen tap. She wrung it out and tied several good hard knots in one end and tried it out with a whack on the edge of the table. She walked in and stood over the bed and brought the knotted towel down in Mr. Halloran's face with all her might. He stirred and muttered, ill at ease. 'That's for the flatiron, Halloran,' she told him, in a cautious voice as if she were talking to herself, and whack, down came the towel again. 'That's for the half-dollar,' she said, and whack, 'that's for your drunkenness. . . .' Her arm swung around regularly, ending with a heavy thud on the face that was beginning to squirm, gasp, lift itself from the pillow and fall back again, in a puzzled kind of torment. 'For your sock feet,' Mrs. Halloran told him, whack, 'and your laziness, and this is for missing Mass and'—here she swung half a dozen times—'that is for your daughter and your part in her. . . .'

She stood back breathless, the lump on her forehead burning in its furious colours. When Mr. Halloran attempted to rise, shielding his head with his arms, she gave him a push and he fell back again. 'Stay there and don't give me a word,' said Mrs. Halloran. He pulled the pillow over his face and subsided again, this time for good.

Mrs. Halloran moved about very deliberately. She tied the wet towel around her head, the knotted end hanging over her shoulder. Her hand ran into her apron pocket and came out again with the money. There was a five-dollar bill with three one-dollar bills rolled in it, and the half-dollar she had thought spent long since. 'A poor start, but something,' she said, and opened the cupboard door with a long key. Reaching in, she pulled a loosely fitted board out of the wall, and removed a black-painted metal box. She unlocked this, took out one five-cent piece from a welter of notes and coins. She then placed the new money in the box, locked it, put it away, replaced the board, shut the cupboard door and locked that. She went out to the telephone, dropped the nickel in the slot, asked for a number, and waited.

'Is that you, Maggie? Well, are things any better with you now? I'm glad to hear it. It's late to be calling, but there's news about your father. No, no, nothing of that kind, he's got a job. I said a *job*. Yes, at last, after all my urging him onward. . . . I've got him bedded down to sleep it off so he'll be ready for work tomorrow. . . . Yes, it's political work, towards the election time, with Gerald McCorkery. But that's no harm, getting votes and all, he'll be in the open air and it doesn't mean I'll have to associate with low people, now or ever. It's clean enough work, with good pay; if it's not just what I prayed for, still it beats nothing, Maggie. After all my trying . . . it's like a miracle. You see what can be done with patience and doing your duty, Maggie. Now mind you do as well by your own husband.'

Dry September

WILLIAM FAULKNER

(1897–1962)

I

THROUGH the bloody September twilight, aftermath of sixty-two rainless days, it had gone like a fire in dry grass—the rumour, the story, whatever it was. Something about Miss Minnie Cooper and a Negro. Attacked, insulted, frightened: none of them, gathered in the barber shop on that Saturday evening where the ceiling fan stirred, without freshening it, the vitiated air, sending back upon them, in recurrent surges of stale pomade and lotion, their own stale breath and odours, knew exactly what had happened.

'Except it wasn't Will Mayes,' a barber said. He was a man of middle age; a thin, sand-coloured man with a mild face, who was shaving a client. 'I know Will Mayes. He's a good nigger. And I know Miss Minnie Cooper, too.'

'What do you know about her?' a second barber said.

'Who is she?' the client said. 'A young girl?'

'No,' the barber said. 'She's about forty, I reckon. She ain't married. That's why I don't believe—'

'Believe, hell!' a hulking youth in a sweat-stained silk shirt said. 'Won't you take a white woman's word before a nigger's?'

'I don't believe Will Mayes did it,' the barber said. 'I know Will Mayes.'

'Maybe you know who did it, then. Maybe you already got him out of town, you damn niggerlover.'

'I don't believe anybody did anything. I don't believe anything happened. I leave it to you fellows if them ladies that get old without getting married don't have notions that a man can't—'

'Then you are a hell of a white man,' the client said. He moved under the cloth. The youth had sprung to his feet.

'You don't?' he said. 'Do you accuse a white woman of lying?'

The barber held the razor poised above the half-risen client. He did not look around.

'It's this durn weather,' another said. 'It's enough to make a man do anything. Even to her.'

Nobody laughed. The barber said in his mild, stubborn tone: 'I ain't accusing nobody of nothing. I just know and you fellows know how a woman that never—'

'You damn niggerlover!' the youth said.

'Shut up, Butch,' another said. 'We'll get the facts in plenty of time to act.'

'Who is? Who's getting them?' the youth said. 'Facts, hell! I—'

'You're a fine white man,' the client said. 'Ain't you?' In his frothy beard he looked like a desert rat in the moving pictures. 'You tell them, Jack,' he said to the youth. 'If there ain't any white men in this town, you can count on me, even if I ain't only a drummer and a stranger.'

'That's right, boys,' the barber said. 'Find out the truth first. I know Will Mayes.'

'Well, by God!' the youth shouted. 'To think that a white man in this town—'

'Shut up, Butch,' the second speaker said. 'We got plenty of time.'

The client sat up. He looked at the speaker. 'Do you

claim that anything excuses a nigger attacking a white woman? Do you mean to tell me you are a white man and you'll stand for it? You better go back North where you came from. The South don't want your kind here.'

'North what?' the second said. 'I was born and raised in this town.'

'Well, by God!' the youth said. He looked about with a strained, baffled gaze, as if he was trying to remember what it was he wanted to say or to do. He drew his sleeve across his sweating face. 'Damn if I'm going to let a white woman—'

'You tell them, Jack,' the drummer said. 'By God, if they—'

The screen door crashed open. A man stood in the floor, his feet apart and his heavy-set body poised easily. His white shirt was open at the throat; he wore a felt hat. His hot, bold glance swept the group. His name was McLendon. He had commanded troops at the front in France and had been decorated for valour.

'Well,' he said, 'are you going to sit there and let a black son rape a white woman on the streets of Jefferson?'

Butch sprang up again. The silk of his shirt clung flat to his heavy shoulders. At each armpit was a dark half moon. 'That's what I been telling them! That's what I—'

'Did it really happen?' a third said. 'This ain't the first man scare she ever had, like Hawkshaw says. Wasn't there something about a man on the kitchen roof, watching her undress, about a year ago?'

'What?' the client said. 'What's that?' The barber had been slowly forcing him back into the chair; he arrested himself reclining, his head lifted, the barber still pressing him down.

McLendon whirled on the third speaker. 'Happen?

What the hell difference does it make? Are you going to
let the black sons get away with it until one really
does it?'

'That's what I'm telling them!' Butch shouted. He
cursed, long and steady, pointless.

'Here, here,' a fourth said. 'Not so loud. Don't talk so
loud.'

'Sure,' McLendon said; 'no talking necessary at all.
I've done my talking. Who's with me?' He poised on the
balls of his feet, roving his gaze.

The barber held the drummer's face down, the razor
poised. 'Find out the facts first, boys. I know Willy
Mayes. It wasn't him. Let's get the sheriff and do this
thing right.'

McLendon whirled upon him his furious, rigid face.
The barber did not look away. They looked like men of
different races. The other barbers had ceased also above
their prone clients. 'You mean to tell me,' McLendon
said, 'that you'd take a nigger's word before a white
woman's? Why, you damn niggerloving—'

The third speaker rose and grasped McLendon's arm;
he too had been a soldier. 'Now, now. Let's figure this
thing out. Who knows anything about what really
happened?'

'Figure out hell!' McLendon jerked his arm free. 'All
that're with me get up from there. The ones that ain't—'
He roved his gaze, dragging his sleeve across his face.

Three men rose. The drummer in the chair sat up.
'Here,' he said, jerking at the cloth about his neck; 'get
this rag off me. I'm with him. I don't live here, but by
God, if our mothers and wives and sisters—' He smeared
the cloth over his face and flung it to the floor. McLendon
stood in the floor and cursed the others. Another rose and
moved toward him. The remainder sat uncomfortable,

not looking at one another, then one by one they rose and joined him.

The barber picked the cloth from the floor. He began to fold it neatly. 'Boys, don't do that. Will Mayes never done it. I know.'

'Come on,' McLendon said. He whirled. From his hip pocket protruded the butt of a heavy automatic pistol. They went out. The screen door crashed behind them reverberant in the dead air.

The barber wiped the razor carefully and swiftly, and put it away, and ran to the rear, and took his hat from the wall. 'I'll be back as soon as I can,' he said to the other barbers. 'I can't let—' He went out, running. The two other barbers followed him to the door and caught it on the rebound, leaning out and looking up the street after him. The air was flat and dead. It had a metallic taste at the base of the tongue.

'What can he do?' the first said. The second one was saying 'Jees Christ, Jees Christ' under his breath. 'I'd just as lief be Will Mayes as Hawk, if he gets McLendon riled.'

'Jees Christ, Jees Christ,' the second whispered.

'You reckon he really done it to her?' the first said.

II

She was thirty-eight or thirty-nine. She lived in a small frame house with her invalid mother and a thin, sallow, unflagging aunt, where each morning between ten and eleven she would appear on the porch in a lace-trimmed boudoir cap, to sit swinging in the porch swing until noon. After dinner she lay down for a while, until the afternoon began to cool. Then, in one of the three or four new voile dresses which she had each summer, she would go downtown to spend the afternoon in the stores with

the other ladies, where they would handle the goods and
haggle over the prices in cold, immediate voices, without
any intention of buying.

She was of comfortable people—not the best in Jefferson, but good people enough—and she was still on the
slender side of ordinary looking, with a bright, faintly
haggard manner and dress. When she was young she had
had a slender, nervous body and a sort of hard vivacity
which had enabled her for a time to ride upon the crest
of the town's social life as exemplified by the high school
party and church social period of her contemporaries
while still children enough to be unclassconscious.

She was the last to realize that she was losing ground;
that those among whom she had been a little brighter and
louder flame than any other were beginning to learn the
pleasure of snobbery—male—and retaliation—female.
That was when her face began to wear that bright, haggard look. She still carried it to parties on shadowy
porticoes and summer lawns, like a mask or a flag, with
that bafflement of furious repudiation of truth in her
eyes. One evening at a party she heard a boy and two
girls, all schoolmates, talking. She never accepted another
invitation.

She watched the girls with whom she had grown up as
they married and got homes and children, but no man
ever called on her steadily until the children of the other
girls had been calling her 'aunty' for several years, the
while their mothers told them in bright voices about how
popular Aunt Minnie had been as a girl. Then the town
began to see her driving on Sunday afternoons with the
cashier in the bank. He was a widower of about forty—
a high-coloured man, smelling always faintly of the
barber shop or of whisky. He owned the first automobile
in town, a red runabout; Minnie had the first motoring

bonnet and veil the town ever saw. Then the town began to say: 'Poor Minnie.' 'But she is old enough to take care of herself,' others said. That was when she began to ask her old schoolmates that their children call her 'cousin' instead of 'aunty'.

It was twelve years now since she had been relegated into adultery by public opinion, and eight years since the cashier had gone to a Memphis bank, returning for one day each Christmas, which he spent at an annual bachelors' party at a hunting club on the river. From behind their curtains the neighbours would see the party pass, and during the over-the-way Christmas day visiting they would tell her about him, about how well he looked, and how they heard that he was prospering in the city, watching with bright, secret eyes her haggard, bright face. Usually by that hour there would be the scent of whisky on her breath. It was supplied her by a youth, a clerk at the soda fountain: 'Sure; I buy it for the old gal. I reckon she's entitled to a little fun.'

Her mother kept to her room altogether now; the gaunt aunt ran the house. Against that background Minnie's bright dresses, her idle and empty days, had a quality of furious unreality. She went out in the evenings only with women now, neighbours, to the moving pictures. Each afternoon she dressed in one of the new dresses and went downtown alone, where her young 'cousins' were already strolling in the late afternoons with their delicate, silken heads and thin, awkward arms and conscious hips, clinging to one another or shrieking and giggling with paired boys in the soda fountain when she passed and went on along the serried store fronts, in the doors of which the sitting and lounging men did not even follow her with their eyes any more.

III

The barber went swiftly up the street where the sparse lights, insect-swirled, glared in rigid and violent suspension in the lifeless air. The day had died in a pall of dust; above the darkened square, shrouded by the spent dust, the sky was as clear as the inside of a brass bell. Below the east was a rumour of the twice-waxed moon.

When he overtook them McLendon and three others were getting into a car parked in an alley. McLendon stooped his thick head, peering out beneath the top. 'Changed your mind, did you?' he said. 'Damn good thing; by God, tomorrow when this town hears about how you talked tonight—'

'Now, now,' the other ex-soldier said. 'Hawkshaw's all right. Come on, Hawk; jump in.'

'Will Mayes never done it, boys,' the barber said. 'If anybody done it. Why, you all know well as I do there ain't any town where they got better niggers than us. And you know how a lady will kind of think things about men when there ain't any reason to, and Miss Minnie anyway—'

'Sure, sure,' the soldier said. 'We're just going to talk to him a little; that's all.'

'Talk hell!' Butch said. 'When we're through with the—'

'Shut up, for God's sake!' the soldier said. 'Do you want everybody in town—'

'Tell them, by God!' McLendon said. 'Tell every one of the sons that'll let a white woman—'

'Let's go; let's go: here's the other car.' The second car slid squealing out of a cloud of dust at the alley mouth. McLendon started his car and took the lead.

Dust lay like fog in the street. The street lights hung nimbused as in water. They drove on out of town.

A rutted lane turned at right angles. Dust hung above it too, and above all the land. The dark bulk of the ice plant, where the Negro Mayes was night watchman, rose against the sky. 'Better stop here, hadn't we?' the soldier said. McLendon did not reply. He hurled the car up and slammed to a stop, the headlights glaring on the blank wall.

'Listen here, boys,' the barber said; 'if he's here, don't that prove he never done it? Don't it? If it was him, he would run. Don't you see he would?' The second car came up and stopped. McLendon got down; Butch sprang down beside him. 'Listen, boys,' the barber said.

'Cut the lights off!' McLendon said. The breathless dark rushed down. There was no sound in it save their lungs as they sought air in the parched dust in which for two months they had lived; then the diminishing crunch of McLendon's and Butch's feet, and a moment later McLendon's voice:

'Will! . . . Will!'

Below the east the wan haemorrhage of the moon increased. It heaved above the ridge, silvering the air, the dust, so that they seemed to breathe, live, in a bowl of molten lead. There was no sound of nightbird nor insect, no sound save their breathing and a faint ticking of contracting metal about the cars. Where their bodies touched one another they seemed to sweat dryly, for no more moisture came. 'Christ!' a voice said; 'let's get out of here.'

But they didn't move until vague noises began to grow out of the darkness ahead; then they got out and waited tensely in the breathless dark. There was another sound: a blow, a hissing expulsion of breath and McLendon cursing in undertone. They stood a moment longer, then they ran forward. They ran in a stumbling clump, as though they were fleeing something. 'Kill him, kill the son,' a voice whispered. McLendon flung them back.

'Not here,' he said. 'Get him into the car.' 'Kill him, kill the black son!' the voice murmured. They dragged the Negro to the car. The barber had waited beside the car. He could feel himself sweating and he knew he was going to be sick at the stomach.

'What is it, captains?' the Negro said. 'I ain't done nothing. 'Fore God, Mr. John.' Someone produced handcuffs. They worked busily about the Negro as though he were a post, quiet, intent, getting in one another's way. He submitted to the handcuffs, looking swiftly and constantly from dim face to dim face. 'Who's here, captains?' he said, leaning to peer into the faces until they could feel his breath and smell his sweaty reek. He spoke a name or two. 'What you all say I done, Mr. John?'

McLendon jerked the car door open. 'Get in!' he said.

The Negro did not move. 'What you all going to do with me, Mr. John? I ain't done nothing. White folks, captains, I ain't done nothing: I swear 'fore God.' He called another name.

'Get in!' McLendon said. He struck the Negro. The others expelled their breath in a dry hissing and struck him with random blows and he whirled and cursed them, and swept his manacled hands across their faces and slashed the barber upon the mouth, and the barber struck him also. 'Get him in there,' McLendon said. They pushed at him. He ceased struggling and got in and sat quietly as the others took their places. He sat between the barber and the soldier, drawing his limbs in so as not to touch them, his eyes going swiftly and constantly from face to face. Butch clung to the running board. The car moved on. The barber nursed his mouth with his handkerchief.

'What's the matter, Hawk?' the soldier said.

'Nothing,' the barber said. They regained the high-road and turned away from town. The second car dropped back out of the dust. They went on, gaining speed; the final fringe of houses dropped behind.

'Goddamn, he stinks!' the soldier said.

'We'll fix that,' the drummer in front beside McLendon said. On the running board Butch cursed into the hot rush of air. The barber leaned suddenly forward and touched McLendon's arm.

'Let me out, John,' he said.

'Jump out, niggerlover,' McLendon said without turning his head. He drove swiftly. Behind them the source-less lights of the second car glared in the dust. Presently McLendon turned into a narrow road. It was rutted with disuse. It led back to an abandoned brick kiln—a series of reddish mounds and weed- and vine-choked vats without bottom. It had been used for pasture once, until one day the owner missed one of his mules. Although he prodded carefully in the vats with a long pole, he could not even find the bottom of them.

'John,' the barber said.

'Jump out, then,' McLendon said, hurling the car along the ruts. Beside the barber the Negro spoke:

'Mr. Henry.'

The barber sat forward. The narrow tunnel of the road rushed up and past. Their motion was like an extinct furnace blast: cooler, but utterly dead. The car bounded from rut to rut.

'Mr. Henry,' the Negro said.

The barber began to tug furiously at the door. 'Look

out, there!' the soldier said, but the barber had already kicked the door open and swung onto the running board. The soldier leaned across the Negro and grasped at him, but he had already jumped. The car went on without checking speed.

The impetus hurled him crashing through dust-sheathed weeds, into the ditch. Dust puffed about him, and in a thin, vicious crackling of sapless stems he lay choking and retching until the second car passed and died away. Then he rose and limped on until he reached the highroad and turned toward town, brushing at his clothes with his hands. The moon was higher, riding high and clear of the dust at last, and after a while the town began to glare beneath the dust. He went on, limping. Presently he heard cars and the glow of them grew in the dust behind him and he left the road and crouched again in the weeds until they passed. McLendon's car came last now. There were four people in it and Butch was not on the running board.

They went on; the dust swallowed them; the glare and the sound died away. The dust of them hung for a while, but soon the eternal dust absorbed it again. The barber climbed back onto the road and limped on toward town.

IV

As she dressed for supper on that Saturday evening, her own flesh felt like fever. Her hands trembled among the hooks and eyes, and her eyes had a feverish look, and her hair swirled crisp and crackling under the comb. While she was still dressing the friends called for her and sat while she donned her sheerest underthings and stockings and a new voile dress. 'Do you feel strong enough to go out?' they said, their eyes bright too, with a dark glitter. 'When you have had time to get over the shock, you must tell us what happened. What he said and did; everything.'

In the leafed darkness, as they walked toward the square, she began to breathe deeply, something like a swimmer preparing to dive, until she ceased trembling, the four of them walking slowly because of the terrible heat and out of solicitude for her. But as they neared the square she began to tremble again, walking with her head up, her hands clenched at her sides, their voices about her murmurous, also with that feverish, glittering quality of their eyes.

They entered the square, she in the centre of the group, fragile in her fresh dress. She was trembling worse. She walked slower and slower, as children eat ice cream, her head up and her eyes bright in the haggard banner of her face, passing the hotel and the coatless drummers in chairs along the kerb looking around at her: 'That's the one: see? The one in pink in the middle.' 'Is that her? What did they do with the nigger? Did they—?' 'Sure. He's all right.' 'All right, is he?' 'Sure. He went on a little trip.' Then the drug store, where even the young men lounging in the doorway tipped their hats and followed with their eyes the motion of her hips and legs when she passed.

They went on, passing the lifted hats of the gentlemen, the suddenly ceased voices, deferent, protective. 'Do you see?' the friends said. Their voices sounded like long, hovering sighs of hissing exultation. 'There's not a Negro on the square. Not one.'

They reached the picture show. It was like a miniature fairyland with its lighted lobby and coloured lithographs of life caught in its terrible and beautiful mutations. Her lips began to tingle. In the dark, when the picture began, it would be all right; she could hold back the laughing so it would not waste away so fast and so soon. So she hurried on before the turning faces, the undertones of low astonishment, and they took their accustomed places where she could see the aisle against the silver glare and the young men and girls coming in two and two against it.

The lights flicked away; the screen glowed silver, and soon life began to unfold, beautiful and passionate and sad, while still the young men and girls entered, scented and sibilant in the half dark, their paired backs in silhouette delicate and sleek, their slim, quick bodies awkward, divinely young, while beyond them the silver dream accumulated, inevitably on and on. She began to laugh. In trying to suppress it, it made more noise than ever; heads began to turn. Still laughing, her friends raised her and led her out, and she stood at the kerb, laughing on a high, sustained note, until the taxi came up and they helped her in.

They removed the pink voile and the sheer under-things and the stockings, and put her to bed, and cracked ice for her temples, and sent for the doctor. He was hard to locate, so they ministered to her with hushed ejaculations, renewing the ice and fanning her. While the ice was fresh and cold she stopped laughing and lay still for a time, moaning only a little. But soon the laughing welled again and her voice rose screaming.

'Shhhhhhhhhhh! Shhhhhhhhhhhhhhh!' they said, freshening the icepack, smoothing her hair, examining it for grey; 'poor girl!' Then to one another: 'Do you suppose anything really happened?' their eyes darkly aglitter, secret and passionate. 'Shhhhhhhhhh! Poor girl! Poor Minnie!'

V

It was midnight when McLendon drove up to his neat new house. It was trim and fresh as a birdcage and almost as small, with its clean, green-and-white paint. He locked the car and mounted the porch and entered. His wife rose from a chair beside the reading lamp. McLendon stopped in the floor and stared at her until she looked down.

'Look at that clock,' he said, lifting his arm, pointing. She stood before him, her face lowered, a magazine in her hands. Her face was pale, strained, and weary-looking. 'Haven't I told you about sitting up like this, waiting to see when I come in?'

'John,' she said. She laid the magazine down. Poised on the balls of his feet, he glared at her with his hot eyes, his sweating face.

'Didn't I tell you?' He went toward her. She looked up then. He caught her shoulder. She stood passive, looking at him.

'Don't, John. I couldn't sleep. . . . The heat; something. Please, John. You're hurting me.'

'Didn't I tell you?' He released her and half struck, half flung her across the chair, and she lay there and watched him quietly as he left the room.

He went on through the house, ripping off his shirt, and on the dark, screened porch at the rear he stood and mopped his head and shoulders with the shirt and flung it away. He took the pistol from his hip and laid it on the table beside the bed, and sat on the bed and removed his shoes, and rose and slipped his trousers off. He was sweating again already, and he stooped and hunted furiously for the shirt. At last he found it and wiped his body again, and, with his body pressed against the dusty screen, he stood panting. There was no movement, no sound, not even an insect. The dark world seemed to lie stricken beneath the cold moon and the lidless stars.

The Short Happy Life of
Francis Macomber

ERNEST HEMINGWAY

(1898–1961)

It was now lunch-time and they were all sitting under the double green fly of the dining-tent pretending that nothing had happened.

'Will you have lime juice or lemon squash?' Macomber asked.

'I'll have a gimlet,' Robert Wilson told him.

'I'll have a gimlet too. I need something,' Macomber's wife said.

'I suppose it's the thing to do,' Macomber agreed. 'Tell him to make three gimlets.'

The mess boy had started them already, lifting the bottles out of the canvas cooling bags that sweated wet in the wind that blew through the trees that shaded the tents.

'What had I ought to give them?' Macomber asked.

'A quid would be plenty,' Wilson told him. 'You don't want to spoil them.'

'Will the headman distribute it?'

'Absolutely.'

Francis Macomber had, half-an-hour before, been carried to his tent from the edge of the camp in triumph on the arms and shoulders of the cook, the personal boys, the skinner and the porters. The gun-bearers had taken no part in the demonstration. When the native boys put him down at the door of his tent, he had shaken all their hands, received their congratulations, and then gone into the tent and sat on the bed until his wife came in. She did not speak to him when she came in and he left the tent at once to wash his face and hands in the portable wash basin outside and go over to the dining-tent to sit in a comfortable canvas chair in the breeze and the shade.

'You've got your lion,' Robert Wilson said to him, 'and a damned fine one too.'

Mrs. Macomber looked at Wilson quickly. She was an extremely handsome and well-kept woman of the beauty and social position which had, five years before, commanded five thousand dollars as the price of endorsing, with photographs, a beauty product which she had never used. She had been married to Francis Macomber for eleven years.

'He is a good lion, isn't he?' Macomber said. His wife looked at him now. She looked at both these men as though she had never seen them before.

One, Wilson, the white hunter, she knew she had never truly seen before. He was about middle height with sandy hair, a stubby moustache, a very red face and extremely cold blue eyes with faint white wrinkles at the corners that grooved merrily when he smiled. He smiled at her now and she looked away from his face at the way his shoulders sloped in the loose tunic he wore with the four big cartridges held in loops where the left breast pocket should have been, at his big brown hands, his old slacks, his very dirty boots and back to his red face again. She noticed where the baked red of his face stopped in a white line that marked the circle left by his Stetson hat that hung now from one of the pegs of the tent pole.

'Well, here's to the lion,' Robert Wilson said. He smiled at her again and, not smiling, she looked curiously at her husband.

Francis Macomber was very tall, very well built if you did not mind that length of bone, dark, his hair cropped like an oarsman, rather thin-lipped, and was considered handsome. He was dressed in the same sort of safari clothes that Wilson wore except that his were new, he was thirty-five years old, kept himself very fit, was good at court games, had a number of big-game fishing records, and had just shown himself, very publicly, to be a coward.

'Here's to the lion,' he said. 'I can't ever thank you for what you did.'

Margaret, his wife, looked away from him and back to Wilson.

'Let's not talk about the lion,' she said.

Wilson looked over at her without smiling and now she smiled at him.

'It's been a very strange day,' she said. 'Hadn't you ought to put your hat on even under the canvas at noon? You told me that, you know.'

'Might put it on,' said Wilson.

'You know you have a very red face, Mr. Wilson,' she told him and smiled again.

'Drink,' said Wilson.

'I don't think so,' she said. 'Francis drinks a great deal, but his face is never red.'

'It's red today,' Macomber tried a joke.

'No,' said Margaret. 'It's mine that's red today. But Mr. Wilson's is always red.'

'Must be racial,' said Wilson. 'I say, you wouldn't like to drop my beauty as a topic, would you?'

'I've just started on it.'

'Let's chuck it,' said Wilson.

'Conversation is going to be so difficult,' Margaret said.

'Don't be silly, Margot,' her husband said.

'No difficulty,' Wilson said. 'Got a damn fine lion.'

Margot looked at them both and they both saw that she was going to cry. Wilson had seen it coming for a long time and he dreaded it. Macomber was past dreading it.

'I wish it hadn't happened. Oh, I wish it hadn't happened,' she said and started for her tent. She made no noise of crying but they could see that her shoulders were shaking under the rose-coloured, sun-proofed shirt she wore.

'Women upset,' said Wilson to the tall man. 'Amounts to nothing. Strain on the nerves and one thing'n another.'

'No,' said Macomber. 'I suppose that I rate that for the rest of my life now.'

'Nonsense. Let's have a spot of the giant killer,' said Wilson. 'Forget the whole thing. Nothing to it anyway.'

'We might try,' said Macomber. 'I won't forget what you did for me though.'

'Nothing,' said Wilson. 'All nonsense.'

So they sat there in the shade where the camp was pitched under some wide-topped acacia trees with a boulder-strewn cliff behind them, and a stretch of grass that ran to the bank of a boulder-filled stream in front with forest beyond it, and drank their just-cool lime drinks and avoided one another's eyes while the boys set the table for lunch. Wilson could tell that the boys all knew about it now and when he saw Macomber's personal boy looking curiously at his master while he was putting dishes on the table he snapped at him in Swahili. The boy turned away with his face blank.

'What were you telling him?' Macomber asked.

'Nothing. Told him to look alive or I'd see he got about fifteen of the best.'

'What's that? Lashes?'

'It's quite illegal,' Wilson said. 'You're supposed to fine them.'

'Do you still have them whipped?'

'Oh, yes. They could raise a row if they chose to complain. But they don't. They prefer it to the fines.'

'How strange!' said Macomber.

'Not strange, really,' Wilson said. 'Which would you rather do? Take a good birching or lose your pay?'

Then he felt embarrassed at asking it and before Macomber could answer he went on, 'We all take a beating every day, you know, one way or another.'

This was no better. 'Good God,' he thought. 'I am a diplomat, aren't I?'

'Yes, we take a beating,' said Macomber, still not looking at him. 'I'm awfully sorry about that lion business. It doesn't have to go any further, does it? I mean no one will hear about it, will they?'

'You mean will I tell it at the Mathaiga Club?' Wilson looked at him now coldly. He had not expected this. So he's a bloody four-letter man as well as a bloody coward, he thought. I rather liked him too until today. But how is one to know about an American?

'No,' said Wilson. 'I'm a professional hunter. We never talk about our clients. You can be quite easy on that. It's supposed to be bad form to ask us not to talk though.'

He had decided now that to break would be much easier. He would eat, then, by himself and could read a book with his meals. They would eat by themselves. He would see them through the safari on a very formal basis—what was it the French called it? Distinguished

---

consideration—and it would be a damn sight easier than having to go through this emotional trash. He'd insult him and make a good clean break. Then he could read a book with his meals and he'd still be drinking their whisky. That was the phrase for it when a safari went bad. You ran into another white hunter and you asked, 'How is everything going?' and he answered, 'Oh, I'm still drinking their whisky,' and you knew everything had gone to pot.

'I'm sorry,' Macomber said and looked at him with his American face that would stay adolescent until it became middle-aged, and Wilson noted his crew-cropped hair, fine eyes only faintly shifty, good nose, thin lips and handsome jaw. 'I'm sorry I didn't realize that. There are lots of things I don't know.'

So what could he do, Wilson thought. He was all ready to break it off quickly and neatly and here the beggar was apologizing after he had just insulted him. He made one more attempt. 'Don't worry about me talking,' he said. 'I have a living to make. You know in Africa no woman ever misses her lion and no white man ever bolts.'

'I bolted like a rabbit,' Macomber said.

Now what in hell were you going to do about a man who talked like that? Wilson wondered.

Wilson looked at Macomber with his flat, blue, machine-gunner's eyes and the other smiled back at him. He had a pleasant smile if you did not notice how his eyes showed when he was hurt.

'Maybe I can fix it up on buffalo,' he said. 'We're after them next aren't we?'

'In the morning if you like,' Wilson told him. Perhaps he had been wrong. This was certainly the way to take it. You most certainly could not tell a damned thing about an American. He was all for Macomber again. If you could forget the morning. But, of course, you couldn't. The morning had been about as bad as they come.

'Here comes the Memsahib,' he said. She was walking over from her tent looking refreshed and cheerful and quite lovely. She had a very perfect oval face, so perfect that you expected her to be stupid. But she wasn't stupid, Wilson thought, no, not stupid.

'How is the beautiful red-faced Mr. Wilson? Are you feeling better, Francis, my pearl?'

'Oh, much,' said Macomber.

'I've dropped the whole thing,' she said, sitting down at the table. 'What importance is there to whether Francis is any good at killing lions? That's not his trade. That's Mr. Wilson's trade. Mr. Wilson is really very impressive killing anything. You do kill anything, don't you?'

'Oh, anything,' said Wilson. 'Simply anything.' They are, he thought, the hardest in the world; the hardest, the cruellest, the most predatory, and the most attractive and their men have softened or gone to pieces nervously as they have hardened. Or is it that they pick men they can handle? They can't know that much at the age they marry, he thought. He was grateful that he had gone through his education on American women before now because this was a very attractive one.

'We're going after buff in the morning,' he told her.

'I'm coming,' she said.

'No, you're not.'

'Oh, yes, I am. Mayn't I, Francis?'

'Why not stay in camp?'

'Not for anything,' she said. 'I wouldn't miss something like today for anything.'

When she left, Wilson was thinking, when she went off to cry, she seemed a hell of a fine woman. She seemed to understand, to realize, to be hurt for him and for herself and to know how things really stood. She is away for twenty minutes and now she is back, simply enamelled in that American female cruelty. They are the damnedest women. Really the damnedest.

'We'll put on another show for you tomorrow,' Francis Macomber said.

'You're not coming,' Wilson said.

'You're very mistaken,' she told him. 'And I want *so* to see you perform again. You were lovely this morning. That is if blowing things' heads off is lovely.'

'Here's the lunch,' said Wilson. 'You're very merry, aren't you?'

'Why not? I didn't come out here to be dull.'

'Well, it hasn't been dull,' Wilson said. He could see the boulders in the river and the high bank beyond with the trees and he remembered the morning.

'Oh, no,' she said. 'It's been charming. And tomorrow. You don't know how I look forward to tomorrow.'

'That's eland he's offering you,' Wilson said.

'They're the big cowy things that jump like hares, aren't they?'

'I suppose that describes them,' Wilson said.

'It's very good meat,' Macomber said.

'Did you shoot it, Francis?' she asked.

'Yes.'

'They're not dangerous, are they?'

'Only if they fall on you,' Wilson told her.

'I'm so glad.'

'Why not let up on the bitchery just a little, Margot,' Macomber said, cutting the eland steak and putting some mashed potato, gravy, and carrot on the down-turned fork that tined through the piece of meat.

'I suppose I could,' she said, 'since you put it so prettily.'

'Tonight we'll have champagne for the lion,' Wilson said. 'It's a bit too hot at noon.'

'Oh, the lion,' Margot said. 'I'd forgotten the lion!'

So, Robert Wilson thought to himself, she *is* giving him a ride, isn't she? Or do you suppose that's her idea of putting up a good show? How should a woman act when she discovers her husband is a bloody coward? She's damned cruel but they're all cruel. They govern, of course, and to govern one has to be cruel sometimes. Still, I've seen enough of their damn terrorism.

'Have some more eland,' he said to her politely.

That afternoon, late, Wilson and Macomber went out in the motor car with the native driver and the two gun-bearers. Mrs. Macomber stayed in the camp. It was too hot to go out, she said, and she was going with them in the early morning. As they drove off Wilson saw her standing under the big tree, looking pretty rather than beautiful in her faintly rosy khaki, her dark hair drawn back off her forehead and gathered in a knot low on her neck, her face as fresh, he thought, as though she were in England. She waved to them as the car went off through the swale of high grass and curved around through the trees into the small hills of orchard bush.

In the orchard bush they found a herd of impala, and leaving the car they stalked one old ram with long, widespread horns and Macomber killed it with a very creditable shot that knocked the buck down at a good two hundred yards and sent the herd off bounding wildly and leaping over one another's backs in long, leg-drawn-up leaps as unbelievable and as floating as those one makes sometimes in dreams.

'That was a good shot,' Wilson said. 'They're a small target.'

'Is it a worth-while head?' Macomber asked.

'It's excellent,' Wilson told him. 'You shoot like that and you'll have no trouble.'

'Do you think we'll find buffalo tomorrow?'

'There's a good chance of it. They feed out early in the morning and with luck we may catch them in the open.'

'I'd like to clear away that lion business,' Macomber said. 'It's not very pleasant to have your wife see you do something like that.'

I should think it would be even more unpleasant to do it, Wilson thought, wife or no wife, or to talk about it having done it. But he said, 'I wouldn't think about that any more. Anyone could be upset by his first lion. That's all over.'

But that night after dinner and a whisky and soda by the fire before going to bed, as Francis Macomber lay on his cot with the mosquito bar over him and listened to the night noises it was not all over. It was neither all over nor was it beginning. It was there exactly as it happened with some parts of it indelibly emphasized and he was miserably ashamed at it. But more than shame he felt cold, hollow fear in him. The fear was still there like a cold slimy hollow in all the emptiness where once his confidence had been and it made him feel sick. It was still there with him now.

It had started the night before when he had wakened and heard the lion roaring somewhere up along the river. It was a deep sound and at the end there were sort of coughing grunts that made him seem just outside the tent, and when Francis Macomber woke in the night to hear it he was afraid. He could hear his wife breathing

quietly, asleep. There was no one to tell he was afraid,
nor to be afraid with him, and, lying alone, he did not
know the Somali proverb that says a brave man is always
frightened three times by a lion; when he first sees his
track when he first hears him roar and when he first
confronts him. Then while they were eating breakfast
by lantern light out in the dining-tent, before the sun
was up, the lion roared again and Francis thought he was
just at the edge of camp.

'Sounds like an old-timer,' Robert Wilson said, looking
up from his kippers and coffee. 'Listen to him cough.'

'Is he very close?'

'A mile or so up the stream.'

'Will we see him?'

'We'll have a look.'

'Does his roaring carry that far? It sounds as though
he were right in camp.'

'Carries a hell of a long way,' said Robert Wilson.
'It's strange the way it carries. Hope he's a shootable
cat. The boys said there was a very big one about here.'

'If I get a shot, where should I hit him,' Macomber
asked, 'to stop him?'

'In the shoulders,' Wilson said. 'In the neck if you can
make it. Shoot for bone. Break him down.'

'I hope I can place it properly,' Macomber said.

'You shoot very well,' Wilson told him. 'Take your
time. Make sure of him. The first one in is the one that
counts.'

'What range will it be?'

'Can't tell. Lion has something to say about that.
Don't shoot unless it's close enough so you can make
sure.'

'At under a hundred yards?' Macomber asked.

Wilson looked at him quickly.

'Hundred's about right. Might have to take him a bit under. Shouldn't chance a shot at much over that. A hundred's a decent range. You can hit him whenever you want at that. Here comes the Memsahib.'

'Good morning,' she said. 'Are we going after that lion?'

'As soon as you deal with your breakfast,' Wilson said. 'How are you feeling?'

'Marvellous,' she said. 'I'm very excited.'

'I'll just go and see that everything is ready,' Wilson went off. As he left the lion roared again.

'Noisy beggar,' Wilson said. 'We'll put a stop to that.'

'What's the matter, Francis?' his wife asked him.

'Nothing,' Macomber said.

'Yes, there is,' she said. 'What are you upset about?'

'Nothing,' he said.

'Tell me,' she looked at him. 'Don't you feel well?'

'It's that damned roaring,' he said. 'It's been going on all night, you know.'

'Why didn't you wake me,' she said. 'I'd love to have heard it.'

'I've got to kill the damned thing,' Macomber said, miserably.

'Well, that's what you're out here for, isn't it?'

'Yes. But I'm nervous. Hearing the thing roar gets on my nerves.'

'Well then, as Wilson said, kill him and stop his roaring.'

'Yes, darling,' said Francis Macomber. 'It sounds easy, doesn't it?'

'You're not afraid, are you?'

'Of course not. But I'm nervous from hearing him roar all night.'

'You'll kill him marvellously,' she said. 'I know you will. I'm awfully anxious to see it.'

'Finish your breakfast and we'll be starting.'

'It's not light yet,' she said. 'This is a ridiculous hour.'

Just then the lion roared in a deep-chested moaning, suddenly guttural, ascending vibration that seemed to shake the air and ended in a sigh and a heavy, deep-chested grunt.

'He sounds almost here,' Macomber's wife said.

'My God,' said Macomber. 'I hate that damned noise.'

'It's very impressive.'

'Impressive. It's frightful.'

Robert Wilson came up then carrying his short, ugly, shockingly big-bored ·505 Gibbs and grinning.

'Come on,' he said. 'Your gun-bearer has your Spring-field and the big gun. Everything's in the car. Have you solids?'

'Yes.'

'I'm ready,' Mrs. Macomber said.

'Must make him stop that racket,' Wilson said. 'You get in front. The Memsahib can sit back here with me.'

They climbed into the motor car and, in the grey first daylight, moved off up the river through the trees. Macomber opened the breech of his rifle and saw he had metal-cased bullets, shut the bolt and put the rifle on safety. He saw his hand was trembling. He felt in his pocket for more cartridges and moved his fingers over the cartridges in the loops of his tunic front. He turned back to where Wilson sat in the rear seat of the doorless, box-bodied motor car beside his wife, them both grinning with excitement, and Wilson leaned forward and whispered.

'See the birds dropping. Means the old boy has left his kill.'

On the far bank of the stream Macomber could see, above the trees, vultures circling and plummeting down.

'Chances are he'll come to drink along here,' Wilson whispered. 'Before he goes to lay up. Keep an eye out.'

They were driving slowly along the high bank of the stream which here cut deeply to its boulder-filled bed, and they wound in and out through big trees as they drove. Macomber was watching the opposite bank when he felt Wilson take hold of his arm. The car stopped.

'There he is,' he heard the whisper. 'Ahead and to the right. Get out and take him. He's a marvellous lion.'

Macomber saw the lion now. He was standing almost broadside, his great head up and turned toward them. The early morning breeze that blew toward them was just stirring his dark mane, and the lion looked huge, silhouetted on the rise of bank in the grey morning light, his shoulders heavy, his barrel of a body bulking smoothly.

'How far is he?' asked Macomber, raising his rifle.

'About seventy-five. Get out and take him.'

'Why not shoot from where I am?'

'You don't shoot them from cars,' he heard Wilson saying in his ear. 'Get out. He's not going to stay there all day.'

Macomber stepped out of the curved opening at the side of the front seat, on to the step and down on to the ground. The lion still stood looking majestically and coolly toward this object that his eyes only showed in silhouette, bulking like some super-rhino. There was no man smell carried toward him and he watched the object, moving his great head a little from side to side. Then watching the object, not afraid, but hesitating before going down the bank to drink with such a thing opposite him, he saw a man figure detach itself from it and he turned his heavy head and swung away toward the cover of the trees as he heard a cracking crash and felt the slam of a ·30–06 220-grain solid bullet that bit his flank and ripped in sudden hot scalding nausea through his stomach. He trotted, heavy, big-footed, swinging wounded full-bellied, through the trees toward the tall grass and cover, and the crash came again to go past him ripping the air apart. Then it crashed again and he felt the blow as it hit his lower ribs and ripped on through, blood sudden hot and frothy in his mouth, and he galloped toward the high grass where he could crouch and not be seen and make them bring the crashing thing close enough so he could make a rush and get the man that held it.

Macomber had not thought how the lion felt as he got out of the car. He only knew his hands were shaking and as he walked away from the car it was almost impossible for him to make his legs move. They were stiff in the thighs, but he could feel the muscles fluttering. He raised the rifle, sighted on the junction of the lion's head and shoulders and pulled the trigger. Nothing happened though he pulled until he thought his finger would break. Then he knew he had the safety on and as he lowered the rifle to move the safety over he moved another frozen pace forward, and the lion seeing his silhouette now clear of the silhouette of the car, turned and started off at a trot, and, as Macomber fired, he heard a whunk that meant that the bullet was home; but the lion kept on going. Macomber shot again and everyone saw the bullet throw a spout of dirt beyond the trotting lion. He shot again, remembering to lower his aim, and they all heard the bullet hit, and the lion went into a gallop and was in the tall grass before he had the bolt pushed forward.

Macomber stood there feeling sick at his stomach, his hands that held the Springfield still cocked, shaking, and his wife and Robert Wilson were standing by him. Beside him too were the two gun-bearers chattering in Wakamba.

'I hit him,' Macomber said. 'I hit him twice.'

'You gut-shot him and you hit him somewhere forward,' Wilson said without enthusiasm. The gun-bearers looked very grave. They were silent now.

'You may have killed him,' Wilson went on. 'We'll have to wait a while before we go in to find out.'

'What do you mean?'

'Let him get sick before we follow him up.'

'Oh,' said Macomber.

'He's a hell of a fine lion,' Wilson said cheerfully. 'He's gotten into a bad place though.'

'Why is it bad?'

'Can't see him until you're on him.'

'Oh,' said Macomber.

'Come on,' said Wilson. 'The Memsahib can stay here in the car. We'll go to have a look at the blood spoor.'

'Stay here, Margot,' Macomber said to his wife. His mouth was very dry and it was hard for him to talk.

'Why?' she asked.

'Wilson says to.'

'We're going to have a look,' Wilson said. 'You stay here. You can see even better from here.'

'All right.'

Wilson spoke in Swahili to the driver. He nodded and said, 'Yes, Bwana.'

Then they went down the steep bank and across the stream, climbing over and around the boulders and up the other bank, pulling up by some projecting roots, and along it until they found where the lion had been trotting when Macomber first shot. There was dark blood on the short grass that the gun-bearers pointed out with grass stems, and that ran away behind the river bank trees.

'What do we do?' asked Macomber.

'Not much choice,' said Wilson. 'We can't bring the car over. Bank's too steep. We'll let him stiffen up a bit and then you and I'll go in and have a look for him.'

'Can't we set the grass on fire?' Macomber asked.

'Too green.'

'Can't we send beaters?'

Wilson looked at him appraisingly. 'Of course we can,' he said. 'But it's just a touch murderous. You see we know the lion's wounded. You can drive an un-wounded lion—he'll move on ahead of a noise—but a wounded lion's going to charge. You can't see him until you're right on him. He'll make himself perfectly flat in cover you wouldn't think would hide a hare. You can't very well send boys in there to that sort of a show. Somebody bound to get mauled.'

'What about the gun-bearers?'

'Oh, they'll go with us. It's their *shauri*. You see, they signed on for it. They don't look too happy though, do they?'

'I don't want to go in there,' said Macomber. It was out before he knew he'd said it.

'Neither do I,' said Wilson very cheerily. 'Really no choice though.' Then, as an afterthought, he glanced at Macomber and saw suddenly how he was trembling and the pitiful look on his face.

'You don't have to go in, of course,' he said. 'That's what I'm hired for, you know. That's why I'm so expensive.'

'You mean you'd go in by yourself? Why not leave him there?'

Robert Wilson, whose entire occupation had been with the lion and the problem he presented, and who had not been thinking about Macomber except to note that he was rather windy, suddenly felt as though he had opened the wrong door in a hotel and seen something shameful.

'What do you mean?'

'Why not just leave him?'

'You mean pretend to ourselves he hasn't been hit?'

'No. Just drop it.'

'It isn't done.'

'Why not?'

'For one thing, he's certain to be suffering. For another, someone else might run on to him.'

'I see.'

'But you don't have to have anything to do with it.'

'I'd like to,' Macomber said. 'I'm just scared, you know.'

'I'll go ahead when we go in,' Wilson said, 'with Kongoni tracking. You keep behind me and a little to one side. Chances are we'll hear him growl. If we see him we'll both shoot. Don't worry about anything. I'll keep you backed up. As a matter of fact, you know, perhaps you'd better not go. It might be much better. Why don't you go over and join the Memsahib while I just get it over with?'

'No, I want to go.'

'All right,' said Wilson. 'But don't go in if you don't want to. This is my *shauri* now, you know.'

'I want to go,' said Macomber.

They sat under a tree and smoked.

'Want to go back and speak to the Memsahib while we're waiting?' Wilson asked.

'No.'

'I'll just step back and tell her to be patient.'

'Good,' said Macomber. He sat there, sweating under his arms, his mouth dry, his stomach hollow feeling, wanting to find courage to tell Wilson to go on and finish off the lion without him. He could not know that Wilson was furious because he had not noticed the state he was in earlier and sent him back to his wife. While he sat there Wilson came up. 'I have your big gun,' he said. 'Take it. We've given him time, I think. Come on.'

Macomber took the big gun and Wilson said:

'Keep behind me and about five yards to the right and do exactly as I tell you.' Then he spoke in Swahili to the two gun-bearers who looked the picture of gloom.

'Let's go,' he said.

'Could I have a drink of water?' Macomber asked. Wilson spoke to the older gun-bearer, who wore a canteen on his belt, and the man unbuckled it, unscrewed the top and handed it to Macomber, who took it noticing how heavy it seemed and how hairy and shoddy the felt covering was in his hand. He raised it to drink and looked ahead at the high grass with the flat-topped trees behind it. A breeze was blowing toward them and the grass rippled gently in the wind. He looked at the gun-bearer and he could see the gun-bearer was suffering too with fear.

Thirty-five yards into the grass the big lion lay flattened out along the ground. His ears were back and his only movement was a slight twitching up and down of his long, black-tufted tail. He had turned at bay as soon as he had reached this cover and he was sick with the wound through his full belly, and weakening with the wound through his lungs that brought a thin foamy red to his mouth each time he breathed. His flanks were wet and hot and flies were on the little openings the solid bullets had made in his tawny hide, and his big yellow eyes, narrowed with hate, looked straight ahead, only blinking when the pain came as he breathed, and his claws dug in the soft baked earth. All of him, pain, sickness, hatred and all of his remaining strength, was tightening into an absolute concentration for a rush. He could hear the men talking and he waited, gathering all of himself into this preparation for a charge as soon as the men would come into the grass. As he heard their voices his tail stiffened to twitch up and down, and, as they came into the edge of the grass, he made a coughing grunt and charged.

Kongoni, the old gun-bearer, in the lead watching the blood spoor, Wilson watching the grass for any movement, his big gun ready, the second gun-bearer looking ahead and listening, Macomber close to Wilson, his rifle cocked, they had just moved into the grass when Macomber heard the blood-choked coughing grunt, and saw the swishing rush in the grass. The next thing he knew he was running; running wildly, in panic in the open, running toward the stream.

He heard the *carawong!* of Wilson's big rifle, and again in a second crashing *carawong!* and turning saw the lion, horrible-looking now, with half his head seeming to be gone, crawling toward Wilson in the edge of the tall grass while the red-faced man worked the bolt on the short ugly rifle and aimed carefully as another blasting *carawong!* came from the muzzle, and the crawling, heavy, yellow bulk of the lion stiffened and the huge mutilated head slid forward and Macomber, standing by himself in the clearing where he had run, holding a loaded rifle, while two black men and a white man looked back at him in contempt, knew the lion was dead.

He came toward Wilson, his tallness all seeming a naked reproach, and Wilson looked at him and said:

'Want to take pictures?'

'No,' he said.

That was all anyone had said until they reached the motor car. Then Wilson had said:

'Hell of a fine lion. Boys will skin him out. We might as well stay here in the shade.'

Macomber's wife had not looked at him nor he at her and he had sat by her in the back seat with Wilson sitting in the front seat. Once he had reached over and taken his wife's hand without looking at her and she had removed her hand from his. Looking across the stream to where the gun-bearers were skinning out the lion he could see that she had been able to see the whole thing. While they sat there his wife had reached forward and put her hand on Wilson's shoulder. He turned and she had leaned forward over the low seat and kissed him on the mouth.

'Oh, I say,' said Wilson, going redder than his natural baked colour.

'Mr. Robert Wilson,' she said. 'The beautiful red-faced Mr. Robert Wilson.'

Then she sat down beside Macomber again and looked away across the stream to where the lion lay, with uplifted, white-muscled, tendon-marked naked forearms, and white bloating belly, as the black men fleshed away the skin. Finally the gun-bearers brought the skin over, wet and heavy, and climbed in behind with it, rolling it up before they got in, and the motor car started. No one had said anything more until they were back in camp.

That was the story of the lion. Macomber did not know how the lion had felt before he started his rush, nor during it when the unbelievable smash of the ·505

with a muzzle velocity of two tons had hit him in the
mouth, nor what kept him coming after that, when the
second ripping crash had smashed his hind quarters
and he had come crawling on toward the crashing, blasting thing that had destroyed him. Wilson knew something about it and only expressed it by saying, 'Damned
fine lion,' but Macomber did not know how Wilson felt
about things either. He did not know how his wife felt
except that she was through with him.

His wife had been through with him before but it never
lasted. He was very wealthy, and would be much
wealthier, and he knew she would not leave him ever
now. That was one of the few things that he really knew.
He knew about that, about motor-cycles—that was
earliest—about motor-cars, about duck-shooting, about
fishing, trout, salmon and big-sea, about sex in books,
many books, too many books, about all court games,
about dogs, not much about horses, about hanging on
to his money, about most of the other things his world
dealt in, and about his wife not leaving him. His wife
had been a great beauty and she was still a great beauty
in Africa, but she was not a great enough beauty any
more at home to be able to leave him and better herself
and she knew it and he knew it. She had missed the
chance to leave him and he knew it. If he had been better
with women she would probably have started to worry
about him getting another new, beautiful wife; but she
knew too much about him to worry about him either.
Also, he had always had a great tolerance which seemed
the nicest thing about him if it were not the most
sinister.

All in all they were known as a comparatively happily
married couple, one of those whose disruption is often
rumoured but never occurs, and as the society columnist

put it, they were adding more than a spice of *adventure* to their much envied and ever-enduring *Romance* by a *Safari* in what was known as *Darkest Africa* until the Martin Johnsons lighted it on so many silver screens where they were pursuing *Old Simba* the lion, the buffalo, *Tembo* the elephant and as well collecting specimens for the Museum of Natural History. This same columnist had reported them *on the verge* at least three times in the past and they had been. But they always made it up. They had a sound basis of union. Margot was too beautiful for Macomber to divorce her and Macomber had too much money for Margot ever to leave him.

It was now about three o'clock in the morning and Francis Macomber, who had been asleep a little while after he had stopped thinking about the lion, wakened and then slept again, woke suddenly, frightened in a dream of the bloody-headed lion standing over him, and listening while his heart pounded, he realized that his wife was not in the other cot in the tent. He lay awake with that knowledge for two hours.

At the end of that time his wife came into the tent, lifted her mosquito bar and crawled cosily into bed.

'Where have you been?' Macomber asked in the darkness.

'Hello,' she said. 'Are you awake?'

'Where have you been?'

'I just went out to get a breath of air.'

'You did, like hell.'

'What do you want me to say, darling?'

'Where have you been?'

'Out to get a breath of air.'

'That's a new name for it. You *are* a bitch.'

'Well, you're a coward.'

'All right,' he said. 'What of it?'

'Nothing as far as I'm concerned. But please let's not talk, darling, because I'm very sleepy.'

'You think that I'll take anything.'

'I know you will, sweet.'

'Well, I won't.'

'Please, darling, let's not talk. I'm so very sleepy.'

'There wasn't going to be any of that. You promised there wouldn't be.'

'Well, there is now,' she said sweetly.

'You said if we made this trip that there would be none of that. You promised.'

'Yes, darling. That's the way I meant it to be. But the trip was spoiled yesterday. We don't have to talk about it, do we?'

'You don't wait long when you have an advantage, do you?'

'Please let's not talk. I'm so sleepy, darling.'

'I'm going to talk.'

'Don't mind me then, because I'm going to sleep.' And she did.

At breakfast they were all three at the table before daylight and Francis Macomber found that, of all the many men that he had hated, he hated Robert Wilson the most.

'Sleep well?' Wilson asked in his throaty voice, filling a pipe.

'Did you?'

'Topping,' the white hunter told him.

You bastard, thought Macomber, you insolent bastard.

So she woke him when she came in, Wilson thought, looking at them both with his flat, cold eyes. Well, why doesn't he keep his wife where she belongs? What does he think I am, a bloody plaster saint? Let him keep her where she belongs. It's his own fault.

'Do you think we'll find buffalo?' Margot asked, pushing away a dish of apricots.

'Chance of it,' Wilson said and smiled at her. 'Why don't you stay in camp?'

'Not for anything,' she told him.

'Why not order her to stay in camp?' Wilson said to Macomber.

'You order her,' said Macomber coldly.

'Let's not have any ordering, nor,' turning to Macomber, 'any silliness, Francis,' Margot said quite pleasantly.

'Are you ready to start?' Macomber asked.

'Any time,' Wilson told him. 'Do you want the Memsahib to go?'

'Does it make any difference whether I do or not?'

The hell with it, thought Robert Wilson. The utter complete hell with it. So this is what it's going to be like. Well, this is what it's going to be like, then.

'Makes no difference,' he said.

'You're sure you wouldn't like to stay in camp with her yourself and let me go out and hunt the buffalo?' Macomber asked.

'Can't do that,' said Wilson. 'Wouldn't talk rot if I were you.'

'I'm not talking rot. I'm disgusted.'

'Bad word, disgusted.'

'Francis, will you please try to speak sensibly?' his wife said.

'I speak too damned sensibly,' Macomber said. 'Did you ever eat such filthy food?'

'Something wrong with the food?' asked Wilson quietly.

'No more than with everything else.'

'I'd pull yourself together, laddybuck,' Wilson said

very quietly. 'There's a boy waits at table that understands a little English.'

'The hell with him.'

Wilson stood up and puffing on his pipe strolled away, speaking a few words in Swahili to one of the gun-bearers who was standing waiting for him. Macomber and his wife sat on at the table. He was staring at his coffee cup.

'If you make a scene I'll leave you, darling,' Margot said quietly.

'No, you won't.'

'You can try it and see.'

'You won't leave me.'

'No,' she said. 'I won't leave you and you'll behave yourself.'

'Behave myself? That's a way to talk. Behave myself.'

'Yes. Behave yourself.'

'Why don't *you* try behaving?'

'I've tried it so long. So very long.'

'I hate that red-faced swine,' Macomber said. 'I loathe the sight of him.'

'He's really *very* nice.'

'Oh, *shut up*,' Macomber almost shouted. Just then the car came up and stopped in front of the dining-tent and the driver and the two gun-bearers got out. Wilson walked over and looked at the husband and wife sitting there at the table.

'Going shooting?' he asked.

'Yes,' said Macomber, standing up. 'Yes.'

'Better bring a woolly. It will be cool in the car,' Wilson said.

'I'll get my leather jacket,' Margot said.

'The boy has it,' Wilson told her. He climbed into the front with the driver and Francis Macomber and his wife sat, not speaking, in the back seat.

Hope the silly beggar doesn't take a notion to blow the back of my head off, Wilson thought to himself. Women *are* a nuisance on safari.

The car was grinding down to cross the river at a pebbly ford in the grey daylight and then climbed, angling up the steep bank, where Wilson had ordered a way shovelled out the day before so they could reach the parklike wooded rolling country on the far side.

It was a good morning, Wilson thought. There was a heavy dew and as the wheels went through the grass and low bushes he could smell the odour of the crushed fronds. It was an odour like verbena and he liked this early morning smell of the dew, the crushed bracken and the look of the tree trunks showing black through the early morning mist, as the car made its way through the un-tracked, parklike country. He had put the two in the back seat out of his mind now and was thinking about buffalo. The buffalo that he was after stayed in the day-time in a thick swamp where it was impossible to get a shot, but in the night they fed out into an open stretch of country and if he could come between them and their swamp with the car, Macomber would have a good chance at them in the open. He did not want to hunt buff with Macomber in thick cover. He did not want to hunt buff or anything else with Macomber at all, but he was a professional hunter and he had hunted with some rare ones in his time. If they got buff today there would only be rhino to come and the poor man would have gone through his dangerous game and things might pick up. He'd have nothing more to do with the woman and Macomber would get over that too. He must have gone through plenty of that before by the look of things. Poor beggar. He must have a way of getting over it. Well, it was the poor sod's own bloody fault.

He, Robert Wilson, carried a double size cot on safari to accommodate any windfalls he might receive. He had hunted for a certain clientele, the international, fast, sporting set, where the women did not feel they were getting their money's worth unless they had shared that cot with the white hunter. He despised them when he was away from them although he liked some of them well enough at the time, but he made his living by them; and their standards were his standards as long as they were hiring him.

They were his standards in all except the shooting. He had his own standards about the killing and they could live up to them or get someone else to hunt them. He knew, too, that they all respected him for this. This Macomber was an odd one though. Damned if he wasn't. Now the wife. Well, the wife. Yes, the wife. Hm, the wife. Well, he'd dropped all that. He looked around at them. Macomber sat grim and furious. Margot smiled at him. She looked younger today, more innocent and fresher and not so professionally beautiful. What's in her heart God knows, Wilson thought. She hadn't talked much last night. At that it was a pleasure to see her.

The motor car climbed up a slight rise and went on through the trees and then out into a grassy prairie-like opening and kept in the shelter of the trees along the edge, the driver going slowly and Wilson looking carefully out across the prairie and all along its far side. He stopped the car and studied the opening with his field glasses. Then he motioned to the driver to go on and the car moved slowly along, the driver avoiding warthog holes and driving around the mud castles ants had built. Then, looking across the opening, Wilson suddenly turned and said,

'By God, there they are!'

And looking where he pointed, while the car jumped forward and Wilson spoke in rapid Swahili to the driver, Macomber saw three huge black animals looking almost cylindrical in their long heaviness, like big black tank cars, moving at a gallop across the far edge of the open prairie. They moved at a stiff-necked, stiff-bodied gallop and he could see the upswept wide black horns on their heads as they galloped heads out; the heads not moving.

'They're three old bulls,' Wilson said. 'We'll cut them off before they get to the swamp.'

The car was going a wild forty-five miles an hour across the open and as Macomber watched, the buffalo got bigger and bigger until he could see the grey, hairless, scabby look of one huge bull and how his neck was a part of his shoulders and the shiny black of his horns as he galloped a little behind the others that were strung out in that steady plunging gait; and then, the car swaying as though it had just jumped a road, they drew up close and he could see the plunging hugeness of the bull, and the dust in his sparsely haired hide, the wide boss of horn and his outstretched, wide-nostrilled muzzle, and he was raising his rifle when Wilson shouted, 'Not from the car, you fool!' and he had no fear, only hatred of Wilson, while the brakes clamped on and the car skidded, ploughing sideways to an almost stop and Wilson was out on one side and he on the other, stumbling as his feet hit the still speeding-by of the earth, and then he was shooting at the bull as he moved away, hearing the bullets whunk into him, emptying his rifle at him as he moved steadily away, finally remembering to get his shots forward into the shoulder, and as he fumbled to re-load, he saw the bull was down. Down on his knees, his big head tossing, and seeing the other two still galloping he shot at the leader and hit him. He shot again and missed and he heard the *carawonging* roar as Wilson shot and saw the leading bull slide forward on to his nose.

'Get that other,' Wilson said. 'Now you're shooting!'

But the other bull was moving steadily at the same gallop and he missed, throwing a spout of dirt, and Wilson missed and the dust rose in a cloud and Wilson shouted, 'Come on. He's too far!' and grabbed his arm and they were in the car again, Macomber and Wilson hanging on the sides and rocketing swayingly over the uneven ground, drawing up on the steady, plunging, heavy-necked, straight-moving gallop of the bull.

They were behind him and Macomber was filling his rifle, dropping shells on to the ground, jamming it, clearing the jam, then they were almost up with the bull when Wilson yelled 'Stop,' and the car skidded so that it almost swung over and Macomber fell forward on to his feet, slammed his bolt forward and fired as far forward as he could aim into the galloping, rounded black back, aimed and shot again, then again, then again, and the bullets, all of them hitting, had no effect on the buffalo that he could see. Then Wilson shot, the roar deafening him, and he could see the bull stagger. Macomber shot again, aiming carefully, and down he came, on to his knees.

'All right,' Wilson said. 'Nice work. That's the three.'

Macomber felt a drunken elation.

'How many times did you shoot?' he asked.

'Just three,' Wilson said. 'You killed the first bull. The biggest one. I helped you finish the other two. Afraid they might have got into cover. You had them killed. I was just mopping up a little. You shot damn well.'

'Let's go to the car,' said Macomber. 'I want a drink.'

'Got to finish off that buff first,' Wilson told him. The buffalo was on his knees and he jerked his head furiously and bellowed in pig-eyed, roaring rage as they came toward him.

'Watch he doesn't get up,' Wilson said. Then, 'Get a little broadside and take him in the neck just behind the ear.'

Macomber aimed carefully at the centre of the huge, jerking, rage-driven neck and shot. At the shot the head dropped forward.

'That does it,' said Wilson. 'Got the spine. They're a hell of a looking thing, aren't they?'

'Let's get the drink,' said Macomber. In his life he had never felt so good.

In the car Macomber's wife sat very white faced. 'You were marvellous, darling,' she said to Macomber. 'What a ride.'

'Was it rough?' Wilson asked.

'It was frightful. I've never been more frightened in my life.'

'Let's all have a drink,' Macomber said.

'By all means,' said Wilson. 'Give it to the Memsahib.' She drank the neat whisky from the flask and shuddered a little when she swallowed. She handed the flask to Macomber who handed it to Wilson.

'It was frightfully exciting,' she said. 'It's given me a dreadful headache. I didn't know you were allowed to shoot them from the cars though.'

'No one shot from cars,' said Wilson coldly.

'I mean chase them from cars.'

'Wouldn't ordinarily,' Wilson said. 'Seemed sporting enough to me though while we were doing it. Taking more chance driving that way across the plain full of holes and one thing and another than hunting on foot.

Buffalo could have charged us each time we shot if he liked. Gave him every chance. Wouldn't mention it to anyone though. It's illegal if that's what you mean.'

'It seemed very unfair to me,' Margot said, 'chasing those big helpless things in a motor car.'

'Did it?' said Wilson.

'What would happen if they heard about it in Nairobi?'

'I'd lose my licence for one thing. Other unpleasant-nesses,' Wilson said, taking a drink from the flask. 'I'd be out of business.'

'Really?'

'Yes, really.'

'Well,' said Macomber, and he smiled for the first time all day. 'Now she has something on you.'

'You have such a pretty way of putting things, Fran-cis,' Margot Macomber said. Wilson looked at them both. If a four-letter man marries a five-letter woman, he was thinking, what number of letters would their children be? What he said was, 'We lost a gun-bearer. Did you notice it?'

'My God, no,' Macomber said.

'Here he comes,' Wilson said. 'He's all right. He must have fallen off when we left the first bull.'

Approaching them was the middle-aged gun-bearer, limping along in his knitted cap, khaki tunic, shorts and rubber sandals, gloomy-faced and disgusted looking. As he came up he called out to Wilson in Swahili and they all saw the change in the white hunter's face.

'What does he say?' asked Margot.

'He says the first bull got up and went into the bush,' Wilson said with no expression in his voice.

'Oh,' said Macomber blankly.

'Then it's going to be just like the lion,' said Margot, full of anticipation.

'It's not going to be a damned bit like the lion,' Wilson told her. 'Did you want another drink, Macomber?'

'Thanks, yes,' Macomber said. He expected the feeling he had had about the lion to come back but it did not. For the first time in his life he really felt wholly without fear. Instead of fear he had a feeling of definite elation.

'We'll go and have a look at the second bull,' Wilson said. 'I'll tell the driver to put the car in the shade.'

'What are you going to do?' asked Margaret Macomber.

'Take a look at the buff,' Wilson said.

'I'll come.'

'Come along.'

The three of them walked over to where the second buffalo bulked blackly in the open, head forward on the grass, the massive horns swung wide.

'He's a very good head,' Wilson said. 'That's close to a fifty-inch spread.'

Macomber was looking at him with delight.

'He's hateful looking,' said Margot. 'Can't we go into the shade?'

'Of course,' Wilson said. 'Look,' he said to Macomber, and pointed. 'See that patch of bush?'

'Yes.'

'That's where the first bull went in. The gun-bearer said when he fell off the bull was down. He was watching us helling along and the other two buff galloping. When he looked up there was the bull up and looking at him. Gun-bearer ran like hell and the bull went off slowly into that bush.'

'Can we go in after him now?' asked Macomber eagerly.

Wilson looked at him appraisingly. Damned if this

392 ERNEST HEMINGWAY

isn't a strange one, he thought. Yesterday he's scared sick and today he's a ruddy fire-eater.

'No, we'll give him a while.'

'Let's please go into the shade,' Margot said. Her face was white and she looked ill.

They made their way to the car where it stood under a single, widespreading tree and all climbed in.

'Chances are he's dead in there,' Wilson remarked. 'After a little we'll have a look.'

Macomber felt a wild unreasonable happiness that he had never known before.

'By God, that was a chase,' he said. 'I've never felt any such feeling. Wasn't it marvellous, Margot?'

'I hated it.'

'Why?'

'I hated it,' she said bitterly. 'I loathed it.'

'You know I don't think I'd ever be afraid of anything again,' Macomber said to Wilson. 'Something happened in me after we first saw the buff and started after him. Like a dam bursting. It was pure excitement.'

'Cleans out your liver,' said Wilson. 'Damn funny things happen to people.'

Macomber's face was shining. 'You know something did happen to me,' he said. 'I feel absolutely different.'

His wife said nothing and eyed him strangely. She was sitting far back in the seat and Macomber was sitting forward talking to Wilson who turned sideways talking over the back of the front seat.

'You know, I'd like to try another lion,' Macomber said. 'I'm really not afraid of them now. After all, what can they do to you?'

'That's it,' said Wilson. 'Worst one can do is kill you. How does it go? Shakespeare. Damned good. See if I can remember. Oh, damned good. Used to quote it to myself at one time. Let's see. "By my troth, I care not; a man can die but once; we owe God a death and let it go which way it will he that dies this year is quit for the next." Damned fine, eh?'

He was very embarrassed, having brought out this thing he had lived by, but he had seen men come of age before and it always moved him. It was not a matter of their twenty-first birthday.

It had taken a strange chance of hunting, a sudden precipitation into action without opportunity for worrying beforehand, to bring this about with Macomber, but regardless of how it had happened it had most certainly happened. Look at the beggar now, Wilson thought. It's that some of them stay little boys so long, Wilson thought. Sometimes all their lives. Their figures stay boyish when they're fifty. The great American boy-men. Damned strange people. But he liked this Macomber now. Damned strange fellow. Probably meant the end of cuckoldry too. Well, that would be a damned good thing. Damned good thing. Beggar had probably been afraid all his life. Don't know what started it. But over now. Hadn't had time to be afraid with the buff. That and being angry too. Motor car too. Motor cars made it familiar. Be a damn fire-eater now. He'd seen it in the war work the same way. More of a change than any loss of virginity. Fear gone like an operation. Something else grew in its place. Main thing a man had. Made him into a man. Women knew it too. No bloody fear.

From the far corner of the seat Margaret Macomber looked at the two of them. There was no change in Wilson. She saw Wilson as she had seen him the day before when she had first realized what his great talent was. But she saw the change in Francis Macomber now.

'Do you have that feeling of happiness about what's

going to happen?' Macomber asked, still exploring his new wealth.

'You're not supposed to mention it,' Wilson said, looking in the other's face. 'Much more fashionable to say you're scared. Mind you, you'll be scared too, plenty of times.'

'But you *have* a feeling of happiness about action to come?'

'Yes,' said Wilson. 'There's that. Doesn't do to talk too much about all this. Talk the whole thing away. No pleasure in anything if you mouth it up too much.'

'You're both talking rot,' said Margot. 'Just because you've chased some helpless animals in a motor car you talk like heroes.'

'Sorry,' said Wilson. 'I have been gassing too much.' She's worried about it already, he thought.

'If you don't know what we're talking about why not keep out of it?' Macomber asked his wife.

'You've gotten awfully brave, awfully suddenly,' his wife said contemptuously, but her contempt was not secure. She was very afraid of something.

Macomber laughed, a very natural hearty laugh. 'You know I *have*,' he said. 'I really have.'

'Isn't it sort of late?' Margot said bitterly. Because she had done the best she could for many years back and the way they were together now was no one person's fault.

'Not for me,' said Macomber.

Margot said nothing but sat back in the corner of the seat.

'Do you think we've given him time enough?' Macomber asked Wilson cheerfully.

'We might have a look,' Wilson said. 'Have you any solids left?'

'The gun-bearer has some.'

Wilson called in Swahili and the older gun-bearer, who was skinning out one of the heads, straightened up, pulled a box of solids out of his pocket and brought them over to Macomber, who filled his magazine and put the remaining shells in his pocket.

'You might as well shoot the Springfield,' Wilson said. 'You're used to it. We'll leave the Mannlicher in the car with the Memsahib. Your gun-bearer can carry your heavy gun. I've this damned cannon. Now let me tell you about them.' He had saved this until the last because he did not want to worry Macomber. 'When a buff comes he comes with his head high and thrust straight out. The boss of the horns covers any sort of a brain shot. The only shot is straight into the nose. The only other shot is into his chest or, if you're to one side, into the neck or the shoulders. After they've been hit once they take a hell of a lot of killing. Don't try anything fancy. Take the easiest shot there is. They've finished skinning out that head now. Should we get started?'

He called to the gun-bearers, who came up wiping their hands, and the older one got into the back.

'I'll only take Kongoni,' Wilson said. 'The other can watch to keep the birds away.'

As the car moved slowly across the open space toward the island of brushy trees that ran in a tongue of foliage along a dry water course that cut the open swale, Macomber felt his heart pounding and his mouth was dry again, but it was excitement, not fear.

'Here's where he went in,' Wilson said. Then to the gun-bearer in Swahili, 'Take the blood spoor.'

The car was parallel to the patch of bush. Macomber, Wilson and the gun-bearer got down. Macomber, looking back, saw his wife, with the rifle by her side, looking at him. He waved to her and she did not wave back.

The brush was very thick ahead and the ground was dry. The middle-aged gun-bearer was sweating heavily and Wilson had his hat down over his eyes and his red neck showed just ahead of Macomber. Suddenly the gun-bearer said something in Swahili to Wilson and ran forward.

'He's dead in there,' Wilson said. 'Good work,' and he turned to grip Macomber's hand and as they shook hands, grinning at each other, the gun-bearer shouted wildly and they saw him coming out of the bush sideways, fast as a crab, and the bull coming, nose out, mouth tight closed, blood dripping, massive head straight out, coming in a charge, his little pig eyes bloodshot as he looked at them. Wilson, who was ahead, was kneeling shooting, and Macomber, as he fired, unhearing his shot in the roaring of Wilson's gun, saw fragments like slate burst from the huge boss of the horns, and the head jerked, he shot again at the wide nostrils and saw the horns jolt again and fragments fly, and he did not see Wilson now and, aiming carefully, shot again with the buffalo's huge bulk almost on him and his rifle almost level with the oncoming head, nose out, and he could see the little wicked eyes and the head started to lower and he felt a sudden white-hot, blinding flash explode inside his head and that was all he ever felt.

Wilson had ducked to one side to get in a shoulder shot. Macomber had stood solid and shot for the nose, shooting a touch high each time and hitting the heavy horns, splintering and chipping them like hitting a slate roof, and Mrs. Macomber, in the car, had shot at the buffalo with the 6·5 Mannlicher as it seemed about to gore Macomber and had hit her husband about two inches up and a little to one side of the base of his skull.

Francis Macomber lay now, face down, not two yards

from where the buffalo lay on his side and his wife knelt over him with Wilson beside her.

'I wouldn't turn him over,' Wilson said.

The woman was crying hysterically.

'I'd get back in the car,' Wilson said. 'Where's the rifle?'

She shook her head, her face contorted. The gun-bearer picked up the rifle.

'Leave it as it is,' said Wilson. Then, 'Go get Abdulla so that he may witness the manner of the accident.'

He knelt down, took a handkerchief from his pocket, and spread it over Francis Macomber's crew-cropped head where it lay. The blood sank into the dry, loose earth.

Wilson stood up and saw the buffalo on his side, his legs out, his thinly-haired belly crawling with ticks. 'Hell of a good bull,' his brain registered automatically. 'A good fifty inches, or better. Better.' He called to the driver and told him to spread a blanket over the body and stay by it. Then he walked over to the motor car where the woman sat crying in the corner.

'That was a pretty thing to do,' he said in a toneless voice. 'He *would* have left you too.'

'Stop it,' she said.

'Of course it's an accident,' he said. 'I know that.'

'Stop it,' she said.

'Don't worry,' he said. 'There will be a certain amount of unpleasantness but I will have some photographs taken that will be very useful at the inquest. There's the testimony of the gun-bearers and the driver too. You're perfectly all right.'

'Stop it,' she said.

'There's a hell of a lot to be done,' he said. 'And I'll have to send a truck off to the lake to wireless for a plane to take the three of us into Nairobi. Why didn't you poison him? That's what they do in England.'

'Stop it. Stop it. Stop it,' the woman cried.

Wilson looked at her with his flat blue eyes.

'I'm through now,' he said. 'I was a little angry. I'd begun to like your husband.'

'Oh, please stop it,' she said. 'Please, please stop it.'

'That's better,' Wilson said. 'Please is much better. Now I'll stop.'

PRINTED LITHOGRAPHICALLY IN GREAT BRITAIN
AT THE UNIVERSITY PRESS, OXFORD
BY VIVIAN RIDLER
PRINTER TO THE UNIVERSITY